Praise for Louise Hare

'Full of life and love . . . It made my heart soar'
Stacey Halls, *Sunday Times* bestselling author of *Mrs England*

'Superb . . . compelling storytelling, beautifully drawn characters
and atmosphere that's deeply immersive'
Harriet Tyce, bestselling author of *Blood Orange*

'A beguiling, atmospheric and important novel, with wonderful,
memorable characters and a vital message about love, loyalty and
hope'
Caroline Lea, author of *The Glass Woman*

'A joy to devour. The characters are beautifully drawn. The tender,
compelling storytelling is immersive and atmospheric. I believe Hare
is a major new talent'
Adele Parks, *Platinum*

'Poignant and authentic . . . it's [Hare's] steady, calm prose and the
animating authenticity of her material that make it so hard to resist'
Observer

'Convincing and involving'
The Sunday Times

'Hare's enthralling novel pulls off the rare trick of being a clever
murder mystery, an evocative portrayal of Windrush London
and a genuinely touching love story'
i

'Full to the brim with such complete joys and heart-aching
tragedies . . . you can feel the warmth and colour emanating from
the pages . . . a transporting debut novel with lovable characters and
musical depth splattered across the pages'
***Magic Radio* Book Club**

Praise for Louise Hare

'Mistress of suspense, Hare keeps us guessing to the last page'
Daily Mail

'A timely first novel of real promise. Confidently written,
compellingly plotted and atmospheric'
Mail on Sunday

'Expect to be obsessed . . . [a book] you need to know about'
Good Housekeeping

'[An] atmospheric debut novel . . . a thought-provoking mystery'
Woman & Home

'Louise Hare writes so effortlessly. It was a joy to read'
Woman's Weekly

'Atmospheric . . . a mystery with characters you can't help but feel
drawn to'
Woman

'Fans of Zadie Smith and Andrea Levy won't want to miss Louise
Hare's enthralling debut novel'
Elle

'Beautifully told . . . heartwarming, heartbreaking and wonderfully
atmospheric'
Heat

'Poignant and compelling'
HELLO!

'Heartfelt . . . brimming with nostalgia'
Prima

Louise Hare is a London-based writer and has an MA in Creative Writing from Birkbeck, University of London. Originally from Warrington, the capital is the inspiration for much of her work, including *This Lovely City* and *Miss Aldridge Regrets*.

This Lovely City was featured on the inaugural BBC TWO TV book club show, *Between the Covers*, and was shortlisted for the RSL Ondaatje Prize. Louise was selected for the *Observer* Top 10 Best Debut Novelists list in 2020, securing her place as an author to watch. *Miss Aldridge Regrets* is her second novel.

Also by Louise Hare

This Lovely City

MISS ALDRIDGE REGRETS

LOUISE HARE

ONE PLACE. MANY STORIES

HQ
An imprint of HarperCollins*Publishers* Ltd
1 London Bridge Street
London SE1 9GF

www.harpercollins.co.uk

HarperCollins*Publishers*
1st Floor, Watermarque Building, Ringsend Road
Dublin 4, Ireland

This edition 2022

1
First published in Great Britain by
HQ, an imprint of HarperCollins*Publishers* Ltd 2022

ISBN: HB: 978-0-00-833261-7
TPB: 978-0-00-833262-4
Signed edition: 978-0-00-855300-5

MIX
Paper from
responsible sources
FSC™ C007454

This book is produced from independently certified FSC™ paper to ensure responsible forest management.

For more information visit: www.harpercollins.co.uk/green

Printed and Bound in the UK using 100% Renewable Electricity at CPI Group (UK) Ltd, Croydon, CR0 4YY

To all my friends.

The doorman barely glanced at me as I approached, slipping past him and down the stairs into the basement club, the stale air thick with cigarette smoke. No one here knew who I was; no one cared. It was a risk, but I'd had to come. The wig that concealed my real hair, the long trench coat that hung almost to my ankles, the glasses from a dress-up box, they lent to me a new persona. My own mother wouldn't have recognised me, let alone Lena Aldridge. She may have possessed both common sense and ambition, but from what I'd learned about her, she rarely used the two together. Why else would she still be working at the Canary Club?

The place was a dive but it was packed. The drinks were cheap and the clientele was mostly made up of young couples, none of whom gave me a second glance. I lurked at the back of the room, out of place without a companion by my side. The club wasn't as sleazy as I'd expected, a pleasant surprise. Apart from the owner that is. I could see Tommy Scarsdale, sitting right at the front where I'd been told he would be, on show for the crowd. A too-young girl leaned into him and he gave her a sloppy-looking kiss. He was more than old enough to be her father. He deserved everything coming to him.

I slid behind a table in the back, out of sight, as Lena was announced to the stage. I'd heard so much about her that seeing her for the first time, it was as though I already knew her. I ordered a drink from a girl whose skirt was short enough to show off her stocking tops. The waitress's cheeks were rouged like a clown's and her caked mascara had begun to flake in the steam caused by a low ceiling and damp weather, every newcomer laden down with a wet coat and a sodden umbrella to add to the humidity.

Lena can sing, I'll give her that. Her dress was cheap and she looked like she'd rather be somewhere – anywhere – else, but every man in the audience was watching her, most of the women too. What must that feel like, to hold sixty or so random strangers in the palm of your hand? A temporary sort of power, but still…

Beside me, two couples were trying to force themselves into a space made for one, the girlfriends giggling as they squeezed onto the same chair.

'Here.' I offered my table, standing up as I pushed my untouched drink away. 'I'm leaving in a moment anyway.' They smiled and thanked me, then lost interest. I loitered by the exit, my heart beating hard, in time to the drums on stage. Not long now. As long as everything went to plan.

I watched Tommy Scarsdale knock back his drink. An Old Fashioned, to which he had added his own sprinkling of cyanide. A green-bound Agatha Christie novel from Hatchards on Piccadilly gave me the idea, the best sixpence I'd ever spent. It wasn't long before he realised something was wrong, his hand clutching at his neck, ripping at his tie, trying to catch a breath. Lucky for him, it was over quickly, not that I could see. Being right at the back, those closer stood to get a better look at the dying man. Macabre, really.

It didn't matter that I couldn't see the man on the floor, that I had to imagine his body seizing in the throes of death. I could see Lena just fine. The horror on her face, the realisation that this man she had despised, had so often wished dead, was dying right before her. She stood there, frozen to the spot, then looked across at her friend, the new widow, their eyes meeting. Shared guilt.

The first doorman charged down the stairs and began to push his way through the crowd. When the second doorman appeared, I slipped past him while his back was turned and ran lightly up the steps before anyone could stop me. Outside, the rain had ceased. I took it as a sign of my good fortune continuing and walked home on a cloud of jubilation. I'd done it. I'd actually pulled it off.

There was no turning back now.

Strike Up the Band

1

Wednesday, 2 September
Queen Mary

I stared down into the churning water, wondering how long it would take for an object to strike the surface if it fell from such a height. I had found a spot at the quieter end of the promenade deck, several storeys above the fierce, white-capped waves. Opening my hand, I let the bottle fall, holding my breath as it began to spin, almost hitting the side of the boat. Small and brown, the bottle looked ordinary but its contents were lethal and I welcomed its demise, destined to sink until it came to rest on the floor of the English Channel. I felt a weight lift and wiped tears from my cheeks as my body sagged forward over the railing, my legs shaking. For days I had carried death with me and finally I was free of it.

The ship sailed on towards France, Cherbourg our only port of call before striking west for New York. She brushed the waves aside as gracefully as the women of Hampstead danced their breaststroke across Kenwood Ladies' Pond. Smooth. Effortless. Even so, I hoped that anyone seeing me in such a state would assume an attack of seasickness, that they'd glance out on the relative calm of the sea and take pity on me, wondering how I'd survive once we hit choppier waters. Only I knew that my nausea had nothing to do with the sea.

I had left London that morning, catching the boat train down to Southampton and holding my breath at each station stop until I was sure that the police weren't coming aboard, hot on my trail. Boarding the ship had been finely managed chaos, crowds of people everywhere as families roamed the dock, waiting to wave off their relatives, the *Queen* looming over us, regal and magnificent. I had felt anonymous in the hubbub, trying to look as though I knew what I was doing, accidentally overtipping the porter who carried my solitary trunk. It was never too early to get used to American customs, Maggie had told me as she waved me off in the taxi from Hampstead. *It'll be like learning a role for a play*, she'd said. I was good at that. It was getting the roles in the first place that I'd always struggled with up to now.

I was reaching into my handbag for my cigarettes, hoping the familiar rush would calm me down, when a gust of wind tugged at my headscarf. I put a hand to the knot, checking it was secure. Someone else wasn't so lucky; I heard a cry and saw a navy felt fedora tumble along the deck like a top. A young man, freshly graduated from boyhood, caught it in mid-air, bowing as he handed it back to its blushing owner. She was quite obviously taken by him, but she was a plain girl, bless her. They exchanged a few words, but I saw his gaze wander as she talked, her conversation slowing to a trickle as she realised he wasn't listening.

He glanced in my direction and I turned away, struggling to

light a match in the breeze. I knew his type too well. Handsome, the sort of chap who's used to women fawning over him. Pay him too much attention and he'll extricate himself in a heartbeat, as fedora lady had found out. I'd forgotten that if you turn your back and act as though you couldn't care less, they're as hard to get rid of as a white cat hair on your best black dress.

'Can I offer some assistance?' He appeared by my side, gold lighter in hand.

'Oh, thank you!' I widened my eyes and tried not to smile at his predictability. 'This wind!' I put on my posh voice, the one Maggie and I used when we went to a fancy hotel for afternoon tea.

'You're English?'

I nodded. 'And you're American.' He was too fresh-faced and healthy looking to be anything but. Even wealthy Englishmen have a pallor to their skin that marks them out from any other nationality. Blame it on the grey skies and overabundance of cabbage in the diet.

'That obvious, huh?' He ran a hand through his blond hair, a grin adding to his boyish air. He was tall, almost a foot taller than my five feet and a few inches. 'I admit, I wondered if you were Italian maybe, or Spanish.'

'My grandmother was Italian,' I lied, parroting what I'd been told to say. 'Not that I ever knew her. She died before I was born.'

I leaned my head towards the lighter's flame, my hand brushing his as we protected the flame with our palms. He might be young but he knew a few tricks already. He hadn't told me his name but we were standing so close to one another that his hand brushed my hip as he lowered it. I fought the urge to take a step back.

'Thank you.' I smiled as my anxiety was replaced with a more familiar electric tingle from the nicotine. I held out my hand, forcing some distance between us. 'I'm Lena. Lena Aldridge.'

'Francis Abernathy.' He shook my hand. 'But everyone calls me Frankie.' He lit his own cigarette and leaned next to me on the railing, still slightly too close for comfort. 'So, what's taking you to New York?'

I considered my answer for a moment before deciding to stick with the truth. Frankie was young, after all, less likely to judge me unfavourably for my profession. 'I'm a singer. And I act a little.'

'But you don't call yourself an actress?'

'I've had a few bit parts on the stage but nothing big,' I admitted. 'Yet, I should say. That's why I'm going to New York. I've been offered a job, on Broadway.'

'Really? Broadway?' He looked impressed. 'I'll have to come down and see your show. I'm sure you'll be spectacular. You certainly look spectacular.'

The small relief from my cigarette was waning. I really didn't want to talk to Frankie, but he made no attempt to leave and the silence became excruciating. 'You live in New York?' I asked, snatching at the first question that dropped into my head.

He nodded. 'Just graduated from college. My mother wanted me to go to law school, but I'm done with books. I'm going to work for my grandfather. Earn some money. I think it's important for a man to learn to stand on his own two feet, don't you think?'

Nothing shouted independence like going into the family business. 'I do like a man who knows his own mind.' I smiled sweetly and dropped my cigarette end overboard. 'Well, it was lovely to meet you, Frankie. Thank you for the light.'

I left before he could wipe the look of surprise from his face. He wasn't used to having people walk away from him, I could tell. It was a petty attempt to teach him a lesson, but I craved a moment of control; the last few days had been a nightmare, one where I was falling from a great height, my legs kicking, arms grasping at thin air. I was hoping to wake up before we reached New York. Before I hit the ground.

Anyone could travel on the *Queen Mary*, they said, and that was true enough as long as you knew the rules. Up here, mingling with the likes of Frankie Abernathy, the air was reserved for the wealthy. They called it cabin class, avoiding the crass bluntness of the term 'first', though that was absolutely what it meant. It reminded me of those boorish upper-class men I'd spent too much time with recently, spouting their fake Cockney slang and frequenting the Soho nightclubs, splashing their cash on cheap gin for good-looking girls. When you're at the top of the ladder the only natural way to look is down.

The cabin-class smoking room was set out like the lobby of a luxury hotel, its walls lined with huge surrealist paintings. To complete the picture of English gentility there was a grand fireplace at the far end of the room and they were doing a roaring trade in cocktails from the small bar. I looked around and congratulated myself on my timing, darting forward to grab a table as a couple vacated it. I untied my headscarf and gave my hair a quick pat to make sure my curls were still behaving. I'd spent the previous afternoon in the Hampstead hairdressers that Maggie always used. For the price I'd paid I wanted to get at least a few days' wear.

'A dry Martini, please,' I told the waiter who came trotting over to take my order.

I had no sooner lit another cigarette than Charlie Bacon arrived, pulling up the chair opposite. 'I'll take one of those,' he said to the waiter as he delivered my drink, the sparkling glass adorned with olives on a stick, just like in the movies. 'No regrets?' he asked me.

'No.' I picked at a rough cuticle on my left thumb.

'Good.' I could feel his eyes on me. 'Lena, you need to forget about what happened in London. It wasn't your fault.'

'I'm fine,' I said, wishing he hadn't brought it up. 'It's been a long few days is all.'

Charlie Bacon. Who was he? A fixer, he'd called himself. A man who solved problems, a former New York police detective now working as assistant to a Broadway impresario named Benny Walker. A week ago that name had meant nothing to me, but Walker was the man who'd paid for my passage to New York, apparently on the basis that he'd known my father decades earlier and had sent Charlie Bacon to London to check in on his daughter and see if she was anywhere as good as old Alfie. *It's a new musical,* Charlie had told me when I'd asked if Mr Walker wanted me to do a formal audition. *He needs a singer first and foremost. We can worry 'bout the acting later.* There were plenty of good-looking girls getting jobs in the West End who couldn't act for toffee, so why couldn't it be my turn?

'I sent a telegram to Mr Walker, so he knows we're safely on our way.' Charlie's Martini arrived and he raised his glass. 'To new beginnings.'

I clinked the edge of my glass against his and closed my eyes against the potent fumes that floated up from the glass as I took a generous sip. God, it was good. 'So, what now?'

He shrugged. 'We travel to New York and Benny Walker changes your life. What more could a girl ask for?'

'What if—'

'What if nothing, Lena. I told you. Benny'll look after you.' He drained his glass and gestured for the waiter to bring two more. 'You won the lottery, honey. Learn to appreciate your good fortune.'

'I do.' I really did appreciate the opportunity, even coming out of the blue as it had. They do say that life changes when you least expect it, and enough bad things had happened to me that I deserved some good luck at last.

'And on that note,' he continued, 'I've been down to the dining room to check on the table assignments. They'd shoved us at the back with a bunch of nobodies, but I convinced the guy in charge to move us.' He looked very pleased with himself. I wondered how much it had cost him. In the few days I'd known him, Charlie Bacon had spent more in tips than I usually earned in a month. 'Guess who I arranged for us to sit with?'

'Marlene Dietrich?' I'd overheard one of the other passengers say they'd seen her on their way over to England the month before.

'Lena, be serious.' He shook his head, disappointed in me. 'Francis Parker!'

'Who?' I racked my brain but the name didn't ring any bells.

'Francis Parker, only one of the richest men in New York! God, Lena, you really haven't heard of him?'

'I doubt we mix in the same circles.' I ground out my cigarette and decided to try one of the olives. From past experience I wasn't sure that I liked olives very much, but Charlie already thought me naïve on several counts, a state of affairs that I wasn't keen on. I took a bite and then swallowed the rest whole, swilling it down with the last of my drink to get rid of the taste of stale socks.

Bacon carried on: 'Parker Godwin is one of the biggest firms in New York. *Parker* Godwin. As in, Francis Parker.'

Even I wasn't quite dense enough to miss that connection. 'What do they do?' I asked.

'Day to day? Something to do with roads. They say Parker paved America. But he has deep pockets – he's known for his sponsorship of the arts. He's the kind of man you could benefit from knowing. We dock in New York next Monday. That's five days to win Parker over and convince him to come and see the show. We get Parker's photograph in the papers, with you sparkling beside him, people are gonna want to know who you are. They'll want to come to the show. You want to be a star, don't you?'

'But you said the part is already mine?' I leaned back out of the way as the waiter placed our second round on the table.

'It is, Lena, it is,' Charlie assured me, 'but you want more than a six-month contract, honey. Trust me, this business is only partly about what you can do on stage. It's about who you know. Who can help you out. You want the whole town talking about you. More important, that's what Benny Walker wants. You don't want to let him down, do you?'

'Fine.' I tried to remember why I'd decided to trust Charlie in the first place, then realised that I'd actually had little choice in the matter. I'd needed to leave London and what he was offering was too good to turn down. 'I can be nice. That's all though, isn't it? No funny business? I'm not that sort of girl.'

Charlie laughed. 'God, no. Parker's far too old for that. He's eighty if he's a day and pretty much wheelchair-bound. Just be polite. Listen when he speaks, laugh if he tries to make a joke, that kinda thing.'

I finished my second drink in two gulps. 'I can do that. What time is dinner?'

'I'll meet you outside the dining room at seven o'clock sharp. Be on time and don't drink any more, Lena. You need to make a good impression.'

I opened my mouth to protest that he'd been the one to order the second round of drinks, not me, but decided not to waste my breath. He was the only person I knew on the ship; best not to argue on our first day at sea. If Charlie Bacon really started to annoy me then I'd simply lock myself away in my cabin until we reached New York and emerge fresh-faced and ready to dazzle Benny Walker. I'd seen a parade of shops in the main hall earlier. I could buy a few paperback novels and be a lady of leisure, spend my days with Hercule Poirot and Lord Peter Wimsey. Eat peppermint creams from one of those fancy boxes with the tissue paper while sipping champagne that my steward would fetch whenever I rang the bell. It sounded glorious.

Of course, I should have known better. I thought that the part I had been offered wouldn't begin until I arrived in New York, but the play had already begun. The director had their cast in place and the curtain had been raised for days. This was my role of a lifetime and, indeed, not every player would make it to their curtain call.

2

Everywhere I looked were people: passengers mingling, waiters rushing around, balancing drinks on silver trays, stewards
hurrying past with a smile and a greeting for everyone they
passed, presumably hoping for a generous tip at the end of the
voyage. I wove my way through them all, looking forward to
enjoying the peace and quiet of my own cabin.

Less than an hour from the English coast, everyone still wore
their best travelling costumes, hats pinned to freshly waved hair, the
gents looking dapper with their scarves looped around their necks.
Picture-perfect, and of course there had been a photographer
ready to capture their likenesses before we set off from
Southampton. Souvenirs to show off to the relatives, keepsakes
to display on the mantelpiece at home. I'd ducked out of his way,
not wanting anyone to catch sight of me, even in the background
of someone else's snapshot. Less than a handful of people back in
London knew that I was on this ship. Best to keep it that way.

I called in at W. H. Smith and browsed the novels, purchasing
two that I hadn't yet read. As I passed the main lounge, the

door swung open and I paused as I recognised the music being played on the piano. The song wasn't sad but it brought a tear to my eye. 'Maple Leaf Rag'. Alfie used to play it all the time.

When I was a tiny child, around four years old, I used to curl up on a pile of blankets, dozing fitfully behind the heavy cerise curtain that separated backstage from front of house at the Royalty Theatre. My heart swelled with pride as I heard the audience applaud, stamping their feet in appreciation when he finished playing. It was only when I grew bold one night and peeked through a gap in the curtain that I learned the truth: they weren't cheering for Alfie. It was the men and women who strode across the stage in their fancy costumes, speaking in such an odd manner, pronounced and deliberate, who had brought the audience off their seats. My father and his piano were merely a background detail, as invisible to their captivated gaze as I was, crouching behind that velvet curtain, his music nothing more than an accompaniment to the real drama the people had paid to see.

I never called him Father, nor Daddy, Dad, Papa. He was Alfie and I was Lena. Partners, he called us, because we could rely on one another. Alfie had grand plans, but they were usually stymied by the simple need to keep a roof over our heads. We didn't have much but the few memories I had of that time were fond ones, living in a cramped little room above a French bakery on Old Compton Street. The owner, Pierre, always had a croissant to give me in the morning, and when times were hard we lived off the bread that hadn't sold and would otherwise go stale. On Sunday evenings when the theatre was dark, Alfie would fetch a bottle of Guinness from the pub down the street and pour an inch into a mug for me.

'To you,' he'd say, raising his mug, 'the best daughter in the world.'

'And to you,' I would clink my own mug against his, 'the best father.'

When I started primary school Alfie decided to move us out to Bethnal Green to rent a room in a terraced house with a family, the Harpers, whose father had gone off to war leaving them short of money. There was no room to swing a cat (the household's ancient tabby kept to the yard where he had a habit of lurking inside the outhouse, terrifying anyone who dared venture outside to use the privy at night), but I had an extended family for the first time and our Sunday-night tradition expanded to include all eight of us.

Mrs Harper had five daughters and one of them, Maggie, was the same age as me. Like the best of friendships, we started out wary of one another and ended up joined at the hip thanks to Jilly Bunce from down the street. A common enemy we could unite against. The school bully, she picked on Maggie for being slow at reading and told the whole classroom not to touch me in case they caught my dirty skin. I was only a tiny thing at the time, easy to win a fight against she thought when I challenged her. Except that Alfie was a mean boxer. Childhood bronchitis had left him weak, an obvious target, so he'd learned to protect himself. He'd taught me a thing or two and I showed them to Jilly Bunce. Maggie had bought me a penny ice from the corner shop on the way home from school and we were the best of friends from that day on.

I'd returned to Soho once I was earning my own wages, moving from one tiny rented room to another. Until I'd stepped foot on board the *Queen Mary,* I'd always made do. Shared bathrooms, coins for the meter, tiptoeing up creaky staircases in the early hours of the morning hoping to avoid the judgement of my landlady.

Now all of that was behind me, so Charlie Bacon had said. My cabin on the ship was on the main deck, one flight of stairs down from where I'd left him. The room I'd called home for the past year would have fit inside it four or five times. To the left of the door as I entered was a double bed that felt like a cloud, not a spring out of place. The air smelt like a summer meadow, the cushions on the sofa were plump and the carpet felt like soft lawn beneath my stockinged feet once I'd kicked off my shoes. There was even a private bathroom attached, with hot and cold running water. Available at all hours, with no schedule to stick to or sign on the wall reminding tenants of the house rules.

I turned on the taps above the bath and sprinkled a layer of rose-scented bath salts as the tub began to fill. There was a knock and I let the bath run while I answered the door to my steward, Danny.

Danny and I were already on our way to becoming fast friends. He'd clocked me for a novice as soon as he'd set eyes on me but not let me feel a dunce. Instead, he'd explained how things worked on the ship, offered to unpack my belongings, and he didn't take offence when I declined. He was a Hackney lad, it turned out, so we were as good as family anyway. I hoped this meant he wouldn't hold it against me if I couldn't afford to tip him as highly as my neighbours along the corridor.

'Your dress, ma'am,' he said, handing over the frock I'd sent out for pressing earlier. 'Anything else I can get you before dinner? An aperitif, perhaps?'

It was tempting but I could hear Charlie's warning in my head. 'I'd love a pot of coffee please, Danny. Will it take long though? I'm about to take a bath.'

'You go right ahead, ma'am. If it's all right with you, I can let myself in and leave it on the coffee table.'

Being rich must take some getting used to, I thought, lying back in the bath and wallowing in the luxury of the hot, scented water. Being surrounded by people who did whatever you asked them to, whenever you asked them to. Danny always seemed to have a smile on his face, but I supposed that was the training.

The water had cooled and my arms swarmed with goose-bumps before I finally climbed out of the bath, wrapping myself in a soft white towel. Its decadence made me sigh: nothing like the old threadbare towels I used at home, unable to justify the expense of buying new.

I was probably the most lightly packed passenger in cabin class, and even my one trunk had been borrowed. Like a bride I had several old items of clothing, one thing new, most things borrowed and one dress that was blue. The porters had deposited my luggage at the foot of the bed and, since declining Danny's assistance, I had left it untouched. I lifted the lid and rummaged through my own meagre possessions, which had been thrown in haphazardly on top: a battered make-up case and a few cheap bits and bobs that you'd expect to belong to a girl who made her living singing on stage in a cellar nightclub. Beneath the tat were the real treasures, mostly donated by Maggie, or Mrs Thomas Scarsdale as her posh Hampstead neighbours knew her.

Maggie herself had made the selections, choosing those pieces she knew I coveted the most. Making amends, I thought, glancing at the red silk gown that Danny had brought me earlier, now hanging from the wardrobe door. The label of a very upmarket Regent Street boutique was still pinned to it, and I remembered trying it on a few months before when Maggie had been bedbound and pale, ordering me to cheer her up with a fashion show in her bedroom while her arsehole of a husband was absent.

'Take it, Lee,' she'd urged. 'When am I going to get a chance to wear it?'

'You'll be back in your old clothes in no time, Mags. Your mum's like a rake and she's had five of you.'

I'd lain beside her on the bed sipping cocoa, me on top of the covers, Maggie beneath, the bulky eiderdown concealing the pregnancy that had ended not long afterwards, like the three before it, in a miscarriage just late enough that she'd dared to get her hopes up. I wondered how she was coping now in London all alone. We'd done a good job of keeping up the pretence that everything was normal over the last few days. I might aspire to be an actress, but Maggie was the expert when it came to hiding her feelings. Being married to Tommy had done that to her. I ran my hand over the red silk and took a deep breath, feeling my anger fade away. Tommy was dead now and Maggie was safe. That was what I needed to remember. Murder might be a sin but if it stopped harm coming to others then perhaps it was forgivable.

Danny had nipped in as promised and left a tray with coffee pot, milk jug and sugar. He'd also had the forethought to provide a glass bottle of water, a hefty crystal tumbler already laid out on a coaster to protect the polished wood of the low coffee table. I poured myself a full glass from the bottle and knocked it back in one. Those bloody Martinis had left my mouth like a desert. I refilled the glass and poured a cup of coffee, taking both to the dressing table where I sat and surveyed the damage. My face was puffy and blotched from the heat of the bath, the booze, and several nights with little or no sleep. I mixed up some of my stage make-up with a dab of cold cream and applied it lightly, layering it until I looked more alive. A dab of rouge and a lick of mascara along my lashes and I was done. I wanted to look fresh-faced, not whorish.

Next was the dress. Cut on the bias and sweeping the floor, the front appeared modest but the back plunged so low that I had to twist awkwardly in the mirror to make sure that my knickers weren't on show. A brassiere was out of the question. My only slight concern was that the deep colour of the silk made my skin look darker. Still, I'd fooled that boy up on the deck earlier and that was a good sign.

Charlie Bacon had told me that Americans could be funny about things like that, that even though segregation wasn't strictly a concern in New York the way it was further south, it didn't mean that people would turn a blind eye. To pass, to fit in, was paramount on the voyage itself. The last thing we wanted, Charlie said, was someone making a fuss. Americans most likely, not used to how things were done elsewhere, and with loud voices that were quick to protest. I had the same rights as anyone else on the ship, but it would hardly be the most auspicious of new beginnings. The plan was that Benny Walker would see me when I arrived and gauge the mood of the day before deciding how I was to be announced to the world: the half-caste daughter of his great childhood friend, or his new European protégée. Hence the story of the Italian grandmother, which had passed its first test with flying colours.

I pulled out Maggie's white mink stole from the trunk and held it to my nose, breathing in Je Reviens. Both the stole and the perfume had been gifts from Tommy, the fur after one of his several affairs, and I wondered if she was trying to rid herself of bad memories. Beneath the selection of furs was her old jewellery box, the shiny black japanned box that I'd saved up to give her on her fifteenth birthday, when all either of us owned was cheap trinkets from the market. When I'd checked in my old carpetbag at the purser's office earlier I'd waited behind a line of uniformed valets and maids, queuing to drop off their employers' most treasured possessions for safe-keeping. The ladies of cabin class may not have their very finest jewels on show this evening but at least that meant I could compete. Maggie had gifted me a diamond necklace and a rope of pearls that would more than do for the few days we were at sea.

As I reached for the pearls, my fingers brushed against cool metal. A silver box stashed right at the back, a parcel label tied around it with the note: TAKE ME. How very Alice in Wonderland. I knew before I unlatched the lid what would be inside. A supply of fine white powder, the good stuff. She'd been quite the fiend for it at one stage, before Tommy's girls had become such a thing that she hated showing her face around places where he might have been with someone else on his arm.

In recent months, since the promise of babies had been extinguished, she'd been all about the gin and sleeping tablets, so much so that I had worried she would end up doing something silly. I'd been too afraid to confront her, too scared of losing my job at the Canary and having no way to pay my rent. Too scared that Maggie would ask me what exactly her husband was up to and not knowing what to say. Of course, it had all gone tits up anyway. I sat down at the dressing table, careful not to waste a single grain as I took a couple of generous sniffs of the powder, blinking as my eyes watered and checking that my mascara didn't run. I sat up straight and forced a smile. I was as ready as I'd ever be.

I reached the dining room bang on time as the clock struck seven, Charlie pacing impatiently by the grand doors. Any artificial confidence from the dope had dissipated by the time I'd made my way along the corridor from my cabin to the staircase that led me down to the dining room. My pride in the glamorous red dress evaporated against the finery that the other women wore. Silks from Paris, and a variety of furs that turned the ship's corridors into an exotic menagerie. Maggie's thin diamond necklace was a string of tarnished metal in comparison to the fine jewels that gleamed at throats and swung from earlobes that had been stretched from the weight of such wealth.

'C'mon, Lena, hurry up!' Charlie seemed jittery himself as he took my arm and dragged me into the great dining hall.

Two storeys high and carpeted in thick pile that my silver sandals sank into, the dining room was like nothing I'd seen before. The noise was terrific, the clamour of people laughing and talking as they took their seats at white-clothed tables. Waiters dashed about, pulling out chairs, pouring wine and handing out bread rolls using silver tongs. I felt like Alice once more, in a world that was somewhat recognisable and yet so disorienting that I tightened my grip on Charlie's hand, scared that he might let go and leave me stranded.

'Here we are.' He showed me into a vestibule just off the side of the room, its round table laid out to seat nine.

Two guests were already at the table and I guessed immediately that the man must be the famous Francis Parker. He had been pushed up to the table in his wheelchair, his ancient back hunched as he wrote in a notebook, the entire page covered in tightly scrawled handwriting. He might be ancient but retirement seemed far from his mind. To his right was a woman whose appearance somehow brought to mind both grieving widow and vaudeville girl. Her hair was a glossy raven black and would have looked fabulous in a bob when she was younger, now grown an inch or two longer and clipped back from her pale face with jewelled barrettes. Her lipstick was bright red but her old-fashioned black dress hid her figure. Her gloves were black lace. Gothic glamour straight out of a 'B' movie.

'Can I help you?' She looked up as the pair of us loitered.

'I believe we've been assigned to this table.' Charlie stuck out a hand to Parker, the older man studiously ignoring it until it was awkwardly withdrawn. 'Charles Bacon. I work with Benny Walker? I think that his office has been in touch with yours recently?'

'Mr Parker doesn't concern himself with the office directly these days. Mr Abernathy is the man to talk to about Parker Godwin.' The woman waved a waiter over as Parker himself ignored us all. 'Perrier water for Mr Parker, if you don't mind.'

I tugged at Bacon's arm. 'Maybe we should sit somewhere else—'

'We're assigned to this table,' he repeated.

The woman shrugged. 'Sit down then, am I stopping you?' She shook out Parker's napkin and attempted to place it in his lap.

'Go and sit down!' Bacon hissed at me.

'Where?' I asked in a stage whisper, rolling my eyes as the woman glanced up at me and smiled.

'Honey, come and sit by me. Come on, I don't bite.' The look she gave to Charlie Bacon said otherwise.

'I take it you're Mr Parker's nurse?' Bacon asked her as we took our seats.

'His secretary, actually. Mrs Lancaster. And you are...?'

'Charles Bacon, agent for Benny Walker. He's big in—'

'I didn't catch *your* name.' She turned to me, blanking Charlie.

'Mine? Lena. Lena Aldridge.' I stammered a little and felt my face flush with heat.

'Lovely to meet you, Lena.' She lowered her voice. 'And you can call me Daisy. We don't often have strangers at the table. This will make a pleasant change from the usual family bickering.'

The waiter reappeared with the Perrier, swiftly filling our water glasses, then our wine glasses from a bottle of white that had already been chilling in a bucket to the side.

'I feel as though we're imposing,' I said to Daisy, Charlie's head buried in his menu. 'I didn't realise this was a family table. Will they mind, do you think?'

Daisy cackled. 'Let them! Sorry, that's not fair. They're not so bad, the Abernathys. They'll be along shortly, you'll see what I mean. And I'm always happy to have someone to talk to. Mr Parker is so busy, and I'm only the hired help after all. You, if you don't mind me saying, don't seem half as stuck-up as most. I don't mind a little girl talk every now and then.'

Abernathy. Why did that name ring a bell? I sipped my

wine and picked up the menu. 'Gosh, they really have every-thing I could think of.'

'The kitchens are so big you can get lost in them,' Daisy told me. 'My advice? Order anything you want. Don't be polite and order chicken when you could have a whole goddamned lobster.'

Reading over the choices, I was distracted when the Abernathys did finally arrive, my head only snapping up as a male voice said my name.

'Lena! What a coincidence.'

It was the young man who had lit my cigarette hours earlier up on deck, his name clicking back into my memory. Frankie Abernathy. What a coincidence indeed. It wasn't to be the last.

3

Wednesday, 2 September
Queen Mary

The new arrivals took their seats, Francis Parker finally relin-quishing his notebook to a tall blonde woman. 'Daddy,' she said, passing it to Daisy to put away, 'don't be rude. It appears we have guests this evening.'

'Eliza, you were late,' he complained, his voice creaking as though it needed oil.

'Sorry, Daddy.' She bent to kiss his paper cheek. 'Poor Carrie had a mishap.'

Eliza Abernathy, née Parker, was in her mid-forties, still a stunner as they said round my neck of the woods. Her hair was professionally styled and her skin was as pale as milk. Although she'd acknowledged our presence, she didn't pay me or Charlie much attention, unlike the man I presumed was her husband. An older version of Frankie, he didn't shy away from staring in my direction.

'That's Jack,' Daisy whispered, mistaking my discomfort for curiosity. 'He runs the company now that Mr Parker's supposed to be retired.'

I was glad when Eliza shooed her husband further round the table and I could avoid his gaze. He'd probably once been as handsome as his son, and he definitely thought that he still was. The broken veins in his cheeks marked him out as a drinker even before he called for the waiter to bring more wine for the table and a large whisky for himself.

Directly opposite me sat Jack and Eliza's daughter, Carrie, a slip of a thing, still of school age going by her childish frock, her hair left long though it had recently seen a hot iron, the front ringlets struggling to cling on to her fine hair.

'Where's Dr Wilding?' Eliza asked Daisy, nodding at the sole empty chair left between Jack and Charlie. 'I called his cabin earlier but there was no answer. Carrie was hurt but luckily there's no harm done.'

'Gust of wind slammed a door right into her face.' Frankie's laugh was unkind.

'It was your fault!' Carrie protested, shrinking back into her chair as we all turned to stare at her face. On first glance I'd assumed that her florid complexion was a hand-me-down from her father but now I saw that her nose was swollen, her eyes puffy from crying.

'I am not the doctor's keeper, I'm afraid,' Daisy replied, buttering a bread roll.

Their conversation turned to the practicalities of the next few days and I returned to my menu, turning slightly to pick up on what Charlie was saying to Jack. Perhaps courting the Abernathys would be a nice distraction after all; they certainly didn't seem boring.

'Have I heard of Benny Walker? The name rings a bell,'

Jack said. 'But it's not really the sort of thing we do, you know. Of course, Mr Parker is a great philanthropist but he's very particular about what causes he chooses to support.'

In other words, musicals weren't their thing. Not high class enough for the Parker family name to be associated with. Perhaps if I'd trained as an opera singer…

'Darn, that's too bad,' Charlie sighed. 'I swear Benny said he'd been in touch with someone. But maybe you can just meet the talent now. Lena here's the star of the new show.'

I tried not to smile and show that I'd been eavesdropping. My ego swelled a little more every time Charlie called me a 'star', even though I knew it wouldn't be true until opening night had been and gone, and only then if I wowed the critics.

'She certainly looks the part,' Frankie said, raising his glass to me, and I managed to force a smile in reply. 'Mr Bacon, I'm sorry but I doubt Grandpa would be interested in a Broadway show – he's more of a museums and orchestras kind of guy – but I might be able to help.'

'Frankie…' His father spoke a quiet warning.

'What? You said that I need to come to the firm with ideas. So, what about sponsoring the arts in a new way? Make sure that people of *my* generation know the name Parker Godwin.'

'Son, we build roads. I can't see how the youth of today can help us out with that.'

'But that's exactly it, Dad! No one cares about roads. They're not exciting. No one walks down Fifth Avenue and wonders who paved it. The boardroom is full of men Grandpa's age. We're going to need to replace them sooner rather than later, and who's going to apply for a job at a company that hasn't done anything new since McKinley was president?'

'Sure. We can talk about it later.' Jack clicked his fingers at the closest waiter, waving his empty whisky glass. 'Another. And we're ready to order.'

'You wouldn't regret it,' Charlie said, refusing to drop the subject. 'Theatre attendance is on the up again. There've been some huge hits recently. *Anything Goes,* for one. And *Jumbo.* I mean, that was spectacular. People want to spend their hard-earned money getting wowed and that's our business. It's what we do.'

Charlie nudged me. I knew he wanted me to speak up but what was I supposed to say? I didn't know anything about how to run a theatre or a company. I sang and I could dance a little and I could learn my lines. That was what I was getting hired for. That and the fact that Benny Walker apparently owed my father a favour. I felt unease stir in the pit of my stomach. What if I got to New York and it turned out this had all been a horrid mistake?

He leaned towards me. 'You could stand to flirt a bit,' he whispered. 'I can't do this all alone.'

'You said I wouldn't have to,' I hissed back.

I looked up and saw that Carrie was watching me. She smiled and her pity made me feel ashamed. A young girl like that feeling sorry for me when I should have known better than to get pushed around by Charlie Bacon. I did know better, I reminded myself. This was all a means to an end and I didn't have to do anything I didn't want to.

'Your guy needs to work on his sales spiel,' Daisy said quietly as Charlie excused himself to go to the loo.

'I'm sorry.' I didn't know what else to say.

'Oh gosh, don't worry. He reminds me of my dearly departed husband. Single-minded and damn everyone else. But you don't work for him, do you? You work for this Walker fella?'

'I suppose. My contract is with Benny Walker, at least.' I'd signed it in a daze a few days before. I made a mental note to read over my copy of the paperwork before we arrived in New York. 'And Charlie's okay. He's just anxious. It's his job to make sure that everything goes well.'

A middle-aged man rushed up then, slipping into the empty seat next to Jack Abernathy. The tardy Dr Wilding. His appearance was everything I would have expected: serious expression, dressed smartly but with no regard for fashion, in a tweed jacket, bespectacled. A forgettable face. Brown hair with a slight curl and a beard shot through with grey.

'Sorry I'm late,' he said, taking off his glasses to wipe them on a pristine white handkerchief.

Eliza merely raised her right eyebrow and turned to her daughter, who had the waiter hovering behind her as she deliberated the menu choices. 'Darling, just order the soup and the roast chicken. You were sick last time you ate foie gras.' She leaned back and blew out smoke from her cigarette, her manicured nails tapping an impatient beat on her closed menu.

Carrie hesitated a moment longer before doing as she'd been told, rebelliously asking for the chicken to come with mashed potatoes rather than roast as the waiter had suggested. When it was his turn, Charlie ordered the foie gras followed by the sirloin steak and a Béarnaise sauce.

'So rich,' Eliza muttered.

My mouth had watered at the mention of steak but somehow I found myself asking for the salmon followed by the already approved roast chicken. Why Eliza's acceptance mattered a jot, I couldn't say, but her slight nod of approval calmed my jangling nerves.

'Well, isn't this nice,' Frankie said, grinning at me. 'Someone new to talk to at dinner makes a pleasant change. Here's to new company!' He raised his wine glass and the rest of us automatically followed suit.

'This is my first time at sea,' I confessed, and I sensed Charlie shift in his chair, no doubt hoping that I was finally about to dazzle the table with my conversation. 'You'll have to let me know if there are any special customs I should know about.'

'Your first time on a boat, huh?' Frankie seemed the only person keen to talk, which was a shame.

'I think they prefer to refer to the *Queen Mary* as an ocean liner rather than a mere boat.' Dr Wilding poured condescension on Frankie's word choice. I thought it a bit rich, bearing in mind that to the Abernathys he was 'staff', here at their whim. Though it was Frankie, so I couldn't really blame him.

'Ignore Wilding,' Daisy muttered. 'He's been in a foul mood since we left London.'

She started to tell me about her summer, their travels in London and around Italy. I smiled and nodded but I wasn't really listening. A week earlier I would have been backstage at the Canary Club, pulling on my dress and warming up my voice ready to go out and sing. Tommy would have been there and I'd have told him to go home to Maggie instead of slobbering over girls who were half his age. He'd have slammed into his office and I would have had a moment of wishful thinking, of wanting to walk out, catch a cab to Hampstead and tell Maggie what her husband had been up to, but I never had the guts. When it was time, I'd walk on stage and sing by numbers, wishing I was anywhere but there. And now here I was, about to get everything I'd ever dreamed of, and still I couldn't be happy.

The food arrived and more wine was poured. The cutlery was complicated and I was thankful for all the times Maggie had dragged me to fancy restaurants that I hated. Of all of us, it was Francis Parker who struggled the most. He had still barely spoken a word, but I wondered if this was more down to his physical condition. His hand shook as he tried to lift his fork to his mouth, frustration writ large across his face as Daisy leaned over to assist. He had ordered food that was bland, soft, easy to chew and to swallow.

I followed his lead, concentrating on eating rather than trying to join in one of the conversations that were happening around the table: Carrie and Eliza discussing whether to invite so-and-so for dinner the following week; Jack and Frankie batting away Charlie Bacon's continued attempts to interest them in the theatre business. Dr Wilding had produced a medical journal from his pocket and folded it in such a way that he could prop it up on the table in front of him. I may as well have not been there at all.

'Are you going to come with us, Lena?' I looked up into Daisy's pleading eyes, surprised. Dinner was now drawing to a close, our dessert plates scraped clean, the waiters clearing the tables around us.

'Isn't it a little early?' Eliza checked the time on her slim gold wristwatch. 'There'll be nobody up there yet.'

'By the time we get old Francis up there...' Jack shoved his chair back impatiently. Both his wine and whisky glasses had run dry and no new drinks orders were being taken.

'C'mon, Lena,' Frankie encouraged. 'You'll love the Starlight Club. They have a live band and it's not as busy as the ballroom.'

I looked at Charlie, who nodded. 'All right then, just this once.'

We made a crocodile, trailing in pairs behind the family patriarch, pushed by Daisy. It took some skill to fit the wheelchair into the electric elevator, only Daisy and Eliza managing to squeeze in alongside. The rest of us waited for the second car to arrive.

I have never had a great love for lifts. It's the sound of the mechanics that spooks me, the clanking and groaning of the chains, together with the jerky motion and the confined space. My phobias were not helped by being squeezed in among three taller men. Carrie was at the front, talking to the lift operator, with Charlie ahead of me. To my left was Frankie who, somewhat recklessly, had decided to glue his hand firmly to my bottom. There was no room to wriggle away and I knew that Charlie would kill me if I made a scene. I watched the floors tick up slowly as we rose, my skin crawling as I felt a thumb brush the bare skin of my lower back. When we reached the sun deck I stumbled out into the vestibule where the others were waiting for us.

'Are you all right, Lena?' Daisy asked me. 'You look rather flushed.'

'I don't like small spaces,' I told her, trying to hide my confusion. For as we'd tumbled out of the lift, I'd realised that it hadn't been Frankie's hand I'd felt; he'd walked out of the lift ahead of me.

It was Jack Abernathy who winked at me slyly as we gathered and made our way towards the nightclub.

4

Friday, 28 August
Quo Vadis, Soho

Autumn had arrived early in London, the wind yanking at my umbrella as I tried to avoid the puddles, only for a careless driver to speed past as I waited to cross the road, spraying my calves with cold, dank water. An omen if ever I'd seen one.

'Bad luck, love,' the woman behind me said sympathetically as I suppressed a cry of desperate rage.

I was running late, no time to nip home for a change of clothes, even though it would take me less than ten minutes. I was always punctual and Maggie would smell a rat. I didn't want her to start asking questions. It was a little after midday but already it had been a hideous morning, the sort that made you want to crawl back into bed and pull the covers up nice and tight, waiting for the next to dawn.

If I'd had any inkling as to how the rest of the day would unfold, I'd have taken things a step further and run for the tube to Victoria, jumping on the first train heading to the Sussex coast. It was where me and Alfie had gone when things got too much to bear in the city.

'The only food the English know how to cook,' Alfie would say as we walked along the pier eating chips out of day-old newspaper and sucking the vinegar from our fingers.

'Don't you like a good old jellied eel?' I'd joke, knowing the very idea made him retch.

My father never passed as an Englishman, even with a knotted handkerchief on his head and trousers rolled up to the knee like all the other dads on the pebbled beach. His skin was far too dark. The other dads sat sweating on the pebbled beach, their skin glowing lobster red at the mere hint of sunshine, but Alfie and I would walk all along the shoreline, heads tilted up in worship to the sun, before heading to the Palace Pier theatre for a show. He would never say if he wished we looked more alike. It had made my life easier to look like all the other girls at school but lately it made me sad that I didn't see him easily when I peered into the mirror. A little in the tilt of my eyes, in the fullness of my lips, that was all. And now he was gone.

I blinked away a rogue tear and pressed on. Dean Street was busy and I danced through the crowds, light-footed as I avoided people hunched up against the wind, not looking where they were going. Through the gloom the restaurant lights were a welcome beacon, cutting through the overcast skies, midday looking closer to midnight. I pushed open the door and walked through the lobby, waving at the maître d' and pointing towards Maggie, who was already sitting at a table in the middle of the restaurant, halfway down what I hoped was her first glass of champagne. I was starving and the warm aroma of garlic and red wine should have set my mouth watering, but I felt ambivalent to the idea of eating. The paintings on the wall, their bright colours clashing and churning, didn't help. I forced a smile onto my face as Maggie looked up and saw me.

She arched an eyebrow and made a show of checking her watch. 'What time d'you call this?'

'Sorry.' I let the waiter pull out my chair even though I always worried that they wouldn't push it back far enough as I sat and I'd end up on the floor.

'Were you at the cemetery?' Her voice softened and I looked away. The cemetery was exactly where I should have been.

The waiter set a champagne flute by my hand and I wondered if this was the sort of occasion that lent itself to a toast. If Alfie had survived, then his forty-seventh birthday would indeed have been deserving of celebration, but he hadn't. The tuberculosis had wrought its devastation over many months, until Alfie had been glad to receive a blessed relief at the very end of the previous year, the sound of revellers forming the background music to his final breaths, his life drifting away with the dying seconds of 1935. The doctors had let him go home for those last few weeks, to our old rented room in Maggie's mother's house, and I was glad that he'd died amongst family. As 'Auld Lang Syne' filled the street outside, I'd wanted to walk outside and scream. How dare they celebrate when my father lay so still, his body shrunken from disease, his rich, full-chested laugh silenced forever?

This was the first birthday that he'd missed. I hadn't planned to mark the occasion but Maggie, God bless her, had thought to book a nice restaurant to cheer me up. It was what we had always done, father and daughter, just the two of us no matter what else was going on. A posh meal for birthdays, hard up or not. Sunday best would be worn whether we were eating a three-course meal and drinking wine or sharing a pudding with a glass of pop. It was a non-negotiable event, even as our situations had changed and I had grown up and he had grown smaller, his once strong body failing until, on my last birthday, I had sat at his bedside and spooned soup into his mouth, Alfie too weak to hold the cutlery.

I looked up at Maggie, a lump in my throat as solid as one of Mrs Harper's suet dumplings, and tried to smile. She was absolutely right. I should have been at the cemetery, paying my respects. The opportunity to come clean and tell Maggie the truth came and went. *I told you so,* was never a nice phrase to hear from someone else's lips.

'Drink up.' Maggie raised her own glass.

'Champagne's supposed to be for celebrations.' I took a sip nonetheless, the bubbles sour on my tongue.

'It's only booze, love, hair of the dog, God knows you look like you need it. Besides, we can raise a glass to old friends, can't we? To Alfie? That's a celebration of sorts. To his memory.'

'I suppose so.' I tried to fake a smile.

'Oh cheer up! You never know, you might see someone famous.' She leaned forward across the table and whispered, 'I heard that Evelyn Laye comes in here.' She knew how I idolised Evelyn Laye. It was a dream of mine to follow in her footsteps, moving from the small theatres, the music halls, to the real thing: the West End stage. Many would have scoffed and said, at the age of twenty-six, I was already too old for such ambitions, but hope can be a stubborn habit to break.

'Wouldn't that be something?' I smiled at a passing waiter and he stopped to take our order.

Nothing on the menu appealed but the sooner we ate, the sooner I could escape the steamy restaurant, the crammed-in tables and warm bodies overcompensating for the foul weather outside. I wanted to go home and crawl under those blankets on my bed, pull the pillow over my head, and sob to my heart's content. Except that I'd still have the evening at the club to get through.

'... and then the veal, but make sure it's not pink in the middle. Turns my stomach, food that's still bleeding.' Maggie handed her menu back to the waiter.

'I'll have the same, but rare,' I said. 'Bloodier the better.' I smiled as Maggie pulled a face. If only this really was like the old days and we could stuff our faces and talk and drink champagne until we couldn't stand.

The waiter topped up Maggie's glass before he left and I saw that the bottle was almost empty. She'd had a couple of glasses before I'd got there then.

'Why aren't you drinking?' she accused. 'You've barely taken a sip!'

'Some of us have to work in a few hours,' I reminded her, glad of the excuse. 'Even if it is only the Canary.'

'Can't you skive off for once?' She lit a cigarette.

'It's your husband who pays my wages,' I pointed out.

She proffered her cigarette case. 'Exactly. Which in a roundabout way makes me your boss. I could give you permission.' I helped myself to her fancy gold lighter.

It was tempting to take her up on the offer, but I knew that Tommy wouldn't agree with his wife's appraisal of the situation. As far as he was concerned, Maggie's job was to keep house and his job was to manage his business affairs: the club as well as some other, less legal ventures.

Pride comes before a fall. Mrs Harper, Maggie's mother, said that often to the pair of us as we grew from children into young women, confident in our looks and our wit. If only either of us had paid attention. But why listen to proverbs when things are going so swimmingly? Not a year before I'd felt on the verge of something big. I was following in Alfie's footsteps, working my way around Soho. I could dance a little, was a decent actress, could sing really well. I'd auditioned at every big theatre and, while luck hadn't been on my side, it seemed only a matter of time. Except then Alfie got ill and with the increasing medical bills as well as the rent, it hadn't taken much skill in mathematics to work out where I needed to be. The odd walk-on role paid less well than a regular nightclub gig. Besides, the only time I'd had a halfway decent role in a play, I'd met James. And that had been a disaster.

'What's up with you then?' I finally took the bait. There had to be a reason why she was chucking overpriced wine down her throat as though she was afraid it was about to run out.

'Take a guess.' She flicked ash into the butter dish. 'Oh, don't look at me like that! They'll clear it away and bring a fresh one. That's what they get paid for, isn't it?'

'There's a perfectly good ashtray.' I shoved the dish behind the salt and pepper so that I didn't have to look at it. 'It's not the waiter's fault you're in a funny mood.'

'You weren't at the cemetery, were you?' She arched an eyebrow, her eyes narrowed. 'You were with that toff of yours. You went out with him last night and drank too much. That's why you look like you want to be sick.'

'It's not like I lied. You were the one who mentioned the cemetery, not me.' I knew I sounded childish, but I couldn't help it.

Maggie reached over and pressed her cigarette butt into the melting butter. 'You hardly rushed to correct me, did you?' She lit another cigarette and blew the smoke up towards the ceiling. 'So? Were you with him?'

'James? Yes, I was. Why does that matter? Alfie's gone, no matter whether I spend the night with a man or not. Acting like a nun won't resurrect him.'

'He's married, Lee!' She held up a hand to silence me. 'I know, I know, I'm not your mother. But what do you think you're going to get out of this? Do you want him to leave his wife for you? His children?'

'No. It's over anyway.' I looked down at my place setting and scraped at a tiny mark on the tablecloth with a chipped fingernail. 'He turned up at the Canary last night and he'd remembered, you know? He'd remembered about Alfie and he said I shouldn't be alone. He bought me a drink and then it got late and… Well, you know how it is. Anyway, it was the last time, he made that very clear this morning. He'd felt sorry for me, he said.'

I'd known all along that I was making a bad mistake but I couldn't help myself. James Harrington. A decade older than me, not even a man you'd give a second glance to walking along the street, but he knew how to charm. The timing had been good, on his part; I'd been waving off yet another short-term fling at the station, on his way home to America now that jazz wasn't paying the bills in Europe. Penniless musicians had to go where the money was, but I couldn't leave London, not when Alfie was ill. I suppose I wanted my next romance to last. Which makes it even more difficult to explain why I chose James, a man who was never free to be mine alone.

It had started off with flowers delivered to the stage door of the Arts Theatre every night for a week, almost two years ago. I was playing Christine in *Miss Julie,* my first and only non-musical acting role. A short run, and at the end of the week I agreed to go for a drink. I wasn't as easy as all that though – I'd made him suffer three months of dancing and drinking our way through Soho before I'd agreed to go back to his flat, the flat that for weeks I'd thought was his actual home, until he'd come clean and admitted that actually he stayed there because he needed to be close to Westminster and his constituency home was too far to travel to and from each day.

There had never been a future for us, but I'd still let him into my life. He knew that it wasn't Italian blood that darkened my skin and he didn't care. He knew about Maggie and Tommy, had been a shoulder to cry on when I knew Alfie wasn't long for this world and Maggie had her own problems to deal with. He'd even offered to help with the hospital bills, but I'd refused. How could I let him pay for the care of a man I could never introduce him to? The idea of it, presenting my married lover to my dying father, made my body tremble with shame.

'Does his wife know about you?' Maggie asked.

It would devastate poor Tabs if she ever found out, he'd said, as though the wrecking of his marriage had nothing to do with him. And his three children would be bullied at their exclusive boarding schools.

'Not that I'm aware of. Besides, like I said, it's over now.' I fiddled with my cutlery and willed her to leave me alone and not press for the details. 'And you never answered my question.'

She'd been stalling, I could see it in her eyes. Suddenly I began to wonder if this was really about Alfie at all. But no, that wasn't fair. Maggie had loved Alfie like a father. During the war, Alfie had taken on that role for the Harper daughters, his weak lungs and foreign status allowing him to remain in London while so many of the men on our street disappeared, many never to return, including Mr Harper.

'Maybe I care about you. Maybe I think you should be aiming higher than to be treated like some tart that can be bought with a few drinks and a bunch of flowers.' Maggie's voice was getting louder and I saw a woman at the next table glance across.

'It wasn't like that, you know it wasn't.'

Was it love? I didn't think so. My heart wasn't broken, it was my pride that was dented. What I had loved was the escapism. Never having to worry if he could afford to pay for the drinks or for dinner. Going to places that I couldn't usually afford. I had loved the way James had looked at me, the way he'd talked to me as an equal and how he'd admired me as a woman. I'd never meant it to last as long as it had. I'd thought that we'd gradually get bored of the club life and part with a handshake and a kiss on the cheek. Very British about it all. Instead, I felt as though I'd been in a car crash, the brakes slammed on before I was ready.

46

'I'm sorry. I don't mean to be harsh, but that man never gave two shits about you, Lee. He just wanted the convenience of a warm body to drag back to his flat when he felt lonely. Buying you a few drinks was cheaper than paying for a decent whore.'

'Thanks for that. Really, you've made me feel so much better.' I picked up my glass and emptied it in one go, gagging a little as the bubbles fizzed in the back of my throat. I stood and reached for the bottle, tipping out the dregs. 'Another please,' I told the waiter who had started towards me.

Our soup arrived but neither of us moved to eat. The waiter brought the new bottle of champagne and poured fresh glasses. We looked quite the tableau of bourgeois London society, from a distance.

'Look, are you going to talk to me or what?' I asked, as soon as the waiter was out of earshot. 'Stop trying to throw me off the scent and tell me what the hell's going on.'

She shifted in her seat and lit yet another cigarette before answering: 'Tommy wants a divorce.'

Little Girl Blue

5

Wednesday, 2 September
Queen Mary

The Starlight Club was as far removed from the Canary Club as the Ritz is from a cheap B&B round the back of Kings Cross Station. My feet did not stick to the floor. The waiters were dressed as smartly as they had been down in the dining room, easy smiles lighting their faces as they greeted their guests. A pianist played a jaunty Noël Coward tune. Everyone was so bloody *civilised*. The lighting was low, each table adorned with tiny candles that created a sophisticated ambience where everyone looked better: wrinkles disappeared, skin less dry. Who needed to be able to read a menu when you could appear ten years younger? Most of the tables were set up for two. It was a romantic setting, which made me feel very wary when I realised that Frankie had conspired to sit beside me at the table that had been reserved for the Parker/Abernathys. My only relief was that Jack would have to sit at the very end, with his wife and daughter between us. At the last moment he'd remembered that his cigars were still in his cabin and gone back to get them.

A waiter arrived and Charlie, opposite me, tried to communicate something across the table. I did my best to ignore him by looking the other way. I didn't know who was paying for the drinks, so I waited for Eliza to order a gin gimlet and then asked for the same. No one could accuse me of leaching off the Abernathys' tab if I was just following my hostess's lead. I reached for my cigarettes and felt Charlie kick me under the table. His gesture was clear this time: strike up conversation. I tried out a few ideas in my head, but they all sounded mundane or inappropriate. Discussions about the weather were dull. I daren't bring up what little I knew about politics, and I doubted these people cared much for jazz. I remembered the silver box, safely tucked away in my handbag. Maybe a pinch of powder would help me out. Maggie had always sworn by it when Tommy had dragged her out to dinner parties with prospective business partners. She'd been expected to make small talk with the wives and leave a good impression. It wasn't very different to what Charlie wanted from me.

'Darn it, I must have left Mr Parker's tonic behind.' Daisy rummaged through her large black handbag. 'I'll have to run and fetch it.'

'Can't even do a simple job properly. It's not like we don't pay her enough,' Eliza muttered under her breath once Daisy was out of earshot.

'This is what happens when you let the help sit up at the table,' Frankie told her with a smirk. I accidentally caught his eye. 'Lena, fancy dancing with me later?'

'Oh? Maybe. I suppose… Would you excuse me? Just need to use the…' Did Americans say loo? I pushed my chair back quickly, praying he wouldn't try to follow. The last thing I wanted was to get trapped on the dance floor with Frankie Abernathy.

The toilets were outside the club, along a corridor, and

as I approached the ladies' I noticed a door to my right, leading out onto the deck. Some fresh air might clear my head and lend me a spark of conversational wit. My head felt clearer immediately, even as my skin reacted to the chill sea breeze, goose pimples erupting as I found myself at almost the very top of the ship, the deck practically empty at that hour.

I stood in the alcove by the door, out of the wind, and managed to light a cigarette. Leaving my fur stole in the club had been an error, but then I hadn't expected to end up outside. The light above the door was bright and I took a step forward towards the railing, blinking as my sight adjusted to the gloom, slowly picking out the clouds above, shades of cobalt and navy blue against an indigo sky. I began to walk along the deck, trying to keep warm.

'Hey there. Got a light?'

I jumped at the sound of the voice, deep and male. American.

'Here you are.' I dared to step forward, holding up my box of matches.

The man who emerged from the shadows towered over me by almost a foot. He reached out a hand for the matchbox, an electric tingle running up my arm as his fingertips brushed against my palm. He lit his cigarette expertly, knowing how to hold his hand against the wind so that the flame caressed the tobacco lovingly, the tip burning bright. I wanted to say something clever and impressive, but I was tongue-tied and silent. His skin was darker than Alfie's, a burnished smooth umber that caught the light in an impossible way and made me wonder why I'd ever given the pasty-faced James Harrington the time of day. The coat and tails he wore were smart enough but I could see the loose threads around the buttons, the shiny patches that told its age. Much like the black dress I'd worn every night at the Canary. A costume for a stage.

'I haven't seen you around before,' he observed.

'Should you have?'

He shrugged. 'I know most folk on this ship by now. You weren't on the last couple crossings.'

'Of course not.' I laughed at the absurdity of his suggestion. 'Why would I travel all the way from New York to England and then head right back again?'

The relaxed look on his face disappeared, confusion fleeting, replaced by an expression of wariness. He took a step back, standing up straight. 'You're a passenger?'

'As opposed to...' Then it dawned on me. 'You thought what – that I work on the ship?'

'No, no,' he said hurriedly. 'Well... I mean, you don't get many folk like us up here. Not 'less we're working. So I just assumed. I'm sorry.'

'Like us?' I stared at him wide-eyed, the words coming out as a bark. 'What do you mean by that?'

The man raised his eyebrow and half smiled. 'No. Sorry, forgive me, I made a mistake. Good evening, ma'am.' He moved forward and I took a step away from him as he flicked his half-smoked cigarette past me, over the rail, before turning on his heel and walking away in the direction he'd appeared from.

He'd seen me for what I was. Did everyone know and they were just being polite? No; Frankie had guessed Italian. And people weren't polite about things like that, especially people like Frankie Abernathy. They didn't see the need to be. But this man had known immediately. He had taken one look and assumed we were merely different shades of the same. Black. Coloured. Whatever. It didn't matter, I reminded myself. *This is England!* Alfie had always told me. We could do what we pleased, same as anyone else. Which didn't necessarily stop people from staring, or whispering things about us as we walked by on the street, but we could sit where we liked on the bus or the tube.

Alfie had told me that there were two sets of rules in America, one for them and one for us. In England, there simply weren't enough coloured people for them to have thought about it that hard. That was why Alfie hated it when another black musician turned up in Soho. He was always welcoming to their face, but I knew that he worried about the delicate balance. A few of us were a novelty, something new. Too many of us and we'd start to become a problem.

When we moved to Bethnal Green from the mixing pot of Soho I began to understand it more. Most people were friendly enough, they just liked to ask questions: Where are you from? Can I touch your hair? Does the brown rub off? *Irritating but harmless,* Alfie used to say. *You are special,* he told me whenever the questions became less harmless, the taunts more hurtful. *And they are jealous. But you are as English as they are.*

I am English, the *Queen Mary* a tiny corner of that green and pleasant land. That was what Charlie had assured me. The concealment was purely for peace of mind, he'd said. It wasn't a problem, but some Americans weren't used to a coloured person sitting at their table. They might not take well to it, and we didn't need the hassle. Smooth sailing. He'd laughed at his own weak joke. No one back home cared who my father was or if I tanned a little darker than the average person in the summer. In New York it would be different. It was why Alfie had left there in the first place.

I raised my cigarette to my lips, for the first time tasting ash and the bitterness of the tobacco. I flung it away, letting my body sag over the railing. A week ago my life had been so normal. A regular schedule of late mornings, combing the pages of *The Stage* and *The ERA* for jobs and opportunities, attending a decreasing number of auditions for roles that I didn't particularly want, my evenings wasted on the Canary or any of the handful of Soho clubs where I was known. Only five days had passed since that had all turned upside down. A visit from a stranger that had changed everything. The sudden death that had forced my hand.

I felt my top lip prickle with sweat as my skin burned, my breathing quickening as I remembered Tommy. My stomach turned over and I gripped the railing tightly until the panic passed. Tommy was dead and it was my fault. There was no getting away from that.

I'd been gone far too long, I realised. Charlie would be fuming and the Abernathys would think there was something wrong with me, to spend so long in the loo. I turned to head back, pausing as I heard a giggle up ahead. Walking into the light were a couple, hand in hand. I watched as Daisy Lancaster led her beau towards the door and the bright light above it. Just as he moved into sight he pulled her back, turning her round and kissing her hard on the mouth. When she pulled away, her laugh growing louder as she teased him, I was shocked to see

Jack Abernathy's face revealed. Apart from the fact that he was married, it wasn't that long since he'd been trying to grope me in the lift. Slinking back into the shadows, I hid until the pair of them had disappeared inside before following them back to the Starlight, weary with this new knowledge. Yet another secret to add to my load.

My drink had arrived by the time I returned to the table and I took a restorative gulp as I sat down, ignoring Charlie's glare.

'I was beginning to wonder if you'd gotten bored and left us,' Frankie drawled.

I smiled politely. 'Goodness no. I suddenly remembered that I'd left something back in my cabin, that's all.'

'It seems to be quite the contagion this evening, this forgetfulness.' Eliza's words were venomous but her dagger-sharp gaze was aimed at Daisy, not me. She knew what was going on between her husband and her father's secretary, I was sure of it. I recognised that look well. Maggie had honed her own evil eye over the years, bitterness a fine whetstone.

'Perhaps it's all the travelling,' I suggested, eager to break the tense silence that Eliza's words had prompted. 'London to Southampton isn't so far, but when you think you have to get a taxi to the train station, then the train, then off the other end. Then onto the ship...'

'Exactly!' Daisy pounced. 'I swear to God, that maid we had this summer was as useless as they come. She packed everything in the wrong trunks – she'd have had half of Mr Parker's medications locked away in the hold. It's lucky I checked, or we'd be relying on the ship's doctor—'

'My dear, we haven't been properly introduced,' Eliza said, interrupting Daisy and addressing me directly. 'Elizabeth Abernathy, though everyone calls me Eliza.'

'Lena Aldridge,' I replied. 'Pleased to meet you. Thank you so much for allowing me to sit with your family this evening.'

'Think nothing of it.' She spoke slowly, thoughtfully. 'Aldridge, you said?'

'Yes.' I felt uneasy, as though I were being weighed up.

'Lena here is our big star,' Charlie chimed in. 'Maybe you didn't hear us talking over dinner, but in a few months' time everyone will be talking about her on Broadway.'

I blushed. 'Well, I don't know about that. I hope so, that is, but...'

'You're an actress?' Eliza leaned forward.

My first thought was to contradict her, but I bit my tongue in time. This was my chance to make Charlie proud and repay Benny Walker for the opportunity. 'Yes, I am. And I sing as well.'

'And she dances. A triple threat!' Charlie told her.

'I do love a trip to the theatre,' Eliza said.

'Darling, we went over all this at dinner. Mr Bacon here is looking for investment and we're not looking at the arts right now.' Jack clicked his fingers once more for the waiter.

'Well, I didn't talk about it at dinner. And I do have my own money, Lena. Perhaps we should get to know one another, you and I. We have time after all.' She patted my hand with hers.

'I'd like that very much.' My mood lifted and Charlie winked at me. Finally, he was happy with me.

'Another drink, Lena?' Frankie asked, and I realised that I'd finished my gimlet already, drinking it down like water. I nodded.

'No more for you, missy,' Eliza told Carrie, whose face scrunched up in displeasure.

'Mama, really? It's not even that late. Just one more Coca-Cola? Please?'

'No, darling. It's after nine o'clock now and you know what a terror you'll be in the morning if you're not tucked in by ten.'

'Daddy, please? I'm not a little kid anymore!'

Jack's expression wavered at Carrie's appeal. She was a daddy's girl then, like I had been.

'Carrie, I won't tell you again.' Eliza raised her voice and Carrie pouted, slamming her chair hard against the table as she was dismissed.

'Honestly, she becomes more argumentative the older she gets,' Eliza complained. 'When I was her age, I did as I was told. Didn't you, Lena?'

If I'd been honest, at fifteen I was already lying about my age to get into nightclubs and bunking off from the factory to go to auditions. Alfie made his peace with that because he didn't have time to keep a constant eye on me. He kept me safe by letting me work at places he knew, with people he was familiar with. Meeting me after midnight to walk with me to catch the bus home was his way of keeping me out of harm's way. I'd never known my mother and Alfie had never liked talking about her. She'd been too young to cope with a baby and a husband who was out most nights, that was about all he would say about her. When it was clear we didn't have long left, that the doctors had no further treatment to offer, I'd thought about asking him for the real story behind her desertion but found that I didn't care enough. At least, not enough to risk upsetting what we had.

'Is there anything?' I'd dared to ask one day, close to the end. 'Anything I should know. Or anyone you want to see?'

'You have always been enough,' he'd said, every word a struggle. 'I hope I've been enough for you.'

And then how could I ask him about her? Because he had been more than enough. Yes, I was curious, but not so much that I would risk him thinking that my life might have been better with her in it. For a start, it simply wasn't true. I was glad that our last few days had been full of smiles and laughter.

'Carrie's more obedient than you were.' Francis Parker's voice silenced the table. 'Let us hope that a slammed chair is the worst of your daughter's bad behaviour.'

'Carrie has two parents who love her. She needs to stop acting like a spoiled brat.' Eliza flushed red, glaring at her father.

'"How sharper than a serpent's tooth it is to have a thankless child."'

'Be careful, Father, I'll start to believe that's the only line from Shakespeare you actually know.' Eliza slammed down her empty glass. 'How long does it take to get a drink around here?'

The atmosphere at the table grew heavy, no one brave enough to speak. Charlie cleared his throat, as though about to sacrifice himself for the benefit of the rest of us, but he was interrupted by a flurry of activity below us, in the area beside the small dance floor. A drum kit was being swiftly assembled, the rest of the band made up of a clarinettist, a double bass player and a pianist with his back to me. It was only as he turned to address his fellow band members that I recognised the man I'd spoken to outside. I couldn't hear what he said but the others laughed and I felt a pull on my chest; envy that I wasn't down there with them to share in the joke.

The man stood and addressed his seated audience: 'Ladies and gentlemen, we are the Starlight Band and we're very glad to have you listen to us this evening. My name is Will Goodman.' He went on and introduced the rest of the band, but I wasn't listening. I couldn't rip my eyes from him, even as I dreaded him looking up and catching sight of me.

'Same old coon band, I see,' Frankie said loudly, nudging me as if expecting me to laugh. 'Can't they think of something more original?'

If I'd had another drink in me I might have told him the truth, just to see his jaw drop. See if he'd dare call me names to my face. Ignoring his proffered lighter, I lit my own cigarette, leaning my elbow on the back of my chair as I let the opening chords of 'The Very Thought of You' wash over me. Will Goodman. I wasn't sure if it was foolish or clever, but I made up my mind to find him again. Somewhere we could talk frankly and I could find out exactly how he'd seen what I was when not a single one of the Abernathys had.

I can hardly believe she's actually here. Setting a plan out on paper is one thing, to watch it come to life before my eyes is another altogether. Not only is she here, but she looks the part. I had hoped that she would, and the clothes help, of course. I suppose she got them from that unfortunate friend of hers. The new widow.

Lena turned up on time to dinner, spoke when she was spoken to, knew how to hold a knife and fork. Her voice was the most miraculous transformation. When I heard her speak at the club she sounded like a Cockney sparrow, like the girls who work on the market stalls round Covent Garden. Common as muck, as they say. Yes, there's still a trace of London streets in there, enough to give her away, but she could be exactly what she says she is — a successful actress moving to New York to star on Broadway. It seems almost a shame, but I must remember she is here simply to serve a purpose. Getting attached to her would not be sensible. There is no Broadway show. She may find fame, but it will not be the sort that she dreams of.

I do wonder though. If I had known her for longer, might I feel differently? Might I grow to like her? You could argue that she is an innocent, after all. Not responsible for the actions of her father or mother. But that is not the point. The point is that, whether she knows it or not, Lena Aldridge has a very good motive for murder and it would be a shame to waste it. When the truth comes out, no one will believe she's innocent.

The stage is set then. All the cast are present and correct and so far not a single person has broken character. So predictable it almost pains me! Still, it is all to my benefit. Tomorrow night Lena will get to be a real star. What a shame she won't have a chance to read the script until it's too late.

6

Thursday, 3 September
Queen Mary

I woke late on my first morning at sea, confused at first by the softness of the mattress, the silken feel of the expensive cotton sheets and the gentle motion of the ship. I had been rocked to sleep, anaesthetised after drinking a third gin gimlet as I watched Will Goodman play his piano, Frankie's further attempts to distract me thwarted.

I closed my eyes and pulled a pillow over my face with a groan. I was supposed to be enjoying a quiet few days at sea, trying to forget about what had happened at the Canary Club, looking forward to meeting Benny Walker. Instead, Charlie Bacon had got me mixed up in the Abernathys' problems. I had Frankie trying to cosy up to me, Jack taking his chances with Daisy behind his wife's back, and now this damned pianist whom I couldn't get out of my head. So much for a quiet life.

Maggie would have cackled and shaken her head. *Only you could get yourself in such a mess without even trying, Lee.* What was she doing now? She'd had a smile on her face as she'd waved me off the day before but I worried that it was only a mask, hiding her real emotions from me. How could she be all right? Her husband was dead. Murdered. What if it wasn't as simple as we'd thought? I had run away and left her with a huge mess to clear up. Even if she had pushed me to leave, it must rankle with her that I'd agreed to the plan so easily. But what else was I supposed to do?

I sat up and squinted at the wall clock, trying to make out the numbers. My eyesight was far from perfect, but glasses were for spinsters, Maggie said, and I tended to agree. I reached for my wristwatch to confirm the time: half past eight. Not a lie-in by my usual standards, but then I had turned in before midnight, the earliest I'd been to bed in months. My mouth tasted sour from the previous night's gin and cigarettes and my throat was drier than the Sahara. I pressed the call bell beside the bed and got up. The thick pile of the carpet tickled the soles of my feet as I made my way to the sofa, retrieving the peach silk robe from where I had flung it the day before. I'd no sooner tied it on than the knock came.

'Blimey, that was quick,' I told Danny, returning his grin.

'You were in luck, madam. I was on my way back from delivering breakfast to one of your neighbours.' He'd even brought a fresh jug of water with him; it was as though he could read my mind.

'I can have breakfast here? In my cabin?' The thought would never have occurred to me, but it was very appealing. I'd far rather lie in bed like an empress, eating toast dripping with butter, than drag myself back down to the dining room for another awkward meal with the Abernathys.

'We can do a continental breakfast. Croissants and coffee, that sort of thing,' Danny offered.

'Sounds wonderful.' I retreated to the sofa while Danny went off to do my bidding.

Lying back against the cushions, I sipped water and let my thoughts drift to Will Goodman. He played piano as well as Alfie had, though his voice had a deeper tone. There was a comfort in that, in knowing that even though Alfie was gone forever, that the music that reminded me of him would go on. Towards the end of the night, Will had asked for requests and the band played anything that was shouted out. No tune had been rejected on the grounds that the band didn't know it. Will was nothing like my father but his musical skill brought back memories, some of them good and some of them less so.

Back in Alfie's theatre days, at the end of a run there was always a party held on the empty stage. That was when Alfie came into his own, playing all the popular songs while the others danced and sang and drank too much. I was allowed to stay up and watch – this was before we moved to Bethnal Green and there was no Mrs Harper to keep an eye on me at night. The ladies thought me a little doll. They'd dress me up in whatever finery they could find in the theatre wardrobe and I would play at being a princess and eat the sweet cakes they gave me, accepting their attention graciously as befit a royal guest. I was too young yet to realise that their eyes were sliding from me to Alfie all the time, hoping that he might notice the care and attention they bestowed upon me, his precious daughter.

I'd been sitting upon my throne when I first found out what we were, Alfie and I. Miss Izzy had just finished arranging a moth-eaten cloak around my shoulders, pinning it with a brooch, its white and red paste stones glittered admirably beneath the lights.

'There we go, dearie,' she said, kissing the top of my head and looking over her shoulder to smile at Alfie. He laughed and blew me a kiss.

I couldn't remember the man's name, the actor who had played the lead role in that long-forgotten play, but he and Izzy both mistook that kiss as being meant for her. That was why he went marching up to Alfie and had a good go at hitting him. Luckily he had half a bottle of rum in him and wasn't fighting fit; I thought it was a game, watching Alfie duck and dive, sidestepping the man's heavy punches, knowing better than to go on the attack himself. I began to laugh at the comedy of it, Izzy soon joining in, and it wasn't long before the whole company were laughing at this drunken oaf of a man who couldn't get within an inch of my father.

Giving up, the man came stalking over to me, ripping the cloak from my shoulders before I could shrink back. 'Thievin' bastards, the lot of you.' He pointed a finger in Izzy's face, his cheeks purple with embarrassment. 'You should be ashamed of yourself. Fancy one of these half-breeds for yourself, do you?'

'That's enough!' Alfie came over and swept me up in his arms. 'You don't talk like that in front of my daughter.'

'I'll speak how I like. If you don't like it you can go back to where you came from and take your snot-nosed brat with you. Niggers ain't welcome in this country.'

That was when Alfie hit him. Only the once, and then we left, the man crying and moaning on the floor as Izzy held a reddening handkerchief to his injured nose. We never set foot in the Royalty Theatre again. For a long time I thought it was Alfie's choice, a protest against the way I'd been treated. Later I realised it was because they'd told him not to bother going back.

The telephone rang just as Danny knocked on the door. My breakfast took priority and I let him in first before running to answer the insistent ringing.

'Hello?'

'Lena?' Charlie's voice was loud in my ear. 'Where the hell are you?'

'I'm in my cabin, Charlie,' I said, rolling my eyes. 'I thought that would have been obvious.'

His sigh was long and weary. 'Why didn't you come down to breakfast? I thought that was the plan.'

'I don't remember us agreeing to that.' I had a vague recollection of Charlie talking at me while Will Goodman was singing the last bars of 'Someone to Watch Over Me', my attention compromised. I remembered nodding and hoping he'd think that I was listening. It wasn't my fault if he hadn't checked to make sure I actually was.

'Lena, honey, you gotta help me out.' Every now and then I'd noticed his accent changed, moving from matinee idol to something rougher. I wasn't sure that Charlie Bacon wasn't just as much of a faker as I was. 'I can't do this on my own. You're the face of this production! The voice! I need you to make a good impression.' I heard him sigh. 'Look, this is the first time Benny's trusted me with a job this big. He's taking a chance on both of us, not just you. You get seen alongside Eliza Abernathy, or it gets about that Francis Parker is investing in you, people want to know who you are. They want to know your name. That's how it works. Benny has money but a show needs an audience. If it's going to be your name above the theatre doors, then people need to have heard of you. *That's* my job.'

I should have been flattered. Grateful even. And I was, only at the same time it was annoying that Charlie had never mentioned any of this to me in London. He'd told me to pack some books and look forward to five days with nothing to think about but what to eat for my next meal. Nothing about cosying up to a load of rich people and hoping they'd help me become famous.

'Thank you.' I mouthed to Danny as he left. The air was now fragrant with the aroma of strong brewed coffee and my stomach rumbled as I gazed upon the basket of perfectly curved croissants and shiny glazed pastries. 'I'm sorry, Charlie. I'll make it up to you later. Luncheon starts at one o'clock, doesn't it? Promise I'll be there, right on time.'

'Meet me at midday,' he ordered. 'I'll be in the long gallery. That's up on the promenade deck, can't miss it. I have a plan.' He hung up and I stared at the receiver for a moment before replacing it on the apparatus.

Sunshine beamed through the porthole and I smoked a cigarette with my first cup of coffee, wondering if there was any better way to start the day. I could feel my body coming awake with each sip and realised I had actually had a decent night's sleep, the first such night in almost a week. No wonder I felt like a new person. I thought about Maggie and hoped that she was sleeping easier now that she didn't have me moping around her house. Looking at the telephone again I felt the impulse to pick it up and place a call to England. I'd been told it was possible, if extortionately expensive. But what would I say to her?

'Don't worry about me, I'll be fine,' she'd said on the doorstep, the hum of the taxi engine filling the silence between us, but I hadn't believed her. She said she had it all under control, but did she really?

'I'll telephone as soon as I arrive,' I'd said eventually, and she'd nodded and we'd hugged before I'd climbed into the car and told the driver to take me to Waterloo.

By the time I'd left we'd spent days navigating around one another, terrified of saying the wrong thing, the final thing that might shatter our friendship for good. So much left unspoken, and it was only now, when we were apart, that the words circled me like hungry birds. There was so much that I longed to say to Maggie. So many questions that I had for her that I had been too scared to ask a few days earlier. I should write them all down, but what if someone found the paper? They might work out what we'd done. No, I'd be patient until we got to New York and hope that a few days wouldn't make any difference.

I ran a bath and ate a croissant while I waited for the tub to fill, watching the mirror steam up. Still hungry, I ate a pain au chocolat in the bath and read a few chapters of the novel I'd picked up at W.H. Smith the day before, a new Poirot. The *Queen Mary* would have been a perfect setting for one of Hercule's ingenious feats of mystery solving. Perhaps one day Mrs Christie would send him off across the Atlantic and I could read all about it. Although, thinking about it, I was glad that he wasn't on my crossing. I had enough on my plate without having a master detective on my trail.

★

The long gallery was busy when I arrived, all the old dears taking their time over morning tea before the doors to the dining room opened for luncheon. It would be very possible to fill an entire day on board simply by moving from meal to meal. Charlie saw me and waved from a table in the centre of the room.

'Tea with lemon, please.' I'd barely sat down before a waiter was there, ready to take my order.

Charlie made a point of checking his watch and I smiled, knowing I was a few minutes early.

'Are you going to tell me what this is all about?' I lit a cigarette and crossed my legs, attempting to look bored.

'I don't know why you have to be so difficult, Lena. You haven't even set foot on a stage yet so you might want to lose those airs and graces until the reviews are in. You know how much it costs to put on a Broadway show? Whatever number you're thinking of, add a zero, maybe two. That's why it's so important that you realise what Benny Walker is risking with you.'

I shrugged. 'I don't know anything about business. And if I'm such a risk, then why is Mr Walker doing all this for me?'

Charlie sighed and curled his lip. 'I told you. He's making amends. I think he's crazy, truth be told, but here we are. I'm not asking you to climb Everest, honey, I'm only asking you to make a little bit of an effort. Look pretty. Talk nice. Get up and sing a song one night with the band. We want people to see your face and hear your name.'

It sounded perfectly reasonable when he put it like that.

'Fine, I just didn't like the idea of asking for money.' I shifted uncomfortably, remembering Jack's wandering hand. Men like him already thought that women like me would do anything for a few banknotes. I didn't want to reinforce that idea.

'It was a way in, that's all. Money and sex are the two great currencies and Francis Parker has no use for the second.' Charlie was irritated now. 'My new plan is to have you seen with him. In a respectable way, of course. Lucky you, you get a second chance to charm him now.'

'What?' I looked over my shoulder, following Charlie's gaze.

'Ahoy there!' It was Daisy Lancaster, wheeling her charge towards our table, the old man looking less than pleased to see us.

'Good morning Miss Lancaster, Mr Parker.' Charlie turned his toothy grin on them both. I had the distinct impression that their appearance wasn't a surprise to him.

'May we sit with you?' Daisy didn't wait for an answer before pushing one of the empty armchairs aside to make way for the wheelchair. 'And I must correct you, Mr Bacon, I'm *Mrs* Lancaster. Mr Lancaster is unfortunately no longer with us, but I think it's only proper to keep my title in honour of poor Gerald.'

The memory of her in Jack Abernathy's arms, their lips locked together tighter than a nun's chastity belt, rather ruined the saintly effect she was going for.

'Forgive me, Mrs Lancaster, but you hardly look old enough to be a widow. And that surely isn't a New York accent, is it?'

'You caught me out, Mr Bacon. I grew up in Tulsa, Oklahoma. Came to New York as a newlywed a little over ten years ago. And call me Daisy.' She all but batted her eyelashes at him.

'If you'll call me Charlie.' He grinned and winked, her antagonism towards him the previous night instantly forgotten.

I hated them both.

'Daisy, my pills.' Francis Parker also looked less than impressed with their little flirtation and I wondered how on earth this staid old man had ended up with the merry widow as his secretary, her lips painted fire-engine red before it was even noon.

'One moment.' She rummaged in her large handbag, which, from the rattle it made, contained quite the pharmaceutical cornucopia. 'Here we go.' She tapped a couple of small white tablets into her palm before handing them to Parker. 'Let me get you a glass of... oh, well don't pay me any attention.' Parker had swallowed them both dry in an instant.

'Mr Parker, we didn't have much opportunity to speak last night. I'm Charlie Bacon. I work with Benny Walker and we were—'

'Charlie.' Daisy interrupted him with a shake of her head, placing a hand on his arm. 'Mr Parker isn't to be bothered about business. I'm under strict instructions.' She lowered her voice to a whisper. 'His health isn't what it was, you understand?' I looked at Parker, who was staring down at the age-stained hands which rested in his lap. Maybe he was going deaf and genuinely couldn't hear what was going on.

'I'm sorry,' I told her, embarrassed about Charlie's persistence. 'My father was ill for the last few years and I would have been grateful to have someone to care for him as well as you are caring for Mr Parker.'

'Why thank you.' She seemed flattered. 'Do you mind me asking, is your father...'

'He died shortly after Christmas,' I told her. 'It was a long illness and I think that he was glad in the end. Good old Alfie, I hope he's looking down on me now and feeling proud.'

'Oh honey!' Daisy patted my hand. 'Rest in peace, dear Alfie.' She made the sign of the cross and I tried not to grimace.

'What's your name again?' Parker suddenly became alert, staring at me with narrowed eyes.

'Lena. Lena Aldridge.'

I waited for him to carry on talking, but Francis Parker seemed to have lost interest in me, turning his attention to the view out of the window. My tea arrived and I drank it quickly before Charlie could make another excruciating attempt to get Parker's attention, getting up to leave with the excuse that I wanted to stretch my legs before sitting down to a big meal. Charlie followed me out into the corridor.

'I gotta hand it to you, you really do know how to act,' he said, full of glee.

'Excuse me?'

'That whole sob story. I mean, yeah, it's sad about Alfie, but did you see their faces? They lapped it up. Pity loosens a wallet like you wouldn't believe.'

'That's not... I didn't...'

I gave up, knowing he couldn't possibly understand. Let Charlie think what he wanted if it got him off my back. I couldn't help feeling a little sick about it though. I had meant what I'd said to Daisy, and it didn't seem fair that Charlie Bacon could cheapen my words so easily. Benny Walker would understand. I had been chosen precisely because of the debt he felt he owed to my father; the guilt he felt at having left it too late to patch up their differences. I was looking forward to meeting him.

Perhaps he could tell me more about Alfie's life before he'd come to England.

Thinking about that broken friendship drew me back to Maggie. What would she do if she were in my shoes?

Tell him to sod off, she'd say about Charlie. *Order another drink and raise your glass to Alfie, the only decent man we've ever known.*

And she'd be absolutely right.

7

Friday, 28 August
Quo Vadis, Soho

I stared at Maggie dumbly. 'A divorce?'

Maggie reached down underneath her chair and retrieved a manila envelope. 'Looks like he finally found a slut he wants to be married to more than me.'

My first thought was that Maggie's mother would hit the roof. God help Tommy Scarsdale once Mrs Harper got hold of him. I caught the envelope from her trembling hand as it threatened to land in her cream of tomato soup.

Inside the packet I wasn't surprised to find a selection of candid photographs, but I was shocked by their subject. That Tommy had been cheating behind Maggie's back on and off for years was well known to everyone, including his wife. That Maggie had finally decided to get her own back was news to me. I couldn't see the face of the man, only the back of his head as he crossed the threshold of Maggie's home in the first photograph. The next shot showed a naked male torso at her bedroom window, reaching to draw the curtains closed. Not Tommy, I could tell from the lack of flab. The most devastating evidence, a trio of photos that had been taken in the alleyway behind the Canary, Tommy's own club, Maggie's face perfectly caught, her head thrown back as the same mysterious man pushed her up against the wall, her legs around his waist. I shoved the photographs back in the envelope.

'Who the hell is he?'

'Does it matter?' There were tears streaming down her face. 'He turned up one day at my front door and told me that he was a friend of Tommy's. He said that a threat had been made and it was nothing to worry about but better safe than sorry. He said that Tommy had sent him round to check the security on the house.'

'Well, he checked something all right,' I muttered. I should have felt pity but all I could think of was what she'd just been saying to me about James and the sanctity of marriage. Never mind that under normal circumstances I'd have been cheering at the idea of her getting rid of Tommy.

'Those first few photos, I never did anything. Not in my own house, Lee! You know me better than that. He stitched me up! I offered him a cup of tea and he said he'd go and check upstairs while it was brewing.'

'And he posed there in the window, knowing there was someone hiding in the bushes with a camera.' It did explain how the man had managed to avoid getting his face in any of the pictures. 'But what about the alleyway?'

She scraped her spoon across the surface of the soup, picking up the skin and depositing it on the edge of the bowl. 'Last Friday afternoon it was. I'd been to the hairdressers after lunch and when I got home, Mrs Wood told me that this man, Brian, rang while I was out. He'd asked for me to go to the club as soon as possible so he could meet with both me and Tommy. To talk about the security thing. So I took a cab straight over. The door was locked but there was a sign saying to go up to the flat above the club.'

My heart sank. I'd never set foot in that flat, but I knew what went on up there. Various girls came and went, none of them over the age of eighteen, so I'd heard. Tommy's latest fling, Serena, was one of them, saving herself from the roulette wheel of vice by hooking herself to Tommy's side where it was safer than servicing whichever man turned up with a wad of banknotes in his pocket each night.

'I should have known what was going on,' Maggie said, smiling ruefully. 'I mean, I always knew, but you hardly want to admit to yourself that your husband's running a knocking shop. I got to the top of the stairs and there was this old man, rancid he was, strolling out of one of the bedrooms with this grin on his face. I could see this young girl behind him, sitting on the edge of the bed in her undies, counting the money. It was too much, Lee – I ran out. And then Brian arrived, or so it seemed. I ran straight into him. And he saw the look on my face and was ever so apologetic. Said he'd been told that the flat would be empty. He suggested that we go for a drink round the corner, for the shock. He was ever so nice, Lee, and when I wanted to go and confront Tommy after a few gins he said all right, but that we should go in the back way. Only we never actually made it to the club. I came over all groggy. I don't really remember what happened. Even looking at the photos, I don't remember any of it. I woke up the next day in bed and a vague recollection of being in a taxi. That's it.'

'Christ, Maggie.' I looked down at the envelope, still in my hands. 'But he – did you...?'

She shook her head. 'I don't think anything actually happened. Not *that* anyway. I think it was posed, to get the photograph.' She stared down at her hands and I wondered how sure she was.

'He stitched you up good and proper,' I said eventually. 'How long have you known about these?'

'Tommy came home early last night. Can you believe I got all excited? I heard the door go and I ran downstairs to greet him. I was thinking if there was anything in the larder that I could throw together to make him a nice dinner, but he flung those in my face and told me I had a week to get out.' She wiped her face with her napkin, leaving streaks of mascara on the white linen. 'He said whores get nothing.'

'Can he do that?'

'How should I know, Lee? Not like I've done this before.' The tears were flowing again, her face contorting so that she reminded me of a Picasso painting. 'I feel like such an idiot. You and Mum've been telling me to leave him for years. And now I'm going to have nothing to show for it.'

'He won't get away with this.' What an absolute bas-tard. I could feel anger begin to run hot in my veins, fuelled by my own hurt and humiliation. I didn't know what exactly, but surely there was something we could do, so that at least Maggie would get the money to start over.

'How old is she? The girl he's seeing,' she asked me.

'Serena?' I'm ashamed to admit that I'd known all about her

but, as a messenger who'd been shot at plenty of times, I'd also known better than to say anything to Maggie about it. 'Sixteen or so?' She was very young, I knew that much, but then so had Maggie been.

I'd always thought I knew what it was that Maggie saw in Tommy. She liked the furs and the new clothes and the nice restaurants. Summer holidays in the south of France, going to parties where you might spot someone famous, never worrying about how to pay the rent. It had suited me to think this of her because I didn't understand it otherwise. Seeing how devastated she looked now made me feel terrible.

'You told me not to marry him.' She offered me the cigarette case, almost emptying it into my soup as her hands trembled.

'That was a long time ago.' I took one and lit hers first.

Eleven and a half years, to be exact. Just turned fifteen, finished with school and scraping by with evening factory shifts while we ran around in the day searching out auditions. Any time a sign went up at a club or a theatre, looking for girls who could act, sing or dance, Maggie and I were there. She couldn't hold a note really, or act, but Maggie had the 'look'. Shiny dark hair that held a wave, bright blue eyes, and a figure that drew attention. Alfie had warned me off certain of the Soho clubs, the Canary amongst them, but we'd happened upon it by chance.

Our days of petty crime are far behind us now, but back then it was how we paid for the little extras. Wages were for handing over to our parents, for food and the electric meter. Lipstick and stockings, a new hair clip or a brooch to brighten up an old dress, those came through shoplifting or pickpocketing. Maggie had been caught with her hand in some old chap's pocket on

Regent Street and we'd legged it into Soho, hoping to lose the bobby who was chasing after us. Diving down a side street, we'd fetched up at the back of the Canary Club where a gaggle of girls were standing outside waiting to go in and show their talent. How could we resist? And a decade later, here we were. My career had made a brief rise before dumping me back where I'd started, and Maggie had a failed marriage to the club's owner. Crime really didn't pay.

'So what happens now?' I asked.

'I'll sort something out,' she said.

'He can't kick you out of your own home.' I said it firmly, but I wasn't at all sure.

She laughed. 'Don't worry, I'll be all right, Lee. Like I said, I'll sort it out. But I wanted you to know. You're my best friend, after all. My only friend. I wanted you to understand why I'm a bit out of sorts today, that's all.'

She pulled out her compact and dabbed away any signs that she'd shed a tear over her marriage. Tommy was a coward, always had been, and this sly game of his didn't surprise me. Why handle your own dirty business when you could pay someone else to get rid of your wife for you? I'd disliked him before but now I hated him. Doing this to Maggie in such a callous way. Watching her sob in the middle of a crowded restaurant, knowing that the room was less noisy now because everyone else was staring at our table and whispering about us, made my blood boil.

'I'm going to come to the Canary tonight. Have it out with him face to face.' She blew her nose and sniffed, nodding her head as she made the decision.

'Tonight?'

'It'll be impossible to find him now. He plays golf in Wimbledon on Fridays, or at least he sits drinking in the club-house, and then he goes straight to the Canary.'

'That's a bad idea,' I told her, trying not to think about the worst that could happen and failing. With ammunition as explosive as those photographs, Maggie should have been trying to calm things down, not throw petrol on the flames. 'Serena will be there and… why not let me talk to him? I'll tell him to go home and be a man about things. That would be better, wouldn't it? You don't want Serena there gloating.'

'Worried I'll start a catfight?' She snapped the compact shut. 'I'd win.'

'I don't doubt it. But that doesn't make it a good idea.' I picked up my spoon, trailing it across the surface of my soup. 'I'm not really that hungry.'

'Me neither.' Maggie waved the waiter over. 'Sorry, love, we're not in the mood. I'll pay for the food we ordered, but could you take these away and don't bother bringing the rest. We'd like a bottle of your most expensive champagne.' She winked at me. 'I'm going to spend as much of his money as I can before it's too late.'

She beamed at me and my heart sank. 'Promise me you won't come to the club tonight?'

'I promise I'll think about it,' she said.

8

Thursday, 3 September
Queen Mary

It was James who had informed me that it wasn't polite to talk about politics at the dinner table. This after he'd called an end to my argument with one of his friends who had the wild notion that he could hitchhike his way to Spain and fight Franco. (The man in question had never even worked a day in his life, so how he'd cope in an actual war was beyond me; the idiot seemed to think all he had to do was show up and talk some British sense into the fascists.) Apparently nobody had ever passed that advice on to Frankie Abernathy.

'It's not politics, Mother. Not when I'm talking about our friends,' Frankie argued.

'Of course it is.' Eliza glanced at Dr Wilding, who looked as though he'd rather be anywhere else in the world. 'What Seb and Anna do is their own business. We don't need to talk about it now when we might not all agree.'

'Wilding doesn't mind, do you?' Frankie addressed the doctor, who declined to answer. The clench of his jaw spoke volumes. 'There are two sides to every story, isn't that what they say? So Herr Hitler had a few Jews locked up. What did they do first? That's what you have to ask yourself. A strong leader has to make hard decisions. And look, it's working. He's turned Germany's fortunes around and people are proud to be German for the first time since the war. That's all Seb was saying. As proud Americans ourselves, surely we can appreciate the value of patriotism. I'm telling you, those condemning his policies blindly should take a good hard look at their own country's failings.'

'The last time I saw you this excited was when I took you to the Moulin Rouge,' Jack said drily. 'Who'd have thought a funny-looking German could compare to a dancing girl.'

'I don't like Hitler,' Carrie piped up. 'He gives me the creeps.'

'I agree,' I said. 'It's the moustache and eyes that bulge when he gets over-excited. And the way he shouts all the time, I bet you'd end up covered in spit if you tried to have a conversation with him.' Charlie kicked me under the table but Carrie giggled and even Wilding had to stifle a smile as the air was let completely out of Frankie's balloon. 'Sorry, I probably shouldn't have said that while people are eating.' I grinned at Carrie. She was the only person at the table who seemed genuine, not bothering to hide behind a façade. When I'd been her age I'd already been a master at showing people what they wanted to see.

'I'm going to take some photographs around the ship this afternoon,' Carrie announced, pulling a smart leather case from the back of her chair where it had been hanging, presumably containing a camera. 'And then I'm going to go swimming.'

'There's a swimming pool on board?' I asked. There was still so much of the ship that I hadn't explored. I couldn't imagine it, a smaller body of water contained within the ship as it sailed across the ocean. It seemed fantastical.

'The entrance is literally right across from the dining room.' Carrie pointed in the general direction. 'You should come, Lena, then I'd have someone to talk to. When we sailed to England in June there were only ever old women in there. Gosh, they swim so slowly I don't know why they bother!'

'Oh, I don't think so.' I patted my hair lightly. 'I'd want to have an appointment booked at the salon for immediately afterwards.' It wasn't that I couldn't swim; Maggie and I had often spent long summer afternoons loitering by the side of the bathing lake in Victoria Park. Our main interest hadn't been in exercising though. Not when there were so many young men about to talk to. And look at. And smile in the direction of.

'I feel exactly the same way, Lena. Darling, don't forget to wait for an hour else you'll get a cramp.' Eliza patted her daughter's hand and I felt a wave of envy wash over me.

'Yes, Mama.' Carrie smiled sweetly. 'Anyway, I want to see if I can find any famous people up on the promenade. I swear I saw Clark Gable on the sailing in June, but I didn't have my camera to take a photo and no one believed me. I want there to be proof next time I spot someone from the movies.'

I meant to wish her well on her hunt but was distracted by the sudden realisation that Francis Parker was staring at me. It was disconcerting, the way he hardly spoke and yet that gaze of his was so sharp, the rest of the family in thrall to him when he did deign to open that wizened mouth of his. I couldn't put my finger on it but there was something odd about the way he stared, as though he thought he recognised me but couldn't quite remember from where.

'Penny for your thoughts, Lena?' Carrie caught me out.

'I was trying to remember what entertainment they had listed for this afternoon,' I bluffed.

'Good thing I brought my *Ocean Times* down with me.' Charlie produced his copy of the ship's daily newspaper with a flourish, turning pages until he found what he was looking for. 'At four o'clock they have orchestral music in the main lounge, followed by the cinema at five. *Mr Deeds Goes to Town*. I saw it already, but I thought it was marvellous. All about a small-town guy who suddenly inherits a fortune and ends up in New York surrounded by people scheming to take it all from him.'

'We could have a girls' afternoon at the movies,' Eliza suggested. 'Carrie?'

Carrie wrinkled her nose. 'Mama, you know I hate the movies. Such a waste of time. Watching fake people in their fake lives.'

'Who can hate the movies?' her brother teased, regaining his bluster. 'Honestly, Carrie, one day you'll learn that not everything in life has to have a purpose. You can do things for fun, you know.'

'But I love taking photographs. And I'm going swimming afterward,' she argued. 'I think that's fun.'

'But you don't do it for fun, baby sister, do you? You swim because you read somewhere that it was good for your health. And you take photographs because you hope one day someone will be foolish enough to want to display them.'

'Can't something be fun *and* good for you?'

86

'I'd like to see the movie,' I said suddenly, raising my voice above their sniping. 'I haven't seen it before and there's not much else to do, so...'

'Fabulous.' Eliza beamed at me and folded her napkin. 'I'll see you in the main lounge then. Shall we say half past four?'

I nodded, remembering what she'd said the evening before, about wanting to get to know me better. Perhaps having a drink or two with Eliza Abernathy would be enough to get Charlie off my back. I glanced across and was rewarded with a thin-lipped smile from him. I hated to admit it after my resolution to ignore his demands, but it was a relief to know that I was in his good books.

After luncheon I found a relatively secluded section of the long gallery and tucked myself away, reading my book. I wasn't hiding as such, more taking a breather from other people, but I couldn't concentrate at all. My fingers turned pages but when I reached the end of a chapter I found I had no recollection of what I'd read. I put my book down with a sigh. The clock close by told me it was almost four o'clock. Was it too early for a drink?

'Fancy seeing you here!'

I glanced up to see Daisy Lancaster approaching, her jet-beaded shawl billowing behind her as she walked so that she looked like a glamorous crow. I wondered if she chose to dress in black because she had loved her husband so much, a modern-day Queen Victoria, or if it was more for the dramatic effect. My money was on the latter.

She sat down and waved a waiter over. 'Time for a small drink, don't you think? I don't have long. Mr Parker takes a nap at the same time every day. Like clockwork he is, but he'll be wide awake by five o'clock.'

'You won't be joining us for the movie then?'

She looked at me as though I were mad. 'I don't think Eliza would like that.'

I remembered the glare Eliza had given Daisy the night before and was glad that the waiter saved me from having to pass comment. 'A Martini, please,' I told him.

'Oh snap! I'll have the same,' Daisy said. 'I've spent the last hour with Dick Wilding and that man's enough to send anyone running for the nearest drink.'

'You two don't get along?'

She snorted a laugh as she lit a cigarette. 'We get by, mostly by having as little to do with one another as possible. He prescribes the medication to Mr Parker and I administer it.'

'I don't think I realised how ill Mr Parker is,' I said, 'to need his own private doctor to travel with him. And it must be strange for you, having to live with someone you don't get on with that well.'

'Oh, I don't know. I have been married after all.' Daisy laughed at her own joke. 'In New York I barely have to see Wilding. He's married and lives at home, but he travels to England with us each summer. I'm sure his wife has a gay old time without him. Between you and me,' she said, lowering her voice, 'he isn't averse to a little self-medication, if you know what I mean. The perks of being a man of medicine, I suppose. Even so, he thinks very highly of himself. Stays in the Mayfair house, eats dinner with us like he's a part of the family, when really he's just a jumped-up servant.'

I thought it best not to point out that Daisy herself fell into that category. 'What exactly is wrong with Mr Parker?'

'A little bit of old age, a little bit of overworking.' She shrugged. 'He had an apoplectic fit last fall and ever since then he's been in a wheelchair. It took him months to regain his voice and even now it's very shaky. He's hardly the same man at all. Used to be he ruled the family. What he said went. But then he had to cede control of the company to Jack, and I swear that came closer to killing him than his illness did.'

'I can imagine,' I said. Anyone could see what a fool Jack was.

Daisy rifled in her handbag and produced a deck of playing cards. 'Gin rummy? Carrie used to indulge me but recently she's been kind of stand-offish with me. It's her age, I expect. Girls get funny ideas in their heads once they get interested in boys. They don't have time for other women the way they used to.'

Or, more likely, Carrie knew about her father's affair with the so-called secretary, but I wasn't about to let on that I knew. She began to shuffle and our drinks arrived, accompanied by a bowl of peanuts, which I couldn't resist dipping into.

'So tell me more about this Broadway play of yours. Charlie says this time next year everyone'll know your name.' She dealt the cards expertly, her eyes on me rather than the deck.

'I don't know about that.' I tried to play it down even though the thought of it brought a smile to my face. 'It's a great opportunity though. I know it might not turn out to be all that Charlie makes out, it's his job to make me sound more important than I am, but I hope I don't make a pig's ear of it.'

'Honey, don't think like that,' she scolded. 'You gotta have confidence in yourself. Broadway! My God, there are girls where

I'm from who'd kill to get a shot like that. Literally. And who doesn't love a good musical? A Saturday matinee is the high point of my week. Carrie comes over to see her grandfather and I can slip away for the afternoon. You can guarantee I'll see your show. What's it called?'

I opened my mouth to answer before realising I actually didn't know. 'They've not settled on the name yet but it's going to be very similar to *As Thousands Cheer.*'

'Oh, I loved that! I saw that three times, in fact; twice on Broadway and then again last summer when we were in London.'

'You were in London last year as well?'

I tried to remember what I'd been doing the summer before. Could it be that I'd run into Francis Parker then, before his illness, and not recognised him? I'd taken a few jobs in hotel bars the summer before to pay for Alfie's care. Perhaps he'd seen me there and that was why he'd been staring at me earlier, trying to remember where he knew me from. I hoped the memory would continue to elude him.

'Mr Parker spends every summer in London. His wife was British, you know. He owns a house in Mayfair and the whole family travel over every year. Parker Godwin have a London office because it would absolutely kill Mr Parker to take any time off. Eliza's flock head off to the Continent for weeks on end, thank goodness, but Jack usually stays back.' Her cheeks reddened slightly and she took a sip of her drink. Thinking of Jack and what the pair of them got up to when his wife was away, no doubt.

I wondered how it had started between Jack and Daisy. They had been cavorting like newlyweds when I'd caught sight of them on deck; presumably it had been during the recent summer,

Francis Parker hardly able to keep tabs on what his secretary and son-in-law got up to each evening now that he was confined to his wheelchair.

We played cards and stuck to banalities in our conversation: life on the ship, the superior taste of a Martini at sea compared to on dry land (put down to the salt in the air).

'Shouldn't you be running along?' she said, finishing her second Martini.

'Where to?' I'd completely forgotten that I was supposed to be meeting Eliza. It was already half past four. 'Oh gosh! I'm going to be late. Which way's the lounge again?'

'That way.' She pointed. 'Just past the bar.'

I hurried along, hoping that Eliza's timekeeping ability was as shoddy as my own, and my prayers were answered when I saw her arrive from the opposite direction. I waved and she gestured to follow her to a table in the middle of the room, not far from the stage where a string quartet was playing a tune I recognised but couldn't put a name to.

'Novices,' she scoffed, looking at the people who crowded the tables along the windows that lined both sides of the lounge. 'In a few minutes they'll close all the drapes for the movie and we'll have the best view.'

I realised that behind the musicians was a screen upon which the film would be shown. Eliza was right, we'd have a perfect view. I wondered how many times she'd sat in ship lounges like this one, crossing the Atlantic twice a year. First with both her parents as a child, now with a father who might be on his last voyage. I knew what it was like to watch a parent fade away, to have to stand by as everything vital about them was slowly extinguished. I didn't get the impression that Eliza was as close to her father as I had been to Alfie, but appearances were often deceiving.

'Coffee?' Eliza asked. 'It's probably a tad too early for a proper drink, don't you think?'

I agreed profusely, lighting a cigarette hurriedly, hoping that the tobacco smoke would cover up any waft of alcohol from my breath.

'You must be excited. First trip to New York. I sometimes think I prefer London, but Manhattan is home in a way that Mayfair is not.' It was an area of London I'd never spent much time in before meeting James, but from what I'd seen it was full of people like the Abernathys, though even more stuck-up. 'Where are you staying? In a hotel?'

'The Sherry-Netherland? Is that right? It sounds more like a dessert than a hotel.' I was relieved when she laughed. 'I'm booked in there for a week and then I suppose I'll need to find somewhere to rent.'

She waved away my reservations with a well-manicured hand. 'It'll be easy, especially for a young girl like you, free and single. The theatres are full of bright young things just starting out. If I were you, I'd ask around on your first day, see if anyone's looking for a roomie. And worst case you can get a room in a boarding house. In some ways that might be better, if you want to take your career seriously. More rules, no boys allowed.'

'That might be more sensible,' I agreed. I imagined what would have happened if Maggie and I had ever rented a flat together. It would have been fun, sharing clothes and staying up late talking about boys. Alfie would have come over on

Sundays and I'd have cooked, because Maggie couldn't, but she loved spending time with Alfie. The pair of them would have shared a bottle of beer and played Twenty Questions. Alfie was an expert at it and rarely needed even half his questions to win; I refused to play him anymore, but Maggie was determined to beat him one day. I could see it all so vividly that it felt like a real memory. 'Did you ever do that? Live with a roomie, I mean?'

Eliza smiled and looked away. 'I suppose, in a way. Not for very long though. My father... he's not the man he once was. In his prime he could be terrifying. And he didn't like me living away from home. After a while it seemed easier to go back rather than to keep arguing.'

'Daisy told me he fell ill last year. It must be strange, for you as well as him.' I took a deep breath and made her an offering. 'My own father died recently after a long illness. I don't know if I preferred it that way, having time to prepare, or if it would have been easier if it had come out of the blue. Sudden but surely less suffering for him to go through.'

For a moment I wondered if I'd been too familiar. Eliza bit her lip. 'I found it shocking at first. The man whose voice was the only one worth listening to, and now he barely speaks. His mind is the same but his body... Well, you can see for yourself. I suppose it's less cruel than the other way around, but I know it drives him mad.' Her smile was unreadable. 'A lot of people would say he deserves it.'

Was she one of those people? I wondered, glad when the waiter arrived with our coffee and a plate of lemon shortbread. What had Francis Parker done to make so many enemies?

'What do your family think about you leaving them?' she asked suddenly.

What would Alfie say if he could see me now? Being honest with myself, so many of my doubts were stubborn because I didn't know what he would think. Whether this opportunity would be the making or breaking of me.

Not everyone needs to be a star, he'd always say. *Sometimes it's better to shine a little less brightly. That way, you won't burn out.*

I'd put his words more down to his – our – lack of opportunities though. Playing piano in theatres and dingy cinemas in the East End was hardly what Alfie had dreamed of when he'd left New York all those years ago. Surely even he would bite off the hand that offered him Broadway.

'It was only the two of us,' I told her. 'I hope that my father would have been excited for me. But he'd have told me to be more cautious.'

'You don't have any living family left?'

She was busy pouring the coffee and I was glad she wasn't looking at me. A lump the size of one of those Martini olives had jammed itself in the back of my throat. Until a week ago I'd have said I had a pretty thick skin. I didn't get upset over trivial things, especially ancient history. A woman I'd never even known.

'I never had a mother,' I said. 'She left me and my father when I was a baby and Alfie never wanted to talk about her. And I'm an only child. Like you.'

Eliza swore under her breath as her grip slipped and coffee spilled into my saucer. 'I'm so sorry! Usually I have a steady hand, Lena. Can I blame the rocking of the boat?'

I used the paper doilies from the biscuit plate to mop up the mess, hoping she wouldn't ask me any more questions about Alfie. 'I have to say, the motion of being at sea isn't anywhere near as bad as I expected. I haven't felt seasick once.'

'You're lucky.' Her face brightened and it seemed that she was as happy as I to move the conversation onto a lighter topic. 'A modern ship like this is built for comfort. I remember some terrible crossings when I was a child. And of course we had the spectre of the *Titanic* hanging over us for years. Safety standards are a lot higher these days, thank goodness.'

'Thank goodness,' I echoed, trying to remember what we'd been told on that very first afternoon as we carried out the lifeboat drill. My thoughts had all been focused on that damned poison bottle and the best way to get rid of it.

I helped myself to a biscuit as the lights in the lounge were dimmed, the curtains pulled across to create the atmosphere of a cinema, waiters carrying around trays of ice cream and handing out boiled sweets. There was safety in the darkness, but I wished I'd been braver. I'd been more than happy to avoid more talk about family, but I had the feeling that Eliza had been even keener than I to change the subject.

9

Thursday, 3 September
Queen Mary

Everyone cheered when Mr Deeds punched the bad guy in the face and by the time the credits started to roll there was only half an hour before dinner.

'Honestly, dear, I doubt I'll be down before eight,' Eliza told me as we filed out of the lounge with the rest of the moviegoers. 'Don't rush to get ready.'

That was fine for her, but I had a feeling Charlie would not be so understanding. I went for a more subtle look that evening, a pale blue gown of silk overlaid with lace, capped shoulders giving a more demure appearance than the night before. When I looked in the mirror, I hardly recognised myself. Then again, I wasn't supposed to be presenting the real me. Charlie wanted the Broadway version. The glamorous actress who could make witty conversation but knew when to shut her mouth. A quick snort of Maggie's white powder warded off the insecurities and I was ready.

'How was your swim?' I asked Carrie as we took our places at the dinner table, Eliza included. Thank goodness I hadn't taken her at her word and turned up late.

'Delicious,' she said. 'Lena, you must come and try it. It's so tranquil down there and so relaxing. Hardly anyone seems to go in the afternoons.'

'I'm afraid I don't have a swimming costume,' I replied, with false regret.

'You can buy one,' she told me triumphantly. 'They sell them in the shop upstairs, I saw them this afternoon. They have bathing caps too, so you can keep your hair dry, if that's what's worrying you.'

'Ah, well in that case maybe I will investigate the situation tomorrow.' I let the waiter shake my napkin out and place it in my lap, hoping someone would change the subject.

'Carrie got carried away watching the swimming this summer. We were in Berlin for the Olympics and now she thinks she's in with a chance of trying out for the national team.'

Frankie's tone was sneering and childish and I wished I had been quick enough to avoid sitting next to him. He leaned towards me every time he spoke and was being extraordinarily clumsy, dropping both his knife and his napkin so far. It gave him an excuse to brush my thigh with his fingers each time he bent to retrieve a lost item and it was taking sheer willpower for me not to dig my nails into the back of his hand. I could almost see the angry red half-moon markings my talons would leave as he rested his hand on the table, straightening out his cutlery. Tempting, but Charlie would have killed me.

'The Olympics?' I said to Carrie. 'That must have been an amazing experience.'

'Lena, you've never seen anything like it, honestly, it was the best ever,' she gushed. 'I went every day that the swimming was on. Mama and Frankie went to the diving as well, but I wasn't interested in that.'

'Darling, didn't we decide not to bore people to death about it?' Eliza rolled her eyes, but her tone was kinder than her son's. 'You really had to be there. Talking about people splashing around in pools just isn't that interesting.'

'Oh, I don't mind,' I said, rewarded by a smile from Carrie.

'If we'd had any dignity as a nation, we'd have boycotted.'

Everyone fell silent and turned towards Dr Wilding, who looked surprised, as though he hadn't meant to speak out loud. He grabbed at his wine glass and took a gulp.

'Boycott? Why the hell would we? They let the blacks and the Jews compete. Wasn't that the whole point of any boycott?' Frankie jumped in first, not that there was a queue of people eager to get involved. First politics, now race and religion – Frankie really was a dinner party conversation novice.

'But the nations with the most power have to set the example. They might still have held the Olympics without America, but it would have sent the world a signal. The games would have lost their prestige. It would have meant a great deal to a lot of people,' Wilding argued, growing braver.

I thought of Vic, the barman at the Canary. He had left Germany the year before, after his brother had died. He didn't talk about it, would change the subject if ever it came up, but I knew he had left for a good reason and didn't expect to return any time soon. Tommy had taken to praising Hitler in front of him to wind him up, but Vic just swore under his breath in German and got on with his work.

'Come on, Doctor, you can't not send a delegation to the

biggest international event of the year unless you want to look weak. Besides, these things get blown out of proportion. We were told Hitler wanted to ban Jews, but like Frankie said, that never actually happened. You can't believe everything you read, you know. Newspapermen have their own agendas.' Jack ripped apart a bread roll and bit off a chunk. 'They tell us what they want us to think.'

'Besides, look what Jesse Owens did. Right in front of the Führer, and everyone cheered like crazy,' Frankie added. 'The German people were very friendly and respectful. They deserved to be punished after the war, but that's history now. Let them enjoy their rallies and funny arm-waving. It keeps the people happy and productive. And even if Hitler doesn't like Jews, so what? It doesn't affect you; you live in America. Besides, I'm pretty sure I've seen you eat a pork chop, Wilding. Not exactly kosher.'

'Frankie!' Eliza admonished her son.

'Firstly, it's none of your business what I eat or how obser-vant I am.' Wilding paused to compose himself. 'It worries me that if we make these small allowances, letting this man persecute his own citizens—'

'God, here we go,' Frankie muttered, nudging me as if I was in on the joke. I turned away from him and hoped he got the message. It wasn't enough, though, I knew.

Wilding raised his voice. 'We say that it's not our place, let the Germans deal with Germany. America makes allowances, but when do we stop? Where does it end? There are stories emerging that aren't being printed in the newspapers. It's not just "funny arm waving" and fun days out at rallies.'

Wilding looked around the table, seeking support, though I could see from his face it was a futile hope. Like dominoes they all turned away from him, one after the other.

'My friend Vic had to leave Germany,' I said, finally finding my voice. 'Because of Hitler. He really is as bad as they say.' I wished again that I'd spoken to Vic about it. That I had real knowledge to add to Dr Wilding's cause.

No one spoke, their empty plates suddenly fascinating. Dr Wilding raised his glass to me, so slightly that I might have imagined it, but I felt better. At least I'd said something, spoken up for once. I'd not just let Frankie Abernathy fortify a vision of the world that didn't match what I knew to be the truth.

'I haven't taken my pills. Daisy! My pills!' Francis Parker broke the terrible silence, Daisy immediately tipping half the contents of her handbag onto the table to look for them.

Conversation began again quietly, Dr Wilding holding his silence. I felt ashamed of myself. Shame for not speaking up earlier, shame for being too scared to risk my precarious position at the Canary, shame for hiding in plain sight and not being proud to be my father's daughter. For not telling Maggie what her husband was up to, not asking Vic about his life in Germany, not checking that those poor girls in the flat upstairs were all right. I'd become an expert at ignoring whatever made me feel uncomfortable, and that ability was about to cause me a lot more trouble.

The rest of dinner passed without any further drama. Daisy made the mistake of asking Charlie what his job actually entailed and he waxed lyrical for almost half an hour about who he knew and how he'd graduated from a city beat cop, via five years as a private detective for the Pinkertons, to being able to afford to have his suits tailored in London. A rags-to-riches story. His accent at dinner was impeccably movie-star American, the Charlie Bacon I witnessed amongst polite company matching the version I had met in London. I wondered why he'd decided to drop the façade with me alone. Was it because he felt comfortable to do so, or was it simply that he knew that my opinion didn't matter?

Whichever it was, Daisy Lancaster was an expert questioner. I discovered that Charlie was divorced, living alone in a part of Manhattan called Chelsea, in an apartment block that had doormen dressed as bobbies. Apparently there was a Soho in New York too. Maybe I would end up living in an American version of my London life. Though hopefully with more success.

'Part of the bullet's still in there,' he told his rapt audience, recounting the tale of the injury that had forced him into retirement from detecting, a gunshot wound to the left shoulder. 'When the weather's cold and damp, I feel it worst. But I shot the other guy dead, so things turned out worse for him.'

'It must be agony,' Daisy sympathised.

From the corner of my eye I saw Jack frown, unhappy with the attention Charlie was receiving. He was on his third whisky and the booze had washed away his poker face. Daisy might have been smiling at Charlie but the little side glances she shot towards her lover, checking that he was still watching, were obvious to everyone except for Jack himself. Eliza's face was a stone mask. She chain-smoked through dessert and didn't say a word. I wasn't sure I'd ever had to sit through a stranger meal, and I'd once had to go to dinner with James and his friend, a fellow MP who was having an affair with his daughter's college friend from Oxford and had brought both girls along with him.

Charlie flashed his now famous white-tooth grin. 'We can't keep talking about me all evening. You must have had some adventures in London this summer, Daisy.'

'Oh, not really. I take my work very seriously.' Eliza snorted, and Daisy pressed her lips together, annoyed. 'Mr Parker and I keep to a schedule, wherever we are in the world. It doesn't allow much for spontaneity but it's the way we like it. Won't you tell us another story? You never told us what happened to the movie producer whose wife was having the affair.'

Charlie Bacon was beginning to remind me of some of the ageing actors I'd known in the past. Finding himself in the spotlight, he hogged it for as long as he could, latching onto every admiring comment while protesting that he didn't deserve it. He'd obviously decided that I was letting the side down and had made it his duty to impress the Abernathys himself. What a shame his ego wouldn't allow him to see that Jack Abernathy was hating every second of his performance.

'I need a proper drink,' Jack said, getting to his feet while coffee was still being served. 'I'll be up at the Starlight.'

'Wait up, Pa, I'll come too.' Frankie turned to me. 'Lena?'

The last thing I wanted was to get stuck in the lift with Jack and Frankie.

'We'll all go,' Eliza decided. 'Why don't you two boys go on ahead and make sure they have our table ready.'

Jack gave a curt nod, shooting Daisy one last baleful glance, and left with Frankie close on his heels. The rest of us followed a few minutes later, Charlie being a gentleman and pushing Francis Parker's wheelchair to save Daisy's poor arms, much to the old man's annoyance.

'You'd do well to be wary of the Abernathys,' Wilding said quietly to me as we followed the family out of the dining room.

I looked up at him, surprised. 'You really don't like them, do you.'

'It's not a matter of like or dislike. It's about trust. Once you understand that there isn't a member of that family who wouldn't put themselves first in any given situation, they become a damned sight easier to deal with. Some friendly advice, that's all,' he said, walking ahead to call the elevator.

Friendly advice. But I looked at Eliza and Carrie, teasing one another as we waited for our turn to ascend, and I couldn't summon any sense of dread. Wilding had obviously decided that I was an ally after my exchange with Frankie over dinner, but if he had a grudge against his employer then that was nothing to do with me. Besides, once we left the ship I'd likely never see any of them again. What was the worst that could happen in four days?

10

Friday, 28 August
Brewer Street, Soho

I was drunk. The cold moisture in the air soaked into my skin as the wind whipped wild along the street, the light beginning to fade as a storm brewed. The days had already begun to shorten, on the downhill slide that would lead eventually to Christmas. Was it really only a week since I'd sat on a bench in Regent's Park, licking ice cream from a cone and wondering what was to become of me? No husband, a job that barely covered the rent, living in a box room that was like a furnace in summer but an icebox in winter. Such small worries compared to what Maggie was facing.

She'd tearfully apologised for taking over Alfie's memorial and we'd sunk the rest of the champagne, chased down with sickly limoncello. She'd seemed calm enough when I left the restaurant, but she had refused to talk about Tommy any longer. I wasn't convinced that meant she wouldn't turn up at the club that night. Apart from anything else, I knew that Tommy would blame me if she made a scene, and it was the last thing I needed. The Canary Club was the only reason I still had a roof over my head. Another reminder of my precarious position. Choosing between my friend and my job, now perhaps an impossible task.

I rented an attic room that, had I been from a family of note, would have rendered me a bohemian. James thought me hilarious when I told him how I lived. *One room?* he'd said, incredulous. *One bloody room? How on earth can you live like that, Lee Lee?* James found it quaint to be courting a girl of little means. I was Cinderella to his Prince Charming. We went to dinners in exclusive bistros and danced in cellar nightclubs where the bottle parties went on until dawn and the heat of so many bodies in such a small space gave up a condensation of perspiration that fell like raindrops from the low ceilings. The sort of club where no one batted an eyelid about a couple dancing too close, or kissing in public, or anything at all really. In short, we frequented places where none of James's more upstanding acquaintances would bump into us. The few friends of his that I met were all the same; posh boys who were either slumming it before marrying one of their acceptable social circle, or like James, bored of the realities of marital life and looking for excitement. I had always known that our relationship was a fun diversion, for me as much as for him. Sometimes it was nice to go out with a man who paid, especially when all my money was going to Alfie and his treatment. In my head, it had always been a temporary arrangement – I wasn't a fool, I knew he'd never leave his wife, and I knew I didn't want to commit to James in that way – but it still stung to be rejected.

And so here I was, alone again with only a couple of hours to go before I was due at the Canary Club. Swaying and tipsy and sad, the three flights of stairs to my attic room taking forever to climb, my head beginning to ache from lack of sleep, the anxiety of making a wrong decision, and an excess of champagne.

'Miss Aldridge, is that you?'

I groaned at the sound of my landlady's voice. She would wait until I was on the top landing, wouldn't she, when she must have heard the door go. Why not call out straight away? Mrs Haskell and I were barely on speaking terms, most of our conversations conducted between gritted teeth. I paid my rent on time, which I felt she should have been more grateful for. And believe it or not, there were worse places to live in Soho. Hence, we were stuck with one another.

'Can I help you, Mrs Haskell?' I waited, hoping that the situation could be resolved on the staircase.

'You've a gentleman caller.' No wonder she wasn't best pleased. I'd be in for a lecture later, about how this wasn't that type of household. She'd most likely be clutching her battered Bible as she instructed me on the way a young lady was expected to behave. I knew from the framed photographs on her living room mantelpiece that Mrs Haskell had two daughters, married off and probably now with children of their own, but they never visited her. I'd also never dared to ask how a woman so devoted to the Lord had ended up in Soho, but I had an inkling. Conversion wafted from her like stale sweat from a working man. Whatever she thought I was going to get up to with my 'gentleman caller', I was sure she'd done worse in her time.

'I'm not expecting anyone,' I called down, my hand gripping

the newel post until my knuckles paled. As far as I was concerned, James and I had a frank and clear discussion that morning. Had he come running back so soon?

'Sorry to bother you, Miss Aldridge. You don't know me, but I wonder if I might trouble you for a few minutes of your time?'

I didn't recognise the voice. The accent was American but the voice didn't belong to any of the musicians I knew in London. One of Alfie's old friends then? I hadn't seen any of them since the funeral.

'You'll have to take your visitor elsewhere, Miss Aldridge, you know the rules.' Mrs Haskell's voice grew higher in pitch by the word.

The stranger was waiting for me at the foot of the stairs. I don't know what I was expecting but it wasn't this chap. He was in his late forties, I guessed, his dark brown hair greying at the temples. He had a well-kept moustache and a sharp parting in his hair, like an older version of Clark Gable. His suit looked fine as well. I had no idea who he was but at least he wasn't James.

'Miss Aldridge, I'm Charles Bacon,' he told me, shaking my hand, his grip dry and firm. 'I'm awfully sorry to have bothered you both. Mrs Haskell, please don't blame Miss Aldridge, she didn't know I was coming. I was a fool not to write first and let you know, only I was excited to surprise you.'

'I certainly am surprised,' I told him. 'Are you sure it's me you're looking for? We haven't met before. Have we?' Doubt began to creep in. There had been a lot of late nights out recently, with and without James, and I tried to avoid Mrs Haskell's basilisk gaze.

'You are the daughter of Alfred Aldridge, aren't you?' I nodded. 'I work for an old friend of your father's, from New York. He only recently became aware of Mr Aldridge's untimely passing and wanted me to come in person to pass on his condolences.' Charles Bacon paused and smiled. 'Is there somewhere we can go and talk? A diner— no, you don't really have those here, do you?'

'There's a café down the street,' I said, glad that I hadn't had time to take my coat off. 'We can go there. I'd like to hear more about this friend of Alfie's.'

I pushed past Mrs Haskell and led Mr Bacon outside and two doors down. The windows of the café were already blazing with light, the warm punch of ground coffee beans hitting me in the face as I held the door open for my unexpected acquaintance. Mrs DeMarco called out a greeting over the comforting whoosh of the great silver machine that served the local workers their pre-shift coffees.

Soho never slept, various businesses operating at all hours to satisfy the needs of London, from food and clothing to drink and dancing, not to mention the sort of trades you didn't talk about in polite company. This late-afternoon espresso crowd was made up of bartenders and waitresses, those who'd be on their feet for long hours to come and needed a quick pick-me-up to get them going. Later on would come the musicians and entertainers, some of them fortifying their coffee with a generous pour of grappa from Mrs DeMarco's never-ending supply. Once everyone else was hard at work, out having a good time, or safe at home tucked up in bed, the girls would come in off the street, especially if the weather was bad and the rain or cold put off the punters. It could be a grim business, street work. Just ask Mrs Haskell.

I'd seen it myself, the way the girls arrived in London with their grand dreams. Schoolgirls, as good as, all rosy cheeks and smiles, full of ambition and with names like Kathy or Sally or Pamela. They wanted to meet a rich husband or tread the boards, and that wasn't going to happen in Reading or Stoke-on-Trent. All it took was a run of bad luck, getting knocked back from every audition, unable to hold a drinks order in her head, getting her head turned by a fella who looked smart enough and would buy her a drink, or encourage her to try something more. Poor Kathy thought her fortunes were changing, but then her beau would show his true colours, let her know that he expected to be paid back, with interest. He'd use his fists and she'd go along with it, anything to clear the debt. It didn't take long for those girls to be broken. A few months and they'd look like all the rest: cynical, tired, hard. Sometimes I thought the only reason I'd escaped their fate was because I'd seen it happen with Maggie. The only luck she'd had was that Tommy had been in the market for a wife when she turned up.

I sat down facing the door and watched Charles Bacon struggle to fold his tall body to fit the chair, the tables in the café pushed close together. Mrs DeMarco always joked that she'd done it on purpose, that she'd know if she was getting fat when she could no longer squeeze between them.

'They sure pack 'em in,' he joked, settling in but looking uncomfortable.

'So who's this boss of yours?' I asked him, getting straight down to business. 'How did he know Alfie?'

'What do you want to drink? My treat.' He waved to get Mrs DeMarco's attention, calling out my order. 'Your Mrs Haskell made me drink a cup of tea while I waited for you.' He pulled a face and I couldn't help but smile. She must really have taken to him if he'd had the red carpet treatment.

'I don't have long,' I warned. 'I have to be on stage in two hours.'

'Of course.' He glanced at his wristwatch. 'I won't keep you long, but I promise you it'll be worthwhile. You'll have plenty of time to get over to the Canary Club.'

'You know where I work?' And where I lived, I remembered.

'Let me explain.' He paused as Mrs DeMarco brought over our coffees, then rifled in his jacket pocket, dragging out a battered notebook. 'Old habits die hard,' he said, waving it in the air. 'Need to make sure I don't forget anything, I'm under strict instruction.' He licked his right index finger, using it to flick through the first few pages. 'Ah, here we are. I'll start with who sent me here. A man named Benny Walker. You ever hear of him?'

I shook my head. 'He used to be friends with Alfie?'

'They started out working in the same restaurant, over thirty years ago now. Two young boys looking for their first break, one Negro, one poor. Alfie was determined to make his name as a musician, but Benny never had any musical talent – he worked on getting to know people in the movie industry, producers mostly. He got fixed up as an assistant to one of them eventually, and from there he worked his way up. Went out to Hollywood for a while but came back to New York last year to set up a new office. Plan is to get into Broadway shows as a producer. Quite an achievement for a man who came from nothing.'

I nodded. It did sound impressive, even though I wasn't sure what Walker actually did or why he was interested in me all of a sudden. 'Alfie never mentioned a Benny Walker. I suppose they hadn't spoken for a while.'

Bacon's smile faltered. 'There was a falling out. I'm not sure of the ins and outs of it, but I'm sure Benny will tell you if you care to ask. Alfie left New York back in 1908 and they never spoke again.'

'What a shame. What made Benny suddenly want to get in touch after all this time?'

'Benny is a proud man, but he has a sentimental streak. He often thought about seeing what his old friend was up to, but he couldn't bring himself to be the first to break the deadlock. It wasn't until he bumped into a fella by the name of John Sawyer – you know him?' The name rang a bell. A trumpet player if I wasn't mistaken. 'He was the one who told Benny the sad news. That Alfie had passed on. Tuberculosis? And he mentioned you, the daughter Benny had never known about. Said you sang like an angel with a twenty-a-day habit.' He paused to check I hadn't taken offence but I recognised the quote, lifted straight from the newspaper review of a show I'd done a few years earlier at the Royale. It had been a good review, four stars, and for a while I had hoped it might lead somewhere. I still had the clipping. 'This was a couple months ago, in case you're wondering what took him so long to send me to find you.'

'I still don't understand. What does Benny Walker want with me? We have a perfectly good postal system in this country. He could have sent a card. Some flowers.' My headache was getting worse. I sipped my coffee and willed him to get to the point, if there was one.

'He wants to make you an offer and he thought it would be better if that offer were made face to face, only he's a busy man. He can't just up and leave the business for weeks on end to try and track down the daughter of a long-lost friend. Can you imagine that, Miss – hey, can I call you, Lena? Is that all right?' I nodded. 'And I'm Charlie. We may as well get to being friends, speed things along, since you don't have much time.'

He spoke quickly and I was struggling to focus on what he was trying to tell me. It was easier to smile and let him carry on, hoping it would all make sense by the end.

'Lena, to cut a long story short, Benny feels badly about how things were left. Whatever it was that went on between them, whoever was at fault, Benny feels guilty about it. So, since he can never make it up to Alfie, he figured that maybe he could do a good turn for his daughter instead.'

'A good turn?' Possibilities began to race through my mind and I sat up in my chair. If Benny Walker was big on Broadway, then wouldn't he know people on the West End? This could be my chance to get back on the stage. A proper stage, that is. One that was a bit bigger than the postage-stamp-sized step that I stood on at the Canary.

'He wants to give you a break. A new musical.' Charlie grinned as I let out an involuntary gasp. 'Hang on! I haven't told you what the show is yet.'

'It's nothing dodgy, is it?' I paused. 'I've had my fair share of offers. I don't need a stranger's help with that.' There were so-called clubs that put on shows where those in the know could go and see young ladies perform in the altogether. I wasn't ever going to be that desperate.

'Ha! No, Lena. This is a real musical. With dancers, actors, costumes, orchestra, the lot. You ever hear of *As Thousands Cheer*? Though I think they called it something else here...'

'*Stop Press*. Yes, I saw it. Twice.' I'd auditioned for it as well, but I didn't intend to tell Charlie Bacon that.

'Ethel Waters is one of the big stars on Broadway right now. A few years ago you'd say that a coloured gal like her wouldn't have a hope in hell of getting that sort of a role on Broadway. A singing spot in Harlem, sure, but there's a reason they call it the Great White Way, and it ain't just the lights.' He chuckled at his own joke.

'So... what? Benny Walker thinks I could be the next Ethel Waters?' I laughed.

'Why not? Chance is what makes most careers, you know, not talent alone. I can't tell you too much right now, mainly 'cause I don't know all the ins and outs. These days I work for Mr Walker, but I used to be a cop. A detective. That's why he sent me to find you. I used the little bit of information John Sawyer was able to provide and here we are! Now all I need to do is get you to New York. If you're willing, I'll be escorting you back there next week. The sailing's on Wednesday.'

'New York?' My eyebrows shot up. 'On Wednesday?'

'I know it's short notice, but Benny's a busy guy and this new show, they start rehearsals a week Monday. You'll miss the first day, that ain't the end of the world, but if you don't make the Wednesday ship then that's a week lost and...' He didn't need to finish the sentence. There'd be no point in going at all.

He talked some more, telling me what life could be like in New York, extolling more of Benny Walker's virtues, a man I'd never heard of before that afternoon, giving me the details of the ship that he was booked onto.

'I'm holding a cabin for you, but they can only keep it until tomorrow afternoon. First class on the *Queen Mary*. I don't need an answer right now. Think about it overnight and then come see me tomorrow,' he said, scribbling on a leaf of his notebook before ripping it out and sliding it across the table. 'My room number at the Savoy. Come anytime tomorrow before noon and I'll be there. Just ask for me at the front desk.'

Charlie got up, paying Mrs DeMarco on his way out. I sat there with my empty coffee cup, trying to make sense of the day. Charlie Bacon's proposition was both madness and everything I'd ever dreamed of. Could I simply up and leave London in a few days' time? I didn't even have a passport. And what about poor Maggie? She was going through hell. Was I such a bad friend that I could desert her with hardly any warning?

A group of young men walked in, noisy in their laughter and the cavalier way they scraped back chairs and knocked against the tables. They roused me in time to realise that I was going to be late if I didn't get home immediately.

Mrs Haskell was waiting, of course, arms folded behind her back like an army major. 'I've said it before, Miss Aldridge, and I'll say it again. This is a reputable establishment and—'

'I know, I know. I didn't invite him though, did I?' I really wasn't in the mood. 'Look, I know the rules and I stick to them.' For the most part. 'What more do you want?'

'I want you to stop cavorting around town with married men, you sinful girl.'

'What *are* you on about?' I bit back the last part of the sentence: *you old bag.*

'People talk and I don't want my name associated with that kind of behaviour. I should have known better than to trust your sort. You're paid up 'til next week, after that I want you out. Understand?'

'Fine with me.' To her disappointment I merely nodded and climbed the stairs to my room. In front of the door was a bunch of flowers and a box of Belgian chocolates from the chocolatier near to James's flat. The card on the box was left blank. An apology? I picked them up off the floor wearily. Either way, he clearly hadn't been bothered to bring them himself. That trip to New York was sounding more perfect with every moment that passed.

11

Jack had secured the same table as the night before and was
already nursing a large Scotch, glaring at Charlie as he wheeled
Francis Parker up to the head of the table. Frankie tried to catch
my eye as he pulled out a chair beside him, but I managed to
execute a neat sidestep around Daisy and take a seat on the
opposite side of the table, between Eliza and Carrie, so that he
wouldn't dare try anything on.

'Oh!' Daisy slapped her forehead with the heel of her palm.
'Gosh, I'm such a scatterbrain. I left Mr Parker's tonic back in
the cabin.'

'Again?' Wilding sat down opposite me, and I swear he
cracked a sliver of a smile when I accidentally let out a laugh,
covering it up badly with a cough. Maybe he wasn't as miserable
as he seemed; he simply had a dry sense of humour. I was sure
it couldn't be much fun for him, being forced to spend so much
time with the Abernathys. Francis Parker must be paying him
very well.

Jack opened his mouth, presumably to give voice to an excuse that would allow him to leave the table also, but Charlie was quicker: 'And tonight it seems that I'm the fool to have left my cigars. May I escort you, Mrs Lancaster?'

I couldn't help but raise an eyebrow. Charlie's choice of words had been a direct shot in the direction of Jack Abernathy, which went against everything he'd told me he wanted to do. Had he given up on trying to impress the Abernathys? A discreet glance around the table: Jack staring into the depths of his whisky as though hoping to get sucked down into the amber; Eliza patting her husband's arm lightly before smirking as she lit a cigarette. If looks could kill then Frankie's could have filleted Daisy as expertly as the trout I'd eaten at dinner. Wilding merely yawned, feigning boredom but watching Jack, almost smiling. Francis Parker curled his lip and gazed upon his son-in-law with contempt. Even young, sweet, innocent Carrie muttered something unintelligible under her breath.

'Thank you kindly, Mr Bacon.' Daisy smiled and let him take her arm.

They left and our drinks arrived, but conversation remained non-existent apart from a minor spat between Eliza and Carrie. Eliza had wanted to book a mother and daughter's day at the salon that she thought might be fun; Carrie disagreed. Sitting trapped between them felt a little like umpiring a Wimbledon tennis match, Carrie finally declared the winner. The club was beginning to fill and a second round of drinks was ordered, Daisy and Charlie still missing from the table. The atmosphere was strained and I reckoned, assuming the band came on at the same time every night, we were still about quarter of an hour from being saved from the bitter silence. Which gave me an idea...

'Excuse me a moment.' I got up in a rush before anyone could ask where I was going or try and tag along.

Retracing my steps from the previous evening, I ended up out on deck, the ocean breeze far stronger than the night before so that I had to fight against it as I made my way along, breathlessly. I held my breath as I reached the corner and turned it, glad to find that my efforts were rewarded.

'Hello again,' I said, hoping that I sounded nonchalant rather than nervous. Now that I had found him, my mind went blank. All I could think of was my clammy palms and how far from confident I felt.

'Hello again.' Will Goodman was civil enough. His face was unreadable.

'You found yourself a lighter.' I took out my cigarette case, fumbling with it and breathing a sigh of relief as I managed not to drop it. Will handed me his lighter. It was heavy in my palm, solid silver. 'Very fancy.'

'A tip, of sorts,' he told me. 'A passenger gave it to me.' He turned it over in my hand and I saw that two initials were engraved: W.G. 'Their initials as well as mine.'

'What was his name?' I asked. 'Wilbur Grant?' The first name that popped into my head.

'*Her* name. Winnifred Grayson.' He took the lighter back and put it away in his pocket, his eyes searching my face for a reaction.

'My apologies to Winnifred,' I said, trying not to wonder who the hell she was and what she'd been to Will. 'Are your band playing this evening?'

'My band play every night. And every afternoon. And in

between that I give music lessons to wealthy women named Winnifred and their even wealthier husbands named Archibald.' He leaned back and blew a smoke ring that was immediately obliterated by the wind.

'You're a busy man.' I could have kicked myself. In the movies they made it seem so easy, the way the femme fatale barely spoke to her man and yet he fell for her in seconds. In Soho you only had to stand by the bar and some fella or other would come crawling over.

'What are you doing out here?' he asked.

'I wanted some fresh air,' I replied. 'Is that so unusual?'

'Actually, it is. Baby, nobody ever comes out here. Nobody who paid for a first-class ticket, that is.'

'I'll let you into a secret,' I told him. 'I didn't pay for my ticket.'

'Then that makes you a stowaway or a kept woman. I'm guessing you ain't no stowaway, not with that lump of gold hanging round your neck.'

My mouth fell open. 'Excuse me, I am neither. If you must know, a man by the name of Benny Walker is paying for me to travel to New York to be in his new show. On Broadway.'

'Benny Walker? Never heard of him.' Will didn't look half as impressed as I'd hoped. 'You sure it's a Broadway show he's booked you for?'

'You know I didn't come out here to be insulted.' I silently cursed myself for getting distracted and forgetting my real purpose. 'If I'm being honest, I actually came to find you. I wanted to apologise, though I'm not so sure I want to now.'

'Apologise? For what?' He took a last drag and flicked his cigarette butt over the side.

'For what?' It was a good question. 'I thought I might have offended you last night. By saying... Well, I mean, of course you were right. What you said about me, about being like you. About being coloured, or half at least. My reaction was a little abrupt because... Well, never mind all that. But you were right.' The words came out in a mess and I could have kicked myself.

'I was right?' He nodded, a slow smile creasing his face. 'I was right. I often am, to be fair.' He laughed at the glare I shot him. 'Baby, don't be like that. I'm only repeating what you already said.'

'You're not very modest,' I told him. 'You're supposed to accept an apology graciously, you know.' Or reject it outright, but I thought it best not to give the option.

'I'm just joking around. Look, maybe we got off on the wrong foot.' He held out his hand to me. 'Will Goodman.'

I shook his hand. 'Lena Aldridge.'

'Nice to meet you, Lena, and thank you. And I guess I owe you an apology in return. I didn't mean to imply that you were anything other than a lady.'

'Apology accepted. I may be travelling on the whim of someone else, but it's all above board. It's a proper musical,' I said, emphasis on *proper*. 'I'm a singer like you, though I don't play piano nearly as well. My father despaired of me in that regard.' I could almost hear Alfie's sigh, the one he couldn't hold back whenever my fingers stumbled over the keys, tying themselves in knots, the notes as heavy as Mrs Harper's suet pudding.

'A singer, huh. You must be pretty damn special to get a free first-class ticket,' he said.

'It's made me a living up until now. But I got lucky. This Benny Walker chap used to be friends with my father. Now he's a big producer on Broadway. He feels guilty and wants to do me a favour. My father died recently you see.'

'This Walker guy have him killed or something?'

'No! That's not… Is that something that happens in New York?' I laughed and then remembered Tommy, but that was different. Sort of. 'But no, he felt guilty because they hadn't talked in years. There was an argument and they didn't make it up in time.'

Will nodded then checked his watch. 'Lena, it's been a pleasure, but it's time for me to go to work. Nice to meet you properly, and maybe I'll see you around?'

'I hope so,' I said, but he was already walking away, my words stolen by the greedy sea air.

If Maggie had been on board the ship, she'd have a few things to say about Will Goodman, mostly unrepeatable in polite company. She'd have given me a sharp elbow to the side and told me to go after him. I knew she despaired of my unmarried status, even though it didn't bother me in the slightest. She had hardly been a walking advertisement for a happy marriage, though I'd never have said as much to her face. Maybe in a few months she could come out to New York like we'd talked about. We could hit the town and flirt with all the boys, nothing and no one holding us back.

When I got back to the Starlight Club, Daisy and Charlie had returned to the table but, if anything, the atmosphere had deteriorated. At least there was a drink waiting for me, a gin fizz, sour and sharp in equal measure. Daisy was back on duty,.

spooning tonic from a bottle for Francis Parker to slurp down, holding a glass of water to his lips as he began to cough, thumping weakly against his chest with a clawed fist.

'Do you have any plans for tomorrow, Lena?' Carrie asked.

'Not really. I thought I might explore the ship a little more. I still haven't seen the ballroom or the library.'

'I could give you a tour,' she said, her face brightening. 'When we sailed over to England our steward gave me the grand tour and it took almost three hours. He even let me visit the kennels, and one of the owners let me walk her dog every day. He was called Bertie and he was a chocolate Labrador. She said that usually her gardener walked him when they were home, but no one brings their gardener away with them, of course.'

'Of course,' I echoed, thinking of Maggie's dog, Cecil (after B. DeMille – Maggie saw *Cleopatra* sixteen times at the pictures, dragging me along to at least half of those showings). Maggie's surrogate child, she'd never have let an employee take her precious Westie out alone. Even when she'd been on bed rest, making every effort to keep her last pregnancy to term, she'd baulked at letting anyone else take Cecil for his walks.

'They all treat him like a dog,' she'd complained to me.

'He is a dog, love,' I'd said, but then Cecil had barked at me and I'd wondered if Maggie wasn't right, that he knew what was what. Certainly, he hated Tommy and took great delight in shredding his master's slippers whenever he forgot and left his bedroom door open, Cecil stealing in like a tiny burglar to seek them out.

I'd taken Cecil for walks in the end, since Tommy flatly refused, and Cecil and I learned to get along for the sake of

Maggie. For the first week I'd seen her watching out for us as I returned from Hampstead Heath, her white face pressed against the bedroom window until she caught sight of us and ducked away. By the end of the second week the inevitable had occurred and Maggie was recovering from the loss of yet another child, her head buried in the pillows as she waited for her beloved pet to bound upstairs and clamber up to lie with her. With Tommy gone, Cecil was all she had now.

I'd opened my mouth to say yes to Carrie, that I'd love to have her company on a tour of the ship, but my attention was grabbed by Parker's worsening coughing fit. His hacks had grown louder, drowning out conversation at the neighbouring tables so that he had gained quite an audience. Daisy was rubbing his back fruitlessly as Parker tried in vain to loosen his tie.

'He can't breathe, woman! What are you even…?' Wilding got up and hauled Daisy bodily away from his patient, quickly freeing Parker from his tie and the top button of his shirt. 'What the hell did you give him?'

'His usual tonic.' Daisy's voice was high-pitched.

Everyone was standing now, all of us unconsciously moving away from the stricken man as his body convulsed in his chair. I saw foam at his mouth and thought of Tommy, my chest tightening as I remembered that night at the Canary, fear bringing me out in a cold sweat.

'Help him, Dr Wilding! He must be choking on something,' Eliza cried out, her face white.

Wilding pulled the wheelchair away from the table and shrugged off his dinner jacket. 'Daisy, go and call for the ship's doctor.'

Carrie was sobbing beside me and it felt natural to reach out and take her hand. Wilding rolled up his shirt sleeves and held Francis Parker's head in his hands, pulling open his mouth, presumably to check for an obstruction. I couldn't tear my eyes away, even as a horrific realisation struck me with the force of a cricket bat to the stomach. This was exactly what had happened to Tommy. The same struggle for breath, the arrhythmia of his fitting, the wide-eyed stare, full of fear. But I had thrown the bottle overboard. Hadn't I? The memory was faint but it was real. I remembered walking the length of the deck, the feel of the smooth glass against my palm, watching it spin and hit the water. Wilding moved Parker to the floor and tried to tilt his patient's head back to ease his breathing, but he couldn't keep Parker's body still. My palms started to sweat and I pulled my hand away from Carrie's before she noticed.

When the silence fell it was suffocating, a heavy weight pressing down on my chest as I held my own breath and watched as Wilding hung his head in defeat. He reached out a hand to Parker's neck.

It seemed inevitable, that tiny, almost imperceptible shake of the head. I had seen it days earlier in a club hundreds of miles away. Eliza's wail was like an echo in a tunnel, sounding from far away and yet so close, and it was the last thing I heard before I welcomed in the blackness, my body falling under its protection.

It is done, and yet even though it is by my own hand, I can't believe he's really dead. Free from the pain and suffering that have been his for the past year. Rotting away in that chair while everyone around him breathed a sigh of relief that the patriarch had been silenced. They may cry in public but their tears are for show; all these years spent on the end of a financial leash and now they are free. He looked straight at me as he realised what was happening to him. Did he know it was me? We had discussed it; not the specific method, but that if it came to it, if there was another fit, then he would rather be allowed to pass quietly. I had said that I would make sure that he wasn't left to suffer on, incapacitated. I'd promised it. He must have known, but I didn't detect any accusation in his eyes. I hope he was grateful, though I doubt he has woken up in the blessed afterlife he believed in. If heaven and hell really do exist, then I'm afraid he will find himself in the latter.

One day someone may find this diary of mine. In fact, I hope that they will. If I were asked to defend my actions, or to explain why I chose such an excruciating death when I could have made it easy on him, I will say this: what difference does it make? A few minutes of agony, it's hardly any suffering at all compared to eternal oblivion. Besides, the spectacle was necessary. His God granted him one last summer in the city he loved more than anyone living and made sure he died surrounded by his family. Who wouldn't want to go that way, given the choice?

Still, I miss him already. It would be impossible not to when he has left such an indelible impression upon my life. Where would I be without him? The man who taught me everything I need to know about the world we live in. Money is one of the only things in life worth having. That was his mantra. Money and power, he told me, knowing that the only money or power I ever had was handed to me from him. That without his generosity I would have nothing.

The easy part is done and the game is afoot, as they say. Two deaths, by the same method, and Lena is the only person known to have been present at both. She knows it too. I'd love to know what she's thinking now, if she realises that she's being set up. She must be so confused. I almost feel sorry about it, but there is no other option. She has a purpose to serve. Tomorrow I commence the slow unveiling of her motive and by the time we reach New York there won't be a soul who believes in her innocence. The police will be handed a cold-blooded murderess at the dock and nobody will think to look elsewhere.

Stormy Weather

12

Friday, 4 September
Queen Mary

The ring of the telephone woke me, interrupting my dreamless sleep like a banshee wail. It took me a moment to work out what the godawful noise was through the dregs of the sleeping draught that Dr Wilding had prescribed, the medical equivalent of a mallet to the head in its efficiency at knocking me unconscious. The bell ceased just as I reached out an unsteady hand, only to start up again a minute later.

'Hello?' My voice was hoarse.

'Miss Aldridge?' I didn't recognise the man's voice, formal and clipped.

'Yes?'

'Apologies if I woke you.' He didn't sound particularly sorry.

I glanced at my wristwatch: well after ten o'clock. Was there somewhere I was supposed to be? Searching my brain for clues, I stumbled across a nightmarish memory and the horror came flooding back and I dropped the receiver with a gasp.

'Miss Aldridge?' The voice sounded tinny as I struggled to grab the cord. 'Should I send someone to your cabin?'

'No, I...' I pushed the receiver against my ear. 'Is this about last night. About...' I couldn't bring myself to speak his name.

'Yes, ma'am. We are gathering all the passengers who sat with Mr Parker last night. You're to come to the port-side writing room on the main deck at eleven hundred hours. The chief officer will explain once you get there. I trust you will be able to attend?'

'Of course.' I doubted I had any choice in the matter, despite his phrasing the summons as an 'invitation'.

I bathed as quickly as I could. I felt horrendously hungover even though I'd drunk comparatively little the night before. When I sat down at the dressing table, I couldn't help but groan at the hideous sight that greeted me in the mirror. My hair was flat, there were dark circles under my eyes and my skin looked sallow. So much for beauty sleep, even though I must have had a good ten hours. We'd been released from the Starlight shortly before eleven o'clock, Francis Parker's body carried out before us on a stretcher by two of the crew.

I had come round quickly after my faint, more embarrassed than anything else. Charlie had hovered over me, doing his duty, even though I could see that he was dying to comfort Daisy, who was crying hysterically. Everyone else was giving her a wide berth, presumably since it looked as though she might be responsible for her employer's death. This wasn't déjà vu. I couldn't even begin to convince myself of it. Francis Parker, his struggles for breath, the swiftness of his death, it was all too familiar. He had died in exactly the same way Tommy Scarsdale had the week before.

'It's the same bottle as always, I swear,' Daisy had cried out, answering the unspoken accusation. 'Look! It's half-full. I've been giving him two spoonfuls three times a day since Dr Wilding prescribed it for Mr Parker's indigestion. We brought bottles of the stuff over to London with us.'

'An open bottle is easy enough to tamper with.' Eliza's voice was blade sharp.

The bottle sat there on the table. Larger than the bottle of bitters that had been used to poison Tommy, but just as likely to contain a fatal ingredient. My limbs felt weak and I was glad to already be sitting down. How was this possible? I knew that I hadn't done it. I couldn't have. But then how had the same method been employed, on two different occasions, when I was the only person common to both?

'Eliza, darling, we don't know what happened to Francis.' Jack put his arm around his wife and drew her away from Daisy. 'He might easily have had another attack. His health hasn't been good, you know that.'

Wilding quashed that idea quickly. 'This wasn't apoplexy.' He picked up the glass that Francis Parker had been drinking brandy from and sniffed cautiously before taking a sip, the rest of us gasping at his recklessness. 'Not his drink.' He picked up the bottle of tonic, lifted it to his nose, then recapped it before slipping it into his jacket pocket. 'We'll need to keep this until we reach New York. The police can have it tested for poison.'

'You know what it is,' I said. I needed him to say it out loud. To confirm what I already knew.

'I think it could be cyanide,' he told me. 'In fact, I'm pretty much convinced of it.'

'How can you tell?' Frankie asked. 'I mean, if you know so much about poisons, doesn't that make you a suspect?'

'Hardly, when it's my job.' But Wilding did look a little unnerved.

'It was the smell,' I said. 'Bitter almonds, isn't it? That's what I've read anyway.' I didn't mention that my knowledge came from cheap paperback novels.

'Exactly.' The doctor looked relieved, nodding his thanks to me. 'But like I say, the relevant authorities will be able to confirm once we reach New York.'

The arrival of the porters had silenced any further conversation and I'd taken the opportunity to escape, Dr Wilding showing his gratitude by sending the sleeping draught to my cabin.

I rubbed cold cream into my face and wondered if the ship's doctor had officially determined the cause of death yet. Was there any chance that Wilding was wrong after all, that it had actually been a natural death, a consequence of old age and general bad health leading to the fit that had preceded Parker's expiration? I knew that if anyone ever found out about what had happened at the Canary Club, I would fall under suspicion. But nobody knew about that, apart from Charlie. I just had to make sure it stayed that way.

I was the first to arrive. A handwritten sign had been placed on the writing room door: CLOSED UNTIL FURTHER NOTICE. When I knocked, one of the young officers who had carried the body the previous night, notable for his terrible complexion, opened the door.

'Lena Aldridge,' I told him. 'I was told to come here to speak to the chief officer.'

He nodded and stepped aside to let me in. Chairs had been arranged in a lopsided semicircle. Morning tea had been set out on one of the desks, as though this were simply an informal gathering: silver pots labelled tea and coffee, fine bone china cups and saucers, sugar and a jug of milk. My empty stomach rumbled at the sight of the biscuit plate, and they'd also laid out a sturdy-looking fruit loaf and a Victoria sponge. I hoped the amount of food wasn't directly related to the length of time they expected us to be confined to the room.

'Take a seat, miss, and help yourself to the refreshments. The chief officer will be along shortly.' The young officer repositioned himself by the door like a guard. Or a jailor.

I helped myself to a cup of tea and balanced a couple of biscuits on the saucer before sitting at one end of the semicircle. The empty chairs were more daunting than the people who would soon fill them.

Charlie arrived next, patting my shoulder awkwardly as he sat down beside me. 'This is an unfortunate situation, Lena, I don't have to tell you that.'

'Not as unfortunate as for Francis Parker's family,' I reminded him.

'No. But the last thing you need right now is to be involved in a scandal. Before we even reach New York! Benny'll kill me.'

'Why would anyone think that I did it?' I retorted. 'I barely knew the man. Why would I want to kill him?'

'I don't know, but these people...' He checked over his shoulder even though the door was firmly closed. 'These are the sorts of people who can point the finger of blame away from themselves and nobody bats an eyelid. People of influence. Of power.'

'I suppose. But they've got two perfectly good scapegoats already,' I reasoned. 'Daisy isn't exactly in Eliza's good books. And Wilding's the doctor who prescribed the tonic. I can see how they might throw either of them under the bus, but surely nobody will be looking at me or you when we don't have any motive.'

'You've thought this through pretty well.' Charlie stared at me, horrified or impressed.

I didn't reply. After going through police questioning the week before I'd learned the hard way to think of every eventuality. 'I hope Daisy's checked her back for knives, that's all,' I said.

The woman in question arrived, her face half hidden by a black veil pinned to her hat. She had forsaken the red lipstick for once and her pale lips left her looking like a tragic consumptive. She took her seat silently, choosing the opposite end of the semicircle.

'How are you this morning, Daisy? It's been a terrible shock, for you more than us, I guess.' Charlie spoke loudly, his words stilted.

She lifted the veil to show her eyes, swollen and bloodshot from crying. 'How do you think I feel, Mr Bacon? They'll try and blame me for this, I know it. As if I would harm Mr Parker! If anything, I'm the last person who would. This is the best job I ever had. A steady wage. A roof over my head. Would I risk everything to end up penniless and alone again? I swear to you, I only gave him medication that was prescribed to him by Dr Wilding.'

She shut up suddenly as the Abernathys finally arrived, twenty minutes late, accompanied by Dr Wilding. The division in their entourage couldn't have been made clearer and I feared greatly for Daisy. She had dropped her veil back down, turning away from the family. It was just as well; if looks could kill, then she would have been joining Francis Parker in whatever they used as a morgue at sea, Eliza Abernathy convicted and hung for her murder at a later date.

'Excuse me, son. Can you tell the man in charge that we're here? I don't want this to take any longer than necessary. My wife's very upset, as you can understand.' Jack watched as the spotty youth left us, then grabbed a biscuit, shoving it into his mouth whole. He took the cup of coffee Eliza had poured for him and plonked himself in the centre, casually reaching into his jacket pocket for a hipflask from which he added a generous pour of booze to his cup.

Charlie got up to get himself a drink and Carrie swooped into his seat, sharing a small smile with me. Eliza sat on her other side, then Frankie. Wilding surveyed the arrangements before deciding to leave a spare chair between him and Daisy.

'How are you feeling today, Miss Aldridge? Did you manage to sleep?' Wilding asked me politely. With any luck he was beginning to see me as an ally amongst the group. I'd stood up for him against Frankie twice; I hoped that if I needed his support in the coming days he would return the favour.

'I did, thank you. That sleeping draught you gave me worked wonders.'

'Just common or garden veronal. I always have plenty on hand.' His eyes slid towards Eliza before darting away. Presumably she was a regular consumer of the stuff. If Eliza was a little dozy, the doctor was quite the opposite. He crossed his legs, tapping his top foot against his leg, unable to keep still. He reminded me of how I'd felt the first time I'd drunk an espresso at Mrs DeMarco's café, my body feeling as though an electric current ran through it. Jittery was the word for his demeanour, and I wondered why he was so worried.

The chief officer appeared finally, a middle-aged man in pristine uniform who stood to attention in the centre of the room, the arrangement of the chairs giving him a good look at each of us.

'Ladies and gentlemen, I realise this is an upsetting time for all of you, especially those of you who are related to the deceased. However, it is important that we establish a few facts while they're fresh in your minds. The police in New York have been informed and if we can share information with them before our arrival, then it will be best all round, though they'll no doubt still want to speak to you.' He nodded in the direction of his spotty junior officer. 'Wilson here will stay with you in case you need anything. I'll call each of you in turn to another room to ensure privacy. Anything you say will be kept completely confidential, but I will expect you to answer my questions fully.'

'What about my daughter?' Eliza asked, her voice barely above a whisper. 'She's only a child.'

'I have no objection to Miss Abernathy being interviewed with her mother present,' he suggested. 'Perhaps you want to go first?'

The pair of them followed the chief officer out of the room, Carrie shooting me a worried glance as she went. I'd go and find her later, I decided, and see how she was holding up. Wilson stayed behind, standing quietly at the door. *In case you need anything*, the chief officer had said, but I was sure he was also there to make sure we didn't confer on our stories.

If he was hoping for something to report back on, he'd be disappointed. Everyone kept their silence, the only sounds made by Frankie as he loudly munched his way through the biscuits, then moved on to the fruit loaf. For the first time I felt something other than annoyance towards him. He hadn't said a word since arriving in the writing room, and he looked rather green, though that might have been down to the sheer amount of sugar he'd consumed. The motion of the ship was more noticeable than on previous days and my own stomach felt a little turbulent.

Charlie sat back down and nudged me, gesturing towards Jack Abernathy. 'Say something!' he hissed under his breath.

I turned to face Jack. 'I'm so sorry about your father-in-law. It must be a terrible shock for you all.'

'A lot of people would say he had it coming,' Jack said, crossing his legs as he lit a cigarette.

'Father.' Frankie shot a warning glance at Wilson, who was definitely listening in; I could practically see his ears twitching at these emerging signs of excitement.

'What? Why they might think one of us would have done him in is beyond me. The man was old and sick. He was going to drop dead any day, so why hurry it along? We'll get to New York and a proper doctor will declare it a heart attack. Natural causes.'

'It wasn't a heart attack,' Wilding said, quietly but firmly, his foot tapping more urgently.

'How the hell would you know? You act all high and mighty, Wilding, but what are you anyway? All you do is dole out sleeping draughts and useless tonics for rich old men and their spoiled daughters. You're a leech, that's all you are. Hanging around the wealthy and prescribing drugs for yourself on someone else's dime. Besides, no decent person could have worked for my father-in-law. He was a total bastard. You'd have to be after his money to put up with him, I know from personal experience.'

'Father, please!' Frankie rolled his eyes as Daisy began to sob. 'Now look what you've gone and done.'

'Oh God,' Jack sighed. 'Daisy, I wasn't talking about you.'

Wilding passed Daisy his handkerchief and smiled thinly. 'It just so happens that the ship's physician agrees with my assessment. Of course, there's a very slim chance that we're both wrong. Once we get to New York an autopsy will give us the answer, one way or the other.'

'For the love of God, Wilding, why don't you shut the fuck up!' Jack ran a hand through his hair, leaving a furrow. He suddenly noticed Wilson by the door. 'Son, make yourself useful and fetch me a drink. In fact, tell the bar to send up a bottle. Whisky. They know what I like. If I'm going to be here for much longer, I'll need something stronger than coffee.'

It took a quarter of an hour but a waiter duly arrived with a bottle of Scotch, crystal glasses and a bucket of ice. Jack was the only one to indulge to begin with, but Charlie wasn't far behind. Daisy said she'd have a small drink for the shock and upset. Wilding poured two more fingers into the three remaining glasses and handed them to me and Frankie. 'Medicinal,' he told us.

'Is Eliza telling them her whole life story?' Jack grumbled, but then there was a knock on the door and Frankie was sent for, clutching his glass for dear life.

After Frankie went Jack, the tension lifting in his absence. The male Abernathys got the proceedings going at a faster clip, in and out in a fraction of the time of the women. Wilding volunteered Daisy to go next.

'Lena, then you, Doctor,' Charlie said.

'Oh no, I'll go last,' Wilding told him. 'I already gave a detailed statement to the ship's doctor last night and it'll be interesting to discover if anything of interest has cropped up during these interviews.'

'You think they'd tell you anything?' Charlie was surprised.

'Maybe.' The doctor sounded defensive. 'Whatever Jack Abernathy says to the contrary, I had no reason to want my employer dead. I witnessed the last version of Mr Parker's will, so I know for a fact that I'm not in it.' He crossed his legs and sat back, closing his eyes. He looked as though he could have benefitted from a good night's sleep himself.

It was after one o'clock and we were going to miss luncheon, although I couldn't think of anything less appealing than the prospect of sitting at that white-clothed table, staring at the empty space where Francis Parker should have been. No sooner had Wilding remarked on the time than a waiter appeared, wheeling in a trolley bearing enough sandwiches and cakes to feed a scout troop, and fresh pots of tea and coffee.

My stomach still felt queasy but I managed a smoked salmon sandwich – and just as well, for Daisy took almost an hour to give her testimony. Charlie was pacing by then. Wilding had decided to use the room for its original purpose and sat at one of the desks to write, filling page after page with his scribbled handwriting. I was wondering if I should do the same and write home to Maggie when suddenly it was my turn.

I followed the officer who wasn't Wilson along the corridor to a door off the main drag. He knocked and waited for the invitation to enter, opening the door for me before closing me in. This new room was small and the chief officer had set himself up with a desk and chairs that took up most of the space. I took a seat opposite him and he turned to a new page of his notebook before looking up at me.

'Miss Lena Aldridge?' I nodded and he wrote my name at the top of his page before sitting back and looking me straight in the eye. 'So, first things first. Can you tell me what was in the bottle that you were seen throwing overboard two days ago?'

13

Friday, 28 August
Canary Club, Soho

I arrived at the Canary Club shortly after seven that evening, a little late but the club was quiet and I couldn't see Tommy anywhere. Maybe he'd decided not to show up. It wouldn't be the first time. Tommy was lazy as well as no good and usually if we saw him on two consecutive nights he'd be complaining of being overworked. A more charitable person than I would wonder if he'd decided to go home and actually show his wife the respect she deserved; talk about a fair way to go about getting divorced. But Tommy wasn't that sort of a man.

Empty of clientele, the doors only just officially open, the Canary looked exactly what it was: a sad cellar room stinking of spilled beer and stale cigarettes. Vic was busy stocking the bar for the night while Clive, who worked the door with his even burlier brother Eric, lent his heft to stacking crates of tonic water and ginger ale behind the counter, the small bottles rattling a tune. I called out a hello and weaved my way through the maze of tables to the threadbare black curtain that hid backstage from front of house. I make it sound more than it is. Backstage was a narrow dark corridor with black mould infesting the walls, a stinking hole that passed for the toilet (staff only, though the customer WC was scarcely any better) and Tommy's office.

My heart sank as I walked through. The cause of many of Maggie's troubles, Serena Mayhew, was leaning against the wall outside Tommy's office holding an open compact up to her face. If she was hanging about then it meant he'd bothered to turn up to work. She smirked at me and went back to checking her spots in the mirror. Her black silk dress exposed an anaemic expanse of goose-pimpled skin on her arms despite the fox fur tippet around her shoulders. Strange thing was, if Maggie and Serena had stood side by side they could have been sisters. Apart from the decade or so age gap, the main difference as far as I could see was that Serena's eyebrows were drawn far too high and you could tell when she'd been on the dope because one would be lower than the other.

Shoving past Serena, I chucked my ancient carpetbag down on the scuffed stone floor and crouched to pull out a long evening gown, one of two that I reserved to sing at the Canary. In the right lighting, by which I mean the dim spotlights of the Canary, it looked five times its real price. It was made out of a cheap bit of dark emerald silk, an offcut on sale at Wickham's in the Mile End Road, that I'd run up into a dress using Maggie's mother's sewing machine.

'Buy yourself something new sometime won't you, Lena?' Serena drawled. 'That old thing looks like it'll fall off you at any moment, and Tommy ain't running that sort of club.'

'Could've fooled me,' I replied, thinking of the upstairs flat and the rumours that Serena was quite familiar with it. Of all the women Tommy would leave Maggie for, I'd never imagined it to be Serena.

'Why don't you get that fancy man of yours to buy you something nice – or has he ditched you?' she sneered.

I clenched my fists and thought how satisfying it would be to give her a good hard slap. 'I don't need a man to buy my clothes for me.' I unbuttoned my day dress and let it fall to the floor, not caring that anyone could walk in. There was nowhere else to go and I wasn't going to close myself into the foetid toilet. Apart from anything else, the floor was always wet, and I doubted it was only water. None of the male musicians ever showed up until at least five minutes before we were due on stage, Vic wasn't into girls, though he wasn't daft enough to admit as much in public, and Tommy would be on the phone in his office, which was why Madame Serena had been kicked out into the corridor.

'You're only still here 'cause it's all the rage amongst the posh set these days. You know that, don't you?' I heard the rasp of her lighter, Serena pausing to inhale from her cigarette, and fought the urge to fill the silence by telling her to mind her own business, only using less refined language. 'They all like a coloured girl on the side. Ask your bloke. If you weren't a bit exotic he wouldn't want to show you off to all his mates. That's the only reason Tommy hasn't sacked you yet. You bring in the fellas who fancy a bit of—'

'Why don't you fuck off, Serena, and annoy someone else. Tommy, perhaps – or has he kicked you out of his office?' I saw red, rounding on her before I could stop myself. Silly little cow, hanging around in a stinking corridor for a man who didn't give a damn about her… She wasn't worth it. I took a deep breath and turned my back.

I wrestled with the side fastening, my heart stopping for a second as I thought I'd ripped the fragile stitching. Serena was right, this dress was on its last legs. I could feel my frustration start to simmer up again and took some deep breaths, trying to calm down. At least my silence finally paid off. Serena grew bored and flounced off by the time I'd put my shoes on, silver sandals that were a hand-me-down from Maggie. The light in the corridor was too dim so I had to hold my breath and make up my face in the cesspit of a loo, under the harsh bulb that swung madly when Tommy slammed out of his office.

'Lena?' he barked.

'Right here.'

'Smells like someone died in here.' His nose wrinkled in disgust as he poked his head through the door.

'You could always pay for a plumber.' I fixed my eyes on my own reflection, unable to bear looking him in the face.

'Did you see Maggie earlier?' he asked, trying to sound less interested than he clearly was.

'Yep.' I kept it short, hoping he'd go away.

'And? What did she have to say?'

I felt my rage rise again and turned to look him in the eye. 'You really are despicable, Tommy, d'you know that?'

I pushed past him and packed my make-up away in my carpetbag. Maggie joked that my life was in that bag, and it was true I'd be lost without it. A change of clothes, a spare pair of shoes, my make-up and a small jewellery box containing the few pairs of earrings I owned along with a real string of pearls that James had bought me and which I didn't dare leave in my room at Mrs Haskell's in case they went 'missing'.

'What d'you mean?' He grabbed my upper arm, tight enough to pinch. 'What's she been saying about me?'

I shook him off. 'I know she made a mistake but she's still your wife, Tommy, and you've hardly been a saint. I mean, don't you care about her at all?'

'What the fuck are you on about?'

I looked him up and down. 'You're a dog, Tommy. For weeks Serena's been hanging off your arm. I don't know how you can stand there and act like the wronged party in all this.'

'My marriage is none of your fucking business,' he argued.

'You're the one who started asking *me* questions! And I'm not particularly over the moon that you've made me look like the worst sort of friend, knowing what you were up to and not telling her.' I let my anger take over. 'I thought you loved her deep down. I thought Serena would be a flash in the pan like all the others, but no. What's she got on you, eh? Is it to do with what's going on upstairs? Do the police know?'

A stupid question really. Everyone knew that nothing went on in Soho without one copper or another getting a cut of the profits. If Tommy was running an underage knocking shop above his club, then there was a dodgy detective getting rich by turning a blind eye. Conducting illegal business was never a problem in this part of town, not until someone got too greedy.

Tommy didn't say a word but I saw his mouth twitch. What an old fool he'd become. I almost felt sorry for him. So desperate to get into a young girl's knickers that he didn't see how people looked at him. That mix of disgust and fascination. He acted like the big man around town but he was small fry really, with no family or gang to back him up. Maggie would be safer without him. It was only a matter of time before Tommy stepped on the wrong toes, and in Soho that didn't usually end well. Wives were considered fair game in a turf war and Maggie knew this; it was why she'd fallen for the fake security man's shtick. She was still young. Too young to let this lowlife bring her down.

'You think you're so clever,' he said. 'A right know-it-all.'

'Seems to me that almost everybody around here knows more than you.' I should have kept my mouth shut but the champagne I'd drunk earlier hadn't quite worn off.

'If you're so much better than me, why are you still working here?'

'I don't know, actually,' I shot back, thinking about Charlie Bacon and New York. 'There can't be many worse places out there.'

'Then find one of them to sing out of tune in,' he told me. 'This is your last evening at the Canary. Collect your pay and get out, soon as you finish your set.'

'Fine with me.' I stormed through the curtain, Serena watching from the bar where Vic had just presented her with a gin gimlet. Judging from the smirk on her face, she'd heard the entire exchange. 'You know what?' I turned back to Tommy, who had followed me through into the club. 'You don't get to tell me what to do. I'm not in the wrong here. You should be ashamed of yourself for what you've done.'

'I should kick you out right now,' he blustered.

'You don't have time to find a replacement.' Now it was my

turn to smirk. I knew I should make more effort to take the high road but sometimes it felt so much better to sink down into the mud.

'Soon as you're done, Clive'll walk you out,' he warned.

'Fine with me,' I repeated, signalling to Vic that I needed a drink.

'She pays for that,' Tommy warned.

Vic looked at me and I nodded, urging him to keep pouring as I leaned on the bar, smiling sweetly in Serena's direction. I had no intention of paying for Tommy's lousy booze, but it would be easier to make him think that I might and then sneak out afterwards.

'You'll come crawling back soon enough.' Tommy came and stood next to me, his overpowering cologne catching in my throat. 'You're not young enough or talented enough to make it anywhere else.'

'You'd be surprised,' I told him with the sweetest smile on my lips, thinking of New York. Vic handed me a strong gin and lime, the first sour sip making my tongue curl.

Tommy stomped off to his office, Serena trotting after him on cheap heels that were too spindly for her thick ankles. If she'd had an ounce of sense she'd have hit Tommy up for a pair of well-made shoes, the first clue to a woman's class or lack of it.

My last night at the Canary then. I took a good look around and didn't feel any sense of sadness, only a slight tingle of fear that I'd burned my bridges too soon. I'd not even officially agreed to go to New York, but it was fast looking to be my only option. If I stayed in London I had nowhere to live and no job. I'd be daft not to bite Charlie Bacon's hand off. So why hadn't I? And then there was Maggie to think about. A good friend wouldn't disappear across the ocean when she was most in need. But Maggie had her mother and her sisters to look after her. Maybe once I was settled in, she could come and stay with me in the States. A change would do both of us the world of good.

The band arrived and I had another gin to calm me down. When the first punters began to trickle in, I went outside to join the boys in a smoke, snatching the packet from my bag on the way. Of the five of them, three were black; two Americans and Jean, who was half Algerian, half Sierra Leonian. They were all friendly enough but they didn't joke around in front of me the way I'd heard them do with one another when I wasn't right there. Like every other part of my life, I was caught between two worlds. They left me before I'd finished smoking and wandered back inside to tune up. Maybe New York would be different. A new start. Choose a side, instead of straddling both and hoping to keep my balance.

I leaned against the bar and watched Tommy take his seat, Serena on his arm. She held her head high, the queen bee. When Tommy bothered to show up at the club his table was the one directly in front of the stage. In the good old days he'd sat there with Maggie, or on his own. Now his mistress sat by his side. He wanted to make a point about Serena, show anyone who cared that she was the new woman in his life, and I'd have to sing my entire set with that smug, foolish girl sitting three feet from me. It was enough to make me gag on my gin.

'Ah. We are in for a show tonight,' Vic said, leaning across the bar to clear away my empty glass.

I looked around. Maggie had walked in, dolled up in her finery, fur around shoulders and sparkling as brightly as a Hatton

Garden shop window. My heart ached for her but I knew she hadn't seen the show that Serena had just put on. Thank goodness.

'You promised you wouldn't come,' I scolded as she joined me.

'I promised to think about it,' she fired back, nodding for Vic to bring her a drink.

'What are you going to do?' I asked.

Her gaze fell upon her husband at the very moment he leaned over to plant a sloppy kiss on Serena's lips. Maggie's eyes were glassy as she turned towards me, her face hard as the diamonds around her neck. 'Whatever it takes.'

14

Friday, 4 September
Queen Mary

The chief officer stared me directly in the eye as I tried to keep my composure. How the hell did he know about the bottle? For a split second I considered denial but thought better of it. I'd obviously been seen. Better to tell a smaller lie than be caught out in the larger one.

'It was a perfume bottle,' I said, the back of my neck itching, my underarms damp with cold sweat.

'Bit odd. Most people would use a bin.'

'It was right there, in my bag and...' My lip trembled and I hoped he'd make the same common mistake as most men and assume that tears weren't far away. 'It had been a gift. He... It didn't end the way I hoped. Obviously. Otherwise I wouldn't be travelling to New York alone. It was a sort of a... a symbolic gesture.'

'Ah.' He looked uncomfortable. 'Right then.'

Frankie, that little bastard. He'd been out on the promenade deck that day. He must have seen me, right before that woman's hat had blown away and our paths had crossed officially.

What a snake. It proved Charlie was right, that the family would pull together, more than happy to point the finger in any direction other than their own. It wasn't comforting to have it confirmed. I'd have to hope that I could trust Charlie at least to keep his mouth shut. But then it wasn't in his best interests for anyone to find out about the similarities between Tommy's death and that of Francis Parker. After all, his main purpose was to deliver me safely to New York.

'How do you know the Abernathys?'

'I don't. That is, I met Frankie on deck as we sailed towards Cherbourg.' I watched the man's face but he didn't even twitch. 'The rest of the family I met at dinner on that first evening. I'm travelling with Charles Bacon. He's escorting me, I suppose you'd say. In fact, I only met him a week ago.' One week. Since the club, since Tommy had died and since I'd absconded with several thousand pounds of his money. My heart began to race and I could feel sweat begin to prickle on my forehead and upper lip.

'And did you notice anything odd over the last two days, at the table or perhaps you ran into some of the party outside of mealtimes? You've been friendly with Daisy Lancaster, apparently.'

The Abernathys liked to talk, then. Well, anything they could do, I could do better.

'I don't mind her,' I said, 'but I wouldn't call us friends. I think she feels a little isolated, especially now that the family have made it clear she's not one of them.' Was I over-egging it?

'Really? I had the impression that was the usual state of affairs.'

'Affairs.' I latched on to his choice of word and made a split-second decision, hoping it wouldn't come back to bite me. 'Yes, exactly.' I paused to make sure he was paying full attention. 'I'm sure someone must have mentioned what was going on. It was the worst kept secret.'

'I'm afraid you'll have to enlighten me, Miss Aldridge.'

'Daisy and Jack?' I lowered my voice. 'They were discreet enough in company, but I saw them together on the very first night. Everyone else was in the Starlight Club but they made separate excuses to leave the table. I went out onto the deck for a breath of fresh air not long afterwards and there they were. Brazen as anything. I suspect that Eliza knows.'

'Doing what exactly?'

'Kissing. They were in the doorway, right beneath the light, that's how I saw them so clearly.' I ignored the ribbon of guilt that started to unravel in the pit of my stomach. It wasn't my fault if they'd all decided to close ranks. I had to protect myself first.

'And Mrs Lancaster is married or...?'

'Widowed,' I confirmed.

He hadn't written any of this down. He either knew already or he didn't care. I wasn't sure which was more unsettling.

'Mr Parker. How did he seem to you?'

'He was quiet, didn't say much, but they all seemed in awe of him nonetheless. I got the impression that age had only recently begun to catch up with him. He fell ill about a year ago, or at least that's what Daisy told me. I suppose that was why he travelled with Dr Wilding. I barely spoke to him directly though; once, at most.'

He began taking notes again. 'Were there ever any arguments, cross words, that sort of thing?'

'He could be a bit snappy with Daisy and Wilding, but nothing in particular.'

He asked me a few more mundane questions about the general atmosphere and then closed his notebook. 'That's all for now. I may need to speak to you again, Miss Aldridge. I trust you'll make yourself available?'

'I can't exactly leave the ship, can I?' I said, immediately regretting my flippancy.

'No. You can't.' He looked at me impassively and got up to show me out.

I made my escape from the chief officer only to run straight into Daisy at the top of the staircase.

'Lena, thank God!' She practically leapt on me. 'I don't know what to do, he thinks I did it, they all do, and it wasn't me, I promise you, I didn't do it, I wouldn't know how—'

'Calm down.' I grabbed her hand and dragged her after me towards the long gallery, hoping that most people would still be at luncheon or outside, walking it off on deck.

We were lucky; only a few passengers were taking tea and coffee and not one of them looked at us as we entered. I led her to the table where we'd sat the previous afternoon and ordered two Martinis from the waiter.

'I don't think I can drink,' she said.

'It'll help with the nerves.' I held out my cigarette case to her.

She'd been crying again, her face blotchy and swollen. I wondered if she really cared about Francis Parker, or if she was actually crying for herself, presumably out of a job now that her employer was deceased. What if she really had poisoned him and was scared that she hadn't covered her tracks well enough? No, I dismissed the idea. I couldn't believe that Daisy would be so stupid when she was the obvious suspect. She could be annoying, but she wasn't a complete idiot. Francis Parker hadn't been a man to suffer fools gladly and she'd survived several years in close proximity to his impatience.

'What did he say to you, that man?' she asked.

'Not a lot. Nothing I can imagine being much use to him.' I crossed my fingers by my side as I told the lie. Compared to her lengthy interrogation, mine had barely taken half an hour. Short enough to believe I'd had nothing to say.

'Did he ask you anything about me?'

'Not really... He asked if you were married.'

'If I were married? Why? I... I mean... I told him about my husband. That he died, I mean.' She inhaled furiously from her cigarette. 'Why would he ask you about that?'

'I don't know.' I looked down at my right hand, the cigarette smoke twirling as someone opened a door and the draught caught it. 'I suppose... because of Jack.'

'Jack?' The word came out as a squeak. 'What about him?' I saw her hand tremble as she raised it to her throat.

'You aren't – I mean, he made it sound as though something was going on with you two.' I watched her face turn white, her cheeks flush red. 'Is it true?'

For a moment I thought she was going to be sick, but it was only a fresh fit of sobbing that convulsed her body. 'It's all such a mess, Lena.' She pulled an already sodden and mascara-streaked handkerchief from her handbag and blew her nose. 'I never meant for it to happen. He can be very... insistent... at times. And I felt flattered, in a way. Eliza's never liked me, even before Jack and I... And so I felt justified. She hated me anyway, so why not? I know that doesn't make it right, but it's true.'

She fell silent as the waiter approached with our drinks. I let her be for a moment as I took a sip and lit another cigarette. I guessed she was wondering how she had let herself get sucked in. I knew because I'd done exactly the same with James. If I couldn't explain why I'd stayed involved with a man who was a weasel at best, then I could understand why Daisy hadn't refused Jack. At least I'd never had to sit at a dinner table with Tabitha Harrington night after night.

'So how long has it been going on between the two of you?'

She looked up, a slight air of surprise in her eyes, as though she'd forgotten I was there. 'Me and Jack? Oh, since the start of the summer. I thought it was just a fling, on the ship over to London. Then Eliza went away for a month with the children, leaving only the four of us rattling around the house in Mayfair. Mr Parker was in bed by nine o'clock every night. Wilding was always locked away in his bedroom, and he was away most weekends – visiting academic colleagues in other cities, he said, though I think he was up to something. Wouldn't surprise me if he had a lady friend on the sly.'

'Isn't he married?' Also, this wasn't the first unprovable accusation that Daisy had thrown in Wilding's direction.

Daisy gave me a look. 'C'mon, Lena, what are we even talking about?'

'Of course. Sorry. I wasn't trying to insinuate anything. I'm hardly one to talk. The man I left in London was married. I know what it's like, being with someone who isn't free.'

The words were clumsy but Daisy didn't seem to notice. Talking about James, he felt a million miles away, a lover from another lifetime. Did he know that I'd left London? Would he care, or would he breathe a sigh of relief that he'd managed to extricate himself from our relationship so effortlessly? It still niggled; not heartbreak, more a fierce grumbling of indignation in my stomach when I thought about how I'd let things go on too long. I should have been the one to end it.

'It was so damn easy,' Daisy went on. 'Eliza rarely bothered to telephone when they were away. Carrie sent postcards most days, but apart from that he could have been a bachelor. It was almost as though she were giving us her blessing.'

I wasn't sure Eliza saw it that way, though I could see why Daisy liked to think so. 'Do you think she knows?' I was sure that she did, but I wanted Daisy to take me into her confidence. Me and her against the Abernathys.

'Who can tell?' She reached for her Martini and took a sip. 'She makes these barbed comments towards me, so sometimes I think she must know, but then she was always a bitch to me. Jack says there's no way she could know, but he would say that. I don't think he cares either way. He doesn't love her, I know that much. And I doubt she loves him.'

'Then why do they stay married?' From what I'd heard, divorce was all the rage in America, no longer the social death it still was in London, that it would have been for Maggie.

'Divorce? God, no!' Each sip of her drink emboldened her. 'Mr Parker would have cut them both off without a second thought if there'd been even a whiff of anything like that. This might be the twentieth century, but a lot of Mr Parker's circle are still firmly back in the nineteenth when it comes to marriage. Besides, between you and me, I'm not sure love ever came into it. Jack basically told me their marriage was a business transaction.'

'It sounds like something out of Jane Austen.' Daisy looked at me blankly. 'I mean, was he saying it was an arranged marriage? Two families deciding it would be best all round if their offspring were paired off?'

'Jack's family weren't wealthy. They weren't exactly poor, but his father was a draughtsman and his mother was a nurse before she married. Working people, not like the Parkers.'

So how did they meet then, Eliza and Jack?'

'Mr Parker introduced them. Jack went for an interview at Parker Godwin straight out of college. He's no dummy, you know, he got a scholarship to Harvard and that ain't easy. Anyway, he got the job and pulled off some big deal in his first month. That's how he caught the eye of Mr Parker. Next thing you know, he's being invited to dinner *chez Parker* and Eliza's there and he thinks she's pretty enough. I mean, I hate to say it, 'cause I think she's a godawful bore, but she is beautiful. And you know how men are. Most of 'em'd sacrifice decent conversation for something that looks good on their arm. Mr Parker as good as told him that if he married his daughter he'd be set for life.'

From the little I'd seen of Jack Abernathy he seemed exactly the sort of man who'd leap at an opportunity like that and worry about the consequences later. Eliza, though, was a conundrum. I'd talked to her enough to know that Daisy's accusation was nothing more than wishful thinking. Eliza was typical of other rich women I'd met but she wasn't a bore. Rather, she gave the impression of being a woman who had once had a lot to say but had learned to keep her thoughts to herself. The effect of years of living with a controlling father? She'd married young, so it wasn't out of desperation at being left on the shelf. What had happened to Eliza Parker to make her marry a man she didn't love?

'I suppose there are the children to consider as well,' I mused aloud, trying to keep Daisy talking.

Daisy rolled her eyes. 'A pair of spoiled brats, if you ask me. I mean, Carrie's sweet, don't get me wrong, but the arguments! You haven't seen that side of her yet, but my God was I glad when they all left for the Continent. Pitting her poor grandfather against Jack. Taking advantage, I call it.'

'What did they argue about?' I asked, curious. Carrie, of everyone in that family, didn't seem to have a bad side. Maybe she'd pouted a little the other night when sent to bed but show me a fifteen-year-old who wouldn't have done the same.

'Nothing important. I think she was just attention-seeking. Something about wanting to go to college. Eliza was in favour of it but Jack thought it was a waste of time, which it would have been. I mean, girls like Carrie will never know what it is to *need* a job, but she begged to differ. Said she'd find a way to go to college, even if she had to apply for every scholarship under the sun. Jack said she was a silly little fool who'd never had to go without and she'd be taking the place of some young man who really needed it. Etcetera, etcetera, you learn to tune this stuff out after the fifth night in a row.'

Daisy didn't seem impressed in the least, but I had to wonder about poor Carrie. The more I learned about the Abernathys, the stranger they seemed. What must it be like to live in that household, with a mother and father who had never loved one another, and with a brother who seemed hell-bent on following in his father's flawed footsteps? She looked so like her mother; could it be that Eliza had once been as feisty as her daughter, before the fight was worn out of her? I hated the idea that Carrie was destined for the same fate. Without Alfie, I was as good as an orphan, alone in the world. Still, I'd rather that than be forced to live my life with a family like Carrie's.

15

Friday, 4 September
Queen Mary

Four Martinis on an empty stomach will always result in poor
decision making. If nothing else is learned from my story, please
take this free advice.

'Let's go and dance!' Daisy giggled.

The long gallery had emptied out as the sun began to fall from
the sky into the sea. We'd wasted the afternoon away talking
and everyone else had gone to dinner. I felt empty inside but it
wasn't hunger, not entirely. I couldn't bear to face the others.
To sit there with the bereaved family seemed ghoulish, whether
they showed their grief or not. I couldn't do it.

I felt as though I were trapped inside my own detective novel.
Would I be the narrator, the unwitting character caught up in
circumstances outside of their control, or was I more important
than that? The next victim? I'd hardly known Francis Parker,
but I couldn't shake the similarity between those two deaths.
Two men dying of natural causes could be put down to simple
coincidence, but not murder, not when the method was identical.
The more I thought about it, the more I found myself unable

to believe that Dr Wilding would have made a mistake. If he believed it to be cyanide, then it was. But where did that leave me?

Daisy clicked her fingers so close to my face that her nail caught my nose, making me blink. 'Wakey wakey! C'mon, Lena let's go.'

'It's too early. Nobody will be dancing yet, they'll all be at dinner. Besides, didn't you say they were closing the Starlight Club tonight as a mark of respect?'

'They are. But I was thinking of somewhere less stuffy.' She giggled and stifled a hiccup. 'Before Jack and I began to – well, forget about that. Let's just say that it can get lonely when you're a woman with only an old man for company. No one knows who you are if you sneak down to the tourist–class lounge. Especially if you give 'em a fake name.'

'What name did you give?' I asked.

'One fella said I reminded him of Kay Francis, and I said, "What a coincidence! My name's Kay, but my surname's O'Connor." Which is my maiden name, by the way.' She was starting to ramble slightly. 'Kay O'Connor, I told him. I never knew anyone called Kay in real life so I figure it's not doing any harm, me borrowing the name.'

'It's so nice to meet you, Kay.' I held out my hand for her to shake. 'But then don't I need a new name?'

Daisy leaned forward and studied my face closely. 'You know, you got a touch of the Hispanic about you, Lena. I love Dolores del Río. What do you think of Dolores for a name?'

'It'll do.' Suddenly the idea of reinvention became intoxicating. 'Dolores on its own. No surname. I'll be an enigma.'

'That's the spirit! Let's go. Those poor fellas are waiting all alone at the bar for a couple of pretty gals like us.'

I looked at Daisy's face, her face powder streaked with salt from her tears. 'Let's take a detour on the way.'

Ten minutes in the ladies' loos to freshen up and we were on our way down to the lounge reserved for second-class passengers. Nobody batted an eyelid as we showed up in our day clothes, the difference between the two classes obvious. There was none of the peacocking and fashion parading that went on upstairs.

The lounge wasn't as luxurious as its cabin-class counterpart but it was echelons above my usual Soho haunts. Down here the waiters were freer with their chat and their laughter than those in the Starlight Club, sharing jokes with the passengers and taking time to pass the time of day. It was quiet when we arrived, but people were slowly trickling in from the first dinner sitting. The women had dressed up, but their jewellery consisted of affordable costume versions of the precious gems that were on display upstairs, paste replicas that failed to sparkle under the lights. The men wore their best suits, but they had come from the rack of a department store rather than a West End tailor. Daisy and I took a table on the edge of the dance floor and ordered a bottle of wine, foolishly thinking it safer than carrying on with the Martinis.

'It's so much more fun down here, didn't I tell you?' Daisy looked around. 'Though I don't know where all the eligible gents are.'

'Is that so bad?' I cautioned. 'Besides, are you really on the lookout? What about Jack?'

'I don't know. He's gone a bit cold on me the last day or so,' she admitted. 'And now, after what happened... It gives him a motive, doesn't it? With Mr Parker out of the way he could leave Eliza and, even if he didn't get to keep the money, he'd have his job and his shares in the company.'

'You think he would? Keep his job, I mean? He'd be outside of the family, so unless he's named in the will...'

Daisy's forehead wrinkled. 'Well, sure, but Mr Parker named him as successor last year.' She looked worried. 'You don't think there'd be a way around that, do you? That he might have written something in his will, left all his own shares to Eliza?'

'She is – was – his daughter. And I can't see her wanting to pay her former husband's salary if he deserted her.' If Eliza knew about Jack and Daisy then she probably had plans to break free of her loveless marriage now that her father was dead, but I thought it best to keep that idea to myself.

'Well shit.' Daisy chewed her lip. 'That'd be an awful mess for poor Jack.'

'I'm sure it'll all be fine. Jack isn't an idiot. Like you said, he's probably trying to protect the two of you, until the will is read and he knows what's what.' I trod carefully, nervous of spooking Daisy before she spilled what she knew. I didn't think she'd done it herself – she was being too loose-lipped and I doubted she'd have drunk away an afternoon with me if she was guilty – but maybe she thought Jack had done it.

There was a strange vulnerability about Daisy Lancaster. I wondered again what had happened to her husband. She wasn't that much older than I was. Something of her manner reminded me of Maggie. There was a fragility that she failed to hide beneath the war paint. A vague desperation.

The waiter was delivering a second bottle of wine to our table when a middle-aged man mounted the stage to announce the evening's entertainment. The applause was loud and appreciative as Will Goodman's band made their way to the stage. The sound of his name gave me a jolt, surprised to see him in this new setting. I smiled as he caught my eye, giving a small nod of acknowledgement. It only took half a song before couples were crowing the dance floor, three songs before a young dark-haired man approached our table.

'Would you care to dance?' He was looking at me as he spoke.

'Why I'd love to.' Daisy was on her feet immediately. 'I'm Kay.'

'Simon.' He shot me a nervous glance as she whisked him onto the parquet.

I was happy to sit, to sing along quietly and pretend that I wasn't enjoying the sight of Will as much as the music. 'Kay' could keep her man, and good luck to her.

The band kept up a steady stream of favourites and I wished they'd play something slower. I was getting dizzy watching people twirl in front of me, coming close to falling in my lap when they lost their balance. A good number of dancers were making up for their lack of skill with the exuberance that came with large quantities of alcohol. I drank another glass of wine and wondered if something stronger was required.

'Whew! I thought he'd never let me go.' Daisy eventually threw herself down in her chair as the band took a break, out of breath and with perspiration shining on her forehead. 'I'm exhausted.'

'I can tell.' I smiled.

'Oh God, really?' She rummaged in her bag for her compact,

grimacing at her reflection in the mirror. 'Damn it. Kay O'Connor ain't the type of girl to walk around with a sweaty face. Let me go fix this. Back in a jiffy, isn't that what you Brits say?'

She sashayed off, leaving me alone once more with my troubling thoughts. I couldn't stand it any longer. I leaned over and asked the polite French couple at the next table if they'd mind saving our seats, then took myself out of the lounge. I needed fresh air but, more than that, I needed someone to talk to. Someone who wasn't connected to Parker or to Tommy. There was a narrow promenade running the length of the ship on this level and I made my way along, hoping to repeat my luck of the night before. There he was, up ahead. I realised too late that I was drunk and not exactly looking my best. I stumbled a little and thought about turning back. I had hoped to impress him, but it was no good. He'd seen me.

'Slummin' it tonight, are we?' Will grinned, leaning against the railing, cigarette in hand.

I delved down into my vermouth-pickled brain for something witty to say and failed. 'Aren't you slumming it down here too? It's not half as glamorous as the Starlight Club.'

'No,' he conceded, 'but I prefer it down here. The people aren't afraid to have fun and we get more tips too. Upstairs folk are too snooty for their own good.'

I couldn't disagree. 'It's nice to see a familiar face. It's been a very strange day.'

'This to do with that fella that died? I saw what happened.' His voice softened with sympathy. 'He was at your table. You were travelling together?'

'No, no. I'd only just met him but still… It was awful. I spent half the day waiting to give a statement.' I shivered a little and he moved closer, his jacket brushing my shoulder and sending the tiny hairs along my arm aloft. 'They think he was murdered.'

'We never got told nothin' last night, but by this morning the whole place was talkin' 'bout it. Poison, they was saying.'

'That's what the doctor thinks,' I confirmed.

'They know who did it?' he asked.

I shook my head. 'It's all so strange. I don't know if I should be more worried that there's a killer on board, or that I was there and that my name's now on a list of suspects.'

'But you didn't know him?'

'No. Never even heard of him before.' I let Will light my cigarette, glad of the moment's silence. It felt so easy talking to him, but what if I slipped and said too much? 'Gosh, this is so morbid! I came down here to try and take my mind off it all, and here I am, talking your ear off.'

'I don't mind,' he said. 'I come out here alone to clear my head. The fellas in the band are like brothers to me. Always bickering and loud.'

'And then here I come, barging in.' We both laughed.

'Like I say, I don't mind. Murder, huh?' He shook his head in disbelief. 'Baby, that's crazy.'

'I know. I feel like I've wandered onto a film set and I'm the only person who hasn't seen the script.' As I spoke, I realised what had been bothering me so much. The idea that someone else knew exactly what was going on. It was the only explanation, and yet it made no more sense than the idea of coincidence.

Why would any of these people have it in for me? 'The rules here, they seem different than at home.'

'You know, you're going to have to learn fast,' Will told me.

'What do you mean?'

'*I'm not like you.*' He parroted my words back to me, the foolish sentence I'd regretted ever since I'd uttered it. 'It's true enough. I can't hide in plain sight like you do. Once you get to New York you probably shouldn't be seen talking to a guy like me. Not if you don't want anyone to get the wrong idea about you.'

'Wrong idea? What wrong idea?'

'Things are, well, black and white. Literally. You hang around with Negroes and people will think one of two things. The first, I won't say out loud, not in polite company. The second is that they'll realise you're a Negro too. You won't know they've been talking 'bout you until it's too late and you realise every-one's staring at you.'

'I don't care if people stare at me.'

'Don't be a fool.' His tone was gentler than his words. 'Isn't this your one shot at the big time? I'd kill for what you have. You can't throw it away so easily. You're taking a risk now, just standing here with me. Now more than ever, you need them to think you're one of them. You're not safe otherwise.'

'But maybe I like talking to you and maybe it's no one else's business,' I fired back. Okay, perhaps I was being naïve, but could New York really be so different to London? I could cope with a few stares, I was used to that, especially when I was with Alfie, and the odd muttered slur couldn't harm me. 'Besides, if you're so bothered, why are you still here?'

'Haven't you noticed? You're the one who keeps coming after me,' he pointed out.

There was nothing left to say, and even if I could have thought of something clever, my throat had closed up and I knew I was close to tears, stupid though that sounds. Will Goodman was a random stranger, not the friend I had hoped to find. It wasn't his fault; I wasn't even sure myself why I'd sought him out. I shoved past him and went back inside, ordering yet another drink from a passing waiter. The band came back on and Daisy headed for the dance floor, whirling around on the arm of a chap I hadn't seen before. Will was at the piano, but I sat through two songs and another glass of wine and he didn't look my way once.

'Honey, here you are!' Daisy flopped back into her chair, exhausted, her dance partner promising to return with drinks for us all. 'So nice of Bert. A real English gentleman.'

She carried on talking but her voice drifted over me. The music grew louder and I had to blink to keep Will in focus as I willed him to look at me. I was very drunk, I realised, as my body began to feel one with the chair.

'Daisy, I'm ever so tired.' I forced myself to the seat edge, bracing myself to stand. 'You'll be all right with Bert, won't you?' I felt wobbly as I stood, holding onto the arm of the chair, unsure whether it was the ship that was rocking or only me.

I didn't wait to hear her reply. I was too afraid of being sick right in view of everyone, including Will. I made it out of the lounge with my dignity intact but had to make a run for the ladies', emptying my stomach into the toilet. The porcelain was lovely and cool against my sweating forehead as I knelt there, praying to the gods of good times that I might feel better soon. The rocking continued and I could feel the hum of the ship's engines as I curled up on the floor. I knew I wasn't just upset over Will, though his words had cut me. It was the drink, the death of Francis Parker, knowing that I wasn't quite free of the murder of Tommy Scarsdale, all of it weighing down on me like a ten-ton weight. It was hard even taking a breath.

I wished desperately that I'd tried to talk Maggie into coming to New York with me. I needed someone to talk to. Someone who wouldn't judge me. I suppose that was what I'd hoped to find in Will, latching on to the first person who I thought might be trustworthy. Certainly, no one at the Abernathys' table could be trusted an inch.

Only a few more days, I reminded myself, and then I would be safe in a New York hotel and I could write to Maggie back in London and pour all my woes onto the page. It would be easier from a distance, rebuilding our friendship through letters. Learning to forgive over time.

Gingerly I made my way to my cabin, thankful that I didn't have far to go. My head ached and I hadn't dared to glance in the mirror above the sinks in the loo. It wasn't that late, only about eleven o'clock, and I was lucky that the corridor was empty, no one around to see me and cast judgement. I could almost feel the crisp linen on the bed, the smooth pillow that would mould itself to fit my head, the well-sprung mattress that felt as soft as a cloud. I turned the key in the lock.

'Miss Aldridge?'

I forced a smile on my face as I saw Jack Abernathy approach me. 'Hello. I didn't realise anyone would still be up.'

'Oh yes.' He grinned. 'It's not even midnight yet, after all.'

Now that I knew he hadn't been born with a silver spoon in his mouth, I could hear the slight rasp of grit in Jack's voice. He was faking it, same as me, only with decades more practice. What was it like to live like a bought man, to know that your fortune was dependent on the benevolence of your father-in-law?

'So there's something we need to talk about. Something confidential.' He said it as if I should know what was going on.

'All right.' I waited for him to continue. Was this something he had been cooking up with Charlie?

'Aren't you going to invite me in?' He leaned against the wall and gave me a crooked smile.

The last thing I wanted to do was let Jack Abernathy into my cabin. I could see from the sheen on his face and the angry red flush that leached up his neck from beneath his collar that he was half cut. At the same time I was exhausted. If I let him say his piece, at least I could then get rid of him.

'Come on, Lena. I'll be in and out before you know it.' He leaned closer, breathing whisky over me.

'Fine. But please be quick. It's been a very long day and I'm tired.' Every nerve in my body was telling me what a bad idea it was to let him in and yet I didn't pay attention.

He followed me in and pushed the door closed, flinging himself onto the sofa with a groan. 'You got anything to drink?'

'No.' I remained standing, my arms folded across my chest. 'What do you want, Mr Abernathy?'

'Jack. Please.' His smile was sly, like a schoolboy walking up to give the teacher a present, a dirty great spider hidden in his hand. 'Come and sit down.' He patted the cushion beside him.

'I'm sorry, Mr Abernathy, I'm very tired. It's been a very difficult day for all of us and we should both get some sleep.'

'You were drinking with Daisy,' he said. 'I saw you earlier. She knows how to have a good time, or she used to. I guess you two got a lot in common.'

'She was upset. We both were. About what happened to your father-in-law.'

Jack laughed. 'Upset? Nobody's upset about Frank, least of all anyone who actually knew the bastard. It's a miracle it took so long before someone put the old dog down.' He leaned forward and studied my face. 'Has Daisy been talking? She talks too much.' He caught me off guard, suddenly springing to his feet and catching hold of me by the arms.

'What are you doing?' I tried to free myself but he was too strong, his hands gripping my upper arms like manacles as he pushed his soggy lips against mine.

'Quit squirming,' he told me. 'You don't need to act the princess around me. I wouldn't have come if I was the judgemental type.'

I meant to shout but the words sputtered out, a weak protest. 'Please, don't.'

He pushed me against the wall so that he could restrain me with one arm while reaching down to yank up the skirt of my dress. 'I'll vouch for your honour, don't you worry. No one'll think any less of you.'

My heart was pounding as I struggled harder, the fabric of my dress tearing as his hand moved further up my leg, his fingers tugging at my knickers as he panted into my ear.

'No!'

I found a breath and shouted, loud enough this time to startle him. I took advantage of his confusion to free a hand and slap his sweaty cheek. He took a step back, his face a picture of offence. I slid down the wall and tucked my body into a ball, waiting for the retaliation. Instead of the blow from a fist, I heard a knock at the door, the creak of the hinge as it swung open. In his drunken haste, Jack had forgotten to close the door properly, thank God. Daisy stood there in the doorway, a look of surprise on her face.

'Lena?' Her face fell as she took in my appearance, her eyes widening as her gaze fell upon Jack, standing above me with his shirt pulled out and his flies undone.

'Daisy.' Jack looked crestfallen. 'What are you doing here?'

'I could...' She stopped and looked down at me, betrayal in her eyes. 'I thought you were tired.'

'I was. I am.' I struggled to my feet, holding onto the wall for support. 'Jack was just leaving.'

'Yes, that's right. I'd better go check on Eliza.' The coward grabbed his jacket and ran away, leaving Daisy and me facing one another.

'It's not what it looks like. I didn't ask him to come here. I didn't want him to...' I gave up talking. She'd make up her own mind about what she'd seen and I could only feel grateful that she'd saved me.

'You've got lipstick smeared all over your chin.' She turned to go, taking a moment to fire one last shot over her shoulder. 'I thought we'd be friends, you and I.'

I wanted to chase after her and tell her she was wrong about me, but my legs were too weak. I sank to my knees, resting my head on the floor until the room stopped spinning. I shuffled to the door on my hands and made sure it was locked, sitting on the carpet with my back against the hard wood. How could Daisy have seen me on the ground and thought that I'd invited that? Or had I? I could have refused to let him in. I should have refused.

I'm not sure how much time passed before I managed to rouse myself. I knew I had to sleep. I clambered to my feet and walked to the bathroom. The mirror showed the state that Daisy had seen: lipstick like a clown's, kohl weeping from my eyes and down my cheeks. I turned on the bath taps and gave thanks that even though it was almost midnight there was hot water. I ran the bath until the air was thick with steam, scrubbing myself until the water was stone-cold and every inch of my skin felt raw.

It was almost one o'clock when I finally climbed into bed wishing I had another dose to hand of Dr Wilding's sleeping draught. I pulled the sheets tight around me, into a cocoon, and pressed my face into the pillow. What an absolute fool I'd been. It didn't matter about the expensive clothes and the jewellery I'd borrowed from Maggie, the refined accent that Charlie Bacon had said was infallible. Even a drunk like Jack Abernathy had seen straight through my disguise.

All potential suspects have scattered to the four corners of this vast ship. I did not anticipate this. A novice error. I trusted in the safety of routine, the need of humans to be social. I thought that we would cling to our group, us against the onlookers who stare at us now, curious. Instead, I find even myself reluctant to stay too long in the company of the others. Do suspicion and guilt look much the same to the outside eye? I hope so.

It started when we gathered in the writing room, waiting for our detective. The chief officer is not a very impressive man. At least, I'm sure he is excellent at the job he carries out on a daily basis, but he is no great mind when it comes to finding a murderer. I gave him hints that should have been obvious, but he only wrote my words down verbatim in his notebook and moved through his list of questions as though he had no real interest in catching a killer. I almost said something out of turn, the temptation to hand Lena to him almost overwhelming, but it's too soon. I must learn to have patience.

Lena continues to play along, as if she knows the plan and wants me to succeed. I saw from her face that she had recognised the method, the effects of cyanide poisoning, and that she had drawn the link between the two murders. I thought that someone might comment on her behaviour – I couldn't believe my luck when she actually fainted! – but no. The assumption was made that she was just another weak woman, the shock of watching a man die too much for her. Everyone was so kind, as if it were Lena who had lost a relative. Of course, they will find out the truth in due course.

Tonight gave more proof that people are predictable. All it took was a note pushed beneath a cabin door, a quick knock to make sure its occupant found it when I needed him to. And Lena let that drunkard in. I suspected what would follow, but I'm not a monster. Lena was never meant to get hurt – I wasn't going to let that happen. I needed to dent her reputation, as simple as that. Show her lack of morals. Isolate her from anyone who might lend her support. In that respect, tonight was an absolute triumph!

Pick Yourself Up

16

Saturday, 5 September
Queen Mary

I watched the sky through the porthole, marvelling as light cracked the clouds, the new day dawning before I'd had a wink of sleep. My head throbbed and my throat was so dry that I couldn't swallow. At six o'clock I gave up and picked up the telephone, glad that it was Danny at the steward's station. I ordered coffee and a jug of water.

'I'm going to take a bath, Danny, so just let yourself in and leave it on the coffee table,' I told him.

I ran fresh water and added a generous scoop of bath salts. I knew that I couldn't possibly need another bath but I could still feel Jack's fingers on my thighs. I could still smell his harsh cologne, transferred from his skin to mine. I rinsed my mouth out with tap water and brushed my teeth. The taste of sour wine and vomit lingered at the back of my throat. I brushed my teeth again. When I lifted my nightgown over my head I saw bruises on my upper arms, matching blotches staining my left hip and inner thigh. I took a deep breath and stifled a sob. It could have been so much worse. I had been lucky. *I was so lucky.* I whispered the words to myself, over and over, knowing it to be true. *Pull yourself together.* If I said it aloud, would that make it true? *No one can know.* Jack wouldn't say anything but would Daisy? If I told the truth, it would be my word against his. But if she told her version…

I sat on the edge of the bathtub as I waited for it to fill. I heard the door to my cabin open, Danny calling out so that I would know it was him. I didn't reply. I didn't trust my voice not to break. My body ached, the sort of throbbing dull pain that often accompanies a bad winter cold.

The water was welcoming and I lay back with my eyes closed, trying to clear my mind. Tommy Scarsdale, Francis Parker, Daisy Lancaster, their faces on some hellish carousel of guilt revolving in my head. I had hoped for five days of peace while we sailed to New York but disaster had boarded with me in Southampton. Disaster, and a murderer. But who?

There must be something good that I could focus on. *Broadway.* But what did that look like? I didn't even know what the role was. It had seemed like a dream when I signed the contract and went with Charlie to the travel agent to pick up our tickets, but now I knew I should have stayed in London. Whatever she said to the contrary, Maggie had needed me. I hated to admit it, but I'd run away. From what had happened, from what I thought might happen next. I'd thought it would be safe across an ocean; it hadn't occurred to me that whatever malevolent influence had upended our lives in London would follow me onto the *Queen Mary.*

I sat up, water tipping out onto the floor with my unexpected movement. Jack would stay away from me now, I was sure. Men like him only went for easy targets and I wouldn't let my guard down again. I could sort things out with Daisy. And we'd be in New York in two days' time. My new life would begin as soon as the soles of my shoes touched American soil. I had no motive for killing Francis Parker. Whoever had killed him, I wasn't a suspect. I could keep a low profile until Monday morning and then I'd never see any of the Abernathys again.

I stepped out and dried myself off. A bit of make-up and a trip to the beauty salon, that would have me looking back to my best. I poured myself a cup of coffee and lit the first cigarette of the day, walked to the porthole and peered out at the horizon. The sky was clear and the early morning sunshine was warm against my face. I closed my eyes and rested my forehead against the glass. It would be so lovely if I could stay in my cabin all day. Maybe no one would mind if I did just that.

I was pouring myself another cup of coffee when there was a knock on the door. I hesitated before going to answer, peeping through the keyhole to see Charlie Bacon checking his watch and looking like a man who had places to be. I opened the door a crack.

'Lena! Why aren't you dressed?'

'Are we going somewhere?' My voice was hoarse.

'Late night, was it?' His tone wasn't friendly. 'Jesus, what the hell are you playing at? You're supposed to be acting like a professional. At least fake it, can't you?'

I opened the door wider to let him in. It seemed better than letting any passer-by hear him telling me off. 'Why? The Abernathys have bigger problems to worry about, and no one else knows who I am.'

'Nobody *knew* who you *were*,' he corrected, walking past me to check his tie in the dressing table mirror. I pulled my robe tighter, holding it at the top so that the neck wouldn't gape. 'Francis Parker croaking at our table destroyed any anonymity you thought you had. It's all anyone's talking about out there. The famous Parker family and the unknown Broadway starlet.'

It sounded exactly the sort of rumour that Charlie Bacon himself would have started. 'I haven't heard any talk,' I said mutinously, lighting another cigarette as I sat. 'Coffee?'

'This isn't a social call, Lena.' He began to pace. 'Daisy Lancaster came to see me first thing this morning. At seven o'clock, no less. Can you guess what she wanted to talk to me about?' Any sympathy I'd had for Daisy swiftly departed. 'She says she saw Jack Abernathy leaving this very cabin in the early hours of the morning. *Jack. Fucking. Abernathy.*'

'She doesn't know what she saw.' I took a deep inhalation and blew out a stream of smoke as I tried to stay calm. 'Yes, Jack came here. But not at my invitation.'

'Then what did he want?'

There was no way of explaining it so that he would understand, I realised. *Insistent,* Daisy had said about Jack, and yet she had assumed the worst of me. Hadn't even given me a chance to explain before running off to tell tales. There was no chance that Charlie would believe in my innocence and I didn't have the strength to fight my corner. Not yet.

'How can you still not understand how important these people are? How many times do I have to tell you? Do you have any idea what a bad reputation can do to a career?'

'What can they do to me anyway? So they have money?'

I shouted back. 'Benny Walker has money. He paid for all this.' I threw out an arm, indicating the luxury that surrounded us. 'What do I need them for when I've got Benny on my side?'

Charlie opened his mouth, then closed it again, shaking his head. 'It really shouldn't be this difficult, Lena. All I'm asking is for you to show up at meals with a smile on your face and keep your legs closed. Is that so damned hard?'

'I didn't do anything wrong.' I could feel tears coursing down my cheeks and wiped them away angrily. 'I didn't ask him to come here, I swear.'

'Clean yourself up and be down at breakfast within the next half an hour or I'll have to telegraph ahead to New York. Tell Benny I don't think you're the girl he needs.'

'Get out,' I said quietly.

'Half an hour,' he repeated, and left.

I felt shaky after he'd gone, like a ragdoll, weak and useless. My hair was a state but I made do with pinning it back from my face, the kirby grips scratching my scalp as I pushed them in firmly. I managed to telephone the salon and made an appointment for later that day. Amongst Maggie's collection of clothes was a mustard-yellow day dress with a navy belt and long sleeves. I slipped on a pair of low-heeled Oxfords and stood in front of the mirror. My reflection presented a demure image that I hoped would please Charlie and help me to hold my own against Daisy's accusations. With the tiniest hint of rouge on my cheeks and a slick of Vaseline on my lips, I looked younger than twenty-six, positively Carrie-like.

Daisy thought she was so clever running off to Charlie like

that, but Jack would go spare if she made a song and dance about it at the table. And if I was right, and everyone in the family knew about her affair with Jack, it would only look as though she were trying to deflect the attention away from herself. I entered the dining room braced for battle, but when I arrived at the table I only had Charlie to face. I deliberately took a seat on the opposite side of the table.

'Sulking?' he asked.

I beamed a bright smile at the waiter. 'I'll have the scrambled eggs and smoked salmon, please. And a hot chocolate.' I wasn't sure that my stomach could handle anything after the night before, but the last thing I wanted was for Charlie to think he'd beaten me.

'So you're – what is it you Brits say? Sending me to Cheltenham?'

'Coventry,' I said. 'And no. If you'd like to talk to me in a civil manner and not talk down to me like I'm a child, then I'm absolutely happy to engage in conversation with you.'

'Engage in conversation, huh?' He sniggered. 'God, you're good when you want to be. It's a great act, Lena. All I'm asking is you don't let it drop. Not around these people.'

I bit back a retort and smiled demurely at Eliza, who was approaching our table dressed in a simple black frock. Carrie trailed behind in a navy-blue pinafore, her camera case slung over her shoulder.

'Am I glad to see you both.' Eliza sat beside me, Carrie on her other side. 'Jack and Frankie are both a little under the weather, so I dragged Carrie out before I went crazy after being cooped up for so long.' I hoped that Jack was particularly ill, full of the shame that often accompanies over-indulgence.

'How are you? I don't think I had a chance to speak to you yesterday. I'm so sorry for your loss.'

'Thank you, Lena.' She put her arm around her daughter. 'We're holding up as well as can be expected. Poor Carrie here is bereft. They used to be thick as thieves, her and my father.'

Carrie smiled sadly. 'Before he got ill, I would spend every weekend with Grandpa. We'd go to an art gallery or we'd drive around Manhattan. He showed me how to take photographs and how to develop them.'

'Carrie is obsessed with photography,' Eliza said, with an indulgent smile in her daughter's direction.

'What I'd really like is to study it properly. I want to be like Lee Miller. I saw an exhibition of her work a few years ago and I thought it was wonderful. But Daddy says that's not what women like me do. He thinks it would be a waste of time, since I won't be able to have a career once I get married anyway.' Carrie looked in my direction, expecting me to be appalled.

'And Daddy's right. Next year you'll start getting invitations to all the dances and you need to be available. Even Lee Miller gave up her career to get married, so don't look at me like that.' Eliza patted her head.

'Mama, don't you want me to be able to make my own choices?' Carrie shrugged away from her mother's hand. 'I want to travel and see the world and capture it on film. You're hoping I'll meet a nice boy from a good family and get married, even if it makes me miserable.'

'Would it be so bad? Darling, you don't want to hide away

in a darkroom for years and then realise you've left it too late and all the good men are taken. And Daddy said he'd send you to finishing school in Europe if you want to travel so badly.'

'Those aren't proper schools though, are they?' I said, surprising myself and earning a dagger-sharp glare from Charlie. I assumed Jack wanted his daughter to attend the sort of institution that Tabitha Harrington had attended, where they taught you how to manage your servants and make small talk with politicians. Not a real school at all.

'See, Mama! Lena agrees with me.'

'Well unfortunately for you, Lena isn't paying your school fees. It's Daddy you need to convince.' Eliza turned to me, changing the subject. 'You two girls seem to be getting along well. Lena, why don't you let Carrie take you to the swimming pool?' She lowered her voice. 'I'd rather she didn't spend too much time alone, not at the moment.'

'I can hear you quite well, Mama!'

'Well, wouldn't you like to have some company every once in a while?'

'Only if Lena wants to come.' She looked at me beseechingly and I felt my resolve to avoid the Abernathys as much as possible weaken. 'Don't feel you have to.'

'I do have a hair appointment this afternoon, but...'

'We can go before luncheon. I'll meet you at the swimming pool an hour after breakfast' She emphasised this last point to satisfy her mother's worries that she might drown on a full stomach. 'I'll see you in the water!'

I nodded. Carrie seemed a lost little soul and I wondered what her place was within this odd family, amongst her boorish father and older brother, and Eliza, who became more of an enigma the more I saw of her. I felt a strange connection to her, even though our lives were nothing alike. And, I hated to admit it, but my cabin was no longer the sanctuary it had been. At least with Carrie by my side, everyone else would leave me alone and maybe I could find the peace that I longed for.

17

Friday, 28 August
Canary Club, Soho

'I thought we had a deal?'

Maggie shrugged. 'Why should he get to have all the fun?'

'Well, he certainly won't be now.' I tried to ignore the death stare from Serena Mayhew, who had clocked Maggie's arrival and was now whispering in Tommy's ear. 'You're not going to do anything daft, are you?'

'Don't worry, Lee, I won't do anything that gets you into trouble,' she drawled, lighting a cigarette.

'Too late for that.' I handed my empty water glass across the bar for Vic to refill. 'He already sacked me, about half an hour ago.'

'Good.' She put a hand on my arm to lighten the blow. 'You need to get out of here. You're worth more, you know you are. I've got a lot on my plate at the moment but once this is all over, we can spend more time together. Get back to how things used to be. Go on holiday or something. I hear the south of France is lovely this time of year.'

She was right, we hadn't spent time together recently. She'd been grieving the babies she'd lost and the husband who didn't seem to care. On days out that I'd arranged, she'd been listless, and so I'd stopped asking and waited for her to let me know when she was ready. Now Maggie seemed stronger, determined to wage war. Almost back to her old self. I'd have been pleased about it if her timing hadn't been so terrible.

'Behave, won't you,' I warned her.

'I know what I'm doing,' she said.

'Glad someone does,' Vic muttered, passing me the glass of water.

I took a gulp and looked away. Should I tell her about Charles Bacon? New York seemed an impossible dream. Maybe it wasn't such a good idea to leave. This feud between Maggie and Tommy wasn't going to get sorted out overnight, and America, well, it was so far away...

'Now,' Maggie said to Vic, 'are those drinks for my husband and his floozy?' She pulled the tray along the bar, snatching it away from one of the pretty young girls Tommy hired to do bar service.

'Erm... yes?' Vic looked worried, with good reason.

Here was the thing with Tommy. He was lazy and he was a terrible boss, but he was very particular about certain things. He wasn't a lush by any means, but he liked a drink or two of an evening. Always an Old Fashioned when he was at the Canary. And he *always* had the bitters served to him separately, the bottle laid out beside the glass so that he could add to his own particular taste.

'I'll take that.' Maggie waved away the waitress and threw off her fur coat recklessly; I had to catch it before it hit the floor. 'I'll show him service with a smile.'

'Maggie, don't you dare,' I warned.

'What do you think I'm going to do? Throw it in his face?' She belted out a laugh. 'No, though he does deserve it. They both do.'

Vic almost leapt on top of the bar, slamming his hands down on the tray. 'Do whatever you like once we are closed, Mrs Scarsdale, but these people have come for the music. If they wanted to see drama, they'd be at the theatre.'

Maggie stared him down for a moment, then threw her hands up in surrender and smiled sweetly. 'Fine. Like I said, I'm not here to cause a scene. I'll take another drink for my trouble though.'

'Maggie, please,' I begged, 'go home. I'll come over later and we can talk. Have a few drinks if you like.'

'Why are you so keen to get rid of me? Do you know something else? Another secret that Tommy's been hiding?'

'No! Look.' I knew I was running out of time. 'I only want what's best for you. No point upsetting yourself.' The band were walking onstage now, Jean looking annoyed when he saw me loitering by the bar. Maggie hadn't moved a muscle. 'Fine. Have it your way. Sit here and don't move,' I warned her as the waitress dived in and grabbed Tommy's drinks.

Maggie nodded and took a seat at the bar as Vic mixed her a drink. Jean started playing at the piano and I had to move quickly to make it across the floor and step up behind the microphone before my cue arrived. My usual nerves had been replaced by the electric tingle of anticipation: something was about to happen.

We got through the first song without anything out of the ordinary happening. I tried not to look down at Tommy's table too often, but I couldn't help myself. Serena was suffering from a similar affliction, unable to stop herself from staring across at Maggie. It seemed impossible that there wouldn't be a scene at some point in the evening.

'Ladies and gents, thank you for having us here tonight.' I gave the usual spiel, introduced the band and made a tried-and-tested joke about the weather and women's hairstyles which always went down well.

I looked out at the modest crowd and imagined a grand Broadway theatre with hundreds, maybe thousands of seats. A real orchestra playing as the spotlight followed me across a stage that was larger than the entire room I stood in. Was it such a ridiculous notion? It was just my luck to finally get the offer I'd been waiting for, only to have to choose between my career and Maggie. Though she'd put Tommy first for over a decade, I reasoned. It wasn't my fault she'd made such a huge mistake.

We went with a current favourite next, 'Let's Face the Music and Dance'. I let my thoughts drift but I sang the right words in the right order, as far as I could tell from the audience reaction. The band had begun to segue into 'Love Me or Leave Me' when I first noticed something amiss. Over Harold's soft bass came another sound, off-beat, out of place. I frowned at Jerry, but he just shrugged and kept playing his trumpet.

A motion caught my eye and I looked down to see Tommy thumping his chest with a closed fist. Even with the stage lighting in my eyes I could see his face turning red as Serena patted his back uselessly. She held his glass to his lips, but he pushed her away. I stopped singing and watched as he slid to the floor, his body beginning to fit, jerking out of his control. The convulsions grew stronger and his eyes rolled back in his head. People were standing up, craning their necks like vultures, trying to get a better view of what was going on.

'Call an ambulance!' Serena cried out. 'Is there a doctor?' She fell to her knees and began to struggle with Tommy's tie, trying in vain to help him breathe.

I looked over to the bar. Maggie was standing there, horror etched across her face. No matter what he'd done, she was his wife, in sickness and in health – only he had chosen to have Serena by his side.

'Please, is anyone a doctor? Or a nurse?' I spoke into the microphone, my voice sounding unfamiliar to my own ears, panic echoing off the walls.

No one stepped forward, they either stood still, frozen with shock, or moved back. Tommy was thrashing on the floor like a fish landed on a canal bank. Watching him was terrible but I couldn't tear my eyes away. When he finally fell still it was a relief.

Clive and Eric had both abandoned their posts, Clive pushing his way through to where Tommy lay, Eric heading towards the bar where Vic was already on the telephone, his face even paler than normal. Clive crouched and held his fingers against his boss's throat and waited. The expression on his face was resigned. He held a hand over Tommy's mouth, then shook his head.

Serena screamed and a man called out, 'Call the police.' Those words cut through the silence like a butcher's knife through fillet steak. Chairs scraped back and the volume rose as people began the push to get out. Eric ran across and blocked the exit with his bulk.

Clive climbed up and pushed me gently out of the way, speaking into the microphone. 'Ladies and gents, take your seats, please. No one's leaving 'til the police arrive.'

'You can't keep us here,' some bloke piped up from the back. 'That's false imprisonment. This ain't got nothing to do with me.'

I saw a couple of the men look Eric up and down, gauging if it was worth a shot. Eric was a sweetheart but you wouldn't know it by looking at him. He wasn't a big talker and the size of him persuaded most people not to start an argument, only the very stupid or the very drunk ever deciding it was a good idea to mess with him. It was too early for the latter.

'Paid your bill yet, have you?' Clive asked. ''Cause if you haven't and you try to leave, I'd call that doing a runner.'

Between that threat and the very visible presence of Eric, people decided to be sensible and sat back down.

Maggie was no longer at the bar, I realised suddenly. I jumped off the stage and pushed through the curtain to the back. The door to Tommy's office was open and I found her crouched behind the desk, fiddling with the combination lock to the safe.

'What are you doing?' I hissed, closing the door behind me and shooting across the bolt that Tommy often used to keep the rest of us out. Meetings with shady characters, interviews with young girls, 'appointments' with Serena. They all took place behind that bolted door. There was a sofa at the back of the room that I'd not have sat on if you'd paid me.

'Get out of here, Lena,' she said, her words coming out in a snap.

'You do know that Tommy's dead, don't you?' Hadn't she seen? Hadn't she realised?

'I know. I just need to grab something before the coppers get here.' Her attention was firmly on the dial but her first two attempts failed, and she hit the metal with the side of her fist. She took a deep breath and turned to me. 'What d'you reckon? Our wedding anniversary, for old time's sake? Tommy's birthday?'

I sat on the edge of the desk. 'Five. Two. Ten.' Maggie's date of birth.

She spun the dial and smiled wryly as the door clicked open. 'Never knew he still cared. Or couldn't be arsed to change it.' She rummaged and found what she was looking for, sighing as she moved from a crouching position to take a seat in Tommy's big leather chair, the most expensive piece of furniture in the club. She threw a large brown paper bag on the desk.

'Tommy's dead,' I repeated, hearing a note of hysteria in my voice. 'You need to get out of here. Vic's already called the police and—'

'Lena, shut up. I need you to help me and we've not got much time.' She tipped the contents of the paper bag on to the desk, a thick wad of banknotes falling out. 'Reckon there's five grand there, easy. Off the books. No one'll miss it, but if the police find it they might start looking into where it came from.'

'Where did it come from?' I asked.

Maggie didn't speak, but looked up at the ceiling and nodded her head. The rooms upstairs. What would happen to those girls now? But that wasn't my immediate concern.

'What are you going to do with it?'

'If you help me, it's yours. I can't let them shut this place down, it'll take weeks, months to sort out. Give us a hand to get it out of here without them seeing and we'll split it.'

I stared at her, both of us falling silent as we heard voices out in the corridor. The band. 'Lena? Are you out here?'

'It's Jean,' I whispered.

'Get rid of him!'

I slid back the bolt and poked my head out. Jean and Harold were talking quietly by the curtain. 'Have the police arrived?'

Jean turned. 'Not yet. What are you doing? Fred wants everyone to be together.'

'Tell him I'm with Maggie. She – she's not in a good way. She saw what happened with Tommy and...' I sighed and let him leap to assumptions about Maggie's state of mind. 'I'll stay here with her. It's better anyway. Away from you-know-who. Best keep the two of them apart for now.' I knew that Jean was no admirer of Serena, not since she'd compared him and his band to the chimps tea party she'd seen at London Zoo. 'Come and knock when the police get here, is that all right?'

He nodded and disappeared back into the club. I closed the office door and bolted it shut once more. Maggie was smoking, rifling through Tommy's drawers in case there was something she'd missed.

'The police'll be here any minute,' I warned. 'Be careful!'

She closed the last drawer and leaned back in the chair. 'Remember when Alfie caught us pickpocketing?'

'Why are you bringing that up?' I asked. It wasn't the day to be thinking about the times I'd disappointed Alfie.

'We were good at it, remember?' She paused momentarily, then piled the money back into the envelope. 'As long as we stuck together, we were all right.' She shoved the envelope towards me. 'Hide it in that dirty old bag of yours and we'll talk later. About everything.'

I clutched the envelope to my chest and watched as she lit another cigarette from the dying embers of the last. The money would incriminate me if the police found it, but how could I not take it? For one, it was more money than I'd seen in my entire life. But also, I suspected that Maggie knew more about Tommy's death than she was letting on. It's not an easy question to ask a friend, whether they killed their own husband. I reasoned that five thousand pounds would just about buy me the right to ask it.

18

Saturday, 5 September
Queen Mary

It had been someone's job to think of everything a passenger might need for a week trapped at sea and they had left nothing to chance. That included a shop with a small selection of swimming costumes, upstairs in the parade.

'All of our costumes use Lastex for a more flattering fit,' the shop assistant informed me, pushing me gently aside so that she could pull out a specimen for me to examine more closely. 'The green and white is our bestseller, but we have sold quite a few already this week.' She shared a conspiratorial smile. 'You don't look the sort of woman to wear the same as everyone else.'

'I just need something to swim in that doesn't make me look like an old maid,' I said, suspicious that she was about to foist her most expensive model on me.

'Of course. Though this red costume would suit your colouring. It's the latest style.'

The costume she held up looked impossibly brief, with less material in it than in some of my actual underwear. The bottom looked like a large pair of knickers, only tighter fitting, cut high in the leg; the back was a criss-cross of thin strands that looked as though they wouldn't offer much support.

She saw me eyeing the straps suspiciously. 'A little more revealing than the crab back, but the idea is that if one is taking the sun, one can loosen the straps to gain a more even tan. Perhaps not what you're needing on this occasion, but this suit will last a good few seasons and this style is incredibly popular amongst our American customers.'

'Fine, I'll take it.' I tried not to wince as I saw the price tag.

'You'll want a cap as well.' She reached up and snagged an ugly-looking piece of rubber complete with strap. At least I already had my appointment booked at the hair salon. I sighed and let her ring up the items.

The swimming pool was a few steps along from the dining room, the sign on the door proclaiming that for the next hour bathing was strictly female only. A chemical odour lingered outside the entrance, strengthening as I pushed through double doors and found myself on a wide balcony above the pool itself. I could hear the quiet chatter of two women gossiping as they walked up the stairs towards me, their wet costumes wrapped in towels; the rhythmic splashes of an older lady swimming lengths beneath me, her legs frog-like as she moved smoothly through the water. I saw Carrie walking along the side of the pool, her bathing costume and cap a dark navy. Her body still held the awkwardness of childhood, all elbows and knees and very little in the way of curve, but she walked with an air of confidence.

I headed down the stairs. The attendant handed me a towel and took me along a corridor lined with dressing boxes, finding me an empty one before showing me where to find the show-ers. Undressing was the easy part. I struggled into the bath-ing suit, the clammy material clinging to my skin like a slug against a wall. It was the work of a contortionist. I emerged from the box like a shy butterfly, waiting for someone to point and shout, shocked by my proximity to nakedness. I hugged my arms across my chest to hide the purple bruises below the shoulders on both my arms, hoping Carrie wouldn't see.

She was powering through the water now, her arms propel-ling her rapidly along the length of the pool, her body tumbling over as she reached the end, her legs pushing to send her back the way she'd come. She stopped when she reached the shallow end and waved. 'Come in, Lena. There's a ladder here if you don't want to jump.'

I walked to the end of the pool cautiously, the tiles cold and slippery under my bare feet. I was awkward in my descent, yelping as my toes touched the chill water.

'Jump!' Carrie urged. 'You're only making it worse for yourself.'

I ignored her advice, prolonging my suffering by inch-ing myself in gradually, rung by rung, muttering swear words in my head. 'I thought this was supposed to be enjoy-able,' I grumbled, Carrie laughing as she floated towards me. As if my presence had offended them, several of the women departed from the pool.

Carrie caught the frown on my face. 'Oh, they'll have salon appointments to keep before they dare show their faces in the dining room. That's why I love coming here at this time of day. So quiet.'

My own appointment was in two hours' time, I reminded myself. I couldn't miss it or I'd look like a wreck at dinner. As I held onto the side of the pool and let my legs drift upwards, I could see that it would be easy to clear the mind, to forget where you were, to forget everything that had happened so recently. I felt soothed by the cool waters and wondered what Carrie was escaping from.

'Nobody bothers me here,' she said, as though she'd heard my thoughts. 'You've met my family. I love them dearly but they can get a bit much.'

'You and your mother seem close,' I said.

'We get along all right, I guess. She's very happy that I'm spending time with you. She thinks you could be a good influence on me.'

'Really?' It seemed rather unlikely. Eliza barely knew me, and the one thing she did know was that I was a singer and an actress. Hardly a role model for a girl, like Carrie, from a wealthy family.

'She said that I lack confidence and poise.'

'You're still young,' I reminded her. 'Confidence often comes with wisdom, though I'm not sure I have much of either.'

'You're far wiser than most people I know, believe me. I just wish...' She leaned her head back and closed her eyes. 'Confidence can be quiet, you know. It isn't always about being the loudest person in the conversation, though in my family that's the only way to be heard. You've met my brother.' She sighed. 'For years Mama said he'd grow up eventually, but now she's stopped saying anything about him at all. I think she's scared of the truth, that he's going to end up the same as Daddy. A mean lush who can't keep his hands where they belong.'

I didn't know what to say; she'd taken my breath away. I shivered at the memory of Jack's hands on my arms and realised once more how lucky I'd been.

'Daddy's always had affairs but at least he used to have the sense to sneak around. I mean – Daisy!' She caught my surprised glance. 'I saw your face last night when they were carrying on at the table. God, it's public knowledge, Lena, he's hardly discreet. I have a half-brother who works at Parker Godwin. No one's supposed to know about him, but people talk. A kid with no decent education and suddenly he's getting put in charge of a whole department! Frankie found out and there was a big bust-up over it last Christmas. Of course, Daddy had to promise Frankie that he'd put him in charge of a more important division when the time came. And Mama sat there drinking her gin and pretending everything was normal.'

'Your poor mother,' I murmured, and tried not to think about Tabitha Harrington and her disloyal husband. Maybe I deserved what I'd got. But no, that wasn't right. I'd met enough foul men to know that bad things happened to good people with dismaying frequency. Those who deserved it were usually devious enough to know how to avoid getting themselves into trouble. I kept forgetting that I had moved myself out of the category of the good. Perhaps I should learn to become more unscrupulous and walk the path I had chosen with more conviction.

'I don't think Mama knew Daddy at all when she married him,' Carrie confided. 'When she tells the story of how they met, she tries to make it sound romantic: Grandpa bringing his protégé to dinner in the hope that he might fall in love with his daughter. Really, I don't think either of them had much say in it.'

'She could have said no,' I pointed out, trying to remember exactly what Daisy had told me about Jack and Eliza. Something similar, but she had hinted about the arrangement suiting Eliza at the time. Averting some sort of a scandal? I cursed the drink for punching holes in my memory.

Carrie laughed drily. 'Lena, you never met my grandpa. My real grandpa I mean, not what was left of him by the time we boarded this ship. Believe me, he wasn't the same man as he was before he fell ill. If he wanted something to happen, it would happen. If Mama hadn't married Daddy, she'd have been cut off. And they don't train women in anything practical at school. She'd have had no job and nowhere to live. She'd've had to marry the first man who came along anyway and then learn to live without Grandpa's money. And my mother spends money like it's going out of fashion. She couldn't survive more than a few months without it.'

'Money gives people choices.' I remembered Alfie saying that often, usually accompanied by a sigh. Usually when a job had fallen through for one reason or another and he was trying to work out how to keep the roof over our heads. We had no money and so Alfie had no choice but to take what he could, even when it barely paid anything at all. Though from what Carrie was saying, the choices might be more evident when money was involved, but no easier to make.

'Everyone hated Grandpa,' Carrie told me. 'Except for me and maybe Frankie. He didn't care what anyone thought of him, which is just as well, and he was stuck in the last century. Once he told me he wished I'd been born a boy, that I was smarter than the rest of them put together and what a shame it was that a woman could never run Parker Godwin, or even have a seat on the board. But I'm as much a Parker as Frankie is, and what's more I'm far cleverer than he is. Everyone knows.' She shook her head in disbelief. 'He treated Daddy like his own son, forgave him anything, but Mama couldn't do anything right.'

'I thought you wanted to become a photographer,' I said. 'You could still do that, couldn't you?'

'Oh, I will, and I'm good at it. Even Grandpa said my compositions were good. But that doesn't mean it'll be easy. If Daddy won't support me then I don't see how I can carry on with it seriously. A hobby is one thing, but I need someone to teach me, to show me how to get better. When I'm old enough, I want to travel across Europe with my camera and meet people and capture life itself!' Her eyes shone with ambition. 'I know what you're thinking: that I should strike out on my own and damn the rest of them. Maybe I'm a coward for not trying, but I don't know the first thing about getting a job. And why should I when my family could support me if they wanted to? I don't expect luxury, but I want to have enough money to live off.' She leaned back in the water, letting her head submerge partly as her legs floated up. 'Mama's my only hope now.'

'You think that she'll be more supportive now that your grandfather isn't there to disagree with her?' I copied her manoeuvre, enjoying the weightlessness as the water supported my body.

'I hope so.' Carrie sounded unconvinced. 'And I assume she'll inherit most of Grandpa's money, though I know that Mama and Daddy are worried about Daisy. I heard them talking last night through the cabin wall. Daddy said he would not be surprised if she'd got Grandpa to write her into the will. Nobody knows what's actually in it. It's with the lawyers back home. That was all I could make out. Daddy had been shouting because Mama had poured away a bottle of whisky he'd had stashed in the cabin. They were yelling at one another. She said, "You'll live to wish you'd never married into this family." It all went quiet after that.'

When I glanced over, tears were streaming down her face. It felt natural for me to put my arms around her, hugging her close as she sobbed.

'I'm so sorry,' she stammered, trying to regain control. 'It's just... Grandpa. I didn't think I would be this upset. He'd been ill for so long I think we were all resigned to it happening sooner rather than later, but...'

'Grief is an odd thing. When my father died, it was months before I cried, and I felt so guilty for ages, as if he deserved more. As if I should have taken to my bed for half a year in mourning to be a dutiful daughter.'

Saying it out loud for the first time was like a weight off my chest. The strangest thing about death is that no one wants to talk about it and so, when it happens, how are you supposed to know what to do? How often to visit the grave? How long to sit at home being miserable before it's acceptable to have a night out, to meet your best friend for lunch, to sit in a dark picture house and watch Fred Astaire and Ginger Rogers dance through a screen of tears?

Carrie wiped her nose with the back of her hand and smiled weakly. 'Thank you, Lena. You don't know how much better I feel, talking to you. It's so strange but you seem to understand me better than anyone in my own family!'

'I wouldn't say that,' I told her. 'But maybe I understand how you're feeling at the moment. And remember, this has all been a huge shock to everyone. A person might not look sad; it doesn't mean they aren't. Like I said, I worried that I wasn't doing anything properly, that my father would have wanted a different suit to be buried in, or different flowers at the grave. Silly things like that! I mean, he only had the one suit, what else would we put him in?'

Carrie laughed. 'Your father would have known how much you loved him. My daddy doesn't seem to care what I do or think. He only cares that I do as I'm told and marry well.'

'That doesn't mean he doesn't love you. Your grandfather loved you too,' I reminded her. 'And if he knew what your education meant to you, then it's possible he made provisions for it. If not, I wouldn't give up hope of your mother helping you out.'

We fell silent as the last woman swam past us to the ladder, climbing out with far more grace than I'd managed getting in. I closed my eyes and drifted in the water, picturing the scene that Carrie had overheard. An argument with Eliza, keeping a distance from his mistress for fear she might have pulled the wool over his eyes and stolen his inheritance? Was that what had influenced Jack to end up at my door the night before?

I stood up, anger surfacing. I had been nothing but a means to an end, a way of asserting his power when he had been bested by both Eliza and Daisy. He'd thought me a soft touch, in other words.

'Did you want to swim?' Carrie asked.

'No, I… I've suddenly remembered something I need to do before luncheon. I'll see you there?'

She nodded, her brow furrowed as she watched me clamber up the ladder. The frigid air brought me out in goosebumps to go along with my wrinkled fingers, and I could hear the splash of water as Carrie resumed her lengths, a regular mermaid. I hurried to the showers and sighed as the warm water beat off the chill. My hair was already wet, so I threw caution to the wind and leaned under the showerhead, the sounds from the pool fading out as my ears filled up with water. I felt my muscles relax, the tension and fury ebbing away. After a few glorious minutes I wrapped myself in a towel and made my way back towards the dressing boxes. I tipped my head to one side as I walked, emptying out water, the sounds of the pool flooding in suddenly, along with a sharp intake of breath close behind me. Before I could react, a weight struck my head with force, the world turning black in an instant.

19

Saturday, 5 September
Queen Mary

I moved my head slightly and was stunned by shock as much as the pain. The initial stab dulled to a rhythmic pounding inside my skull and my whole body felt rigid, cold from the hard surface beneath me.

'Keep still for a moment, Lena.'

I hadn't even realised I'd been trying to lift my head. And that voice… It took me a few seconds to place it: Dr Wilding, though his tone was gentler than I was used to.

'What happened?' It took effort to speak.

'You don't remember?' Carrie was there. 'Who did this to you?'

'She was struck from behind, Carrie, and I can't see a pair of eyes in the back of her head.' I didn't need to open my eyes to see Dr Wilding's derisory expression. I almost smiled.

'Where am I?' I put out a hand and felt tiled floor. I was lying on my side, a towel placed under my head as a makeshift pillow. I opened my eyes, blinking against the shock of the bright light overhead. 'Oh!' I realised that I was still wearing nothing but the scanty red bathing costume, my damp towel hardly covering me. Wilding didn't look particularly perturbed, but I supposed that as a doctor he'd seen all sorts.

'At the swimming pool,' Carrie reminded me. 'Don't you remember? You said you had something to do, and I stayed in the pool to swim a few more lengths before I realised the time. I found you lying here and ran to get help.'

'Something hit me. Some*one*.' I closed my eyes, my vision spotted, like a pincushion being stabbed by multiple tiny needles. 'I heard them behind me, but I wasn't able to turn around in time.'

'Didn't you see anything?' Wilding asked Carrie.

'I was in the pool. My head was under the water and I didn't hear a thing.' She was apologetic.

That was why I hadn't heard my attacker in time, I remembered. Ears full of water from the shower.

'I'm assuming this is what was used.' I looked up to see Wilding holding a metal pole aloft.

'What on earth is that?' I managed to shuffle into a half-seated position.

'Some sort of pool-cleaning contraption. This is definitely the weapon. I think this is a trace of blood, and look – brunette hair that looks exactly like yours.' He held out the pole to us for inspection but I turned away, not keen on seeing my own blood smeared across the metal. 'This was no accident. You saw nothing, Carrie? Not even anyone walking past the swimming pool?'

'I don't think so.' She bit her lip. 'A shadow, maybe? I thought I saw someone dressed in black, but I was doing backstroke at the time and when I reached the end of the pool there was no one there, so I must have imagined it. A reflection off the water.'

'Probably not though, all things considered.' Wilding propped the pole back in its proper place. 'Someone was incredibly lucky to sneak past both you and the pool attendant without being seen.'

'She went to the bathroom,' Carrie explained to me. 'I told her you'd slipped. I hope you don't mind, only I didn't think you'd want a circus down here. Not with everything else that's going on. But you know, if you want to, I'm sure you could still report the attack. I wanted to check with you first, that's all.'

'It's fine,' I reassured her. I absolutely didn't want to face the chief officer again if it could be helped. 'You did the right thing. I'm sure this was an accident. The pole could have fallen somehow...'

'No.' Wilding was clear. 'Poles don't walk around on their own or fly through the air of their own accord. This black shadow of Carrie's must be the person we're looking for. That's the only logical explanation.' I could see from his frown that he was wondering the same as me: was this attack connected to Francis Parker's murder?

'Oh.' Carrie looked devastated. 'Lena, I'm so sorry. If I'd had any idea then I would have paid more attention. But who on earth could have wanted to hurt you?'

'Whoever it was, it's hardly your fault,' I assured her. 'I can't even guess who it might have been.' Which was the truth, though I was beginning to realise that I might have to think harder. Something was going on, and I was involved, but for the life of me I had no idea how.

'We need to get you up off that cold floor.' Wilding retrieved a pipe from his jacket pocket and produced a box of matches. 'You'll be quite all right, Lena, but you may have a mild concussion. You'll need to take it easy.'

I prodded the back of my head lightly. There was a tender area but only a tiny amount of red smeared my fingers when I checked them. 'I don't think it's too bad. Do you have any aspirin I can take, Doctor?'

'I'll bring some pills to your cabin. Carrie, can you give her a hand? Take your time and I'll meet you up there.' He was like a new man, a doctor with purpose once more. I think he even smiled as he left, though it was so fleeting it could have been a twitch.

Gingerly I climbed to my feet and let Carrie support my weight. The change in altitude made my head feel as though it was about to explode, but I managed to take the few steps to the cubicle, dressing while sitting down on the narrow wooden seat. Carrie took my arm as we made slow progress to the exit, the pool attendant watching us guiltily. I wondered why she'd left her post at that exact moment. Surely it wasn't safe to leave the swimming pool unattended when a passenger, Carrie in this case, was swimming alone? Unless someone else had caused her to leave.

Daisy. She flapped about the ship in her voluminous black dresses like an un-jilted Miss Havisham. There was Carrie's black shadow. And she had cause, or so she thought, to be angry with me. My head hurt too much to think with any clarity and by the time we reached my cabin I felt nauseous again, my balance unsteady. Carrie helped me onto the settee and fetched a blanket from a cupboard I hadn't even noticed before, draping it over my body and tucking it in.

'I don't suppose you're hungry?' she asked. 'It's after midday.'

I grimaced. 'I don't think I could stomach anything. And I definitely can't walk back down to the dining room.'

'The steward can bring you anything you want. I'll ask for water for now.' Carrie called from the telephone and then disappeared into the bathroom, returning with a damp flannel to press against my forehead.

'I'm sure Dr Wilding won't be long. In fact, that's probably him now.' She answered the knock at the door. 'Speak of the devil!'

'Thank you, Miss Abernathy, I thought I could feel my ears burning.' The doctor had really pepped up. He moved quicker than usual and his smile was unmistakably warm. He was a brand-new man.

'I was only saying that you wouldn't be long.' Carrie's face flushed and she almost ran to get the door as another knock came.

'Is everything all right, ma'am?' Danny's eyes were wide as he took in the scene, the doctor rifling through his bag for the promised pills.

'Lena had a little accident at the swimming pool,' Carrie said quickly. 'You can leave the tray there.'

'Thank you, Danny,' I added as he left.

Perhaps when one had servants running around at one's beck and call, manners were not considered a requirement. I caught myself frowning and tried to smooth my forehead. It must have been the headache making me grumpy.

'You know,' Wilding said thoughtfully, 'perhaps it's for the best if we stick to the story that this was a fall. For now, at least. I don't want to worry your mother, Carrie, you know how sensitive she is.'

Carrie shifted her weight and looked uneasy but she finally nodded in agreeance. 'I hate to lie to her but you're right, she would panic that we weren't safe. Is that all right with you, Lena?'

'Fine with me.' It would save a lot of questions. I tried not to consider the possibility that maybe we weren't safe. Or I wasn't.

'Miss Abernathy, shouldn't you go down to luncheon? Your mother will worry about where you are.' Wilding dismissed her with little effort.

'See you later, Lena?' she asked in a small voice.

'I'll come down for dinner,' I promised. 'Carrie, this isn't your fault. Stop fretting!'

She managed a smile and left us, Dr Wilding finally finding the bottle he'd been searching for.

'These are nothing special but they should shift your head-ache,' he told me, shaking two tablets into my open palm. He poured me a glass of water and I swallowed them down, watching as he swallowed a couple of the pills dry. 'I have a bit of a bad head myself. Must be all the excitement over the past day or so.'

'You don't have any more of that stuff you gave me the other night, do you?' I held the cold glass against my head, the flannel having already lost its chill. 'I didn't sleep well at all last night and I'd be surprised if that isn't why I feel especially grotty now.' He didn't need to know the real reason.

Wilding shook his head. 'You need to stay awake. That blow

was hard enough to break the skin and you might have a mild concussion.' He moved to the armchair and I closed my eyes, wishing he'd go away and leave me alone. 'Stay awake, I said! It'd be a fine thing after everything else that's gone on if you were to choke on your own vomit and die.'

My face twisted in disgust at the thought. 'So are you going to sit there all afternoon and watch me?'

'No, you're a fully grown adult, after all. I'll just wait until the pills begin to take effect and then I'll head down to the dining room myself.' He settled himself in and brought out his pipe once more.

'I suppose you have nothing better to do these days now that you're out of a job.' It was a horrible thing to say but the words came out of their own accord. 'Sorry, that was uncalled for.'

'I shall put your mean spirits down to your injury, Miss Aldridge.' He put the unlit pipe in his mouth and bit down, smiling. 'And you are both right and wrong. Mrs Abernathy asked me to stay on as her own personal physician, but I declined. I'll be looking for new employment once we reach dry land. I'm not sure what I'll do next, to be honest, but I know that I don't want to be beholden to one patient any longer.' He chewed the inside of his cheek and I wondered if there was something more to his split from the family. 'Mr Parker was very generous financially though, and I can't say it was difficult work.'

'Did you begin working for him after he fell ill?' I prompted. Perhaps the doctor had some motive I hadn't yet considered.

'Oh no, it's been six years all in.' Wilding scratched his chin, his manicured nails rasping against his beard. 'I inherited him when my partner retired. I used to have a whole practice back then and he was one patient among many, but it was made worth my while to commit to him exclusively. Not that I don't sometimes regret that decision. He wasn't the easiest man to deal with, though strangely he became less demanding the more ill he became.'

'The money must have made it worthwhile.' But as I looked at Wilding I could see that wasn't it.

'I had to leave my own daughter's wedding two years ago because he had what turned out to be a bout of indigestion. I haven't spent a night in the same apartment as my wife for months. But sometimes these situations have to be suffered through.' He sighed deeply and fiddled with his pipe, tamping down the tobacco. 'I had nothing left. The stock market crashed. I know we weren't the only ones, but when you lose all your savings… Well, I borrowed and I gambled and I borrowed again. And then finally the bank called and – and somehow Francis Parker knew all of this. He knew everything about me, in fact. I'd have lost everything if it weren't for him. He gave me a way out.'

It was like popping a champagne cork, his confession spilling out of him unchecked. I didn't know why Wilding was telling me any of this, but it was fascinating. The caustic façade had been stripped away from this shabby yet respectable physician in his ancient tweed. He was a freed man, coming to terms with the severing of his golden tether.

'You aren't devastated by his death, though.'

'I don't think he deserved to die like that,' Wilding told me sternly. 'Poison? It was quick enough, thank God, but he still suffered. With all his afflictions he didn't have long left, I'm sure of it. I was more than happy to wait. And if I'd really wanted to be free of him, I'd have done it before we left New York at the start of the summer. No offence, but I'm really not in love with England. I'd have taken my wife away to the Catskills instead. She goes every year with our daughter and her husband, without me. Can you imagine? Everyone thinks she's a widow it's been so long since they last saw me there!'

'Next year you'll be there with her.' I earned a smile from him. 'You must know the family better than anyone else. Who do you think killed him?'

He took his time thinking, lighting his pipe in the meantime. I poured another glass of water, patient to wait. Wilding was my only ally in this. The family would stick together and, if I was right, Daisy had marked herself out as an enemy. If anyone were to discover that I'd been present at not one but two murder scenes in the past week I would become the obvious suspect, motive or not. Unless, of course, I was meant to be the next victim. Cyanide to a random metal pole was a leap, but it could have been an opportunistic attack. Tommy's murder had made the newspapers. Could this whole thing really be a huge coincidence, or had some disgruntled family member or employee read about Tommy Scarsdale in the paper and decided to try the method out for themselves? Stranger things had happened, but that didn't explain the attack on me. Could Daisy really be behind it all, perhaps having had the time to coolly plan the murder of her employer, before heated passion had led her to attack me more recklessly? I didn't know her well enough – I didn't know *any* of these people well enough – to draw any rational conclusions. All I could do was try to be more careful, keep my back to the wall quite literally, until we reached New York.

'I've removed money from the equation,' Wilding said finally. 'Eliza lives off a trust fund, so she's happy to wait for her inheritance, and Jack has a good salary from Parker Godwin.'

'But Mr Parker could have given him the sack at any time, I assume. If, say, Jack did something to bring the family into disrepute.' Like sleeping with his father-in-law's secretary. 'Wouldn't that give him a reason to want Mr Parker dead?'

Wilding barked a laugh. 'You're thinking of Daisy? Forget it. Jack's had his wicked way with any number of unsuitable women over the years. He's married to the golden goose, but Eliza doesn't seem to care what he gets up to so long as he leaves her alone. Their marriage is a condition of the trust fund, so she won't leave him. Jack Abernathy's living many a man's dream.'

And I knew to my own cost that Jack wasn't exactly head over heels in love with Daisy or looking to forsake all others on her account. I tried to hide my shudder as memories from the night before leapt back into the present. I decided to risk mentioning what Carrie had told me earlier. 'But what about his son. Not Frankie, the other one.'

'How on earth did you find out about – ah, well. The world's worst secret. And again, Francis Parker knew all about it and didn't give a damn.' He puffed away, trying to draw inspiration from the bowl of his pipe.

I was running out of ideas. 'Eliza? I know she has money, but maybe she… snapped. Tired of living with her father's rules. Or maybe she'd had enough of Jack's philandering.'

'I suppose. And that might make sense if it were Jack who was dead. But again, why now? Why kill a dying man, Lena? That is the question I cannot fathom the answer to.' He scratched his beard once more and sighed. 'If this had all happened a year or so ago, I'd say that any of them could have done it. I've never known a man so unlikeable. To wait until he'd already lost his power, I simply can't see what the killer stood to gain.'

'Did he know that they all hated him?' It seemed curious to me that by all accounts the man had found power from controlling his own flesh and blood.

'I don't think he looked at it that way,' Wilding said, chewing on his pipe. 'He was a traditionalist. Hated anything modern. Clung to old ideas and prejudices. I was always surprised that he hired me, as a Jew, but then I also think that was why he chose me. He liked being able to order me about, tell me what to do. He liked to feel superior without having to prove it, that purely by dint of the families we were born into, he was better than I was.'

'And you put up with that?'

'He liked to shout and slam things about, that's all. And I think he knew he'd never find another doctor who was as desperate as I have been these last years.' He barked a laugh. 'You know, at least my family love me. I might have had to neglect them more than I'd like, but they miss me when I'm gone. The people who hate me because I happen to belong to a particular community, they don't bother me. It's nothing more than prejudice, based on superstition and stupidity. Better that than be hated as an individual, because of your own hateful actions. Francis Parker was a man with no moral compass who somehow thought that he was the one in the right. I do wonder if, in those last few moments before he died, he realised how wrong he'd been.'

I remembered the panic-stricken look upon the elderly man's face as his mortality rushed up to greet him. 'What a cruel thought.'

'Indeed.' Wilding moved to the edge of his seat. 'Well, you seem to have perked up a bit. How's the head?'

'Much better, actually.' I tilted it gently from side to side. 'Those pills have worked a miracle.'

'Excellent.' He smoothed down his trousers as he stood. 'Now, no alcohol. Rest up here and drink plenty of water. I'll see you at dinner, Miss Aldridge. And make sure you lock this door behind me. Better to be safe than sorry.'

I did as I was told, sliding on the door chain for good measure. The incident with Jack had been bad but the attack at the pool was something else altogether. How hard did you have to hit someone to actually kill them as opposed to knock them out? I certainly didn't know and I wasn't sure my attacker had either.

20

Saturday, 5 September
Queen Mary

I dozed for a couple of hours after Wilding had left, woken by a loud, shrill noise that shocked me into consciousness. For a moment, I was back in my Bethnal Green childhood, hearing the competing church bells on a Sunday, before I remembered that I was far away from the East End.

I staggered to the telephone, slumping down onto the bed as I mumbled a greeting. 'Lena, I didn't wake you, did I?' Eliza's voice was full of concern.

'No, not at all,' I lied.

'I wanted to see how you were, my dear. Carrie told me about the accident. Your poor head! I'm appalled, honestly. I understand that it's a swimming pool, the floors are bound to be wet, but surely people shouldn't be able to slip and knock themselves out. I shall be mentioning this to the captain when I next see him.'

'Oh no, Eliza,' I said quickly, 'there's no need, really. It was entirely my own fault. I wasn't taking care. Please don't say anything. I feel rather foolish, truth be told.'

'If you're sure.' I heard her sigh. 'Have you eaten? You must be starving. Shall I come and join you? I hate to think of you cooped up alone all afternoon.' I agreed that some companionship might be nice. 'Excellent,' she said, 'and how about a spot of afternoon tea? I'll be right along.'

She put the telephone down before I could think to react. Did I trust Eliza? Wilding didn't think she was a murderer but someone was. On the other hand, would she be so brazen about sashaying along to my cabin to murder me? Unlikely. I almost laughed at the idea. After my nap I found that my appetite had returned and the thought of the thin white bread sandwiches I'd seen them serve in the long gallery made my stomach rumble. I placed a call through to Danny.

'My dear, you're ever so pale! Go and lie down immediately,' Eliza told me as I let her in five minutes later. She held the back of her hand to my forehead and I had to brace myself not to back away, surprised at the sudden contact. 'No fever at least.'

'It was only a bang on the head,' I assured her. 'And I feel quite all right. Dr Wilding gave me something that got rid of the headache in a trice.'

'I bet he did. Now come along, sit down, Lena.' She fussed until I was lying back on the settee, tucking the blanket back around me, just as her daughter had done earlier.

'You make a wonderful nurse,' I joked, and she smiled, turning as there was a knock on the door. 'Oh, I ordered tea for us, like you said.'

'Let me fetch it.' She pressed a kind hand on my shoulder.

'Thank you.' Not that I could have got up very easily, the blanket firmly wrapped around my legs. She stared at me hard for a moment, as if expecting a different reaction, then went to answer the door.

Danny winked at me as he wheeled in a trolley, laying out the teapot and its accompanying china, along with a tiered stand of sandwiches and cakes. 'Tea's been brewing so you should be all right to pour unless you like it very strong. Glad to see you're being taken care of, ma'am,' he said.

'She certainly is,' Eliza informed him, taking a seat and offering me a cigarette from her case. 'Now, would you mind bringing us a couple of brandies as well, young man? I find that it really does work wonders after a shock, and it's rude to let a person drink alone.'

'Manners maketh man,' Danny agreed, wheeling the trolley away. 'I'll be back in a jiffy.'

Eliza poured the tea and placed two smoked salmon sandwiches on a plate for me, pushing the coffee table closer so that I didn't have to strain myself reaching.

'You must do this for Carrie and Frankie when they're ill,' I said.

'Oh, they hate me fussing around them. They'd rather have a maid bring them sustenance than speak to me.' She crossed her legs and played with the teaspoon lying on her saucer, looking into her cup as deeply as a fortune teller studying tea leaves.

'More fool them. I wish I'd had a mother to take care of me when I was young.'

'You didn't have any mother at all?' She took a sip from her cup, watching me over the rim.

'No, Alfie – my father – he always said he was happiest it

just being the two of us. I'm sure he had… friends… you know, but he never brought anyone home.' I hesitated. I didn't want to introduce Alfie to a stranger like that, to have her thinking things about him without having known the man himself.

'Alfie? Alfie Aldridge.' She tried the name out, nodding slowly to herself. There was an odd look on her face. 'Whatever happened to him?'

'He died,' I told her. 'A few days after Christmas. Tuberculosis.'

Her smile was sad. 'A dreadful disease. I'm sorry for your loss.'

'Thank you.' I didn't know what else to say.

Eliza got up suddenly, wiping her face roughly with her hand. 'May I use your bathroom, Lena?'

'Of course.' I watched her, confused. Was that a tear she had shed? That didn't make any sense. Unless – had Eliza's mother died from the dreaded TB as well? I kicked myself for reminding her of such a sad memory, though how could I have known? In twenty years' time would I be like Eliza, going about my business only to be jolted back into grief by an unexpected comment? The thought was both overwhelming and a comfort, that at least Alfie would never be forgotten while I was still alive.

She returned as Danny knocked on the door, delivering two large brandies. Eliza took them from him at the door and pushed the door closed behind him.

'Drink your tea first,' she instructed.

'Dr Wilding told me to steer clear of the booze,' I said.

'Dr Wilding doesn't practise what he preaches, so I'd take his advice with a large pinch of salt.' Eliza kicked off her heels and curled her feet under her on the armchair. 'I'm so sorry, I inter-rupted you before when you were talking about your father. Tell me about Alfie. Sometimes it helps you know, remembering the person. Keeping their memory alive.'

'Alfie?' I shrugged. 'He was...' I was going to say ordinary but of course he hadn't been. Not to me. 'I miss him,' I said, and felt tears brighten in my eyes. 'He was everything to me, and everything I wanted to be. I have this wonderful oppor- tunity because of him. Instead of him. He should be here, not me.' I looked down at my cup and a tear disturbed the surface. 'He was a brilliant pianist. The only other person I've ever heard play half as well is Will Goodman.'

'Will Goodman?' Eliza looked confused and I realised she didn't know who Will was. She lit a cigarette and threw her lighter to me so that I could do the same.

'The man who's giving me my big break was friends with my father when they were both young. Alfie was from New York,' I explained. 'This should have been his big shot, not mine.'

'I know what it is to lose a father, Lena,' Eliza reminded me, her voice almost stern. 'And my mother died when I was younger than you are now. Not much older than Carrie, in fact.'

'I'm sorry, Eliza, forgive me.' I felt wrong-footed, as though I wasn't thinking quickly enough to catch up with Eliza's mood changes. It must have been the bang on the head, scrambling my thoughts.

She sighed and brushed invisible crumbs from her lap. 'No, I'm sorry. I'm being such a coward. If my father's death has taught me one thing it's that even he couldn't resist his own fate. And perhaps I have to accept mine. It was our destiny to end up together on this ship, at the same table, Lena. Did you know that? Isn't that why you're really here?'

'I don't understand.' I stared at her. 'Do you know something I don't?' My hand trembled. Did she know about Tommy's death? But her expression was gentle, almost sad. Not what I'd expect for a cold-blooded murderer. And her eyes shone as if she was close to tears.

'Oh God. You really don't know.' She put down her cup and reached for the brandy glass, lifting it up in a salute. 'Time for the stronger stuff now, Lena, I think.'

Her riddles were making me anxious. 'What's going on, Eliza?'

'I'll tell you everything, but humour me. Have a sip of brandy and then I'll explain.'

I did as I was told, the liquid setting my mouth on fire. Eliza took a gulp and leaned forward, her keen attention making me nervous as she began her tale.

'My family never missed a summer in Europe, not since before I was born. Not even the year my mother died. Pneumonia took her in the February, and a few months later my father was packing up the house as usual and booking tickets on the *Mauretania*. I didn't want to go. I was seventeen years old, an adult I thought. I wanted to stay in New York, and I went so far as to apply for a summer school at Columbia but he refused to pay the fees, though he could well afford it. "Why stay here and mope when I can get you a tutor in London?" That's what he said.' She snorted. 'Can you imagine?'

The brandy warmed my chest, but I wished she would get to the point. I kept my face as neutral as I could, trying not to let my impatience show.

'So, I went to London, against my will. Father, hoping to cheer me up, accepted an invitation to a garden party in Richmond. He hated those sorts of soirées, so this was actually a real sacrifice on his part, believe me. I got there determined to hate every second and the first hour or so was every bit as dreadful as I had hoped. Boorish young gents who asked me to dance because they'd heard American girls had lower morals than the British, or because they'd heard of my father's fortune and wanted it for themselves.' She inhaled deeply and blew out a steady stream of smoke. 'I decided to sneak away, somewhere none of them would think to look. It was back behind the kitchens that I found him, smoking a pipe.'

Alfie had always preferred a pipe. One of my last memories of him was sitting in a wheelchair outside the sanatorium, on the porch where the nurses insisted he spend much of the day, despite the frigid weather. Heavily wrapped up, each breath a hard-earned gasp, he had nevertheless managed to light his pipe, handing it to me every so often to inhale from so that it didn't go out. It was the smell he had wanted, the sense of the everyday to push away the knowledge of his own mortality. I'd hated the taste of the tobacco, but I knew what it meant to him, the time we spent together before visiting hours were over. I'd even smoked a pipe myself after the funeral, closing my eyes so that I could imagine him beside me.

'Every morning he smoked that damned pipe. First thing with a cup of tea and a dry piece of bread.' Eliza's gaze travelled back into the past, recalling an image of my father that was as familiar to me as it was to her. 'Disgusting.'

'Every morning.' I echoed her words, too stupid to put the pieces together. It had been Alfie's routine. Ablutions first, followed by breakfast. Although sometimes Mrs Harper had talked him into porridge in the winter. To put some flesh on his bones, she'd said. She hadn't minded the pipe. Reminded her of her husband, may he rest in peace.

'I hated my life, Lena, you have to understand that first, to forgive me for what I did.' She paused, as if waiting for me to put her out of her misery. But how could I? She was leading me towards a discovery that I didn't want to make. 'I'm talking about your father. I'm talking about Alfie. How we met, how...' Her voice trailed off. 'You really don't know, do you?'

If she didn't actually say it, if I didn't hear the words, then it wasn't true. Ridiculous, I know, but after the past week it seemed as if nothing I thought I'd known was true. Even before setting foot on the ship, I'd felt the ground shifting beneath my feet, my world rocked by uncertainty and confusion. Ever since I'd watched Tommy die.

But Eliza finally drummed up the courage: 'Lena, I'm your mother. And I'm sorry you had to find out this way, but I had the crazy idea that you knew already. That you must have tracked me down somehow and found a way to insinuate yourself into my family. And even if you had done, I wouldn't be angry.'

She looked at me expectantly but my ears were full with the pounding of blood, my heart pumping as I felt the panic rise yet again. I threw back the rest of the brandy and dug my nails into my palms, trying to wake myself up. It couldn't be true. Could it?

Eliza took a deep breath and smiled. 'I get it. I felt the same way when I realised. I tried to kid myself that you might not be her. What's in a surname, after all? But you're the right age. And you're so like him. I mean that favourably. Amongst men,

Alfie was one of a kind, I still think that. It's not why I left.' She held out her hands, palms upwards, beseeching me to confirm or deny that I was the baby she'd walked out on twenty-six years earlier. 'You're my Eleanor.'

The name on my birth certificate. Lena for short.

'Eleanor was my own mother's name,' Eliza told me.

I had wondered a thousand times if this moment would ever come, imagining how it would happen. If I'm honest, my dreams demanded guilt and regret on her part, and my eventual forgiveness. But Eliza showed no remorse. If anything, I felt she expected gratitude. She was unburdening herself in exchange for an absolution that I didn't feel capable of.

'Is this when you tell me that you didn't mean to desert us? That your wicked father came and kidnapped you away and forced you to marry a man you didn't love?' I'd landed a blow, I could see from her face. She'd expected a happy reunion where I threw myself at her feet and cried with joy.

'No, not exactly.' She looked away. 'Please, let me explain.' Her fingers began to pluck at the hem of her skirt. 'Alfie made me laugh that night, for the first time in months. I asked him if he taught piano lessons and he said he could if I wanted. He came to Mayfair only one time. My father found out that I'd invited a Negro into our home and told me in no uncertain terms that if I dared try a thing like that again he'd throw me out and cut me off.' She shrugged, calm now that she had found sanctuary in her version of truth. 'I was young. I'd never had to live without money, but I figured that if other people managed it, how difficult could it be?'

I bit my lip to stop myself from speaking. As if managing to be poor was an achievement! Poverty was a state thrust upon people who had no choice. I looked at her, oblivious to my growing despair. No wonder Alfie hadn't wanted to tell me about her. A spoiled child, nothing more. A woman made up of expensive clothes and jewellery with no further substance.

'Alfie wasn't thrilled when I turned up at the theatre he was playing at that night, but he let me stay and we went for a walk while he showed me a side of London I'd never seen before. He was only a year older than me after all, both of us little more than children. We were ripe for romantic foolery, thinking ourselves Romeo and Juliet when nothing could have been further from the truth. I got home in the early hours of the morning and faced my father's wrath. I lied about who I'd been with, told him I'd been reading about Charles Dickens and how he walked the streets of London at night, gathering ideas for his stories.'

'And he believed you?' A stupid question. Eliza had probably inherited her monomaniacal tendencies from her father. She hadn't even stopped to consider that *Romeo and Juliet* was a tragedy. All she cared about was being the star of this doomed romance.

'My father realised that if he let me go on these walks, I wouldn't mope around the house getting in his way. I wasn't supposed to go alone, but I paid my maid to say she'd gone with me. Really, she took the money and went off on nights out with her own young man. Alfie worked in the evenings, so we'd spend the afternoons together and then I'd go wherever he was playing before he walked me home, as close as he dared. I thought it was only a summer fling, that in the fall I'd leave and my life would go back to normal in New York. Except a week before we were due to leave, I realised that something was very wrong. That I was going to have a baby.'

'Why are you telling me all this?' I wiped my face angrily, cursing myself for showing her that I was upset.

I'd have been none the wiser, would never in a million years have guessed that I'd been sitting at the same table as the mother who'd abandoned me. Horrified, I suddenly realised that Francis Parker hadn't just been some old man, he'd been my grandfather. I'd watched my own relative die right in front of me.

Eliza finished her brandy with a wince. 'God, I really should have gotten that boy to bring us the bottle.' She put the glass down carefully on the table. 'Lena, I wanted what was best for you – I knew that Alfie was a good man. The best of men. He would look after you and I couldn't. You would have had a miserable childhood with me. I'm not a good person.' Her smile twisted. 'I'm sure you've worked that out for yourself.'

'Can you please leave?' I spoke quietly.

'But, Lena—'

'I can't,' I told her. 'I can't pretend that I'm all right with this. I don't understand how this has happened, us being in the same place like this, but it's not fate. This isn't your happy ever after.'

'That's not what I came here for,' she protested. 'Please, Lena, can't we talk things over? I'd like us to be friends at least. I mean, isn't this providential, us being brought together like this? Neither of us planned this and yet here we are. It's as if it was meant to be!'

'Or maybe it's simply a coincidence. Now please, Eliza, can you leave me alone.' She didn't move and I played my trump card. 'Or we can go and ask Carrie and Frankie to join us. I assume they know all about the baby you abandoned in London twenty-six years ago? Jack too?'

Eliza's face paled. 'No, they don't know. I haven't told them. Please, can we keep this between us for now? Just until I have the chance to break it to them gently.'

'I promise they won't hear it from me.' I pointed to the door. 'But only if you get out.'

She hurried away then, the door shutting behind her with a final click as I lay my head back down on the cushions, the tears flowing freely now that it was safe to cry.

All Through the Night

21

Friday, 28 August
Canary Club, Soho

It was still so early when I walked back through the curtain into the club, not even ten o'clock. I'd hidden the wad of money at the bottom of my carpetbag, beneath my everyday clothes and my make-up bag. There was a back door to the club and it had been tempting to slip out through it but, as Maggie pointed out, the easiest way to attract the attention of the police was to make a run for it.

'Shouldn't we at least hide the money out by the bins? In case they decide to search the place?' I'd said.

'What if someone found it? You get all sorts going on by them bins after dark. No, it'll be safer here. And if anything does happen, I'll say it was me who put it there. It's my husband's money after all, and that makes it mine now he's... well, you know.' For the first time she looked flustered. 'I'll be honest, tell 'em it's off the books and that's why I hid it.'

'If you really think it's a good idea.'

There was no time for arguments. All hell had broken loose in the club and Vic was pouring drinks as fast as he could, the poor waitresses running to and fro trying to keep up with demand.

'What on earth's going on?' I shouted across the bar to Vic. The noise was incredible, punters shouting and laughing, nobody taking a blind bit of notice of Tommy's body, still lying there covered over with a dirty sheet that someone must have grabbed from the upstairs flat.

'Clive offered them drinks on the house to stop them rioting, so everyone's necking as much booze as they can before the police arrive.' Vic shook his head. 'Absolute bastards. Look! Tommy is right there, lying on the ground, while they all get legless. I don't care if they don't know him. They got no respect.'

'Maybe they *did* know Tommy,' Maggie muttered under her breath as she lit a cigarette. 'A gin fizz please, Vic, when you get a sec.'

I turned my back to Vic so that he couldn't hear or see what I was saying. 'Maggie, you got to watch what you're saying. You being here, tonight of all nights... You'll be their number one suspect, especially if they hear some of the stuff you've been saying.'

'Number two suspect,' she corrected, looking over her shoulder at Serena Mayhew, who was being comforted by one of her dancer friends. 'Don't you worry, Lee, I wasn't anywhere near him when he died.'

Which would have been all well and good except that it looked very much to me as though whatever had killed him had been in his drink. I racked my brains, trying to remember what exactly Maggie had done when she'd grabbed the tray away from the waitress. Could she have dropped something into the glass? But then if it was in the drink, that gave Vic opportunity as well. Only, why would Vic want to harm Tommy? A few insults here and there weren't motive enough.

'What I've been thinking,' Maggie said, looking me dead in the eye, 'is that it might be all right for the right person to get away with it, as long as the wrong person doesn't go to the gallows.'

'How would that work?' I asked, not liking the way she was staring at me.

'We just muddy the waters a bit. I was over here, you were on stage, Serena had more to lose by his death, Vic needs this job. If there's no poison on the table then how will they know any one of us did it?'

'Do you know who did do it?' I held her gaze though I felt my legs tremble.

She ignored me and took a messy slurp of her gin. 'It seems pretty obvious how it was done. If you wanted to poison Tommy's drink, how would you do it?'

I thought for a moment, about what had happened right before he'd died. 'The bitters,' I said. 'He adds it himself. Poisons himself.' The bottle was still sitting there on the table. I wondered if the murderer's fingerprints would be on the glass along with Tommy's own. If they would turn out to be Maggie's.

'So if we get that bottle, swap it for another one, when they test it it'll come back clean and the police will be none the wiser.' Maggie had never sounded so calm and decisive in her life. Had she sat down and planned this carefully, methodically?

I looked across at the table, trying to take deep breaths and calm my racing heart. The heat in the club was almost unbearable but nobody else seemed to notice. From where we stood it'd be impossible to make the swap unnoticed. So many people sat between us and Tommy's table, and they'd be sure to notice if one of us pushed through and took the bottle. Besides, there must be several sets of fingerprints on the bottle. Vic's, Tommy's, any one of the waitresses could have touched it. 'What if they think Vic did it? He poured the drink, which is still sitting there on the table. He'll be the only person left who could have done it.'

'Or they might decide it was a heart attack.' Maggie sighed heavily, as though I were making it difficult on purpose. 'Vic's got no reason to kill Tommy. And if anything does happen, I'll sort it. I promise.'

'So we're going to stroll over there and grab the bottle? Right in front of a whole crowd of people?' I leaned my back against the bar and looked across the club again. Every table was full. One of us – I was guessing me since Serena would likely claw Maggie's eyes out if she had the chance – would have to weave her way past at least three tables to reach Tommy's. There was no way it could be done without attracting attention, given that Serena would surely have something to say when I got there.

'Come on, Lee, it'll be like the old days. You were a master pickpocket! The Artful Dodger as a girl! Just go behind the bar and get a glass of water. Take it to Serena and make the switch while she's distracted.'

'She might be distracted, but what about everyone else?' I asked.

'Can you see anyone else looking in her direction?' Maggie had a point. Serena's sobbing was uncomfortable to watch and everyone had turned their backs to her so that they wouldn't feel bad about toasting their good fortune with the free drinks.

'Fine,' I said. 'And then what happens to the bad bottle?'

'Stick it back on the shelf, at the back, to make sure Vic doesn't accidentally murder someone else with it. Once the coast's clear, we can get rid of it.'

My palms were damp, fear sending shockwaves through my body like a mild electrical current. 'What if this goes wrong? What if I get caught?'

Maggie looked at me. 'It can't go wrong. Not unless you want one of us to hang for murder.' She plucked a bottle from her handbag and forced it into my hand. Bitters, this bottle presumably unadulterated. 'Go on. Just like the good old days. Please? You know I'd do it myself if I could.'

I should have refused, but she was my best friend. Whatever she'd done, we could sort it out later. Vic didn't even glance in my direction when I went back behind the bar, he was too intent on getting through the orders as they came in thick and fast. I spilled a good third of the water as I elbowed my way to the table where Serena sat, her head buried in the shoulder of her dancer friend, whose name popped into my head at the last moment.

'How are you, Betty?'

'Betsy,' she snapped, glaring daggers.

'Sorry. Betsy.' I smiled weakly, holding the bottle behind my back, pressed out of sight against my body. 'It's been a night, hasn't it? I can barely remember my own name.' Suddenly I recalled the glass in my other hand. 'I brought this. In case...'

I could see the poisoned bottle on the table but it was right next to Serena, only a couple of inches from her hand. There was no way I could make that switch. The Artful Dodger himself couldn't have made that switch.

'Serena, how are you?' Maggie announced her arrival loudly, as grand an entrance as any prima donna at the Royal Opera House. All eyes were on the two women, as Maggie had known they would be. A distraction, like the one she'd used earlier, flinging her fur coat from her shoulders to prevent anyone at the bar from seeing her make the first bottle-switch.

'Was this you?' Serena turned her tear-ravaged face to her rival, shoving Betsy aside as she climbed to her feet. 'Did you kill him?'

'Darling, how could I have? I'd hardly been here a minute when it happened.' Maggie had the gall to bring out her handkerchief, dabbing it to her eyes. 'I only came to tell Tommy that I forgave him. I was happy for you both.'

'Pull the other one, you old bitch!' Serena lunged and I made the switch as Maggie enveloped her replacement in a hug, her arm sweeping Tommy's half-drunk Old Fashioned to the floor in a shatter of glass.

'Serena, I forgive you.' Maggie gripped the younger woman, resisting her struggles. 'I know that you loved Tommy. And he loved you, that's why he wanted to marry you. I can't lie. I was upset at first, but I'm no fool. Things hadn't been right for a long time. I knew that but I wanted to keep the house. And a bit of money.' She smiled as Serena stared at her, speechless. 'That's why I came here tonight. To sit down with Tommy face to face and make a deal. He owed me that much.'

'You're lying.' Doubt crept into Serena's voice. 'He said you'd be fuming.'

'And I was at first. But then I realised it all made sense. I wasn't happy with him, any more than he was with me. I just didn't want to be left with nothing.'

Nobody was watching me while Maggie was centre stage. Even Vic was transfixed, though my heart still pounded as I made my way back behind the bar and shoved the deadly bottle onto the shelf, pushing it behind the Tabasco where it couldn't be seen, using my thumbnail to scratch a corner from the label so that it would be easy to find again.

'Hey! You want another drink? I'll make it.' Vic shooed me out of his domain.

I sidled back to the right side of the bar and watched the scene unfold before me. Serena was now sobbing in Maggie's arms, the two women united in supposed grief for Tommy. I wondered how Maggie really felt, standing so close to the body of the man she'd once loved. My hand tingled where it had held the bottle, as if the poison within had leached out through the glass, and I looked down at my open palm, half expecting to see it branded, marked to show my guilt. Maggie had just made me an accessory to murder.

I lit a cigarette and smoked it right down until it burned my fingertips, lighting another and then another until the police finally arrived. A hush descended as three uniformed coppers walked in, followed by two men in plain clothes. Detectives, wearing three-piece suits that looked like they'd cost a few bob. I recognised one of them, the older of the two, a man in his mid-forties. Clive met with them and a hushed conference was held at the back of the club before he led the older of the detectives to the stage.

'Ladies and gentleman, I'm Detective Inspector Hargreaves.' He tapped on the microphone until everyone stopped talking. 'Thank you for your patience, I'll try not to keep you any longer than is necessary. My constables will come round and take note of your names and addresses, then you can go. It goes without saying, but if you saw something odd tonight, anything at all, then you must mention this to my officers.'

'Is that it?' Vic said quietly.

'I suppose they can't keep everyone here forever. Besides, Tommy might have had a heart attack. A middle-aged man who doesn't look after himself...'

'You know who he is?' Vic nodded towards Hargreaves. 'You know how he affords such a nice suit? This should be interesting.'

'At the very least,' I agreed, hiding my trembling hands behind my back.

Slowly the club began to empty as the three uniformed police-men took down names and addresses. DI Hargreaves had sepa-rated Serena and Maggie and placed them at opposite sides of the club, interviewing Serena first. The ambulance had arrived ten minutes after the police, in no rush since their patient was long past resuscitation, and there was an audible sigh of relief around the room once Tommy's body was removed.

'Which of them do you think did it?' Vic slid another gin towards me, taking his own drink in hand now that his services as barman were no longer required. He was looking at Serena and Maggie.

'Who says it was either of them?' I'd been watching Maggie, who was the very picture of the grieving widow, though I wasn't sure how she expected to pull it off, bearing in mind the detec-tives already knew about Serena and would very soon discover that her husband had made plans to leave her. 'You know, a lot of people wanted Tommy out the way. He was mixed up in all sorts.'

Vic looked shifty. 'What d'you mean?'

'I mean the booze, for one. Them bottles that arrive off the back of a van in the middle of the night, right when the club's closing.'

Vic wasn't an actor and his face confirmed what I already knew; there was a reason he hated anyone coming back behind the bar. He'd worked at the Hotel Adlon in Berlin before coming to London – you couldn't tell me that a man who'd served cocktails to American presidents and some of the most famous people in the world would be happy working at the Canary unless he was being well compensated.

'Everyone does it.' He defended himself, cheeks flushed. 'You think the police will check?'

'Lucky for you, Vic, I doubt they give a shit about some contraband booze. Besides, I've seen Hargreaves with Tommy before. Do you recognise the other one?'

'I never saw their faces,' he admitted. 'I overheard an argument the other day, in the office. Something to do with the business upstairs. They wanted more money and Tommy didn't want to pay. I was carrying crates past the office so I only heard a little bit of it. They usually come in on a Friday afternoon, but Tommy always sent me out on errands when they were here.'

The cash in the safe was probably theirs then. I hoped they didn't expect to find it waiting for them. Hargreaves didn't seem in any rush to head back to the office though.

'You think Tommy was killed over the booze?' Vic looked worried.

'No,' I reassured him, 'I think he was killed for what goes

on upstairs. The young girls he keeps up there. You know. You've seen.'

'I wasn't sure.' His eyes slid away from my gaze.

He'd suspected, same as I had, and neither of us had done a thing about it. If I did get caught, I'd deserve it. I'd turned a blind eye and excused it because everyone else had done the same.

'We both knew what was going on,' I told him.

'I see them arrive, all dressed up in their high heels and their nice dresses and they're laughing. They don't look that young when they have all the make-up on,' he said, looking as ashamed as I felt.

'They're too young,' I said. 'We should have said something.'

But none of us had. Thinking back to that period in my own life, being fourteen or fifteen and feeling grown up, I would have pulled a face at anyone who had called me a child. It was only now that I could look back and cringe at how little I'd known. How the men who had bought me drinks and slid their arms around my waist and, later on, up my skirt, were attracted to me precisely because I hadn't yet learned how to reject their advances. I had still been trapped in that way of thinking, that all adults were right, that these men wanted to look after me. Watching Maggie and Serena, I wondered if any of us had ever escaped. Was that why we had found it so difficult to recognise that we were consigning these fresh young girls to the same fate?

It was easy to justify our actions. My wages from the Canary had paid for Alfie's sanatorium costs and his funeral. Vic had been desperate for a job where no one asked him why he'd left Germany and where he wouldn't bump into anyone he'd known in Berlin. Serena had been one of those girls herself; she'd just been lucky that Tommy took her under his wing as soon as he'd laid eyes on her. She'd not had to sit upstairs in the poky flat, plied with dope and knock-off gin, waiting to see who would walk in through the door expecting to spend the night with her. And as for Maggie... well, I had quite a few questions for my best friend if we made it out of the club without getting arrested.

22

I needed to get out of the cabin. I needed to clear my mind. I felt as though I'd trodden on a land mine, had heard the click and was waiting for it to explode. Eliza's revelation was life-changing, and yet all I felt was numb. I'd never believed Alfie when he'd told me he'd barely known my mother. I'd thought that he was protecting me, so I'd gone along with it, reasoning that she knew where I was if she wanted to find me. Now I realised that he'd been protecting me from the truth. Eliza was still a child, used to having everything handed to her on a silver platter.

What were the chances of our both ending up not only on the same ship but at the same dinner table? Eliza had seemed genuinely surprised and had suspected that it was I who had conspired to meet her. Whatever else I thought of her, she didn't strike me as a skilled dissembler. Surely if it were Eliza behind it all, she would have kept her identity a secret. I would never have guessed if she hadn't come clean. I wondered when exactly it had been that she realised who I was. Before today. When she heard my surname? Was it only when I started spending time

244

with Carrie that she had made the choice to step in and find out what my motives were?

Maybe they'd been in love, maybe not, but Eliza had chosen to leave me and Alfie behind. No one had forced her hand. She even admitted as much. Alfie could have told her to get stuffed and let her deal with the problem they'd made. Plenty of children were brought up in homes and institutions. A man of Francis Parker's influence could have ensured that there was no way to trace a link between his daughter and an unfortunate half-caste child. Alfie had given up so much in order to become a father, and I wished, as I had every day since his passing, that he was still alive. What would I say to him? I wasn't sure if he'd have wanted me to have anything to do with Eliza. She had given me up and agreed to a loveless marriage in order to get back in her father's good books.

My thoughts turned to Tommy, to James, all the men who had decided that their marriage vows were meaningless. Did James's wife, Tabitha, know who I was? She must guess that all his late nights couldn't be spent discussing the future of the country over Scotch and cigars at the Carlton Club. James told me she lived a simple life, that she was happiest when he wasn't there, but I'd never quite been sure whether to believe that or not.

I stepped out onto the sun deck, the light blinding bright and the breeze a mere whisper. The sea was so calm it seemed that we weren't moving at all. The clement conditions had brought a host of passengers out on deck to take the air and all the chairs had been snapped up by the post-luncheon hordes. I struggled to find a quiet spot on the railing, a place to lean as I closed my eyes to think.

I have a mother. I mouthed the words but it didn't make them feel any more real. Eliza wasn't what I'd ever imagined. And why tell me now? Was she just getting her shot in before I jumped to my own conclusion? She'd spent my entire lifetime pretending that I didn't exist. If she'd wanted to find me it wouldn't have been hard. Ask around at any of the places Alfie had worked in when she'd known him and they'd have been able to point her in the right direction, the theatres which became smaller and less salubrious as I grew older and when Alfie first began to show signs of the illness that took his life.

His last years of employment had been spent hopping around the theatres of the East End, the jobs drying up as they closed one by one, reopening as cinemas. People didn't want to pay to see second-rate plays once the talkies came in. Maggie and I had sometimes spent an entire Saturday at the pictures, watching the films and singing, and occasionally liberating the odd punter of their wallet. Such fun we'd had, never once realising that, for Alfie, finding work was growing ever more difficult. He was too good to have to play out of sight in half-full backstreet theatres. If he'd only had himself to worry about, he could have travelled the country, gone to Paris or across to Germany when jazz started to take off like crazy. As soon as I was old enough that Alfie would have risked leaving me, he fell ill, and then I was the one trapped, looking after him. It wasn't strictly fair to blame it all on Eliza, but she had that same air about her that I had hated in James, the assumption that those of us who found ourselves floundering in life only needed to pull ourselves together, forgetting that they'd been born in the lifeboat while some of us had been dropped into the fathomless depths without so much as a rope to grab hold of.

Maggie hadn't liked James. She'd only met him twice but she said that was enough. Could my attraction to James have been my mother's biological influence? She had given me up and married Jack so that she could return to her privileged lifestyle. Was there something within both of us that made us strive for power? Money? But James had never given me either of those things, would never have been able to.

Being stuck in the middle of this vast ocean, days from civilisation, I'd never felt so alone. Without Maggie, I had no one to talk to. I'd have given anything to be able to sit down and tell her everything that had happened. Have her tell me in no uncertain terms that Eliza was a bitch, amongst other choice terms. She'd calm me down and tell me to stop being stupid, to think rationally and keep my head down until I could work out what was going on. Someone at the Abernathys' dinner table was a murderer. But who? The more I puzzled over it, the worse I felt. I needed an escape, a sanctuary away from these horrific people.

There was someone I could talk to, I realised. On my walk back along the deck, chairs had become vacant as passengers began to make their way down to their cabins to change for dinner. I took the stairs to the promenade deck and the main lounge where a few tables were still enjoying tea and cake. Will was up on the stage alone, sitting at the grand Steinway piano and singing Gershwin. I glanced around but none of the Abernathy entourage were present.

I loitered by the stage, darting forward as one of the tables within Will's eyeline became vacant. He smiled as he recognised me and I felt the heavy weight on my chest lighten just a tad.

Maybe this wasn't a stupid idea. As he reached the end of his song he winked at me and made a gesture with his head that I realised meant that he wanted me on stage. I checked by pointing at myself and he nodded, his fingers finding the opening chords of 'Smoke Gets in Your Eyes' as I stumbled towards the steps. Could I get up there and sing in front of Will? I hadn't warmed up my voice. My head hurt and my throat felt tight. What if I sang out of tune? Or forgot the words? Came in on the wrong beat?

My feet hit the stage and I felt my pulse slow, the beating of my heart less frantic. No, this was going to be all right. This was home, even if I'd never stepped onto this particular stage before. Over the years I'd toyed with the idea of getting an ordinary job. Factory or shop work would have paid better. Every time a medical bill arrived I'd considered it, but Alfie had said no. Once I gave up, that would be it. Hope lost forever. I'd known he was right, much as I hated the Canary. Every evening spent at the Canary had felt like singing by numbers, but it was better than giving up.

I glanced at Will and his smile was genuine. This wasn't a test then. Maybe he could see that I needed this. I stood by the piano, my hands resting lightly on the black lacquered wood. I began to sing, my gaze fixed above the few stragglers who made up our audience, each inhalation rejuvenating me, each line I sang pushing out the hurt and betrayal of the past few hours. Gosh, this was what I'd been missing for so long. Singing and having it matter. Wanting it to be the best I'd ever sung. So simple and yet I'd lost it somehow.

Halfway through the song I looked across at Will. He was

watching me, his eyes never leaving my face until the song came to an end, and I felt my heart rate speed up again. It didn't even matter that no one in the audience was really listening. It could have been an empty room, only the two of us, and I would have felt equally exhilarated. People were getting up to leave and Will closed the piano lid carefully, standing to bow to the empty room. I followed him off the stage and out into the corridor.

'That was a bold move,' he said, talking over my head as I trotted beside him, struggling to keep up with his long-legged stride.

'You invited me up there!' I laughed.

'I wanted to see what you would do.' He looked down at me, a half-smile on his face. 'You really can sing though, I'll give you that much.'

'Thanks.' I was good at sarcasm as well. 'Look, can we talk?'

'About?'

'Last night. I realise you were only trying to warn me. Maybe we didn't exactly get off to the best start, but I'd like us to be friends.'

'Friends, huh?' He stopped walking, right in the middle of the main hall.

My face flushed, partly because I was standing a few scant inches from a man who made my skin feel like it might set aflame. I hoped it would be worth it. Not that I wanted to unburden all my troubles on Will, far from it. He would think me insane if I told him even half of what had happened to me in the past week. I just wanted to spend some time with a person who was honest, and definitely not trying to kill me.

'Lena, you'll learn pretty damn quickly once you land in New York that you gotta pick a side. People stick with their own.

And I'm not here to play along with some rich girl's fantasy, I've done that before and it gets old real quick.'

For the first time I could see myself through his eyes. He thought that I was just slumming it for a while with him, the lifestyle equivalent of a hard arm pinch, making me realise how lucky I was before I ran back to my safe cocoon of cabin class. A story to tell at dinner parties, an anecdote wheeled out to show that I knew what life was. He thought that I was an Eliza, and he was too wise to be an Alfie.

'I promise you, I'm not like that,' I told him. 'I know how it was for my father and I know I'm able to pass and that makes a difference. I'm not going to lie and say that I'll arrive in New York and shout from the rooftops that I'm coloured, but I don't intend to hide the truth either.'

Alfie had always said it: *You're lucky, Lena. No one knows what you are and you make sure you don't tell no one, not 'less it suits you.* Hiding in plain sight. Maybe he'd been wrong about that. Of course, anyone who knew me through Alfie knew exactly what I was. It was, I suspected, why the band at the Canary Club, amongst others, didn't quite trust me. If I was happy to live that big a lie, what else might I be willing to hide?

Will chewed the inside of his cheek. 'Come on then.'

Past the parade of shops, past the library, was a door on the right-hand side. Will pulled out a set of keys from his pocket and let us in, flicking on the light before closing us in. I felt my heart rate increase slightly as he turned the key in the lock so that no one could walk in on us. He left the keys in the door and I reminded myself that he wasn't Jack.

'This is the music studio,' he said unnecessarily. It was small and square, dominated by yet another Steinway. Nothing but the best for the *Queen Mary*. I pulled out the stool and sat down. 'Cole Porter sat right there only a few weeks ago, you know.'

'Really?' I ran my hand over the smooth wood. 'You get famous people on the ship all the time, I expect. I haven't seen anyone yet.'

'They're usually not what you imagine.' He sat next to me and I felt my body go rigid. 'Mostly you'd walk straight past them and not even notice. A lot of them don't look like they do in the magazines, you know. You'll find out yourself one day, Broadway star.'

I laughed nervously. I couldn't quite work out if Will was being friendly or testing me. Either way, it wasn't unpleasant. Talking about something other than murder and death and long-lost family felt more than welcome. 'I like the idea of being famous but really isn't it all about making a deal with the devil? You can travel in luxury and afford nice things, but you'll have to put up with people poking their noses into your business and thinking they know you when they've never met you before. It can't be easy.'

'You don't think your star turn on Broadway will make you a household name?' He lifted the piano lid and brushed his fingers noiselessly along the keys, removing non-existent dust.

'Are you mocking me?' I feigned outrage, laughing at his face as he gave in and smiled.

'I'm sorry. I guess I'm a little jealous,' he admitted. 'I used to dream of playing on a big stage myself.' He sighed heavily. 'I'm sorry. I've been rude, I know. You can definitely sing and I do believe that was why you got the job, not just for having a pretty face.'

'Ah! You think I'm pretty?' I laughed at the look of consternation on his own face. 'You said so!'

'Not exactly,' he grumbled.

'Well do you think it or don't you?' I gloated at having taken the upper hand for the first time.

'All right, yes. I think you're pretty and I think you can sing. Happy now?'

'Very. Thank you though. For letting me sing. You didn't have to, and I do appreciate it.'

'That's all right. It's about as exciting as my afternoons get.' He laughed.

His fingers began tinkering on the keys, almost absent-mindedly, and I let him marinate in his apology for a moment. Listening to him play, the two of us alone, felt like an honour. He was far better than Jean at the Canary. I could have sat there for hours.

'I haven't enjoyed singing for a while now,' I confessed. 'Until a moment ago, on that stage with you. I was beginning to think that maybe it had become a job. Like being a waitress or a shop assistant.'

'Not many shop assistants ending up on stage on Broadway,' he said.

'No,' I smiled. 'But that's all thanks to my father, not me.'

'Your father was from New York, you said.'

'Yes. He was like you. A pianist, I mean. He signed up to work on a cargo ship but on his first trip he was so seasick he got off in Hamburg and decided to try and make a living playing the piano in fancy hotels. Then he realised that if he travelled to London it'd be even easier since he couldn't speak German.'

It struck me then that Alfie would have laughed at the absurdity of my situation, finally making that return sea crossing to the city he'd left as a young man. Hoping that music would be my own saviour.

'When did he pass?'

'Last year. TB. It was a long time coming. I think he was ready by the end.' The more I talked about it, the easier it seemed to get. Perhaps one day I would say Alfie's name and not feel that dip in my stomach like going round on the Ferris wheel, the sudden loss of air as though I'd been punched. 'I still miss him terribly.'

Will stopped playing and took hold of my hand. 'I guess I'd like to tell you that it gets easier but I ain't sure that's the case. You'll never forget him. That's something. Sort of a life within yours.'

'I know I'll always remember him but I can't help feeling guilty,' I admitted. 'Like I should have spent more time with him when he was alive.'

I'd been lucky that Victoria Park Hospital was at least easy to get to. But the smell. And the people, the other patients, many of them like Alfie, waiting for their health to decline… when I had to speak to them I found a mawkish tone creeping into my voice and I hated it but couldn't stop myself.

'There's no point clinging onto regrets,' Will told me.

'I hated going to visit him at the hospital, there were so many ill people there. And one week you'd meet a young chap who seemed fine, nothing worse than a bit of a cough and a pale complexion. A few weeks later and he'd be in bed like the rest of them, at death's door. I used to go out the night before a visit and drink too much, dance all night, as if that would help. We'd sit there and he'd know. He could probably smell the gin still on my breath. And the guilt... so I'd make an excuse to leave before visiting hours were up. And he'd pretend like it was fine when we both knew it wasn't.'

'You ever think that maybe the gin and dancing were your way of getting through it all?' Will asked. 'I barely know you, but I don't think you're a bad person, Lena. If you were, you wouldn't feel this guilty about it.' He used his thumbs to gently wipe the tears from my face. 'And think how proud he'd be to see you now. Sailing to New York to sing on Broadway. Going back to his hometown.'

'I suppose.' I smiled. 'You know, you're just a big softie really, aren't you?' He looked at me, askance. 'I mean, the other night when I first met you, I thought you didn't like me at all. I thought you'd sussed me out and decided I was too much of a... a faker.'

I'd been called that before. Faking what I was to fit in with the situation. Acting white or black depending on who I was with. Will had worked me out in an instant. Maybe that was why it was so important to me to change his mind.

'I didn't mean to be rude, but that's how people are. You look at this ship – the folks up here at the top don't want to mix with those in the bottom who aren't as rich, and God forbid they regard someone like me as their equal. You have to keep someone beneath you, else you might end up at the bottom yourself.'

'So I either get stood on, or I have to be the one trampling others down?' It was something I'd never had to consider particularly. In London I'd very much been towards the bottom of the pile. Skin colour aside, a club singer without a penny to her name was nothing.

'I didn't make up the rules, baby. That's the way life is. But let me ask you this: you ever get spat on in the street?' I could tell he was trying to keep the emotion at bay. 'Ever had some stranger you never even met before scream *nigger* in your face?'

'No,' I admitted.

'You should think about that. 'Cause if you tell the truth in America, that's what'll happen. Not every day, of course, but sooner or later something will happen and you'll wonder if it was worth it to be honest. Far as most people are concerned, if your daddy's coloured, that makes you coloured too, and if they don't realise it at first, you'd better tell 'em. 'Cause if they think you tried to fool them?' He rested his hands in his lap and let me draw my own unwelcome conclusion. 'I don't say this to upset you, but you need to understand where you're headed. It's a long way back to England.'

Less than two days and it still didn't feel real. On Monday we'd disembark and I'd go with Charlie to the hotel that had been booked for me. That night I'd be having dinner with Benny Walker. Which version of Lena Aldridge did Mr Walker hope to see? An Englishwoman with olive skin who could throw coy hints to a Mediterranean ancestry? Or a light-skinned black woman who could hold her own against the likes of Bessie Smith and Adelaide Hall? I might have no choice in the matter. And that was without thinking about Eliza Abernathy. I'd been hoping for a new start, but I'd arrive in New York with secrets so heavy I wasn't sure they wouldn't crush me under their weight.

'Don't look so down.' Will nudged me. 'I'm sorry. Lemme cheer you up. How 'bout you come and sing with us tonight? Blow off the cobwebs and show people what you got.'

'At the Starlight?'

'Hell no, you ain't ready for that, sister, not while those people still think you're one of theirs. No, we got our own little English pub down in the crew quarters. We play down there sometimes, try out new stuff, the sort of music they don't like upstairs. Gotta warn you, there won't be many women there, but there're usually a few, mostly passengers who sneak down, so don't be afraid to wear your finery. It'll be late though, after we're done at the Starlight.'

The Starlight. I still had to get through dinner with the Abernathys, sitting near Eliza and pretending that everything was normal. Sitting near Jack when the very thought of him made my skin crawl. Being with Will had been nice because he'd made me forget about them both, despite the memories of Alfie. I liked sharing Alfie with Will; I wasn't sure I wanted to taint the time we'd spent together by telling him about Eliza, and certainly not about Jack.

'I'll be there. What time?' I asked.

'I'll meet you at midnight.' He gave me directions to the tourist-class dining room. 'I'll see you there. Don't be late!'

23

Saturday, 5 September
Queen Mary

I didn't see how I could avoid going down to dinner. Charlie was already angry with me. Dr Wilding would worry about me and my still aching head. Carrie would be confused and Eliza would – well, I wasn't sure I cared what she would think, but it seemed rather cowardly to hide from her. Besides, better to keep an eye on all the potential suspects rather than risk them sneaking up on me again.

Making sure that my cabin door was firmly locked behind me, I sat down heavily at the dressing table and sighed in despair at the state of my hair. The heavy lump that pressed its way out of my scalp, and my missed appointment at the hair salon, meant there was only so much that could be done. Perhaps I could distract by dressing well. Will had said that finery was welcome at the crew pub, so why not take him at his word? Maggie had baulked a little at handing over her pride and joy, a black Schiaparelli dress embellished with a white floral design that she'd bought in Paris the year before. Sleeveless on one side, an artfully draped shawl would hide the bruises on my arms and no one would be any the wiser. Chic and eye-catching without being too daring, I thought. And black. As much a mark of respect as I had available to me. After all, who amongst us had thought to travel with full mourning to hand? Apart from Daisy Lancaster.

I remembered the look on Francis Parker's face when I'd told him my surname. Had he known who I was in that moment? I leaned forward, examining my face closely in the mirror. I had Alfie's eyes, dark brown with long lashes. And his nose, the nose that gave me away, that was surely what had tipped Will off. The cheekbones though, the angle was closer to Eliza's but that was all. I was happy that I took after Alfie more than Eliza. I wasn't sure I should trust her at all. She didn't seem to me the sort of woman who did anything that didn't benefit her somehow. Which begged the question: why had she chosen to reveal herself to me at all when I clearly hadn't guessed who she was? Was she afraid of me? Were we all sitting in our cabins, scared and trying to work out who had killed Francis Parker?

I picked up the marcelling iron but the thought of heat coming anywhere near my broken scalp made me wince. Instead I pulled my hair into a chignon, wetting the front and brushing it back so that it lay flat against my head, using pins to stifle rogue hairs. It would have to do.

I'd already disobeyed Dr Wilding's advice by drinking the brandy and nothing terrible had occurred so, I reasoned, there was little point in paying attention to it at all. I pulled Maggie's silver box from its hiding place and took a generous pinch of its contents, pulling a face as the bitterness hit the back of my throat. I'd never been one of those girls who couldn't leave the house without a pick-me-up, but this was hardly a usual situation I found myself in. It took only a few seconds for me to feel just that tiny bit less nervous. When I left my cabin and walked towards the lifts, I didn't struggle to make eye contact with those I passed. I walked with my head held high and knew that if anyone was staring it was because I looked fabulous in my Schiaparelli. Even as I approached the Abernathy table, almost the last to arrive, my gait only faltered slightly, my smile fading for less than a second.

'Lena!' Eliza had saved a seat for me, between her and Carrie, her gaze beseeching. I couldn't exactly refuse without causing a scene. 'I love that dress.' She reached out and stroked the silk and it took all my efforts not to shrink away from her touch. It was as though she'd forgotten that our last encounter had ended with me screaming for her to leave me alone.

Everyone was present bar Dr Wilding. The chairs had been spaced out so that there was no longer a gap where Francis Parker's wheelchair had sat, a relief to us all. Charlie had been moved around to the other side, opposite me and beside Daisy Lancaster, who glared at me intermittently, like a cat keeping a keen watch on her rival from the safety of a wall. Jack was thankfully far away from me, next to Charlie. He was oddly quiet, ignoring most of us as he slowly and methodically broke a bread roll into crumbs on his plate, a large whisky on the go already. Frankie and Carrie were the only two who seemed less affected by recent events, sheltered from so much. They were indulging in a good-natured argument over which city had the best museums, London or New York. Nobody looked particularly like a cold-blooded killer.

'Well, I can't believe you have anything as impressive as the British Museum in New York,' I joined in, nodding for the waiter to fill my wine glass before Wilding arrived and told me off.

'I agree.' Eliza clinked her glass against mine. 'But you must have a day out with Carrie and me once you're settled in. We can show you all the sights and go for lunch, and you can share all the latest theatre gossip.'

'That's very kind of you.' It was difficult to keep the sarcasm from my voice. What would happen on this outing? Would this be when we let Carrie in on the family secret or would it be another chance for Eliza to show me the life that was only available to her legitimate children?

'Can we order food now?' Jack asked petulantly as the waiter hovered uncertainly beside him.

'We're still waiting for Wilding, aren't we?' Charlie chimed in, oblivious to the tension at the table, dark looks being exchanged between Jack and his wife, Daisy and Eliza, Jack and Daisy, while I averted my own gaze from everything but the menu before me.

'Has anyone seen the doctor this afternoon?' Eliza asked. 'Lena?'

'Not for hours. He brought me some pills for my headache, but that was early afternoon.'

'Lena slipped and fell at the pool this afternoon,' Carrie announced loudly to the table, nudging my arm and smiling conspiratorially when I turned. Our little secret. I tried to smile back, but it felt more like a grimace. I took a large gulp of wine and almost choked on it.

'Are you all right?' Charlie looked concerned. 'Lena, you have to be careful! You can't get your face banged up.'

'I'm fine,' I assured him. 'It was nothing but a silly... slip. An accident. Just a tiny bump on the head.'

I watched Daisy out of the corner of my eye but she didn't even blink. Maybe I'd underestimated her. Because, as much as she'd saved me, why had she turned up at my cabin the night before? Had she been following me? The black shadow at the pool, the access to Francis Parker's medication, her affair with Jack. The pieces were almost fitting together, but could she have known about Eliza being my mother? And Tommy – what possible reason could Daisy have for killing him?

'We should wait for Dr Wilding. It's only polite,' Carrie said.

'You can wait if you like but I'm going to order. Wilding's quarter of an hour late, which makes him incredibly *im*polite. Why should I show him a respect that he couldn't be bothered to extend to us?' Frankie made a show of being bold, his chest puffing as his father nodded in agreement.

'He works for us, not the other way around,' Jack offered, waving his empty glass in front of the waiter, his way of requesting another.

It was just as well that we did order, since Wilding didn't appear at any point during dinner. I was the only person present who appeared to miss him; I'd have been glad of his dry wit as a distraction. And of everyone present, he was the only one who couldn't possibly have attacked me that afternoon. Carrie had called him in his cabin and he'd replied immediately – there hadn't been enough time for him to run from the pool to his cabin and still pick up that telephone. Eliza kept trying to drag me into banal conversation and I really would have preferred to be anywhere other than at that table, forcing down mouthfuls of roast duck, no matter how perfectly cooked it was.

It was after the plates from the main course had been collected and we were waiting for dessert that Eliza decided to liven up the proceedings: 'So, Mrs Lancaster, what are your plans when we reach New York?'

Daisy shrugged. 'I suppose I shall have to look for a new appointment, if you're able to supply a reference, Mrs Abernathy.'

'I should think my husband would be more able than I.' A smile masked the barb of Eliza's words. 'I shall take a look at Father's papers tomorrow and work out what wages you're due.'

'And you will let me know when the will is to be read?' Daisy threw her question like a grenade and I braced myself against the table, waiting for its impact.

'The will?' Eliza looked at Jack, who became very interested in the ice at the bottom of his third empty glass, or was it the fourth?

'Mr Parker told me directly that he'd bequeathed me a modest sum. Nothing for you to be worried about, I'm sure.'

Pudding arrived and we froze into a tableau, waiting for the waiters to deliver desserts and coffee. Of course, Daisy had ordered pancakes Grand Marnier so we all had to wait and then ooh and aah as they were set alight, Daisy's face a picture of macabre satisfaction as Frankie sniggered, waiting for the show to continue. I really did dislike him. Knowing that he was my half-brother made me feel nauseous.

Eliza's knuckles were white as she gripped her spoon and dug into a poached pear. 'When was this?' she asked Daisy finally. 'When was this *bequest* made?'

'A month or so before we left New York. End of April, or beginning of May,' Daisy said breezily, shoving a mass of pancake into her mouth, sticky sauce running down her chin. She wiped it away. 'He didn't tell you?'

Frankie laughed again. 'Your face, Mother, is a picture. Are you really shocked? You knew what a crazy bastard Grandpa was.'

'Don't talk about your grandfather that way, Frankie.' Eliza took a sip of water, eyeing the glass disappointedly as if wishing it were something stronger. 'My father wasn't well this past year. He wasn't crazy, but he was... forgetful. He wasn't his usual self. I'm just sorry that he may not have kept Mrs Lancaster abreast of more recent developments.'

Daisy's face fell a little. 'What's that supposed to mean?'

'I haven't seen the will but I did speak to the family lawyer about my trust before we left London and he had received a newly signed will from my father that very day, sent from England. A brand-new will.' She weighed down *brand-new* to make sure that Daisy got the message.

Daisy looked at Jack. 'She's lying.'

'This is the first I'm hearing,' he said, holding his hands aloft.

'You knew the plan was to replace Mrs Lancaster with a proper nurse, someone to take father through his last few months.' Eliza meant business and she wasn't going to let Jack get away scot-free. The tension grew as the rest of us held our collective breath.

'Replace me?' Daisy shook her head. 'No, he'd have told me. Dr Wilding was there for the medical stuff and I was there to help with everything else.'

'I'm afraid Dr Wilding was going as well. He's had his... issues.' Eliza looked to her husband. 'That was Jack's idea.'

'You're lying!' Daisy lost the fight to keep her composure.

'Well go on, Jack, tell her!'

'I'm sorry,' he murmured, his head hanging down. 'I was going to tell you, only…'

'You're nothing but a snake! To think I ever believed a single word you said to me.' Daisy threw down her napkin and pushed her chair back so violently that it fell. 'You'll all be sorry. I know a whole heap of dirt about this family. I could ruin you all.'

She caught me with the razor edge of her glare and I felt a bolt of ice shoot down my spine. Francis Parker was likely the key to all of this and she was the one person who had access to his private quarters, all his personal papers. She knew the family gossip. She'd been in London all summer.

'Try it,' Eliza told her. 'I think, if you check your contract of employment, you'll find my father took precautions in that area. You'd regret it far more than would we. I look forward to you finally learning your place, Mrs Lancaster.'

Daisy stalked off and left a table of stunned people behind her. All but Eliza, who calmly finished her dessert, unbothered by the potent silence.

Carrie went straight to bed after we left the dinner table. Charlie had been invited to join *the boys,* as Eliza referred to them, but he'd declined, claiming he had paperwork to do for Benny Walker before the ship docked in New York. Jack and Frankie headed off to the smoking room which was, in the evenings, very much a 'gentleman's' domain. Cigars and cognac and card games played for the sort of money that brought serious gamblers onto the ship, Eliza told me as I trailed behind her towards the lounge. Apparently, those who were good could make a living from it.

'Jack will soon cheer up,' Eliza said as we walked into the lounge. 'A few games of cards, and someone else's money in his pocket always does the trick.'

I said nothing but checked my watch. Will would be getting ready to begin his set at the Starlight. Three hours before we were due to meet. Down in the lounge the quieter crowd were being entertained by a Jean Harlow lookalike, a woman who on closer examination was at least ten years older than she wanted her audience to think. She could hold a tune though. We sat at a table to the side, out of the way.

'I'm glad you came. I didn't think you would.' Eliza lit a cigarette and looked nervous.

'It's been quite a day,' I replied. I didn't necessarily think that Eliza knew how we'd ended up on the ship, on the same table together, but she would know who had been aware of the family secret. 'I can hardly believe we're both sitting here after all these years. It's quite a coincidence, don't you think?'

'I find it serendipitous more than anything.' She leaned forward and smiled at the waiter who approached. 'Two gimlets?' I nodded and the waiter disappeared. 'I never expected to stumble across you like this but once I realised who you were, I promise you, I was so happy. You've grown into a fine young woman. I can feel a little more at ease knowing that.'

'If that's all it took to make you happy, then why tell me the truth at all?' I asked. 'I'd never have guessed in a million years. You could have been reassured and kept me in the dark.'

Eliza blew out a steady stream of smoke. 'I don't know. It seemed a good idea at the time, to talk about what happened. My life might look perfect but who am I really? I'm Francis Parker's daughter, Jack's wife, Frankie and Carrie's mother. That's it. Nobody cares who Eliza Abernathy is, or what she wants. Alfie was the only person who ever did. When I told him that I was pregnant he wanted to marry me. We went up to Scotland on the train to do it and it was so romantic that I didn't think about what came next.' She bit her lip. 'By the time you were born I'd decided I couldn't stay. Alfie made it easy on me. I knew when he held you that he would never let you go. I went to my father's lawyer a week later and he arranged for me to travel back to New York and to have the marriage annulled.'

It went a long way to explaining why Eliza and Jack's marriage had been so hastily arranged, why she hadn't put up a fight. It had been a trade-off, an exchange for her father's help and money. 'So what do you want now?'

She shrugged and smiled, showing perfect teeth. 'You know, I have no idea. Can you imagine that? A woman of my age and I have no clue what it is that I want. I've lost my father and found my daughter, all in the space of a few days. It must be a sign of something, but I don't know what.'

'You must have had dreams once. When you left me behind, what were you hoping for?' I tried for lightness but the words refused to come out any other way than harsh.

Eliza winced, turning to face the window to her left, the darkness outside rendering the glass a mirror so that she stared back into her own frowning reflection. 'Would it make you feel better if I told you I regretted that decision?'

'I wouldn't believe you.'

'No, and you'd be right not to. I wish I did, but I couldn't have stayed living in that tiny room with barely enough money for food. I regret that I don't feel worse about it, but I suppose that doesn't make it easier to hear.' She paused to take a drag from her cigarette. 'I would have been the worst mother under those circumstances. I'd have hated every second and I'd have blamed you for it. I'm not a good person, Lena. You were better off without me, you know that, right?'

'I'm getting that impression.' I lit my own cigarette and we sat quietly as the waiter placed our drinks on the table. I'd been able to tell that she hadn't lost years of sleep over her decision; I couldn't help respecting her a little for not being afraid to tell me the truth. 'So what happens now? I don't imagine you want my existence to become common knowledge.'

She pressed her lips together, no doubt trying to find the words to lessen the blow. 'I'd like to help you, Lena. I can give you money, I've got lots of it and probably even more once my father's will is read. I would have done it earlier, but Alfie told me he didn't want anything from me. He said that you'd only ask questions and that it wasn't fair if I didn't want to have a relationship with you.'

I didn't doubt that it was true, that Alfie would rather that we lived off his meagre wages than accept her reparations, but I didn't trust her motives in telling me. Was she trying to pass some of the blame onto him?

'What's the catch?' I asked, sipping my drink for fortification.

'The deal is we don't tell Carrie and Frankie. Not yet. Jack would use it against me and Carrie's at that difficult age... I'd like her to be a little older before I have to sit down and explain all this to her.'

I snorted a laugh. 'You're paying me off.'

'No! Well,' she conceded, 'sort of. I suppose. But I'd like to see you every now and then, if you want to. I'd like us to have some sort of relationship, even if it's not the one you deserve. The money is your birthright. You can get set up with an apartment in a good building. Socialise in the right circles. Make something of yourself.'

'How much money are we talking about?' I asked. Was it mercenary of me to take the money and run? I wanted so desperately to tell her that I didn't want a penny of it, but I'd been hard up for so long... Maybe it was my turn to have nice things. To take Maggie out for dinner whenever I saw her next. To wear jewels and nice dresses that I had paid for myself. Like Eliza said, wasn't it my birthright? But then I thought of Alfie. I could see him shake his head in disappointment. How much money would it take to buy my loyalty?

'Would fifty thousand dollars do?' I almost choked on my gin as Eliza named my price. 'To begin with. Then we can set up a regular allowance.'

'I could manage on that,' I said, my voice croaky.

Eliza sighed heavily. 'I know it won't make up for what I've done but it's a start, isn't it?'

If only Alfie was around, he'd be able to tell me what to do. Would he have thought less of me for taking the money and agreeing to Eliza's terms? I really wasn't sure, but as she turned to stare in the mirrored window once more I found myself feeling sorry for her. She lived in her gilded cage, afraid to leave a husband who disrespected her under her own roof, afraid to change her life from what she knew. I'd always wondered about my mother but, now that she was here, I found that the fantasy was far superior to the reality of this person in front of me, and if I could grab the money and never see Eliza Abernathy again, so much the better.

24

Saturday, 5 September
Queen Mary

I must have walked miles around the ship since leaving Southampton and yet I once again found myself treading new ground as I wound my way down through tourist class to where Will had asked me to wait for him. A privilege of the higher-priced tickets was the ability to roam the ship at will while being able to bar the cabin-class doors to those less fortunate. A visible representation of real life. My relationship with James had taken me to places where I wouldn't have been allowed over the threshold but for his presence by my side. Whereas he was free to enter any backstreet club or dingy pub that he felt like, at any time.

I had remarked on that once. A rainy Sunday morning, lying in bed in the flat his wife never visited. His maid had brought up tea and hot buttered toast, which we gorged on in an attempt to quash our sluggishness and aching heads, caused by too many Martinis at the birthday party of one of his old school chums the night before. Afterwards, I'd lain amongst the crumpled sheets, curled up like a cat against him, closing my eyes as he stroked my skin, his warm fingers tracing from my shoulder to the curve of my waist.

'St John would explode with jealousy if he could see me now,' James muttered, almost to himself.

'St John? Wasn't he there with that blonde girl? She didn't exactly give off the impression of being prudish.' An understatement. I don't know where James's friend had found her, but if money had changed hands I wouldn't have been that surprised. St John looked like a toad, was a damn sight slimier, but was also very rich. I tried to avoid standing too close to him but the girl – Janet? – had been more than happy to cling onto his arm and stop him from getting too touchy-feely with anyone else.

'You know he has a thing for girls like you.'

'Girls like me?'

'You know.' The warning tone in my voice had clearly not penetrated James's hungover haze. 'He refers to you as the *dusky beauty*.' He snorted a laugh. 'He likes a taste of the exotic, that's all.'

'Then he should buy himself a parrot,' I snapped. 'Besides, how the hell does he know what I am?'

I felt James's shoulders shrug. 'People talk, Lena. St John is well known on the scene, we go with the same crowd. We used to watch Alfie play at the 43 Club, long before I met you or knew you were his daughter.'

'Well, tell St John he can stay away from me. I don't want his greasy fat hands anywhere near me.' I shuddered at the thought.

People talk. It was true enough, and from then on I couldn't look at James with his friends without wondering what it was they talked about when I wasn't there. It wasn't as though I expected anything serious to come out of the relationship. I'd gone into it happy to treat it as a bit of fun. But that was when it was on my terms. I couldn't shake the vision of James striding off to meet his fellow MPs at the Carlton Club, on the nights that he didn't spend with me, and relaying every moment of our time together to his chums over several glasses of aged Scotch. I'd poked fun at Janet, but maybe she was laughing at me behind my back, counting her money when I had nothing to show for my evening with James but for an aching head and the nagging sensation that I was being taken for a fool. Now I couldn't understand why I'd put up with him. Why I hadn't told him it was over months before. Loneliness? That addictive thrill of being desired?

Distracted by these thoughts, I realised that I'd wandered too far and had to retrace my steps through the deserted corridors, an almost mirror image of the stretch of passage by the cabin-class dining room. I found the entrance to the tourist-class equivalent and realised that the kitchens must occupy the space between the two, the same chefs preparing food for the masses, perhaps even the same dishes.

'You're early.'

I whirled round and smiled at Will. 'So are you.'

He held out his arm for me to take. 'Off to the famous – or should I say infamous – Pig and Whistle. This is how we lowly crew members entertain ourselves while the rich folk knock back the cocktails upstairs. Now I must warn you, there's nothing fancy 'bout this place. Beer's the safest thing to drink, or rum, but it's the cheap stuff. And you can expect to hear a little coarse language. You ain't gonna have a fainting spell if you hear a bit of cursing, are you?'

'I think I can handle myself.' I smiled at the idea. I'd heard some choice language in my years in the clubs, let alone what Maggie and I had picked up on the streets of Bethnal Green. I'm not afraid to say either that I've used most of the worst words myself when the situation was deserving.

The corridors began to narrow as we made our way deeper into the bowels of the ship, the rich carpet ending as we crossed the border into the crew's domain. A sudden cheer went up ahead of us, a trio of men embracing before a dartboard hung from two large steel doors, firmly bolted shut.

'They bring the luggage through those doors. It comes in here and then there're a couple elevators to take it down to the hold.' Will pointed it all out to me. 'When we're in port this area is for work, but at sea this is where we play. Our promenade, smoking room and nightclub all in one.'

The so-called pub, the 'Pig and Whistle', was a loading bay to the side, the walls of bare steel, the room furnished with a mish-mash of mismatching chairs and tables, exposed lightbulbs illuminating the space. The motion of the ship felt more noticeable here, the hum of the engines louder than on the upper decks. The rest of Will's band had already commandeered a table, two vacant stools saved for me and Will. Introductions were made but nervous excitement forced their names to slip through my memory almost immediately. My attention was firmly focused on Will's left leg, pressing against my right as we sat.

'Beer?' he asked, and I nodded.

Bottles were passed along and Will knocked the caps off against the edge of the table. I shook my head when a glass was offered; no one else was putting on airs and graces. I took a swig from the bottle and tried not to wince at the bitterness of the ale.

In the corner an impromptu orchestra began to play, made up of a fiddler, a chap with an accordion and a third with a bodhrán. It seemed to be a nightly ritual, the air filling immediately with shouted requests, though it seemed to me that the musicians weren't paying them much attention, just playing whatever they fancied. The first song was an old tune. I couldn't remember the name but it was the sort of song that got the audience on their feet and swaying in the music halls of East London. Filthy lyrics and a chorus even the tone-deaf could sing along to.

'Guess we won't be playing tonight,' Will said to me. 'You don't mind, do you?'

'Fine with me.' I was happy just being there, drinking foamy beer from a glass bottle with a peeling label, feeling more comfortable than I had since I'd dragged my suitcase down the rickety stairs at Mrs Haskell's and told my witch of a landlady not to expect me back.

Conversation felt effortless and I quickly got to know the members of the band. Deon was the bass player, as tall and wide as his instrument but with a laugh an octave higher. He was thick as thieves with Leo on trumpet, the pair of them taking the mickey out of anyone within earshot. Bobby was the baby who played clarinet. He'd not long joined the band and this had been his first trip outside of America. He was still in awe of everything, including my accent, even after I let it slip back from Mayfair to the East End. Sammy, the drummer, made up for Bobby's inexperience, up on his feet as soon as the first female passenger appeared, hovering nervously in the doorway, taking her by the hand and leading her towards the small square of floor that had been designated as a dance floor. Blonde hair, well-dressed, there was something familiar about her. It took me a moment to place her, but I realised she'd been at the table next to me and Daisy when we'd been drinking, up in the long gallery. She'd been playing cribbage with an elderly lady. Had that really only been the day before? So much had happened in the past twenty-four hours that it felt like a week ago.

'It's quite common then, passengers coming down here to let their hair down?' I asked Will. Despite what he'd said to me, nobody seemed to bat an eyelid at the sight of this white woman dancing with Bobby.

'No rules down here,' Will told me as a trio of girls filed in, from tourist class this time if I had to guess based on appearance. 'You ain't the only girl who likes to slum it from time to time.'

I opened my mouth to put him straight, realising in the nick of time that he was winding me up. 'Nice try, Mr Goodman. You know I'm no better than you.'

'In that case, may I have this next dance?' Will held out his hand and I took it gladly.

The space was too cramped for real dancing but people were making do, whirling and laughing and bumping into one another, nobody taking any offence. Will kept a tight grip on me and I could feel the solidity of his chest, the strength in his arms, smell the laundry soap that he'd used to wash his shirt.

'You havin' a good time?' he asked, and I nodded, too breathless to speak.

Eventually the tempo slowed, couples embracing as the lone

men slunk back to their chairs, watching on jealously. Will and I looked at one another uncertainly.

'I could do with some air,' I said, pressing the back of my hand to my forehead, horrified to see it come away damp with sweat. The room was sweltering.

'Want company?'

I nodded and we walked out, Leo winking at us as we passed the band's table. Taking the stairs, we made our way up four flights to the promenade deck, diving through the first door we came across. It was after two o'clock now and the deck was deserted, all the evening's official entertainment long finished. After the heat of the pub the chill in the air was welcome, though I was grateful for my shawl. Will lit two cigarettes and handed one to me, checking over his shoulder as he did so. I realised that he was taking a risk standing out there with me.

'It's so much nicer out here without all the people.' I leaned my back against the railing. 'I suppose everyone's fast asleep in bed.'

'You'd be surprised,' Will told me, not quite relaxed. 'It might look quiet, but you can catch people getting up to no good at all hours of the day. One time I left some sheet music in the lounge up here, forgot about it until I was leaving the Pig after a few drinks. I came up to get it and got the fright of my life when I turned on the light! This couple ran out from behind the piano, him as naked as Adam, her with only her panties on. I didn't know where to look.' He laughed. 'I had to grab my music and leave them to gather themselves together.'

'Really? And they were cabin-class passengers?'

'Baby, people with money like to get down and dirty just as

much as those without. The fella, I recognised him, even without his clothes on. He'd given me a hard time that night, wanted me to play some song that they sing down South, a song that only white folks sing, shall we say, and I refused. He threatened to complain about me and I told him to go right ahead. You can understand how satisfied I was to catch him there with a woman who was definitely not his wife.'

'He didn't complain then?'

'No, he did not complain.' Will laughed. 'In fact, he apologised to me the day after. Said he spoke out of turn and could we let bygones be bygones.'

'He learned a lesson, I hope.' I tried not to notice that Will had slowly moved closer to me, our arms almost touching.

'If I had to guess, he learned not to be so cheap. If a fella wants that sort of thing there are always plenty of women who'll take you to their cabins for the right price.'

'For the right price? You mean...'

'Prostitutes. Worst kept secret of the ship. The stewards know who they are, how much they charge. You get a lonely gentleman travelling on his own and all he does is call up the steward, let them know what he's looking for, and the steward makes a recommendation, like he's ordering a bottle of wine. Course, they expect a cut, but these gents can afford it.'

'Well I never.' I shook my head in disbelief. There were more than a few girls back in Soho who'd give their right arm to work on a ship like the *Queen Mary* instead of having to hang around the streets and clubs. 'How do you know so much about it?'

'I been doing this crossing six years now. Different ships, same old story. On a quiet night, those girls come and hang around the Pig, waiting for a call.' He paused and took a drag of his cigarette. 'But d'you think a man like me can afford a girl like that?'

'So you're on the lookout for a cheap woman?' I turned my head a little so he couldn't see the smile on my lips.

'You lookin' to pick another fight with me?' he asked, his voice soft.

I shook my head and shivered as he laced his fingers with mine. 'I can't afford to pick a fight with you. I think you're my only friend on this ship.'

'That woman in black you were sat with last night, she ain't your friend?'

'Not anymore.' I tried to laugh it off. 'We had a disagreement. She thought I did something... and I didn't.' I could feel his curiosity rise. Could I really trust Will? So far nobody had turned out to be what they'd seemed. When I looked up at him I saw an open face, an expression of concern. I took a leap of faith. 'Jack – the son-in-law of the man who died – was having an affair with Daisy – the woman in black – behind his wife's back.'

Will's brow furrowed as he tried to picture the man. 'Likes his drink a little too much. That fella? Shouts when he talks? Gets red in the face?'

I nodded. 'When I went back to my cabin last night, he showed up. Nothing happened, but he tried to...' I took a deep breath, my exhalation shaky as I laid myself bare. Would Will believe me, or would he think the same as Charlie, as Daisy? That I must have done something to make Jack assume I was interested. 'Well, let's just say that I was lucky. Daisy came past and put a stop to it, but she thinks that I tried to steal Jack from her. I can't blame her for being upset about it. I know it can't have looked good, I only wish she'd let me explain.'

Will turned me around gently, his hands running lightly up my arms to the bruises that I had tried to keep covered with my shawl. 'He did this?' He made a low noise, deep in his throat. 'She's welcome to him then, I guess. But love is a drug, don't they say? Makes people go crazy. She'll realise one day that she had a lucky escape.'

'I hope so.' The more I thought about the murder and the incident at the pool, the less I believed they were connected. Who went from plotting with cyanide to grabbing the first weapon that came to hand? No, I was convinced it was Daisy who had struck me. That madness that Will had referred to – love, even though I could barely believe Jack Abernathy to be worthy of anyone's adoration. 'Anyway, they can both take a running jump. I'm not scared of them.'

'You're no damsel in distress then.' Will smiled. 'Shame. I'd love to introduce that fella to my fist.'

'Ah. You want to be my knight in shining armour?' I teased. 'But you'd lose your job and Jack Abernathy would get to feel like the wronged party. I think that would be worse all round.'

'Yes, why is that? That men like him get to be so despicable every day and yet anyone who fights back is the one in the wrong?'

I shrugged. 'Life isn't fair. I'm learning that lesson a lot recently.' I thought of Eliza, of Alfie and Maggie and everything that had happened. These interludes with Will were the only time I felt normal. 'You know what? I reckon we should just try and enjoy what we have.'

'And what do we have?' His voice was teasing yet tender, his body moving ever so slightly closer to mine so that I could feel his breath against my forehead.

'Each other?' I suggested, taking that final small step that closed the gap between us. I could almost feel the blood racing through my veins as my pulse increased. This was either a magnificent decision or a terrible one. I'd never been very good at telling the difference until it was too late.

Will bent his head and touched his lips to mine, his kisses soft but persistent. He took the cigarette from my hand and threw it away, our bodies pressing together. Remembering where we were, I pulled him away from the railing and into a shadowed corner where I wrongly thought that no one would see us.

I lost track of time as we kissed, caught up in the moment and grateful that Will didn't push his luck. Kisses were enough for now, though I tried to forget that we only had another full day before we'd be in New York and after that I might never see Will again.

The skies above the ocean were beginning to lighten as we shared one final embrace, the pair of us parting reluctantly before any early risers could catch us. The corridors were still silent as I tiptoed barefoot back to my cabin, my heart light and my troubles far from thought. It was only as I arrived at my cabin door that these returned, a hundredfold.

The door looked closed from a distance but up close I saw that it was ajar. Surely I had locked it before I left? I pressed my hand against the knob and the door swung open. Some sixth sense prevented me from blundering inside, an action that probably saved me from being locked up below deck for the remainder of the voyage. Instead, I peered in and screamed at the horror within. Jack Abernathy lay upon the sofa, his head thrown back and his eyes staring in my direction, unseeing. His white shirt was dyed red with blood and in his chest was lodged a knife, the handle sticking straight up, like a flagpole missing its standard.

I did something foolhardy. An improvisation that now feels inevitable. Of course he had to die, and Lena made it easy for me. I heard her this afternoon, making plans with that man. The bandleader. Nobody noticed when I took the master key from the steward's station. The hardest part was calculating how much sedative to pour into the decanter; I need to save enough for later.

A phone call, a facecloth over the receiver to muffle my voice as I tried to emulate hers. Such a narcissist to imagine that, after what he had tried the night before, she would actually want him to come anywhere near her! But off he went, and I'd already unlocked her door, left a note on the coffee table as I waited in the bathroom, disturbing the bathwater occasionally with my hand so that he would believe that Lena was readying herself for him. Two glasses laid out, a fresh decanter of Scotch, and he couldn't help but pour himself a glass. I heard the clink of crystal, the slur in his voice as he called out to her to hurry up, the words barely intelligible as his brain tried to force him into unconsciousness.

He couldn't believe it when he saw me. Didn't think I would do it, not until that last moment when the blade pierced his chest. He didn't even try to fight back. Not that he could. And yes, I felt guilty. I still do. But he has hurt so many others that it feels justified. A means to an end.

I'm writing this all down here not to gloat at my brilliance but to make it real. I find that each morning when I wake, the memories of what I have done feel more like a dream, the actions of someone else. A character in one of the trashy novels that Lena reads, perhaps. But I did this. I am forging my own destiny, waging war on those who have tried to keep me down. I am one step closer to achieving what I set out to do, and I won't let anyone stop me.

25

Sunday, 6 September
Queen Mary

They took me to the same small room where I'd been interviewed by the chief officer two days earlier. No accusations
were spoken aloud but the two crew members who escorted
me refused to answer my questions. I sat at the table to wait,
numb with the shock of that indelible image. The body of Jack
Abernathy, his eyes staring up at me.

My throat felt raw. I hadn't even realised I was screaming
until doors began to open up all along the corridor, the great
and good of both sides of the Atlantic emerging to see what
the fuss was all about, rubbing the sleep from their eyes as they
grumbled about noise and the early hour. The man from the
cabin directly across from mine saw in an instant what had
induced my hysteria and dragged me into his own quarters as
his wife tied on her dressing gown. Calm as anything, she sat me
down on the sofa while he telephoned the operator to enquire
matter-of-factly, as only the British can, about the protocol
in a situation such as this.

Major Wrightson was his name and he was a retired war hero.

Mrs Wrightson fetched me a glass of brandy and rubbed my hands between her own until they stopped shaking. When they came to take me away, both the major and his wife protested on my behalf. *Look at the poor girl,* she told them. *She hasn't a single spot of blood on her and that chap's spilled claret all over the ruddy place. One doesn't need to be Sherlock Holmes to work out that she didn't do it,* he told them.

My stomach rumbled. Breakfast time. I felt sick but my belly said otherwise. I leaned my head in my hands and closed my eyes, so tired I couldn't remember what sleep was. The vision of Jack's body appeared once more and I opened my eyes wide, staring at a smudge of dirt on the wall opposite. What had he been doing there? Had he broken in to finish what he'd started the night before? Had the murderer been waiting for me? Had Jack stumbled across him first?

I sat up as I heard voices approach the door, the chief officer looking weary as he walked in, a thick manila folder in hand.

'Miss Aldridge.' He gave a curt nod and I murmured a hello in greeting. 'I've asked for some tea and water to be brought. Are you hungry?'

'Not really,' I said.

'Some toast,' he decided, giving the order to a junior crew member who stood in the doorway waiting. 'Make sure they send up plenty of butter. Nothing worse than dry toast.' The door closed behind the boy and we were alone.

'So.' He sat down wearily and I wasn't sure if the creak came from his chair or his joints. 'Mr Jack Abernathy.'

'He's dead.'

'Yes. Killed rather violently. His throat was slashed first – the cause of death. That the murderer felt the necessity to plant the knife in his chest… It's quite the added flourish.' He looked me up and down. 'You don't have a drop of blood on you.'

'I didn't set foot inside the cabin,' I said quickly. 'I saw that the door was ajar and I was worried that there might be an intruder. That he might still be there. So I pushed the door open, and then I saw him—' My voice cracked. 'I saw him lying there and then I suppose I started screaming.'

He nodded. 'Major Wrightson agrees with that sequence of events, at least once he was awoken. There are many questions that do need answering though. For one, why were you not in your own cabin already at that time of the morning?'

He paused and waited expectantly for an answer. I chewed my lip and wondered what I could tell him. Will wouldn't thank me for involving him in this mess. The ship was his place of work and no matter how liberal relations were between crew and passengers when we mingled down at the Pig and Whistle, the idea of him fraternising with female passengers romantically would not be smiled upon.

'I promise you, I didn't kill Jack Abernathy,' I said finally.

'Miss Aldridge, I've seen a lot in my time. You won't shock me. I'd rather you dealt with your embarrassment now, quickly and painlessly, and told me the honest truth so that when we arrive in New York I can tell the police that I don't believe you to be involved.'

'The police?' I imagined the small room replaced by a real cell in a real jail and shuddered.

'A man has been murdered, only one day after his father-in-law died, probably also murdered. Even without taking into account who they were, this is incredibly serious. I'm not qualified to draw conclusions, that's best left to the police after all, but it seems likely to me that these incidents are linked. Jack Abernathy was found in your cabin. You are the obvious person with whom to begin the investigation.'

'All right,' I said, nodding, trying not to panic. Deep breaths, I reminded myself. 'I suppose there will be plenty of witnesses who saw me at dinner. And I had drinks afterwards with Eliza Abernathy in the lounge.'

'And where was her husband at this point?'

'Not with us. I believe he was with his son, Frankie, in the smoking room. That's where they told us they would be anyway.'

'And was Mrs Abernathy with you all evening?'

'No. She went to bed early. I stayed in the lounge and had another drink. I went down to the Pig and Whistle at midnight and left at around two. Afterwards I went for a walk on the promenade deck to clear my head.'

'Alone?'

Will's name lodged in the back of my throat. 'No, but do I have to say who I was with? I was with a man and I'd rather not involve him in this, for his sake. He did nothing wrong and he wasn't with me when I got back to my cabin.'

'He didn't walk you home?'

'I didn't want anyone to see him. I thought he might get in trouble.'

'Ah.' The chief officer made his notes. 'Well, let's see how we get on. I understand why you don't want to tell me, but he is your alibi at the end of the day.'

'I understand.' My voice faded to a whisper.

Breakfast arrived, delivered by Danny. He smiled at me from behind the chief officer's back and I felt the gloom lift for a second. 'Sir, did you need me to make any arrangements for Miss Aldridge to move cabins?' He poured the tea and placed the sugar bowl beside me.

The CO's brow furrowed. 'I'm not sure that there are any spare cabins.'

'Actually, sir, Mrs Abernathy has offered to move and let Miss Aldridge take her cabin.'

I looked up in surprise. 'She has?'

'She said it would suit her to move to Mr Parker's suite since it's only for one night.'

The chief officer gave me a strange look, then waved a hand in dismissal. 'Very well then, yes. We're almost done here, so if you can get that all arranged...'

I mouthed a thank you as Danny bobbed his head and disappeared. I wasn't sure if I wanted to be any more beholden to Eliza, but anything was better than having to go back to the scene of Jack's murder, and her offer was proof that she believed in my innocence.

'Putting the question of your alibi aside, I do have to ask about your relationship with the deceased.' He cleared his throat. 'And his wife.'

'I met them for the first time on Wednesday.' Stick to what he asks, I reminded myself.

'But you've already developed a relationship with Mrs Abernathy. You spend part of the evening with her. And perhaps you had quite a different relationship with Mr Abernathy? More intimate?' His gaze was glued to his notebook and I realised that I wasn't the first person he'd spoken to that morning. I'd been left in the care of Major and Mrs Wrightson as much to keep me out of his way as to let me regain my senses.

'Eliza and I have been friendly but there was no relationship with Jack. Not the way you seem to be implying.' I spoke carefully, hoping it was Daisy Lancaster who had been dripping poison into his ears and not someone with more credibility. 'I was civil to him at the dinner table but we hardly exchanged a word. We didn't have an awful lot in common, to be honest.'

'But he was seen in your cabin prior to last night.' I'd never understood what people meant by the term piercing gaze until the man looked up from his notebook and I felt that he could see all my secrets.

I nodded and pulled my shawl close, starting to shiver. 'I didn't invite him though, on either that occasion or last night.'

'His attention was unwanted then?'

'Yes.' I let my shawl fall away slightly, showing him the bruises on my arm. 'I didn't make a fuss about it because I wasn't sure anyone would believe me. Not when it was my word against his.'

The chief officer shifted in his chair. 'And this man you were with last night, did he know of the incident with Mr Abernathy. I'm sure he was appalled at what had been done to you.'

I laughed bitterly and ripped a round of toast in half, feeling it turn to crumbs under my fingers. This all felt too unreal. Lack of sleep was making my vision woozy and I could feel tears begin to prickle at the edges of my eyes. I shouldn't have told Will what happened. If the chief officer asked around, it wouldn't take long before someone gave him up.

'Miss Aldridge? I don't see this is as a laughing matter.'

'No,' I agreed. 'But what are you implying? That I seduced some poor man and coerced him into killing Jack Abernathy for me? It's mad. Jack wasn't worth it. You met him, you saw what he was like. He was a drunk and, well, he didn't hurt me badly enough for that sort of revenge.' It felt like a lie but, after all, I hadn't killed him. Had he hurt someone else worse? 'It didn't get beyond these few bruises. Ask Daisy Lancaster. She'll tell you that we were both fully clothed when she saw us together. Besides, as you said, there must be a connection between the two deaths. Someone who stands to benefit from an inheritance perhaps.' I had to hope that Eliza stayed true to her word and kept our relationship a secret.

'Why your cabin?' he asked. 'And what do you think took Mr Abernathy there?'

'I honestly don't know,' I told him, hoping he could read the honesty in my expression. 'I suppose that someone else did know what he did to me. Tried to do. They must have thought I'd make a good scapegoat. Though they would have had plenty of choice. I was telling the truth when I told you that Mrs Lancaster was having an affair with Jack. If anyone felt wronged by his recent behaviour it would be her. Or his wife.' I needed muddy waters to persuade him to look elsewhere for Jack's murderer.

'Perhaps it would be easier to ask who *didn't* bear a grudge against the deceased,' he said drily, closing his notebook and tucking it back into his jacket pocket. 'Well, I reckon that will do for the time being. As you said on our previous encounter, it's not as if you can leave the ship.' He placed his palms firmly on the table, pushing himself upwards to stand. 'I cannot tell you how glad I will be to hand this mess over to the proper authorities and let them sort it all out. I strongly advise you, Miss Aldridge, to get your alibi in order before then. Come.'

I followed him back to the main deck, my legs weakening as we neared my cabin and the bloody scene that I imagined was still on display within. The chief officer made sure to stand on my right, our speed increasing as we passed by. At the end of the corridor we stopped and he knocked at the door of a cabin that was only five doors down from my own.

Frankie answered, dressed in grey trousers that matched his face and a rumpled white shirt. 'Yes?' He made no attempt to let us in. For the first time I felt something for him other than mild dislike; seeing how he suffered now made him seem more human. Less of the traditional 'rich boy' and more like the fatherless child he now was. His eyes were red and swollen, his entire demeanour deflated by tragedy.

'Mr Abernathy, I'm sorry to bother you again so soon but I thought it might help to expedite matters if we could bring everyone together in the one place temporarily.'

'I'll see if my mother is up to it.' Frankie closed the door in our faces.

'We must make allowances for the grief-stricken,' the chief officer said, though I wasn't sure if he was talking to me or trying to convince himself.

My fellow passengers were starting to return from breakfast and I was suddenly very aware that I was still wearing the Schiaparelli gown that I'd paraded all over the ship the night before. I felt a lot less glamorous in the light of day. Standing there in the clothes of the day before, beside the chief officer in his immaculate uniform, I stood out like a sore thumb.

The door was yanked open finally. 'Mother said you can come in.'

We were admitted through a short hallway into a sitting room the same size as my cabin. Two long sofas and an armchair were arranged around a low coffee table, which was dominated by two vases of lilies, their odour filling the air. Eliza lay on the furthest sofa, blankets tucked around her. She hadn't dressed yet, a silk robe saving her dignity. Her face was pale, bare of make-up, and her hair was bound in a turban. Carrie had squeezed onto the end by her mother's feet, an expression of fierce protection on her face.

'Lena, how are you? I heard you found him.' Eliza smiled wanly and gestured to the sofa opposite, meaning for us to sit. 'It must have been an awful shock.'

Frankie moved out of the way with a scowl. 'What I want to know is how my father came to be in your cabin in the first place.' He threw himself into the armchair and crossed his legs, reaching for the ashtray.

I sat on the edge of the sofa, looking to the chief officer for assistance that never came. 'I hardly know what to say to any of you. I'm so terribly sorry for your loss. And I have no idea what happened. I stayed out dancing and when I got back… that's when I found him. Someone had broken into my cabin, I don't know how.'

'Maybe we're looking for a thief,' Carrie suggested, her voice hoarse. I suspected that she, like her brother, had already cried herself out. Her face was pale but a little blotchy. 'Daddy could have stumbled across them. He would have had to walk past Lena's cabin to get back to his own. If he saw the door ajar…' She let the words peter out, realising that she was grasping at straws.

In a way though, it made perfect sense. Jack might indeed have seen an open door, but I wasn't sure I would raise him to hero status. More likely, he'd have taken it as an invitation to finish what he'd started the night before. What a terrible shock he must have had.

'I was with him until quite late,' Frankie said, glaring in my direction. What did he know about what his father got up to at night once his wife and children were safely sent to bed? 'I watched him go into his cabin shortly after one o'clock. That's when I went to bed myself.'

'In which case he must have gone out again for some reason,' the chief officer said calmly. 'Mrs Abernathy, do you remember your husband coming to bed?'

'Oh.' Eliza looked down at her hands. 'Well, we have separate cabins so… I'm a light sleeper.' She sounded like she was clutching at the first excuse that came to mind. 'And Jack does like to stay up late when we're at sea, so…'

'Of course, of course.' I could see that resigned look return to the chief officer's face.

'I did think I heard a telephone during the night,' she said, frowning as she tried to remember. 'But I don't know what time that would have been.'

There came another knock at the door and Frankie resumed his role as gatekeeper, showing in Daisy this time. Perhaps in deference to Eliza's more recent widowhood, she'd toned down her weeds, going without the veil and dressing in a dark navy dress that suited her better. She gave me a wary smile, which confused me greatly, and took the seat the chief officer vacated for her. Charlie was only a few minutes behind, taking a standing position close to Frankie and the ashtray so that he could smoke.

'Now, I believe we're only missing Dr Wilding.' The chief officer looked back to his notebook to confirm. 'I haven't spoken to him at all, in fact. Has anyone seen him this morning?' No one had. 'But he was at dinner last night?'

'Actually, he wasn't,' Eliza told him. 'We assumed he'd had enough of us and decided to take his dinner in his cabin.'

'No. His steward said he hasn't heard from him and he wasn't in his cabin when we checked.' The chief officer paused and looked around at his assembled suspects, his expression grave. 'It rather looks as though the man's gone missing.'

Someone To Watch Over Me

26

By the time the chief officer released us, my meagre belongings had been moved into Eliza's cabin across the corridor, her own spirited away to Francis Parker's vacant suite. Giving up her cabin was the least she could do in exchange for me keeping our true relationship secret. And it was on the tip of my tongue to spit that secret out once Frankie started up his complaining.

'Mother, please!' He had leaned forward, lit cigarette in hand, staring malevolently in my direction. 'She can share Daisy's cabin if she's got nowhere else to go.'

'But there's only one bed in my cabin,' Daisy blurted quickly.

'Hush now, Mrs Lancaster.' Eliza's voice was quiet but strangely soothing. 'Frankie, darling, I'm more than happy to move cabins; it'll give me the chance to go through some of your grandfather's papers. And Lena had nothing to do with your father's— with... well, whatever happened.' She stumbled a little at the end and before she turned away I saw how her eyes shone, the tears held back by strength of will alone. Jack had meant something to her then, even if he wasn't the best husband.

'Lena, do you need any help?' Carrie asked.

'No, that's all right. Stay and look after your mother. I'll come by later and see how you're holding up.' More than anything I needed to be alone for a while. My idea of relaxing in luxury had turned into a living nightmare and it had everything to do with the Abernathys. I was in two minds over whether it was better to avoid them or keep an eye on them. We'd be safely in New York by the next morning and then I'd be free. Had Wilding already made his choice and hidden himself away? Or – a sudden, sickening thought – had he already become the next victim?

Eliza's cabin was adorned with several grand floral displays that must have been delivered in Southampton, their petals beginning to droop and show the first signs of decay. Their fragrance was thankfully fading but it was still a powerful odour and I hoped that Eliza would send for them. I noticed a door behind the bed, presumably leading to another cabin next door. Jack's perhaps? I tried the handle but the door was locked. I pushed my trunk up against it to make sure. I didn't have the key but someone else might.

I felt lightheaded from exhaustion but I needed to feel clean before I could let myself sleep. Slipping off the dress was a relief and it was pure joy to slide into clean hot bathwater. I needed to clear my mind, think what my next move should be. There was a knock at the door. I stifled a groan and wished whoever it was to go away. Couldn't everyone just bloody leave me alone?

There was another knock. 'Lena?' It was Daisy calling, loud enough that I could hear her all the way in the bathroom, which meant that half the corridor could hear her. 'Lena, please. I know you're mad at me but, please – I need to talk to you. I need to apologise.' She could hardly murder me after making such a ruckus in public, I reasoned.

It seemed easier to get it over and done with. I clambered out, water sloshing dangerously close to the rim of the bath. I wrapped myself in a towel before stomping soddenly to the door.

'Come in then.' I threw the door open, little caring anymore that I was half naked, for anyone passing to see. People were already talking about me.

'Sorry. I didn't realise you'd be in the bath.' She walked past me and took a seat on the sofa while I bit back a barbed retort.

'Won't be a mo.' I tried to sound cheerful as I marched past her to the bathroom, drying myself roughly with the towel before snatching my robe from the hook on the back of the door, returning to face her. 'Now. You were going to apologise?'

She'd already lit a cigarette and made herself at home. 'Sit down first, won't you? This is hard enough without you standing over me like my mother used to when she was about to give me a whipping.' Daisy's eyes were swollen and red; she blinked madly against the sting of the cigarette smoke.

I sat down. 'I didn't kill him, by the way.'

'I know.' She bit her lip. 'I know you weren't with Jack last night.' She tilted her head and smiled ruefully. 'I should have known you didn't lead him on. I'm sorry.'

'What made you change your mind? Have you told the chief officer all this?' I was torn between wanting to slap her and shake her.

'Yes. I've just come from there.' She rubbed at her forehead and closed her eyes. 'I couldn't sleep last night. I wanted to talk to Jack, have it out with him, to find out why he'd gone to you instead of me the night before.'

'But you know it wasn't me,' I reminded her quietly.

'Yes. I...' She opened her eyes. 'Lena, I'm sorry. I was upset. I thought that finally things were looking up for me. I thought he loved me, you know? Even after... Well, never mind.' She laughed and took a drag. 'What a dumb bitch.'

'He wasn't a good man,' I said.

'No. He didn't deserve what happened to him, but he wasn't a good man.' Daisy sighed. 'I heard him coming back to his cabin late last night and I went and knocked on his door. He let me in but he told me he wasn't interested. He said he'd realised it couldn't work out between us. He'd been drinking and he didn't hold back on what he thought of me. It wasn't complimentary, I'm afraid. I threw a shoe at his head and told him to get lost.'

'What time was this?' In my head I was trying to work out where I would have been when this was happening.

'Around three in the morning,' she said. 'I looked at the clock when I got back to my cabin and it was half past.'

'What was he doing when you left?'

'The telephone rang,' she explained. 'Which didn't seem that strange at the time, even though it was so late. He answered it and told whoever it was that he'd be right there. Then he threw me out, said we were done. I was so angry, Lena! I thought he'd been cheating on me, met someone else, so I waited until he left and then slipped out to watch where he went.'

'You thought he was going to see me,' I guessed.

She had the decency to blush. 'Yes. And I wasn't wrong.

That's his cabin, next door to this one.' She pointed at the locked door that I'd discovered earlier. 'And mine is opposite and down two. Yours – your old cabin, I mean – is a few doors down the hall. When I stuck my head out of the door I saw him knock, and then he went in.'

'Into my cabin? He just walked in?' It didn't make sense. Even if someone had broken in, it seemed pretty brazen that they'd sit in there, waiting for me to come back. And why hadn't he been surprised to see a person who wasn't me?

Daisy nodded and smiled sadly. 'I was going to march on down there and hammer on the door, but in the end it all seemed too desperate. Do you think if I'd done that Jack would still be alive?'

'It seems more likely that you'd both be dead.'

How had someone gained access to my cabin without breaking the lock? Whoever it was, they must have been the person who'd called Jack. But wouldn't he have realised it wasn't my voice? And who was strong enough to slit the throat of a man who had stood at around six feet tall?

'Out of interest, if you didn't see the person who let Jack in, how did you know it wasn't me who killed him?' It was more hope than anything else. After all, if Daisy had seen the murderer, we wouldn't be talking about it.

'I saw you a few minutes later. Up on the deck.'

'You saw me?' Slowly it dawned on me. I had been up on the promenade deck with Will. My cheeks burned red as I imagined what she must have seen.

'I went for a walk to calm down. I thought some fresh air might help. And then I saw the two of you. It looked as though you'd been there for a while. I'm glad you found someone to treat you well. And he is quite handsome for a… well, you know.' Her smile seemed genuine. 'I'm sorry I behaved so badly. I've known Jack for long enough to know what he's like. Was,' she added after a pause. 'God, it's so strange to think he's gone.'

'Thank you for apologising.' I meant it. For here was not only a mended relationship but my alibi, all in one. With Daisy's account I could leave Will's name out of the whole sordid mess. 'And for clearing my name with the chief officer.'

'It was the least I could do. I'm so sorry, Lena.' She smoothed her skirt and stood. 'I'll let you get dressed. They have a church service every Sunday in the main lounge. There'll be prayers said for Mr Parker and probably for Jack too. You should show your face. As a mark of respect, you know, and to shut the gossips up. It begins in half an hour.'

'I'll see you there.' It was an instinctive gesture, to reach out a hand as she walked past me, but I was glad later that we'd had that true moment of friendship between us.

In good Christian spirit, one Church of England service was held for the masses, with tourist and third-class passengers allowed through the barriers that usually separated us and them. However, like any church worth its salt, a clear hierarchy was established, the lofty cabin-class inhabitants taking the more comfortable chairs at the front, the lower class passengers sitting on wooden fold-out chairs or simply finding standing room at the back. There was safety in numbers and amongst this crowd I could relax a little.

The Abernathys were on the front row. I thought about

joining them but Daisy spotted me, three rows back, and waved me over to where she had saved a seat. My new best friend.

'Any sign of Dr Wilding?' I asked, looking around. Where the hell was he? Nobody else seemed particularly bothered by his absence. Even the chief officer had mumbled something about it being a big ship, and that he'd turn up. But what if he didn't?

'It's like he's vanished into thin air. Apparently the steward was sent in first thing this morning to check his cabin and the bed hadn't been slept in. His cabin's next to mine but I haven't heard anything out of the ordinary.' She chewed her bottom lip, already chapped from worrying. 'You don't think he's involved in all this, do you?' She lowered her voice. 'Could he be the killer?'

'I wouldn't have thought him the type. Though I barely know the man.' Poison might have been Wilding's thing, but I couldn't imagine him fighting Jack, blade in hand. I glanced at the hymn sheet that had been placed on my chair. Old favourites that I remembered from childhood. Which gave me an idea. 'Daisy, I don't suppose your cabin happens to connect to Wilding's?'

'Sure, but it's locked. Honey, I made certain of that – not that I think I'm the doctor's type!' She cocked her head and narrowed her eyes at me. 'Why? What are you thinking?'

'I was thinking that we could engage in a spot of amateur detecting,' I told her.

'You mean go snooping in his cabin? But how would we get in?'

'Leave that to me.' I had to get in there, for my own peace of mind. See if everything was as it should be. I'd heard about people disappearing from ships at sea before. What a perfect murder that would be, tipping a man overboard, no chance of him ever being seen again. I thought about Dr Wilding's long-suffering wife and hoped that, for her sake as much as his, he was just in a drunken stupor somewhere, celebrating his new-found freedom.

The captain mounted the stage, saving me from having to answer the questions that were clearly on the tip of Daisy's tongue. His monotonous sermon soon had me stifling a yawn, more than one elderly parishioner also falling victim, judging by the regular soft snores that punctuated every pause he made to take a breath. The saving grace of the ordeal was seeing Will at the piano, roped into accompanying the hymns, which were sung with surprising gusto. I think the congregation was glad to stand up and shake off the spell of the captain's hypnotic tones.

'Finally, we would like to include in our prayers this morning two of our passengers, Francis Parker and Jack Abernathy, may they rest in peace. The Lord is my Shepherd; I shall not want...'

I looked around as the prayer continued but nobody seemed disturbed by the announcement that two men were dead. As if reading my thoughts, Daisy leaned close: 'Death at sea isn't all that unusual. Though it's usually natural causes, not murder.' Will had said similar.

The service ended and I was itching to go to Daisy's cabin and see if I could pick the lock on the door that led to Dr Wilding's but she hesitated, watching Eliza, Carrie and Frankie as they patiently received the captain's long-winded but well-intentioned words. I saw Will leave the stage, about to slip out of the side door onto the promenade.

'I'll come and find you,' I promised Daisy, before chasing after him.

'Hey!' I darted out of the door after him, the wind stealing the air from my lungs, my hair stinging my face as it whipped against me. I held on to the railing as I ran to catch up with Will.

His face softened into a grin as I tapped his arm and he turned to see me. 'Good morning. Sleep well?'

'Not really.' I waved away his look of concern. 'It's a long story. Can I tell you later? Maybe this afternoon?'

Will took hold of my hands, glancing around quickly to make sure no one was looking. 'Baby, you look exhausted. I hope this isn't my fault?'

'No, no. Something else happened. I promise I'll tell you everything later.' I wanted to reach up and kiss him but it was a bad idea, in broad daylight, right in the middle of the cabin-class section of the deck.

'You remember how to get down to the Pig and Whistle?' I nodded. 'Meet you there at three this afternoon?'

'I'll see you there.' I smiled shyly and let him walk away. I knew it was pointless to let myself fall for him, but I couldn't help it. Besides, he was quite literally the only person who couldn't have killed Jack Abernathy. There was no one who made me feel safer.

27

THE WEEK BEFORE

Saturday, 29 August
Canary Club, Soho

'And you were where exactly?' DI Hargreaves asked me.

'On stage. Standing right there.' I even went to the trouble of pointing.

I knew the detective was only doing his job, but his questions seemed pedantic, wanting me to outline every tiny action I had made since arriving at the club earlier that evening. I just wanted to get the interrogation over with, convinced that the longer I sat there, the more likely I was to say the wrong thing. Like catching a cold from sitting beside someone on the bus, my suspicions about Maggie would transfer across the table to the detective. I sat on my hands, hiding the tremors.

All the punters had left, Clive evicting the hangers-on who were hoping for more free drinks. Maggie was still acting as mother to Serena, who had finally stopped crying and decided to accept her rival's kindness. Vic was conducting a thorough clean of the bar as he waited his turn to speak to the detective.

DI Hargreaves was in youthful middle age, his dark hair

greying at the temples and a twinkle in his eye despite the gravity of the situation. I had the feeling though that his easy manner could quickly disappear if I gave the wrong answer to any of his questions. He didn't strike me as a fool and it worried me that he might already have clocked that Maggie's motherly comforting of Serena was out of the ordinary. Every so often he'd glance over at them, his brow furrowed as he tried to decide who was the most likely to have murdered the club owner: the mistress or the jilted wife.

'How long have you known Tommy Scarsdale?' he asked me.

'Ten, eleven years, give or take. Maggie's my best friend, but I wouldn't say I knew Tommy well outside of work. We didn't socialise together, put it that way.'

'But he gave you a job.'

'Begrudgingly.' I reached for a cigarette and Hargreaves whipped a silver lighter from his pocket. 'I've been working here for the past year or so but I've also done a bit of acting, the odd stint in hotel bars. Tonight was my last night working here, actually.' I leaned forward into the flame to avoid making eye contact. Someone was going to tell him about the argument I'd had with Tommy. Better it came from the horse's mouth, so to speak.

'Your choice?'

I shrugged in what I hoped was a casual way. 'We had an argument. I was annoyed about him parading Serena around when he was married to Maggie. It's disrespectful and, if I'm honest, I wasn't upset about losing the job here.' I couldn't decide if it was a good or bad idea to mention Charlie Bacon's offer. It took away my most obvious motive for killing Tommy, but then if Hargreaves's didn't know that I planned to leave the country, he couldn't stop me.

'So how long has he been seeing Miss Mayhew?'

'A few months as far as I know, but she wasn't the first.'

'He'd never threatened to leave his wife before though?' The DI lit his own cigarette and leaned back, crossing his legs. 'So Miss Mayhew must have meant something more to him than the others. I imagine Mrs Scarsdale wasn't best pleased.'

'She was upset, I suppose.' I tried to hide my surprise. How had he found out about the divorce? I'd not mentioned it and he hadn't spoken to Maggie yet. 'But I don't believe Tommy'd have been so callous as to leave her high and dry.' A blatant lie: Tommy was just that sort of a man.

Hargreaves made a note. 'Talking of high and dry, what are you going to do now? For work, I mean. Surely you weren't expecting to get the sack tonight?'

I realised in time that he was baiting me and bit back a retort that I hadn't been sacked, thank you very much. 'I was offered a new job only this afternoon,' I told him. 'In New York, a Broadway show. They want me to travel there next week, in fact. So yes, I argued with Tommy, but I'd have been leaving anyway.'

'A job overseas. That's lucky.' He meant convenient, I could see it in his face.

'You can double-check if you like. The man who made me the offer, Charlie Bacon, is staying at the Savoy until we sail on Wednesday.' The decision had been made for me, I realised. What else would I do for money? For a roof over my head?

'You're planning to leave the country?' Hargreaves's eyes narrowed.

'Surely you don't think I had anything to do with this?' I tried to force a laugh. 'Tommy wasn't my favourite person in the world but I wouldn't risk getting hanged over him. He didn't matter that much to me.'

'He treated your friend appallingly,' he reminded me.

'Yes, and he had done ever since they got married. I was happy she was getting shot of him. You should be looking at the people he did business with. Tommy stepped on a lot of toes in recent weeks.' I lowered my voice and leaned forward. 'You know what I mean. You must deal with all sorts round here.'

'You think this is what? The work of one of the gangs?' He didn't exactly laugh but the intent was there.

'It seems the most likely explanation to me.' I ground out my cigarette in the ashtray. 'You know what was going on upstairs, don't you? The girls?'

'Mr Scarsdale was running a brothel out of the flat above the club.' Hargreaves stopped taking notes and closed his notebook.

I nodded. 'Quite young girls from what I saw, though I don't know anything for certain. Tommy kept the club separate. Different entrances, but sometimes we crossed paths.'

'How old would you say these girls are?'

'Fourteen? Maybe fifteen? I don't know.' I looked down at my hands, ashamed of my previous indifference.

'You didn't think to report it?'

'To who? The police?' This time my laugh was genuine. 'Come on, you lot know exactly what's going on behind every door in Soho. That's a very nice suit you've got on. Pay for that with your police wages, did you?'

For a moment I thought I'd gone too far, then Hargreaves smiled and raised his hands in surrender. 'You've got me, Miss Aldridge.' He tucked his notebook away. 'Well, it looks as though Tommy Scarsdale's dodgy dealings are at an end. He did wrong and he paid the price. That's how justice works, don't you agree?'

'What are you saying?'

Hargreaves winked, so quick that I almost missed it. 'I'm saying that you don't need to worry. The culprit will be behind bars before the end of the weekend and you'll be on that boat to New York come Wednesday.'

'The culprit?' I leaned forward. 'You know who it is then? Not one of us?'

Hargreaves waved my concerns away. 'All you have to do is keep your gob shut and it'll all be taken care of.' He raised his voice. 'Thank you for your time, Miss Aldridge. I shall check in with this Charlie Bacon tomorrow though, to cross the t's, you understand. The Savoy you said?'

I stared at him a moment too long. 'Yes. The Savoy.'

Dismissing me, Hargreaves called across to Vic, who looked up from his anxious mopping of the floor, panic-stricken. I was shaking as I stood up, ice-cold sweat gathering in the small of my back. What the hell was going on?

With Vic busy, I took advantage of his distraction to pour myself a stiff gin and soda, slipping the bottle of poisoned bitters back off the shelf and under my arm while no one was looking. I left my drink on the bar and disappeared to the back office. Two uniformed policemen were in Tommy's office, joking and talking as they looked through the files in the desk drawers.

'Just grabbing my bag,' I called out to them, shoving the bottle firmly to the bottom of my carpetbag, underneath the envelope of money.

I carried my belongings back through to the bar, swinging my coat on. The temperature in the club had dropped considerably with the lack of warm bodies left in the room. I drank my gin and waited for Vic to return, his face even paler than usual, then for Maggie to be questioned. Hargreaves barely spent ten minutes with her, but then if he already knew who'd killed Tommy, questioning Maggie was a formality.

'Come back to Hampstead, will you?' she asked, pulling on her coat. 'We should talk.'

A mild understatement. I nodded mutely.

Maggie's show of unity done with, we left Serena Mayhew slumped at the table with Hargreaves. She was sobbing once more as he forced her to relive the last few moments of Tommy's life. It seemed cruel, but presumably he had to make sure that no one would question the thoroughness of the investigation.

The street outside was quieter now but still not fast asleep. The early hours of Soho morning were like a snapshot of the city. Smart-suited businessmen scuttling home beneath the amber glow of the street lights, hoping their wives were tucked up in bed and wouldn't have the chance to get a whiff of the cheap perfume on their clothes; city workers out sweeping the streets, chatting to the milkman as he drove his cart around the houses; an anxious new widow and her best friend on the lookout for a cab driver who could deliver them to the north London suburbs where they could plot what to do with a bottle of lethal poison and a wad of illicit banknotes.

'You don't have to look at me like that,' Maggie said as we settled into the back of a cab, our driver heading towards Hampstead.

'Why the hell did you turn up there?' I cleared a circle in the steamed-up window, the streets outside glittering as they did after a rain shower. 'I told you to stay away. You're lucky that copper didn't arrest you.'

'Lena, can we wait until we get home before we get into this? It's been quite an evening.' She wiped at her cheeks and I realised she was crying, the tears streaming silently down her face.

We sat in silence for the rest of the journey, Maggie paying the cab with a crisp banknote, no change asked for, before letting me into the dark house. She didn't bother to switch any lights on, so sure-footed in her own home that I was able to follow her through to the kitchen, the bright light shocking when she flicked the switch on the wall by the door. I could hear the click of Cecil B. DeMille's toenails as he trotted after us from the living room where Maggie let him sleep on the sofa, against her housekeeper's wishes.

Maggie's kitchen was twice the size of the miserable room I rented from Mrs Haskell. The housekeeper came in five days a week, so she hardly had to lift a finger herself to keep the grand house clean. Still, it was a house, not a home. There was a vague emptiness that hung in the air, a loneliness that haunted the rooms. *What do the two of you need with a five-bedroom house anyway,* Maggie's mother had sniffed when she first came round to visit. As far as I knew, she'd hardly visited her daughter in the year since. Maybe that would change now that Tommy was out of the picture.

Maggie stuck the kettle on the stove and I took a seat at the large oak kitchen table. 'You all right with tea or d'you want something stronger to go with it?' She plonked a bottle of Lamb's Navy in front of me and fetched two glasses, generous with her measures.

She took the seat across from me and pulled Cecil into her lap as we waited for the kettle to boil. 'What are you thinking, Lee?'

'I'm wondering…' I stopped, lit a cigarette and took a swig of the rum, knowing that I had to go ahead and spit the words out. 'Did you do it?'

She nodded, unsurprised at my accusation, and drank down her rum in one go, reaching for the bottle to fill our glasses back up. 'Yes, I did it. Because I didn't have a choice. What I told you this afternoon, it was all true. The man coming here posing as security chap. The photographs… It was all them.'

'Them?'

'I don't know exactly. Hargreaves and whoever he works for. You didn't recognise him, did you? He was the man in the photos. They said they'd destroy the pictures if I got rid of Tommy for them, then made the switch with the bottles, nice and easy. I said no, how could they expect me to do such a thing, so they went and sent Tommy copies of the photographs. I thought – well, you'll laugh, but I thought he still loved me deep down. But no. He seemed relieved. An easy escape route, and they'd handed it to him in an envelope.'

'So you changed your mind.' I didn't bother to keep the horror from my voice. 'You've killed someone, Maggie!'

'They'd have got rid of him one way or another. Why should I be left with nothing?' She shook her head and blew smoke up to the ceiling. 'I couldn't let him do that to me. To be forced to move back home and have Mum telling me that I should have listened to her? Needing to find a job when I'm not qualified for anything.'

'Better than being sent down for murder,' I said.

'Is it?' She did at least look a little ashamed.

'Why did Hargreaves want to get rid of Tommy anyway?' I asked.

'I don't know anything for certain, but a few months ago there was suddenly a lot more money coming from somewhere. Tommy had barely touched our bank accounts for weeks but he was bringing home champagne and presents, and I found the receipts from the fancy restaurants he took *her* to. The fur coat and the jewellery that I never saw. I can only assume he got greedy. He wasn't an honourable man, you know, and he wasn't as clever as he thought he was.'

The kettle began its whining screech and Maggie carried the small white dog with her, pouring water into the teapot with one hand, bringing it back to the table, snug in its cosy. She refilled our glasses while we waited for the tea to brew.

I fortified myself with a large mouthful of rum, the heat lubricating my throat. 'Do you know who Hargreaves is planning to frame for this?'

'No,' she said finally, 'but he promised it'd be someone who deserved it. No one we know.' She reached for the teapot, then thought better of it, pushing it to one side. 'The cheating, the dodgy business deals, the brown envelopes full of money. I knew about all of it. But I liked the life, you know? The house and the nice holidays. The clothes. If I'd put my foot down sooner... or ever, maybe this could have been avoided. But d'you really think he'd've listened to me?' She knocked back the rest of her rum and grimaced. 'I'm not even a tiny bit sad that he's dead. Isn't that awful? I'm crying because I'm relieved. It's all over at last.'

'It is all over,' I agreed. 'But what now? What if these men decide you're too useful to set free? They could hold it over you forever. You've killed for them now.'

'They promised not to,' she said, but I could tell that even she wasn't convinced. 'I'll get rid of the club. Sell it. God, Lee, I'll sign it over to them for nothing if that'll put an end to it. If I'm out of Soho, I'm no use to them.'

We smoked in silence until the hallway clock chimed three. 'I'd better go.' I pushed back my chair. 'Can I use your telephone? I'll need to call a cab.'

'Don't,' she said. 'Can you stay? I don't think I want to be on my own, not now. Just stay for tonight? Please? I'm scared that if you leave now, Lee, you won't ever forgive me.'

'It's not for me to forgive you, Maggie,' I said, but I knew what she meant. I felt it too; that if I had left the house then, it would have felt final. A line drawn. 'Let's talk upstairs. Maybe it'll be easier.'

Maggie stood up, letting Cecil down to the floor, and I followed her up the dark staircase. We hadn't slept in the same bed since we were little girls, staying up until all hours telling one another ghost stories and making shadow puppets on the walls with a torchlight. That night we climbed into Maggie's bed, fully clothed and exhausted, Cecil snoring like an old drunk between us as we talked until dawn. By the time we fell asleep I knew that our friendship would be dented, but I had hopes it would survive.

28

Sunday, 6 September
Queen Mary

'You really think you'll be able to do this?' Daisy was blocking my light and I shooed her away through gritted teeth as I knelt in front of the door between her cabin and Dr Wilding's.

'It's been a while, but this lock looks pretty flimsy.'

'I have to say, Lena, I didn't have you down as some sort of master criminal. Should I be worried?'

'Hardly.' Daisy looked at me dubiously and I couldn't blame her. 'It was just something we used to do when we were young. For fun.'

'I believe you.' She held her hands up and moved away finally.

I turned my attention back to the lock, wishing the small porthole let in more light. My lock-picking skills had rusted in the intervening years and all I had to aid me were a couple of cheap hairpins that Daisy had lent me. My companion grew bored of waiting for me to solve the problem and kicked off her shoes, lying back on the bed to file her nails with a metal file that produced a distractingly irritating rasp. Deep breaths, I told myself, and got on with the task in hand. Eventually the lock tumbled over and I jumped to my feet, ecstatic.

'You did it?' Daisy had clearly doubted my abilities.

'Told you.' My smile was smug as I turned the door handle and slowly peered into the cabin beyond. After recent events I was more than a little afraid of what I might find, but the room was empty, no sign of the good doctor anywhere. Daisy pushed me in, impatient to have a nose around.

'It smells very... manly... in here.' Daisy wrinkled her nose at the lingering woody fragrance, Dr Wilding's cologne overlaid with pipe smoke and something sweeter. The empty pipe itself rested on the coffee table next to a pouch of tobacco. What sort of man up and left without his pipe, I wondered. A man in a hurry? But where had he rushed off to and why? Surely there was nowhere to run *to*.

'It's like he walked out for a stroll and forgot to come back.' Daisy pulled open the wardrobe doors to reveal a closet full of neatly hung jackets, more than one man could possibly have needed for a five-day voyage, organised by colour: muted grey, brown, tweed, black. 'His good dinner jacket is here.'

The bed was made and a copy of *The Beautiful and the Damned* lay on the bedside table. I picked it up, feeling from the softening of the paperback cover that this was a loved copy, read multiple times, perhaps a literary comfort for a man tied to a family who could easily provide the fuel for a novel of their own. Anthony and Gloria Patch had nothing on the Abernathys.

I pulled open the left-hand drawer of the dressing table. Everything was laid out inside: clothes brush, manicure set, plain black comb, a small leather-bound case containing a hypodermic syringe and needles, all carefully packaged. His wallet was also there. I picked it up and turned to see Daisy flop down on the sofa.

'This is a waste of time,' she grumbled, swinging her legs over the arm and lying back so that she looked like the dismembered victim of a magician's trick gone wrong. She had a ladder in one stocking, I noticed, right above the ankle.

'Dr Wilding's wallet is here.' I waved it in the air until she popped her head up to see. 'You'd think he'd take this with him at the very least.'

'You don't need money on board.' Daisy peered at me over the top of the sofa, resting her head on her arm and closing her eyes. 'Besides, he can't exactly go shopping when half the ship's on the lookout for him.'

I unfastened the wallet. Inside were two fifty-pound notes, some loose change and a faded photograph tucked in carefully, behind a fold in the leather. I pulled it out: a couple on their wedding day, Richard Wilding and his bride posing for a formal portrait. His usual stern expression was replaced with a grin of such joy that I hardly recognised him. In his youth he'd been gangly and awkward-looking but there was something softer about the version of Wilding in my hand that had been eroded since. His bride was pretty, her hair naturally curly beneath the frothy expanse of lace that made up her veil, the bouquet of flowers in her hand overflowing. She looked so happy; I wondered how she had spent her summer with her husband away. Had she welcomed the freedom or did she count down the days until he returned? Perhaps their daughter now had children of her own, grandchildren for Mrs Wilding to occupy her time with while her husband was in London.

I put the wallet back, feeling like a snoop, and closed the drawer. It was as I did so that I noticed that the wastepaper basket beside the dressing table wasn't quite empty. I knelt down and took a closer look. Two empty glass vials lay at the bottom of the basket. One word I did recognise on the label: morphine. Had the doctor really been sampling his own medications? Daisy had implied it. And what had Eliza said? Something about him not following his own advice.

'Do you think Dick Wilding could be behind all this?' Daisy asked, interrupting my chain of thought. 'He's a stuck-up ass, but I wouldn't have thought him capable of murder.'

I stood up. 'I can't think of a reason why he'd want to kill Jack. Or Francis Parker, for that matter, unless you know something I don't?' I decided not to tell her about the morphine. It didn't necessarily mean anything, and I'd learned to my cost how quickly Daisy liked to jump to a conclusion.

'No. The only person I can think who would have a motive to kill both men is Eliza, but surely...' A tear drifted down her cheek. 'Was this my fault?'

'Don't be daft,' I said. With both her father and husband gone, Eliza was now free of the shackles that had bound her for over two decades. That was certainly motive but I couldn't imagine it, not least because Wilding himself had been so convinced of her innocence. But what if he'd made a mistake? The obvious explanation for him leaving his belongings untouched and in situ was that he had expected to return. Which made it very likely that he had already become the victim of the same person who had done away with Francis Parker and Jack Abernathy.

The stench of the flowers in my cabin had grown stronger in my absence, their sickly fragrance soaking into every corner of the room. It was eerie how much the room resembled my own cabin. Even the clothes hanging in the wardrobe had been put back in the same order they had occupied across the corridor. A horrific thought suddenly occurred and I pulled open the dressing table drawer in a panic. The silver box was gone. I pulled everything out and ran my hands around the inside of the wood, finding nothing but a splinter for my trouble. Someone had taken it. Or confiscated it.

I picked up the telephone and rang the steward's station, sucking at my finger as I tried to evict the tiny sliver of wood.

'Good to hear from you, ma'am. Settling in all right to the new cabin?' Thank goodness it was Danny who answered.

'Yes, thank you. I was hoping you could do a little job for me,' I said, trying not to sound anxious. 'Can you come over?'

He was along in a flash.

'Any chance you could deliver these to Eliza Abernathy's new cabin?' I asked, pointing at the grand vases, hoping they would distract from what I really wanted. 'The smell's giving me a bit of a headache but I probably shouldn't throw them away.'

'They do pong a bit,' he agreed. 'While I'm here, Mrs Abernathy asked me to let you know that she's hosting the captain for dinner tonight in their suite, if you'd care to join?'

I couldn't think of anything worse. 'Has she invited everyone from our party?'

'I believe so. Mr Bacon and Mrs Lancaster – that's the lot now, isn't it?' He nodded sadly. 'Anything else, ma'am?'

'Yes.' Fatigue was creeping up on me once more and I had to think carefully how to phrase my question. 'You didn't happen to be present when my things were moved?'

'I gave a hand, ma'am. We did Mrs Abernathy first, of course, then you.' He looked worried. 'Nothing's missing, is it?'

'No, no,' I lied. 'I just wondered if anyone else had been present, that's all. Not that there's anything particularly private, only I didn't want there to be any vultures poking about in my things. You know, people wanting to see the scene of a crime.'

'Oh yes, miss, I know what you mean.' He bit his lip. 'Nothing like that, only Mr Bacon did come by. Said he was looking for you.'

'But he wasn't doing anything in particular?' I prodded. 'I mean, he didn't... touch anything. Did he?'

'Not that I saw,' Danny told me. 'You're sure nothing's missing?'

'No, nothing of any value,' I assured him. 'I'm tired, that's all. I think I'm getting confused with the new cabin, where everything is.'

'Very good, ma'am. I'll leave you to it then.' He whisked the vases away and I closed the door firmly behind him, sliding the chain back to make doubly sure.

I trusted Danny. I couldn't see why he would lie, but then if he hadn't seen anything out of the ordinary... And then Charlie Bacon had been sniffing around and surely he'd known that I'd be at the church service at that time. I paced up and down on the carpet until an idea occurred to me.

I picked up the telephone once more and dialled the operator. It would cost a fortune to ring London but I needed to hear a familiar voice. I wanted someone back home to know what was going on. If anything happened to me then I wanted a friend who could tell the police everything I knew.

'Swiss Cottage 2987.' The voice was faint.

'Maggie?'

'I'm sorry, Mrs Scarsdale is out at present.' It was Mrs Wood, Maggie's housekeeper.

'Do you know when she'll be back?' I chewed at my thumb-nail and hoped she'd only popped out for a minute.

'I couldn't say, madam, but I'd think she'll be a while. You've only just missed her I'm afraid and she told me she'd see me tomorrow.'

I thanked Mrs Wood and put down the receiver, the wasted money the least of my worries. There was no point in sending Maggie a telegram; by the time she received it the ship would be docking in New York. My stomach rumbled and I realised it was after one o'clock. Luncheon was in full swing by the time I got down to the dining room. None of the Abernathys were present, which was to be expected, but Daisy and Charlie were already eating, their heads close in conversation. Charlie looked up first and moved away from her, looking somewhat perturbed at my intrusion.

'We were about to send out a search party for you,' he said, shoving in a mouthful of food. 'People *are* going missing, you know.'

'Sorry. I lost track of the time.'

I sat around the other side of the table. Maybe there was nothing in it, but knowing that Charlie had been nosing around my belongings made me uneasy. And who was Charlie Bacon anyway? Of everyone who had sat at our table that first even-ing, I realised that I still knew the least about him. He'd shared plenty of facts: where he lived, his previous jobs, but nothing outside of the sort of information a person wrote on their curriculum vitae. I didn't have any sense of who he actually was, as a person.

I ordered an omelette and waved away the bottle of wine that Daisy and Charlie had already partaken of. Charlie was joking around, talking as he chewed so that I had a better than desired view of his roast quail and potatoes as he ate. He seemed very familiar with Daisy all of a sudden and she seemed taken with his attention. The woman who'd seemed so upset about her lover's death earlier had departed, and she was back to her usual self, drinking more than was wise and even flirting a little. I reached for a bread roll and buttered it, my eyes on the knife strokes but my ears tuned carefully in to their conversation. Definite flirting; Charlie joking and Daisy telling him he should be more sober, but giggling as she said it.

I had treated Charlie as an ally because we were travelling together, but if I were looking for a connection between London and the ship, he was it. Leaving Benny Walker out of the equation, my ticket had been bought by Charlie. He had made sure that we sat with the Abernathys in the first place. He'd been in the police as well as being a former private detective. If anyone knew the tricks of the murder trade, surely it would be him. I looked up and he caught my eye, winking before turning his attention back to Daisy.

I picked at my food when it arrived, no longer hungry. Even a starving woman would have struggled to force down food when sitting at a table with a potential murderer.

'Hey! Lena!' Daisy clicked her fingers right in front of my face and I dropped my cutlery, startled, my fork falling to the floor.

'Everything all right?' Charlie asked.

'Yes.' I tried to smile reassuringly.

'We were saying that we should organise a card game this afternoon to take our mind off things,' Daisy said. 'Not for money, just a bit of fun.'

'Oh, I...' I had a ready excuse in Will, but Charlie didn't know about him, unless Daisy had been talking. 'You know, I think I need a lie-down. With everything going on, I haven't slept a wink.' I pushed my chair back. 'I'll feel better once I've had a rest.'

'See you at dinner,' Charlie reminded me.

I could feel Charlie's eyes burning a hole in my back as I walked away and forced myself not to break into a run. All I needed to do was get through the next few hours and then we'd be safe on American soil. I only wished I could shake the horrible suspicion that dinner was going to be eventful for all the wrong reasons.

29

Sunday, 6 September
Queen Mary

The corridor leading to the Pig and Whistle was quiet in the daytime, the crew hard at work elsewhere. I felt out of place wandering alone down there and I hoped Will would hurry up. I waited by the great steel doors where the men had played darts the night before and checked my watch compulsively.

'Hey,' he said, walking towards me without a care in the world a good ten minutes later than we'd agreed. I wanted to be cross but all I felt was an immense sense of relief. 'Sorry, baby, I got caught up.' He held up a small metal pail. 'I hope you'll think it's worth it though.'

'What've you got there?' I asked.

'You looked kind of down this morning and I thought, what always cheers me up?' He showed me a creamy yellow slab inside the pail, like butter, but from the melting edges I could tell immediately what it was. 'Ice cream. We can find somewhere here to sit if you like, or we can go along to my cabin. I promise to be a gentleman.'

'You have your own cabin?'

He pulled a face. 'I share with Leo, but he's busy all afternoon. Some kid with too much money who thinks Leo can teach him to play like Louis Armstrong.'

I followed Will around to another dark narrow corridor, the atmosphere down here far more oppressive and claustrophobic than the wide passageways on the decks above. Pausing at the second door along, he pulled out his keys and let me into the pitch-black room beyond.

'Home, sweet home.' He flicked the switch and the cabin flickered into harsh bright light from a naked bulb overhead.

There was no porthole, no outside light of any kind. No bathroom attached like the cabins several decks above. It reminded me of my Soho room, bare but clean. Neat as a pin, in fact. Shipshape and Bristol fashion, as they said. A bunk bed stood against one wall and at the back, beside a small sink, was a railing on which hung two men's suits, one for Will, the other for Leo. Dress shoes lined up neatly beneath were polished to a high shine. There was hardly room for furniture, but they'd crammed in two wooden chairs and a trunk to use as a table, a pack of cards and an empty ashtray resting on top.

Will pulled out one of the chairs for me and two spoons from his pocket, handing one to me. 'I borrowed these from the kitchen.' He placed the pail between us on the trunk.

'Is that one of the perks of the job?' I asked. 'Being able to help yourself to food from the kitchen?'

'Not strictly speaking, but there's more food in the kitchens right now than can be eaten up before we get to New York. Stuff that would go off otherwise. You get your timing right, you can get hold of some real nice food. Usually we have a party at the Pig and Whistle on the last night, eat up the oysters or smoked salmon, cake that would go stale. Kitchen crew get the first pick but the rest of us don't do too bad.'

I scraped my spoon across the creamy surface of the ice cream and tasted it. Rich and full of flavour, not like the cheap milky stuff they sold in tubs from a tray at the picture house.

In contrast, Will shoved a huge spoonful into his mouth and winced, trying to swallow it quickly. 'Too cold!' His voice was muffled and he squeezed his eyes shut against the pain in his head.

'You're not supposed to shove it all in your mouth in one go.' I showed him how it should be done. 'See. If you eat it slowly, a bit at a time, you'll get to enjoy it and it will last longer. Have patience.'

Will looked dubious even as he copied me. 'I may not know you that well but you don't strike me as the sort of woman who has a lot of patience herself.'

'I suppose I do tend to jump in at the deep end from time to time.' He didn't know the half of it. In fact, he really didn't know a thing about me. If he did, he'd have run a mile.

'Kind of brave though. Moving to a whole new country where you don't know a soul. For a job that you don't seem to know an awful lot about.'

I made an attempt to smile. 'I know. Pot and kettle and all that.'

'You said earlier that something had happened. You want to talk about it?'

I thought about it. 'I don't want to burden you.'

'I'm a good listener. And I got broad shoulders. Burden away.'

I knew that if I didn't tell him anything, I may as well leave. This was my chance to tell him something, get my side of the story in before he no doubt heard the rumours. And what was the worst that could happen? In a few hours we'd each be going our own way, Will back home for a few days before travelling back towards England, me to a fancy hotel and then on to Broadway. Assuming that Charlie was on the up and up, which seemed less and less likely the more I thought about it. Best not to think about it at all.

'You probably heard most of it already on the grapevine. There was a murder last night,' I said. 'Jack Abernathy.' I dug my spoon back into the pail, needing somewhere else to look.

'Yeah, I heard something 'bout a passenger getting stabbed. Some of the crew was talking about it earlier and got told to keep their mouths shut. They don't want to start a panic. You knew the fella?' I waited for the penny to drop, for him to recognise the name. 'Wait, this ain't the sleaze who tried it on with you, is it?'

I nodded and took a chance. 'It happened while we were up on deck last night. Someone saw us, so you're sort of my alibi – but don't worry. I didn't tell anyone who you were, Will, I promise.' He was staring at me, his eyes wide. 'It's all right. They think it was Dr Wilding, he was on our table as well. He's gone missing and so it seems reasonable to assume it was him.' I was rambling now, doing anything to talk the look of pure astonishment from Will's face. I knew I had to tell him everything. 'They found him – Jack – in my cabin. I thought you should know. That's all.' I fell silent finally, holding my breath while I waited for a reaction.

'Good thing you were with me then.'

'Absolutely. Jack was with his son when I was down in the pub with you, and then I... Well, I found him right after I left you.' What was he thinking? He'd only just met me and already I was causing him trouble. 'It was lucky, I suppose, that someone saw us.'

'Well.' He made me wait an age before he spoke again. 'You really like to get yourself in a mess, don't you?' I dared to peer up at him and he laughed. 'My God, girl. How in the hell did you get mixed up with these crazy people? I mean, don't get me wrong. I'm grateful to you for keeping my name out of this mess. Honestly though, you're supposed to be an actress. Keep the drama to the stage, baby, 'stead of real life. It goes easier that way.'

I managed a smile. 'I know, I know. I promise when I get to New York I'm going to live a quiet life. Straight home after every performance. I'll live like a nun.'

'Usually I'd say that's a bit extreme, but in your case it might be sensible.' He ate some more ice cream and shook his head. 'You're sure you're all right? I guess they know you had nothing to do with it, but still. Must have been an awful shock.'

I could only nod, my throat closing up suddenly, taken aback by how much trust he had already placed in me. No suspicion, no condemnation, just acceptance. I wiped away a tear and Will stood and pulled me up, wrapping his arms around me in an embrace that was all comfort. I rested my head on his chest and clung to him for dear life.

'I'm sorry.' I pulled myself together finally. 'I didn't get any sleep last night. As you can imagine, I'm pretty tired.'

'You want to lie down? Get some shut-eye? I can leave you alone if you like?' Will offered me the bed. 'Might be safer down here, no one knowing where you are, I mean. They already got into your cabin once before.'

'No, it's all right, don't go. Can we talk maybe? I like talking to you.' I sat on the edge of the bottom bunk and a wave of exhaustion washed over me. 'I think I will lie down though.' I kicked off my shoes and Will pulled up the chair opposite, my knees pressing against his shins. 'Most men would be running a mile, given what I've just told you.'

'Baby, if I thought you had it in you to kill a man, all you'd see of me is a clean pair of heels.'

'You're safe with me,' I assured him. 'I could never kill a man as beautiful as you.' I took his hands and pulled him towards me, moving so that he could sit beside me on the bed.

'That's what I thought.'

Even though we hardly knew one another, I felt that we were kindred spirits. I felt numb around the Abernathys and Charlie, even Daisy, like a character in a play, but with Will I felt myself. He had listened to me talk about Alfie and he knew most of what had gone on since we'd set sail from Southampton. I wanted to tell him everything. The whole story, right back to Maggie and Tommy, my foolishness over James, Eliza and her rejection and how odd I felt that it really didn't matter. There just wasn't time and so I kissed him instead, hoping that the minutes would pass by more slowly and we might be able to make the most of what we had left.

'I can't figure you out,' he told me when I finally pulled

away, my chin pleasantly sore from his stubble. 'I thought I had, but I really haven't.'

'When we get to New York, I would like to see you again.' I held my breath, waiting for his response.

'You know I sail back to England on Wednesday,' he said, moving away a little. I could feel a channel begin to open up between us and leaned forward, desperate to close it. 'It's not a life, Lena, if you're about to say what I think you are. It's not what anyone should want, this to-ing and fro-ing across an ocean.'

'Then why do you do it?'

'The freedom?' His sigh said the opposite. 'I don't know, I got sick and tired of New York. During Prohibition it was fun. Maybe it's 'cause I was younger then. More foolish. Drinking moonshine and smuggled liquor and playing wherever whenever. All-night parties.' He shook his head. 'Makes me tired just thinking 'bout it now. I figured I was never going to make the big time, so getting this job was like winning a lottery. No worries about where you lay your head, five days out of seven. A good wage to send home – I got a sister and a niece.'

'But what if there was a good job in the city? Wouldn't you like to be with your family?' I asked. 'I could speak to Benny Walker for you, see if there's an opening for a musician. There must be an orchestra for this musical after all.'

'I don't know, Lena. I mean, I got a good thing going on here. This Walker fella ain't gonna give me my own band. I'm no Duke Ellington.' He went shy all of a sudden and I felt there was something else, some other reason that was keeping him on the move, but I had no right to prod.

I reached to straighten his collar where it had folded over, a distraction from what was turning into the beginning of goodbye. 'It's up to you and I can't promise anything. But imagine if he said yes!' My fingers found the top button of his shirt and undid it.

'You want a guy with a steady job, not a musician. I've got nothing, Lena. Some savings put away, but nowhere near enough to keep you in the style you're accustomed to.' He raised a hand to cup my jaw and bent in to kiss me, his actions not following his words.

His shirt came off easily, thrown onto the chair as I kissed him, the buttons rattling against the wood as it made its soft landing. Underneath, Will wore a white cotton vest, yellowing in patches and darned in two obvious places. Embarrassed, he disposed of that garment even quicker than the shirt and I smiled as I reached for his belt buckle, his breath catching in his throat.

'If you want me to stop, you only have to say,' I said, mocking him gently.

His reply was to pull me closer, his hands gripping my hips as he manoeuvred our bodies along the narrow bed, taking care to protect my head from the metal frame, for which I was grateful, the back of my scalp still tender from the attack which felt like a lifetime ago now that I was safe in Will's arms.

'Watch the stockings!' I laughed as we battled with our remaining garments, Will erring on the side of caution, rolling each stocking down carefully, his fingers soft against my bare skin.

He threw them lightly to land on the back of the chair. 'Better safe than sorry.'

I reached behind to unfasten the clasp at the neck of my dress, letting him lift it over my head. There was no hurry to it, certainty allowing us the luxury of patience as we explored and gasped and laughed. Will felt both new and yet so familiar that I forgot to be nervous or embarrassed, even as he touched me, kissed me, in places that I had allowed very few men the privilege to imagine looking upon. I forgot about anyone and anything else; there was just this pleasure to be enjoyed. And as we lay there afterwards, catching our breath, our skin sticky with sweat, I didn't care what went on outside of that small cell of a room and its locked door, keeping the rest of the world at bay.

I Won't Dance

30

Saturday, 29 August
The Savoy, London

The receptionist didn't bat an eyelid as I approached the desk and asked her to contact Mr Charles Bacon. It was almost midday and I was cutting it fine. I hoped Charlie hadn't given up on me already. He had said that the cabin was on hold until the afternoon, I reminded myself, and it was still morning. Just. I waited while the woman behind the desk spoke on the telephone and tried not to look as jittery as I felt.

I'd woken with a splitting headache and a sore throat from smoking too much. It took me a moment to remember where I was, but Cecil's high-pitched barks gave my memory a nudge. Maggie's housekeeper was banging around downstairs, presumably with a broomstick, but it sounded more like she was swinging a sledgehammer off the walls.

'Bloody Mrs Wood,' Maggie had groaned. 'She's a devil when it comes to housework, the dust doesn't stand a chance, but she thinks me a right slovenly cow. I swear she's noisier than she needs to be on purpose, to wake me up.'

'Can't you get her to stop?' I'd pulled the pillow around my head, trying to muffle the sound as it drew closer, Mrs Wood working her way up the stairs towards us. 'You pay her, after all. You're the boss.'

Maggie had just sat there in bed, her head in her hands, until eventually Mrs Wood ran out of floor to sweep and traipsed back down the stairs. In her defence, it was after nine o'clock and any decent person would have been out of bed and well into their daily routine, not still lying among the crumpled sheets.

We lay there in silence, the pair of us stunned after the events of the night before. Cecil butted his wet nose against my hand and I stroked him, wondering if he sensed my anguish and wanted to comfort me.

'I should go,' I said eventually.

'No. Don't do that. Please. Let's have a cup of tea first.'

Maggie got up and threw me her old dressing gown to wear. I followed her downstairs, Mrs Wood's out-of-tune singing echoing around the walls of the bathroom. She wasn't a quiet woman, but at least she wouldn't be able to sneak up on us.

'I'll go and see my solicitor and find out what's what, then I'll come down to the Strand and meet you,' Maggie said as we picked at tea and toast in the kitchen. 'Unless you don't want to.'

'No! I mean – yes. I do.' I bit my lip. I'd told her about New York in the early hours of the morning, Maggie silent in her reaction to the news. This was the first time she'd referred to the fact that I was leaving. 'And I was thinking, should we check in with Hargreaves? To see if they've actually arrested anyone. I hate to ask you to do it, but you know, you are – were – Tommy's wife.'

Maggie nodded soberly. 'Why don't I meet you at that nice little tea shop in Covent Garden that does the cakes you like? Been ages since I had one of their chocolate eclairs and I think we could both use some cheering up, don't you? I'll telephone my solicitor now and see if I can get an appointment. He can call the police on my behalf so it's all done properly. His office isn't far from there.'

I nodded and she got up and went into the hallway. I drank more tea as I tried to eavesdrop on her telephone conversation, but it was too hard to make out the words. Besides, I reminded myself, it was none of my business. My only concern should be to make sure neither I nor Maggie went down for Tommy's murder.

Later, sitting in the lobby of the Savoy, waiting for Charlie Bacon to come down, I began to have second thoughts. Could we really stand by and let someone else take the blame for Tommy's death? Even if that someone wasn't a good person, we'd be sending an innocent person to the gallows.

'Miss Aldridge!' Charlie walked towards me as though he owned the place, smart in a well-pressed three-piece suit and with a broad and open smile on his face.

'Hello again.' I stood and shook his hand. 'I hope I'm not too late.'

'No, not at all. I had a feeling you'd show up.' He turned to the concierge. 'Pierre, is there somewhere I can take Miss Aldridge? Somewhere quiet where we can talk?' To me, he lowered his voice and said: 'Too early for a drink?'

'Perhaps the American Bar would suit, sir?' The concierge led us past huge displays of tastefully arranged flowers and up a short flight of steps, the thick carpet silencing our footsteps.

The bar was quiet but not quite empty. Pierre led us to a table in the corner, a small lamp in its centre lending a cosy air. This was the sort of bar Alfie had played at in his heyday. The sort of bar that would let a man like him through their doors to entertain their customers, but wouldn't let him order a drink. Not that there were any laws against it, but in real life what was law, and what was made up by managers who didn't want their wealthy guests complaining, didn't matter. Even the great Paul Robeson had found that out when he'd tried to meet a friend at the Savoy. For now, I had Pierre fooled.

Charlie picked up the menu. 'Now. Are we celebrating, Lena? I do hope you haven't come to tell me no.'

'No. I mean, yes. I'd love to go to New York.' I laughed nervously. 'There is something you should know though. In case it changes things.'

I'd thought about it carefully and decided that a little bit of truth went a long way. There were still four days before the ship left from Southampton and it seemed too much to hope for that Tommy's murder wouldn't make at least the London papers.

'I don't see how. A yes is all I want to hear from you, my dear.' He beamed up at the waiter. 'A bottle of Dom Pérignon, please.'

Once we were alone I told him about Tommy's death, that it was being treated as suspicious.

'I wanted to be straight with you.' I crossed my fingers under the table. 'But don't worry, the detective in charge, he reckons they'll have the chap who did it very soon.'

'You're out of a job? Then the timing's perfect!' Another bright smile. 'Lena, I'm sorry about your former boss but maybe this is a sign, giving you the push that you... No, I'm sorry, I should show more compassion. This was your friend's husband, did I get that right?'

'Yes.' I played with the edge of the tablecloth. 'It wasn't a happy marriage, but it was a shock of course. Unexpected. I was a bit worried about leaving her, but she wants me to go to New York.'

Charlie offered me one of his cigarettes and lit it for me. 'Lena, a good friend will always think of you first rather than themselves. And it's not like you can't write to her from New York.' The waiter reappeared with the champagne and Charlie raised his glass in a toast. 'To you, Lena. To a new beginning in New York and leaving the past behind.'

I clinked my glass against his and drank deeply. Maybe I was being daft to worry so much. Tommy Scarsdale had been a bad man. The sort of man that mothers warned their daughters about, as Mrs Harper had done with her own daughter, not that she'd taken a blind bit of notice until it was far too late. What Maggie had done was terrible, but if it came to a straight choice between Tommy and Maggie, I'd have put the poison in his Old Fashioned myself. Maggie was safe in her house and she had money. Her mum would come over from Bethnal Green and, if I knew Mrs Harper, she'd give the police a piece of her mind and the rest if they did come sniffing around. No, everything was in hand and all I had to do was get myself to Waterloo station in four days' time to catch the boat train.

'Anything else you're worried about?' Charlie asked.

'I need to get a passport,' I told him.

'I already made you an appointment for Monday morning. All you have to do is show up with your birth certificate and they can do the rest.'

He had a solution to everything. It was all so easy. Too easy. *A good friend will always think of you first rather than themselves.* Charlie had spoken those words with conviction. I didn't think at the time that he might not be talking about me and Maggie. Friendship is such a precious thing, but it can be so easy for best friends to become the worst of enemies.

'Clothes.' Maggie ticked off the items on her fingers, sticky though they were with chocolate icing. 'You'll need evening dresses for dinner.'

'I've got my black dress.' Even I wasn't convinced that would pass muster. Charlie had told me that we were travelling in first class. With properly rich people, not just Maggie rich, the sort of rich that meant houses on different continents and diamonds worn to breakfast.

Maggie rolled her eyes. 'You can borrow some of mine. In fact, I insist you take them. God knows I don't have anywhere to wear them to these days, and I'll have to look like I'm in mourning for a bit. We'll go through my wardrobe when we get home.'

'So I'm staying with you now?' It was strange how normal this was, the two of us sitting there chatting like nothing had happened. I knew that I was excited about New York, but Maggie was positively bubbling over, though there was a twitchiness to her exuberance. Not quite hysterical but something close to.

'We'll go to Soho first, tell that old bag where she can stick her room and grab your things. But yes, you can stay with me.' For the first time, Maggie looked vulnerable. 'I don't want to be alone and I don't want Mum coming over yet. You won't tell her, will you? You know what she's like and I can't bear it. Not yet.'

'You'll have to tell her before I leave. She'll look after you, you know?' I scraped cream off the choux bun in front of me. Usually I loved a good cream cake but I had no appetite.

'I know, I know. I'll give her a ring on Monday, and you'd better be there when she comes round.'

'Charlie's taking me to get a passport on Monday morning,' I told her. The last thing I wanted was to be the buffer between Mrs Harper and her daughter. 'Call her on Tuesday.'

'"Charlie"?' she mocked me.

'Mr Bacon then. The man who I need to be nice to because he's offered me the best job I've ever had,' I snapped at her.

'Sorry.' She licked chocolate from her fingers. 'You're sure he's on the up and up?'

'What do you mean?'

She shrugged. 'Well, he shows up out of the blue, waving a contract and a first-class ticket to New York. It's a bit odd. And he's already plying you with booze.'

'It was two glasses of champagne! Less than we drank yesterday afternoon.' God, had it really been only a day ago? Tommy had still been alive and I'd never heard of Charlie Bacon. To say a lot had happened was more than an understatement.

'You'd better take that money with you, you know, the money I gave you last night,' she said casually, referring to the wad of banknotes that was still in my carpetbag along with the bottle of poison. 'When you get on board, put it somewhere safe. There's enough there that if it does all go wrong, you can get home again.'

'It's too much, Maggie. It's your money,' I reminded her.

'I don't want it. I don't need it anyway,' she said, looking down at her plate. I knew she was worried I would think it was a pay-off for keeping my gob shut. And it was, in a way, though the idea of having a safety net was comforting. I had five shillings left in my purse and I didn't even know how I was going to get my last week's pay from the Canary. 'The least you can do is put it to good use.' She spooned sugar into her tea. 'I rang Clive earlier, before we left the house. I told him to empty the flat and split last night's takings between any girls who were left up there.'

'You think he did what you asked?' I didn't know Clive that well but he was the only person other than Tommy and the girls themselves who went up to the flat above the Canary on a regular basis. 'You don't think he'd just pocket the money himself?'

'I don't know, Lee.' Maggie pinched the bridge of her nose and looked pained at having to explain herself. 'Look, I'm only doing what I think is best. I can't go down there myself, and Clive was the one person I could think of who'd know what I meant without me having to explain. He said he'd do it and I believe him.'

I couldn't promise that I'd have done any different. 'What did your solicitor say then?'

Maggie groaned and lit a cigarette. 'Oh, not a lot. He kept complaining that it's the weekend and he'd need to go through it all on Monday. There's so much to sort out. Death certificate, funeral. Serena'll want to go to that and no doubt make a show of herself.'

'So it all looks straightforward? Nothing out of the ordinary?'

'You mean like Tommy changing his will?' She took a deep drag before she answered, letting the nicotine fortify her. 'I don't expect he did, if I'm being honest. He was the sort of man who'd have made sure I knew about it if he had. He was a bastard like that. A petty man. No, if he'd known he was going to die, then maybe he'd have saved it as one last shitty surprise, but he thought he was too clever.'

'What will happen to the Canary?' I wondered aloud. I felt safer talking about concrete things, practical issues that Maggie might need help sorting out. Solid ground where we didn't have to talk about how we really felt about what had happened.

'What d'you mean?' She shoved half an eclair in her mouth in one go.

'Well, it's yours now, presumably. Do you want to keep it?'

She chewed for a while, finally swallowing. 'Nah. What do I want with a nightclub? 'Specially now it's got a bad reputation. Child prostitutes and murder? Christ, no one'll come, Lee. And even if they do, I don't want to have to get involved in paying off bent coppers like Hargreaves just to stay alive. Better it sees a change of management. New name, lick of paint, all that.'

The end of an era then. Not a particularly happy era, but I'd miss that grimy dark cellar nonetheless. Vic would be all right. He'd got friends all over Soho who could sort him out. Clive and Eric the same. I had been a big fish in a small pond but now I was about to sail off and become a minnow swimming upstream in a New York river. I shivered: just nerves, I told myself. Who wouldn't feel the same, whatever the circumstances?

'Do you trust Hargreaves?' Maggie asked suddenly.

'Do I trust a bent copper?' I raised an eyebrow. 'After what he did to you?'

'He apologised,' Maggie said. 'Which hardly makes up for what he did, but he seemed genuine.' I could tell she was in two minds. She wouldn't have sought my opinion otherwise.

'Are you sad?' I asked, needing to know. 'Do you feel anything at all about Tommy?'

'I've been sad for ever such a long time, Lena. What's one more drop in the ocean, eh?' Her attempted smile was unsteady. 'Come on. Let's go home. You need to try on these dresses and see what fits.'

It was so much easier to agree and go home with her. I was exhausted and if Maggie was happy to trust Hargreaves, then it was up to her. I didn't want to ask too many questions; she might tell me everything, and I was scared that the answers might shatter everything I thought I knew about her.

31

Sunday, 6 September
Queen Mary

'I should go,' I said, unconvincingly.

'Uh-huh.' I could hear his smile.

In Will's defence, I had uttered the same sentence several times without making any real attempt to move from his bed. We had dozed a little but sleep eluded me. My watch told me it was almost six o'clock already. I knew it was important to be on time to dinner at the Abernathys' at seven. Even with my alibi, I couldn't raise any suspicions, though I couldn't help feeling a tremor of fear. There was every chance that a murderer would be at that dinner table.

'You coming to the Pig and Whistle tonight?'

'Of course. Wouldn't miss it.' We lay side by side on the narrow mattress, his left arm thrown lazily across my waist. 'I have to survive dinner with the captain first though, and he almost sent me to sleep during the service this morning.'

'He does go on,' Will agreed. 'But are you sure this is a good idea? You could hide out here. Get some rest.'

The idea was tempting. If I stayed in Will's cabin, no one

would ever find me. Would they even notice me missing? Which brought me back to Dr Wilding. Could he have grown fed up with the Abernathys and taken himself off to another part of the ship? I hoped so. I hoped he was living it up with cocktails and brandy down in tourist class, perhaps enjoying a brief affair with a beautiful widow. The alternative was hideous.

I sat up reluctantly. 'No, I have to do this. And dull as the captain is, I can't see anyone trying anything in front of him.'

'That's a maybe,' he said, his voice slow and soft. 'But watch yourself.' He sat up and rested his forehead against mine. 'Promise me.'

'I promise.' I could feel a lump form in the back of my throat, surprised by how powerful the loss felt already, even while I was still with him.

I got up and began to dress quickly, shoving my stockings in my handbag.

'You'll come to the Pig and Whistle though?' He leaned out of bed and grabbed hold of my hand, squeezing it tight. 'I want to know that you're safe.'

'I'll come down around midnight,' I promised, keeping my head turned away so that he couldn't see my wet eyes. Even if there really was no future for us, I'd happily spend one last night with Will while I could. 'If I don't turn up at the Pig, come looking for me, won't you?' I tried to keep my tone light. 'Main deck. Ask Danny the steward which cabin's mine.'

'You ain't there by five past twelve, I'll bring the boys out to hunt for you.'

I hoped it wouldn't be necessary, but it was somewhat

reassuring to know that at least one person would come looking if something happened to me.

I was running out of time but none of Maggie's frocks seemed right. The red silk was too bright and garish, given the circumstances. I'd worn both my black dresses and, in the upheaval of moving cabins, I hadn't thought to send either of them out for laundering. I found a dark green floor-length gown that had no back to it but, I reasoned, we'd all be sitting at the table and no one would be looking at my bare skin. A black shawl would be sombre enough for drinks if Eliza decided to have an aperitif before we ate. My hair was even more of a disaster after my afternoon of ardour and all I could do was spritz it with water and pin it. The list of things to do when I'd settled into my New York hotel the following day was growing as long as my arm, but I added one more item: to seek out a hairdresser as soon as possible.

I made it to the Abernathys' at ten minutes past seven – fashionably late I hoped, rather than outright rude. I knocked at the door and was surprised when Danny answered.

'Evening, ma'am,' he said with a wink. 'Won't you come through? No coat this evening?'

I smiled, his cheery disposition always a joy. 'The weather in the corridor isn't particularly inclement this evening.'

'You'd be surprised how many have been known to chuck on a full fox fur to walk a few steps.'

He stepped back and admitted me to the sitting room we'd sat in earlier. The captain was boring everyone to death with statistics about the ship. Charlie's eyes had gone glassy and Daisy was paying the cuff of her long-sleeved dress more attention than it warranted. Everyone was present bar Dr Wilding.

Danny poured my champagne from a bottle on the side which I could see had been used to fill everyone's glasses. He lowered his voice. 'Do let me know if you're in need of something stronger.'

'Don't worry, Danny, I will.' I took a sip and moved into the room.

Eliza and Carrie were huddled in one corner of the room, their blonde heads bent together as they talked quietly. I wondered how Eliza really felt about Jack's death. Shocked, certainly, but would she soon come to think of it as a relief? It struck me that she shared something in common with Maggie. Perhaps the situation was too complicated to sum up so easily, years' worth of emotions tied up in these marriages that had been far from the fairy tale most young women dreamed of. Carrie looked up and caught me staring, sharing a small sad smile before turning her attention back to her mother. There was a rawness in that short exchange that made me gasp audibly, the reminder of the loss of my own father overwhelming. Embarrassed, I turned away and hoped no one had heard.

The captain had moved on to Frankie, who looked obviously drunk, clicking his fingers at Danny to fetch him more champagne. Charlie had cosied up to Daisy once more, their knees touching as they gently teased one another. I didn't want to begrudge Daisy this moment of levity but her behaviour surprised me. Was she hedging her bets now that Jack, and the opportunity he'd presented, were out of the picture? I'd seen that cynical flirting before in the Soho clubs. The girls could sniff out the money, with one eye on their prize, the other checking to make sure no one else was trying to elbow in, like a dog guarding a bone.

'Lena!' Eliza stood and walked over, taking my free hand in hers, her eyes a little manic, not quite meeting mine. 'Darling girl, thank goodness, I was beginning to think you'd deserted us.'

'How are you holding up?' I asked.

'Oh, you know.' She waved away my question clumsily – not drunk but something else. Wilding might still be nowhere to be seen but she had obviously found chemical support elsewhere. 'As well as can be expected.' She leaned in closer and lowered her voice. 'We will talk again, Lena, about everything. Not now, though, all right? In New York. You promise me you won't go running off tomorrow without telling me?'

'Of course,' I told her, though I wasn't sure if I meant it. 'You have a lot to deal with. Do you need any help at all? What I mean is that I know how hard it is. There's a lot to arrange and—'

'No,' she said quickly. 'Thank you, but I really think only Jack's family should be involved.' She squeezed my hand and then let it drop, returning to Carrie's side as if to prove her point.

'Top-up, ma'am?' Danny appeared by my side.

I looked down and found that I'd drained my champagne without noticing. 'Please.' I held my glass still while he poured and then took a seat on the edge of the sofa, away from everyone, watching the Abernathys.

Would I want to be part of this family? They hadn't seemed happy, even before the deaths of Francis and Jack. Carrie was a darling. I looked at her and saw a sole spark of hope. Innocence. My sister, though she didn't know it. The care she showed her mother was touching. She had spoken scathingly of her father, but looking at her now, I saw pain in her eyes, her face pale and her fingers worrying away at the hem of her skirt, the nails bitten unevenly. Maybe she'd find it helpful to talk to someone who wasn't as close to the rest of the family. I would like to see her again, more than I would Eliza.

'Of course, I'll have to take over now,' Frankie was telling the captain, loudly, his ability to judge volume impaired. 'Parker Godwin might be a large firm but it's a family firm and Grandpa would turn in his grave if an outsider got hold of it.'

His voice cut through all other conversation, everyone's attention grabbed by the certainty of his statement. Of all the Abernathys, Frankie was the most obviously broken by his father's death. How could he not be? The loss of his mentor had to be a heavy blow. Every time he looked in a mirror he would see a version of his father, the man whose footsteps he had been treading only too neatly in.

'Frankie, darling, we can sort all of that out once we get home. I haven't even notified anyone in New York.' Eliza looked a little dazed now, as though the medication had begun to wear off. 'Perhaps Dr Wilding can assist with the paperwork. A doctor must be used to that sort of thing.'

Glances were exchanged around the room, Eliza oblivious. Surely she knew that Wilding was missing. We'd talked about it only that morning, in that very room. His very absence, in that moment, should have served as a reminder.

'I'm starving, Mother,' Frankie said, filling the awkward silence. 'It's half past seven.'

'You're the man of the house now. Why don't you take everyone through?' She let her son help her to her feet.

We filed through to the adjoining room, a dining room dominated by a long table, set with white tablecloth and silver cutlery. Danny and a young waitress were in attendance. Frankie took the seat at the head of the table, the captain to his right and Eliza to his left. The rest of us sat where we liked, the spare place setting another reminder of the missing doctor.

'In honour of it being a Sunday, I asked Mrs Abernathy if she minded humouring a British tradition,' the captain announced, with much excitement. 'Roast beef with all the trimmings, like we have back home.'

'There's smoked salmon to start,' Danny chimed in, nobody paying any attention.

'We should raise a glass before we eat,' Charlie said, 'to those we've lost.'

Frankie glared and I took some small satisfaction in seeing Charlie deflated. 'Waiter, some wine. And perhaps it would be more suitable if the captain were to lead us in a short prayer in honour of my family. For my father and grandfather, whose deaths we hope will be avenged.'

Carrie appeared as though she were going to say something, then thought better of it. She caught my eye accidentally and quickly looked away, leaving me to wonder if I'd done something wrong. Twice now she'd avoided my gaze.

Danny filled our wine glasses and we bowed our heads as the captain gave a by-the-book plea to God to look after the souls of Francis Parker and Jack Abernathy. I had a strong feeling that he was wasting his breath; both men were surely in the fiery pits below.

The smoked salmon was served in thick slices, with brown bread and butter. We ate in silence, Danny shifting awkwardly as he stood by, until he remembered the gramophone in the corner.

'Some music, sir?'

Frankie nodded and Danny put on a record, Louis Armstrong's distinctive voice papering over the lack of conversation. I wondered who the record belonged to, given that Frankie had made clear his distaste for jazz.

Danny carved the huge joint of beef and laid it on the table. Jugs of gravy appeared, along with roast potatoes, even Yorkshire puddings, though the Americans turned their noses up, apart from Charlie.

'No more for me,' the captain said, turning down the offer of more wine. 'It's a matter of hours before land is in sight and I must stay sober. I wouldn't say no to pudding though.'

'I'll fetch it now, sir. Treacle tart and custard,' Danny told him.

The rest of the party looked as though they'd rather chew on their soiled napkins, but I felt cheered by the stodge and familiarity of the food.

'So heavy,' Eliza complained, letting a spoonful of creamy yellow custard plop back into the bowl. I had already scraped my bowl clean and only held back from asking for seconds because my dress had tightened so considerably around my belly that I feared another bite would rip the seams apart.

'Good English grub,' the captain said. 'Thank you for a wonderful meal, Mrs Abernathy. I'm only sorry it wasn't under better circumstances. Now, I hate to leave you in such a rush, but I really must show my face on the bridge.'

He left, Eliza dismissing Danny and the waitress once they'd cleared the table. I wanted to talk to Carrie, but with so many people still present, Frankie's glare shifting between myself, Daisy and Charlie, it didn't seem possible. I finished my coffee and pushed back my chair.

'Thank you, Eliza. This has been... nice.' It sounded so impersonal, but I didn't know what else to say. The circumstances the Abernathys found themselves in were unthinkable. 'I should leave you to it.'

'Oh, won't you stay for a quick last drink?' Carrie pleaded. I rather had the impression she wasn't keen to be left alone with her mother and brother so soon.

'Brandy?' Charlie asked hopefully.

'That would be nice,' Eliza agreed. 'Frankie, would you do the honours?'

He started to growl a complaint but Carrie sprang to her feet. 'I'll do it, Mama. It was my idea after all.' She disappeared back into the sitting room and returned a few minutes later with the glasses on a tray, an inch of brandy in each.

I took a sniff of mine, then pushed the glass aside slightly. If I drank too much I knew there was no hope of me staying awake and I had to see Will. 'I'm sorry, everyone, but really, I'm completely exhausted. I should go and lie down.'

'I'll let you out.' Carrie stood up quickly and followed me through to the sitting room, closing the door on her mother and brother.

'How are you holding up?' I asked quietly. 'I know we've really only just met, but if you'd like to talk about anything, you know where I am.'

She hesitated for a moment before moving forward and surprising me with a hug. There were no tears, no hysterics, and when I reciprocated she pulled away almost immediately. 'Sorry,' she said. 'You know, of everyone, you're the only person I'd like to talk to, only I don't know that I can. You'd think badly of me.'

'You never know,' I told her. 'I've done and said some awful things in my time. I'm not perfect. I don't expect anyone is.'

'No. That is true.' She nodded and took a sharp breath.

'Carrie!' I heard Eliza call her daughter.

She looked over her shoulder regretfully. 'I guess I'd better go. Goodnight, Lena.'

'Goodnight.' I left the cabin and heard her lock the door behind me.

It was almost ten o'clock and I wasn't sure what to do with myself. If I were to lie down on the bed in my cabin I knew I wouldn't wake until the morning, too late to see Will. I didn't feel much like another drink, but the easiest solution might be to go up to the Starlight Club to see Will and the band play their last few songs.

'Are you really going to bed, Lena?' Daisy caught me dithering in the corridor. 'It's still so early!'

'Oh, I… no. Not yet.' I didn't really want to get stuck with Daisy but after two days without sleep I couldn't come up with a ready excuse.

'Can we talk?' She lit a cigarette and leaned against the wall by my cabin door. It didn't seem as though she intended to give me much choice.

'I'm very tired, Daisy. Is this important?'

'I know your secret,' she said, keeping her voice low but

356

looking towards an older couple who were walking back to their cabin. Major Wrightson and his wife, my saviours of the night before. I raised a hand in greeting and they reciprocated.

'My secret?' I tried to laugh it off, turning away so she couldn't see my face. I unlocked my cabin door, my heart beginning to race. 'Come in then.'

I sat on the sofa and let Daisy decide whether she wanted to sit or stand. I'd seen Tommy deal with people who'd wronged him at the Canary. He'd sit at one of the tables and wait for them to speak. Nine times out of ten they'd end up talking too much and he'd have them over a barrel. The tenth time was the reason Tommy employed a man like Eric, the strong man never more gleeful than when he was let loose, escorting those unfortunate chaps out into the alleyway round the back of the club. I was happy not to know what he did with them once they were out there. Whichever choice they made, to talk or to keep quiet, none of those men showed their faces in the Canary again.

I lit a cigarette and crossed my legs, and eventually Daisy sat down opposite, looking less sure of herself. 'Spit it out then,' I told her.

'I know who you are.' Triumph returned to her face. 'You're Eliza's daughter. *You're* the big secret she's been keeping all these years. The reason she agreed to marry Jack.'

'So?' I shrugged and hoped the heavy thudding of my heart didn't carry across the table. How the hell had she found out?

'So, this changes everything! You're one of the family. You're one of *them*.'

'I'm *not* one of them.' There was a knock at the door and I got up to answer it, flustered. Danny stood there, a box of chocolates in his hand. Peppermint creams, my favourite.

'From Mrs Abernathy,' he said, handing them to me. 'I'm about to clock off for the night. Did you need anything else before I go, ma'am?'

'No, Danny, thank you.' I remembered my manners. 'You will be around tomorrow morning, won't you, before I disembark?'

'I'll be here, don't you worry.' He saluted as he left and I wondered at his carefree demeanour. For the last few days he had brought a lightness to what could have been an even darker time. I'd make sure to tip him well.

'I don't care if you want to tell people,' I told Daisy, throwing the box down on the table. 'Tell the world if you like. It's Eliza who wants the secret kept.' I took a drag of my cigarette. 'You'd be doing me a favour.'

'Aren't you worried she'll cut you off without a dime?' Daisy seemed appalled.

'She's given me nothing for twenty-six years. You don't miss what you've never had.' I stared her out, damned if I was going to give in to her games at this late stage.

'I wasn't going to tell that many people. Only a few. The people who care about that sort of thing.' Her body sagged as she perched on the edge of the sofa, head hanging down. I saw that she was still wearing the same stockings that had laddered, the wound in the silk stretching higher up her leg. 'I just thought that... Look, I'm desperate, Lena, you know? I'm going back to nothing. No job, no Jack...'

'It'll be all right,' I told her, with far more conviction than I felt. 'And you're far better off without Jack. I don't want to say that he deserved what he got, but he was an absolute monster, you know he was.'

'He wasn't that bad,' Daisy protested. 'Really, he was—'

'He was a drunk and a bully and he thought he could take whatever he wanted. You're well rid.' It irritated me beyond reason that she kept defending Jack when she should have been glad to see the back of him.

'I know he wasn't a good person,' Daisy said. 'But I just— I can't help it. And he could be kind. Generous. He wasn't all bad, you know.'

'I'll take your word for it.' I put out my cigarette and wished she'd hurry up and leave. I needed to splash water on my face and I needed time alone to think. Something was nagging at me, but I couldn't quite grasp it. It was frustrating, like trying to thread a narrow needle with thick yarn.

'Can I have one of those?' Daisy pointed to the chocolates. 'I'm not even hungry, but when I get anxious, I eat.'

'Help yourself,' I said absent-mindedly, still plumbing the depths of my mind to figure out what I was missing. 'So who told you about me anyway?'

'I overheard Eliza talking.' She looked ashamed to have been caught eavesdropping. 'You know that my cabin is next to Mr Parker's, and now of course she's staying there.'

I could well imagine Daisy with her ear pressed up against the connecting door, but who had Eliza been talking to?

Daisy popped a shiny-cased chocolate into her mouth and pulled a face. 'What are these? Tastes kind of odd. Peppermint? Yuck.' She chewed on regardless, then took another. 'You got anything to drink?'

'As in a "drink" drink?'

'As in some water. My throat's ever so dry. And some coffee would be good.' She ate another chocolate.

'You should have said a moment ago. Danny was just here.' I took a deep breath and forced a smile. Gosh, she was frustrating. I went to the telephone and called but no one picked up. 'Strange. I wonder if the night steward's running late.'

'It's a busy night. Last evening on board, a lot of people have an early night and get up to watch us come into the city,' Daisy told me. 'This is prime cocoa and supper time, after all.'

'I suppose. Well, I can get you some tap water.'

I went to the bathroom and ran the tap, taking my toothbrush from the small glass by the sink and filling it with water. If it hadn't been for Will, I'd have thrown Daisy out, but she had her uses. At least if I was talking to her then the risk of falling asleep would be minimised. I knocked back the water in one go and refilled the glass before taking it through.

'Here you are.' I put the glass down on a coaster. 'Daisy?'

There was no answer. When I looked down, she was lying back against the cushions, her eyes closed. I shook her and her body flopped forward, completely unconscious. Her eyelids fluttered and I let go of the breath I'd been holding. Still alive then, for now. The empty gaps in the chocolate box tray showed me that she'd eaten six of the bloody things. I swore and ran to the door, wrenching it open only to run immediately into a body. A person who had been standing there, waiting patiently.

32

Wednesday, 2 September
Waterloo Station, London

The train hadn't moved off yet but I was fascinated by the view from the window. The station platform was heaving: excited passengers rushing down to find an empty carriage; family waving off their loved ones; station staff sidestepping their way through the crowds, shouting instructions to one another in a language that belonged to the railway and to these workers and to this station. I also kept watch for any sign of Hargreaves or the police. I didn't trust the man as far as I could throw him. He knew where I was going, the day, the name of the ship. Until I was actually on the *Queen Mary* and we had set sail from Southampton, I wouldn't feel safe.

Boarding the train, I had my first glimpse of life in first class. Charlie and I sat either side of a white-clothed table. I had already been served with Perrier water and coffee, turning down the champagne when I heard the expensively dressed woman on the table opposite announce to her companion that it was far too early for a lady to be drinking. Best to start now with the pretence. Maggie had bought me a box of peppermint creams from Fortnum's for the journey, which I now displayed, their gold logo visible on the packaging.

I watched two friends embrace on the platform, one leaving the other behind to board the train, and wondered if Maggie would have come if I'd asked. As it was, it had been a nice surprise that she had dragged herself out of bed to wave me off in the cab, but I had felt nothing but relief as the driver took the first corner. Did Maggie trust me, knowing that I had seen Tommy and Serena together for weeks and not said a word? Could I trust her, knowing that she was capable of murder? The time apart might give us a chance to reflect.

Maggie had spent most of the past few days isolated and in bed. I took over one of the spare rooms, my meagre belongings spread about the place. Every time there was a knock at the front door, my heart stopped; I'm sure Maggie's had done the same. But it was never the police. The only time I spoke to Maggie was between dinner time and midnight. Mrs Wood would leave the food on the stove before she left and I would dish up for both of us, Maggie sweeping down the stairs in a clean nightgown for the occasion.

We'd gone through no small amount of gin and brandy each evening, as if we could only bear one another's company in the soft focus of inebriation, the alcohol rubbing away the sharp corners of hurt, guilt and fear that made our sober encounters unbearable. The bottles had mounted up until Mrs Wood had knocked them over as she tried to mop the kitchen floor, lost her patience, and made me cart them all back down the road to the pub. I didn't care that the landlord had looked at me like I was a lush. I did care that I couldn't look at Maggie without wondering how easily she'd agreed to kill her husband. I couldn't look at her without feeling guilty that I hadn't noticed how terribly desperate my friend had become.

'We'll be off soon,' Charlie told me, checking his watch. 'Before you know it, we'll be setting sail and you'll be that much closer to New York.'

I smiled even as I felt an almost irresistible urge to get up and flee, to run back to Maggie's and beg to be allowed to stay. I knew that I couldn't though. Each day she'd plied me with gifts – more dresses, a stole, a ruby brooch that I ended up replacing in her jewellery box, tiptoeing into her bedroom as she slept to drop it back. I felt immense sadness that she felt it necessary to try and buy my silence, but I had to accept some of her generosity, knowing that I couldn't afford to kit myself up for the voyage any other way. At least Mrs Harper had shown up the day before, furious with me for not overruling Maggie and calling her as soon as Tommy had died.

'It's always hard, leaving home for the first time,' Charlie told me gently. 'It'll feel strange for a while, until you settle in. But you'll get used to it in time.'

'I suppose. I'm worried about my friend, that's all. I wish I'd a little more time to spend with her, to make sure she's all right,' I said.

The platform outside was almost empty, just a couple running down past our window towards the front of the train, the man dragging his wife as they rushed to find their carriage before the train moved off. No police.

'This will be the friend whose husband died? She'll understand why you had to leave. It's not as though you can bring her husband back to life, after all. She'll want the best for you, whatever that means for her.'

Was that true? And did I deserve such self-sacrifice, on Maggie's part anyway? I had convinced myself that I'd wanted the best for her, but if I'd cared so much before, wouldn't I have made her face up to the truth years earlier? I had watched Tommy conduct his affairs publicly and justified my silence by telling myself that Maggie knew. She'd laughed it off and acted as though it wasn't anything out of the ordinary, that all husbands did it. But if I had really cared, I could have told Mrs Harper what her son-in-law was up to. I could have borrowed James's camera and taken incriminating photographs of Tommy, given her the ammunition that he'd ended up using against her. Any of those things might have helped, but they might also have ended our friendship. It was sad to say, but Maggie was and always had been the only real friend I'd had. She was as good as family.

'I'm sure she'll be fine,' I told Charlie. 'I can't help thinking I should have done more, that's all.'

'A strong friendship will survive time apart,' he assured me. 'And it's not forever. Once you make it big, you'll be in demand in the West End.'

It didn't seem possible, but I nodded as the train began to pull out of the station with a jolt, the chatter around us increasing in volume as we began our journey. The train whistle made me feel like a child, excited and nervous and unsure what to expect. We picked up speed and it felt as though there was no way back. I was heading towards freedom but away from everything I knew.

'Want a peppermint cream?' I offered the box to Charlie.

'Oh no, thanks, I don't like chocolate.'

'Who doesn't like chocolate? These are my favourite. They always cheer me right up.' I shoved two in my mouth, one after the other.

'Let me tell you a story, that'll cheer you up.' Charlie grinned at me.

'Like a fairy tale?' I was dubious.

'No, not a fairy tale.' He laughed at me. 'Let me tell you about Benny Walker and your father, the story as I know it.' I sat up, suddenly interested. 'Two young men, trying to make their way in the world. They crossed paths working in a restaurant. Alfie washed dishes in the kitchen, they wouldn't let him front of house. Benny was a waiter. They used to take smoke breaks outside together and talk about their dreams. Benny was more into the acting side of things while Alfie was all about the music. He had a voice on him, all right. The chefs in the kitchen would shout out their requests and he would sing whatever they wanted. All he asked in return was a fair share of the tips, and that was no problem.'

I could imagine the young Alfie, little more than a boy, washing plates at the sink as he sang. He'd often helped Mrs Harper with the housework and sang as he swept and dusted and mopped. He said that singing could make even the most mundane of tasks interesting, but I'd never found that to be the case. I'd never inherited his sunny disposition.

'So these two young men,' Charlie went on, 'became great friends. And Benny got an audition at a small theatre. Nothing too fancy, but it was something. They paid him for a start, less than he'd been getting at the restaurant, but he figured it'd be worth it. Get his foot on the ladder, so to speak. After that play there was another and another. Benny was doing great, and Alfie was starting to get a bit of work as a pianist, but he was struggling to get by. They were still great friends though. But then Benny started stepping out with this girl – let's call her Isabelle.'

'Isabelle? She sounds very posh,' I laughed.

'Oh, she was a beauty. Everyone thought that Benny had done well for himself because even though she herself was an actress, Izzy usually wouldn't have anything to do with the theatre crowd. She was saving herself for someone with real talent. Someone who would be somebody one day, she always used to say.'

'Did you know her?' I asked. There was something familiar in the way he talked about this woman, a wistful tone to his voice, as if he had been one of those men who'd been turned down by the lovely Isabelle.

'I know her type,' he said. 'Women like that – and I know you're not one, Lena – they talk it up as though they're above everyone else, but really they aren't. Izzy liked that Benny spent every penny he earned on her. Flowers and nice meals out that he couldn't afford. And then a job opened up at the theatre for a pianist and he called his friend Alfie. Benny thought that life couldn't be better. He had his best friend and his girl together at the theatre, and the role that was going to set him on the path to success.' He paused as the waiter approached, ordering a plate of pastries for our table and a fresh pot of coffee.

'But something went wrong?' I prompted, once the waiter had gone. Despite myself, I was keen to know what had led to the end of this friendship that Alfie had never spoken about.

'At the end of the run, Benny found out that Izzy and Alfie had been carrying on behind his back.' Charlie leaned back in his chair and reached into his jacket pocket for his cigars. 'And that was that.'

'Alfie was?' I was astounded. 'That doesn't sound like him.' Alfie had never been a ladies' man as far as I knew. And usually rumours about that sort of thing spread like wildfire around the clubs. Someone would have made sure I knew about his reputation if he'd had one.

'I'm sorry to say it's true. They had an almighty bust-up over it and Izzy ditched both of them. Benny, being a fool, tried to patch things up with her, but she'd moved onto some other guy by then, a theatre manager who'd got her a small part in the next big musical.'

The waiter placed a basket of croissants between us and I helped myself to one, enjoying the pleasure of pulling apart the strands of pastry, the feel of the complex weave of baked dough giving way. There was something very familiar about this story. Was it possible that Alfie had told me his own version years before?

'It sounds to me as though Benny was better off without her,' I said.

'Oh, undoubtedly. He left that theatre, even though they begged him to stay for the next play, and he never looked back. He never saw Alfie again either.'

'This all must have happened thirty years ago. Excuse me if I sound ungrateful – I don't mean to be – but if Benny thinks that he was wronged, why does he need to make amends?'

'I see your point. Maybe there's a part to the story that I've forgotten.' Charlie shrugged and held a lit match to the end of his cigar, taking his time to light it evenly. 'You've taken a real chance getting on this train with me today, I know that. But I promise you, this will all make sense in a few days. By the time you reach New York there'll be no doubt in your mind as to why you're there.'

Of course, if I'd really thought about why the story sounded so familiar, I might have worked out who Charlie Bacon really was. And if I'd managed that, there was no chance that I'd have set foot on the *Queen Mary*. But at the time I had other worries on my mind. Just as I was meant to.

33

Sunday, 6 September
Queen Mary

Charlie stared down at me, surprised, his hands gripping my upper arms as I tried to catch my breath.

'Oh! Thank God, Charlie, something dreadful has happened to Daisy,' I said.

'To Daisy?' His forehead wrinkled with irritation. 'Ah. Damn it, that stupid woman. Come with me, we'd better call someone.'

I followed him along the corridor to his cabin. I was struggling to breathe properly, my lungs diminished and my vision began to close in on me as the panic set in. I could feel my body start to weaken as Charlie took me by the arm, more gently now, and sat me down on the sofa, pushing my head down between my knees.

'Stay there and take deep breaths,' he ordered.

There was a loud buzzing in my ears, my stomach turning over as the weight of my head dragged my body down. I was in big trouble, I knew that. First Jack killed in my cabin, now Daisy. Though maybe she wasn't dead. She had still been breathing. Had I told Charlie that? I could hear his voice, too low to pick out the words as he spoke to someone on the telephone. I heard the click of the receiver as he replaced it.

'A drink?' he suggested.

'Please. A glass of water.' I dared to raise my head, the black spots starting to recede.

There was nothing personal on display in Charlie's cabin. Barely any of his belongings were in sight. A pair of spectacles on the bedside table, which surprised me. There was a scent of something male in the air, the brilliantine he used on his hair, I supposed. He must have packed his belongings, ready to leave the ship bright and early. He poured brown liquid from a decanter on the side and handed me the glass.

'Here. Whisky,' he told me. 'It'll be better for the shock.'

I took it gratefully and sipped, reaching to take a cigarette from the case he held out to me. It was only as he lit it for me that I realised what had changed, my brain sluggish to catch up with what I had been hearing. I looked up and stared at him as he sat down beside me on the sofa.

'Your voice,' I said. 'Your accent. It's changed.'

This man looked like Charlie Bacon. He wore Charlie's suit, had Charlie's thin moustache, but the way he held himself was different. Looser, less formal. He looked smug as he turned to face me.

He smiled. 'It took you a moment to notice, didn't it?' I felt a sharp prod in my side and looked down. He held a gun in his hand. 'I don't want to use this, but I will if I have to.'

'You're English?' English people didn't walk around with guns, did they? My brain struggled to put the pieces together. 'But how?'

'Oh, it's a long story,' he said, but he sounded as though he wanted to tell it. 'You don't know who I am, do you?'

I turned to look at him, very aware of how close the gun was to my waist. 'I... no. Should I?'

He grinned. 'And to think all these years I've been waiting to show what I can do! She never recognised me either, though we only met a few times and it was a long time ago.'

'Who?'

'Eliza.' He was full Cockney now; we might have lived on the same street in Bethnal Green. 'I knew her a little, years back. I mean, she never gave me the time of day, but still, I wasn't sure the moustache and the voice would be enough.'

He'd known Eliza. I tried to work out what that meant, but it was like bobbing for apples, each piece of the puzzle slipping away as I tried to grasp it, until one finally stuck. 'You knew Alfie then?'

'Did I know Alfie?' His laugh was bitter. 'To be fair, you were quite small, the last time you'd have seen me,' he said. 'Five or six maybe. Your father used to drag you out every night, d'you remember? I think he thought people would feel sorry for him. Or sorry for you, whichever.'

'You're from the Royalty.' I looked more carefully at Charlie's face, subtracting twenty years, a different hairstyle, removing the moustache and the beard. 'Oh God. You're that actor. The one who fought Alfie over a girl. Izzy.' The story he'd told me on the train – that was why it had seemed familiar. I had been there, had seen it with my own eyes.

'Isabelle. I thought we were going to get married, me and her. Love at first sight it was.' His gaze was focused twenty years in the past but the pressure of the gun kept up. 'I was going to buy her a ring. I'd already picked it out, you know. But that night, after what happened with Alfie, I lost my temper and – well, I'm not proud of what happened, but she could have given me another chance.' His tone was whining, the voice of a small man who always needs someone else to blame. 'She'd always accused me of not being romantic. What's more romantic than fighting for the woman you love?'

'I'm sorry that things didn't work out,' I said carefully, trying to shift away without him noticing. 'Alfie never kept in touch with Izzy though. Are you sure he was after her? Not just being nice to her because she was nice to me?'

'You were too young to understand what went on,' Charlie told me. 'He was a charmer, Alfie, I'd seen it before. He did it with Eliza. A spoiled rich cow like her, and he got her to give it all up for him, even if it didn't last. She used to turn up everywhere, looking for him. That's how I came to meet her. She came to an opening night and got drunk on two glasses of gin. He wanted rid of her but she said she could change his life. So he stuck it out and ended up saddled with you and no money.' He laughed. 'Served him right, except that then any woman in sight wanted him. *Poor Alfie!* Izzy used to say. *That poor motherless child.* I should have known what was going on.'

'Maybe she did just feel sorry for us. It is possible. It doesn't mean she didn't love you.' She'd had a lucky escape.

'Well, perhaps, but it's far too late for that now. I was a bit drunk. Bit handy with my fists. I wanted to teach her a lesson, that's all, but she left me. She was a diamond, you know? Things could have been different if I'd married her. Instead she went running to your father – and do you know what he did? To me, who was meant to be his mate? Came round and helped her pack up her stuff. Put her on the next train back to her family in Bridlington. She never would've dared leave me if it had been left up to her.'

'But you did hit her,' I said, careful to keep my tone light. If Alfie had put Izzy on a train out of London, then he must have thought that Charlie was dangerous. Come to think of it, it had been around that time that we'd left Soho and gone to Bethnal Green. 'Charlie, what's this all about? What's this got to do with Francis Parker, or Jack. And poor Daisy.'

'Daisy'll be fine,' he said casually. 'You know what they say. Revenge is a dish best served cold and all that.'

'This is revenge then, is it?' The more he talked, the less sense he made. Alfie was dead and had been for months. Why wait all these years and then come after me? 'This is ridiculous! I barely know who you are. Is Charlie even your real name?'

'Charles Walker,' he admitted. 'Bacon was – well, it was just a little joke. Since he was supposed to be an ex-copper. She didn't get it, of course, but Yanks don't have a sense of humour like the English.'

She? He'd let the pronoun slip without noticing. Who? There was no Benny Walker then, I realised. No wonder Will had never heard of him. It had been Charlie all along, and someone else. A woman?

'Was it her idea to do the chocolates?' My mind was running through the possibilities. Daisy? Could she have been faking? Danny had said that Eliza sent the chocolates. 'What's in them anyway?'

Charlie checked his watch, ignoring my questions. 'Hold your horses, she'll be here in a minute. It makes more sense the way she explains it.'

There was a knock on the door, almost perfectly timed, as though the person had been listening in, waiting for their cue. If the gun digging into my ribs hadn't felt very real, I'd have thought I were in some third-rate murder mystery play, the sort that tours the provinces.

'Why don't you go and let her in.' Charlie smiled and moved the gun to his other side, away from me.

I'd thought I'd regained some composure but when I stood, my legs turned to jelly and I stumbled as I crossed the carpet. I opened the door though, and there she was. The last person I'd have thought of.

Carrie Abernathy.

34

Sunday, 6 September
Queen Mary

She stood there in her navy knee-length dress, a barrette holding her hair back. Fresh-faced and fifteen. I took a step away, dumbfounded, and she strode into the room, a brown leather-bound book under her arm, as though she was on her way to a school lesson. Charlie moved up to make room for her and proffered his cigarette case. To my surprise, she took one and accepted his light, inhaling deeply as though she'd been smoking all her life.

'Sorry. It took longer than expected,' she said to Charlie, before turning to address me. 'I don't know if you know this, Lena, but dear Mama has built up quite the resistance to her sleeping draughts over the years. I added a large dash of veronal to her brandy at dinner but I had to talk her into taking more of her own accord, all without her realising that Frankie was already passed out.' She sighed, wearily. 'Don't look at me like that! I need to make sure they don't disturb us. Come and sit down, won't you.'

I glanced at the open door. Three steps and I'd be in the corridor, free to scream out.

'Don't do anything silly, Lena, Charlie's got a gun, remember? He can shoot you before you make a sound – and don't think I haven't a cover story prepared. Sit down. There's a lot for us to talk about and you look as though you're about to pass out.' Carrie pointed to the chair where I was to sit.

'Is Daisy all right? What did you do to her?' I didn't move but I did close the door. I didn't necessarily believe that Charlie would actually shoot me down, but I did believe that Carrie would be able to fool anyone. If it came to my word against hers, I had no chance anyway.

She glanced at Charlie and laughed. 'Don't worry, I didn't want to kill you, Lena. You were supposed to drink the brandy after dinner and then you'd be fast asleep like the others. Unfortunately, you turned down a drink for once and I had to inject the solution into the chocolates. Daisy will be fine.' She pulled a face. 'Though honestly, I can't stand the woman. She sticks her nose in anywhere she'd not wanted. Why do you think I framed her for the swimming pool attack?'

On top of everything else it shouldn't have been any surprise. Carrie had been the only witness. Easy enough to wait until the pool attendant had moved out of sight before sneaking to the changing boxes. Anyone who'd ever met Daisy would have recognised her garb from the description Carrie had given of my so-called attacker.

'She's alive then? You promise?'

'Yes! Now come and sit down.' She blew smoke out in a fast stream, irritated.

'And what about Dr Wilding?'

Carrie shrugged. 'Now that's a mystery that I cannot unravel, I'm afraid. I was hoping you might know where he's run off to.'

I shook my head. 'No, I— So you had nothing to do with his disappearance?' Slowly I walked closer to them, sitting on the edge of the armchair the furthest from the pair of them.

'Not me.' She glanced at Charlie, who shook his head. 'Then I suppose the good doctor has made a run for it. Perhaps Daddy's death was the final straw.'

'Or he knew who had done it,' I pointed out.

'I doubt that very much.' Her voice was brittle, like ice. 'I've known Dick Wilding for years and he never thought me any more than a silly little girl. If it hadn't been for you, I'd have picked him as my scapegoat.'

'What's going on?' I tried to fight off the fear that threatened to paralyse me. I had to keep my wits about me. 'Please, can we just get this over and done with?' I glanced down at my watch. Far too early for Will to come looking. I was on my own.

'You're looking at me as though I'm crazy but I'm not, trust me.' Carrie stubbed out her cigarette and gave me her full attention. 'It's not as bad as you think. Poor Grandpa was miserable. He told me himself. I saved him from months of suffering. A kindness. And Daddy was a scandal waiting to happen. I told you about my so-called half-brother whom Daddy already moved into the firm. Well, from what I hear there are at least two more. As soon as we get back to New York they'll be on the doorstep with their caps held out, but they won't get a penny.'

'You killed him to make sure you got to keep your fortune?' She was so nonchalant about the killing of her own flesh and blood, as if it was a game, a child's experiment with deadly consequences.

She looked at Charlie as if this were all one big joke, and he gave her a lopsided smile. 'Lena, don't you get it? I know who you are. The sister I was never supposed to know about. The bastard half-breed. That's what Grandpa referred to you as, by the way, in case you were still feeling sorry for him. But he was fine with Daddy's mistakes littering the company he built. I call that double standards, I don't know about you.'

'He told you about me?' It seemed unlikely.

'Of course not, I found some papers. When Grandpa got sick I carried on visiting him every weekend. Daisy used that time to go out, so it would be me and him alone in the apartment, same as before, only he slept a lot more. To keep from getting bored, I decided to go through his old papers.' Carrie had a twinkle in her eye. 'He kept all his correspondence, you know, including the begging letters Mama sent him when she was stuck in a London hovel, about to give birth to you. She'd included a forwarding address, which came in very handy when I was trying to find you, except that I found Charlie first.'

'I was working in the pub where I used to go drinking with Alfie,' Charlie told me. 'You and him lived in a flat above the bakery next door at the time. Used to be I'd pick up a few shifts on and off between jobs, but it's become more of an occupation than the acting over the years, thanks to your father. Can you imagine Basil Rathbone or Claude Rains pulling pints in some backstreet boozer?'

I shook my head, realising how unhinged Charlie actually was. How he could think that Alfie had any sort of power to end his acting career was beyond me. Alfie had never even mentioned Charlie, and yet Charlie had clearly never forgotten him. The bogey man who had become a symbol of everything wrong with his life, even those things he had caused himself.

'I thought I'd got over it all,' he said, his voice growing quiet, brittle. 'But as soon as this girl came in, asking if anyone had heard of Alfie Aldridge, well…'

'I thought he was going to jump over the bar and hit me!' Carrie's laugh was high-pitched, and I wondered if she was actually a little scared of Charlie. 'But I got him to calm down and then it turned out that he knew who you were.'

'The two of you cooked up this insane plot together? Two lots of revenge for the price of one?'

'Not entirely, but Charlie did give me the idea, didn't you?' Carrie patted her accomplice on the knee and he sat up taller, looking pleased with himself. 'He really hated your father, you know. He just didn't know what to do with all that anger until I came along.' She reached for another cigarette and leaned into the flame from Charlie's lighter.

'All I wanted was to study photography, but Daddy said that college was a waste of time and money for a girl. Nothing to do with me, or what I can do. I can take a good photograph, but I want to take brilliant photos. I want my pictures to hang on the wall of a gallery someday.' I could see the fierce ambition burning, her hand shaking slightly as she raised the cigarette to her mouth. 'Grandpa was the one who told me to do whatever it took. Or, no, actually, what he said was that it was the difference between men and women. That a man would do whatever it took to get ahead, while a woman would always cave. She'd always take the easy option, not because she was lazy but because she was weak.'

'I doubt he expected his own death to be the result,' I said. Was this what happened when you grew up in the shadow of Francis Parker, learning to value ruthlessness and money in equal part? She wasn't irrational like Charlie, blaming his life's failures on the outcome of one night. She was coolly logical, which gave me hope. Carrie had no bone to pick with me. Did she really want another death on her conscience?

'You've gone quite pale, Lena.' She actually looked concerned. 'Everything's going to be all right though, I promise you. Shall we all have a drink to settle our nerves?' She took up my empty glass and looked over to the sideboard where the decanter of whisky still sat. 'Oh, there are only two glasses. Charlie.' She gave him a hard nudge in the ribs. 'Charlie! We need another glass.'

'I can drink out of my tooth mug.' Charlie handed the gun to Carrie and disappeared into the bathroom. She produced a small bottle from her skirt pocket and went over to the sideboard.

She turned to me and winked, holding her finger to her lips. I watched her as she began to pour whisky, taking the mug from Charlie as he returned. As soon as his back was turned, walking back to take his seat, I saw her pour a clear liquid from the bottle into the mug before swirling it into the whisky.

Chivalry dictated that Charlie of course took the mug while Carrie and I drank from the crystal tumblers. Our eyes met and I waited for her to drink first before I took a sip from my own glass.

'What happens now?' I asked, watching Charlie knock his whisky back in one, wincing as he stared into the mug.

'Drink up,' Carrie told me.

'Mustn't have rinsed it out properly,' Charlie muttered, walking over to the decanter to top himself up.

'I always wanted a sister,' Carrie told me quietly as Charlie sat down. 'Didn't you?'

'I never really thought about it.' I couldn't bear to look at Charlie and yet it was a battle to force my eyes away from him. And she was so calm, like it was nothing, sitting there chatting and waiting for him to fall unconscious.

'Lena, maybe you should get some water. You've gone awfully pale. It's a lot to take in, after all. We're in no rush,' she said.

I followed her instructions as if I were a marionette and she the puppeteer, my legs not my own. I ran the cold tap fast and emptied the whisky down the sink, trying to fill the glass but my hands trembled so much that I dropped it, smashing it into two clean pieces.

'Everything all right?' Carrie called.

'Yes. Sorry. A little accident.' My legs gave way suddenly, my knees smacking against the cold floor tiles, and I hung on to the basin for dear life, blood dripping from a cut on my palm where the glass had sliced me.

Will would be up in the Starlight Club, finishing his last performance before New York. Was he thinking of me or was his mind lost in the music? He wouldn't notice me missing for another hour, and by then it would be too late. Would I ever see him again? This fickle child – my half-sister – held my future in her hands. It was tempting to take one of the glass shards, a makeshift weapon, but I knew it would be a mistake. Carrie had prepared for every eventuality so far; she would know how to shoot the gun.

Slowly I walked back into the room. Charlie's head had fallen back, his mouth open, eyes half shut. He groaned gently, stirring as he fell into a chemically induced slumber.

'You'll want to know what comes next,' Carrie said, getting to her feet. She poured more whisky into her glass. 'Well, let me ask you. What would you like to happen?'

'I'd like to go home,' I said, my voice breaking as my eyes welled up. I sat back down.

'That's it?' She looked surprised. Disappointed. 'Home? To London?' I nodded. 'But you've got nowhere to live. No job to go back to. No money.'

'I can stay with a friend.'

'With Maggie, is that her name?' She leaned against the arm of the sofa opposite me, only two feet away from me, the gun held lightly in her hand, though I didn't doubt she could shoot me if she had to. 'Even though she killed her own husband?'

'How do you...?' My jaw dropped, but of course it made sense. That was why Francis Parker and Tommy Scarsdale had died the same way.

'Charlie and I came up with that part together. His cousin's a policeman. Well, you met him.' She meant Hargreaves, I realised with a shock. 'Charlie thought you'd snatch his hand off as soon as he mentioned Broadway to you, but I knew you weren't that stupid. I was afraid that the offer sounded too good to be true, though we'd taken the precaution of not being specific about the role or the theatre, in case you mentioned it to someone in the business who knew better. I worried that once you told Maggie, she'd convince you to get the job checked out with her lawyers. Better if she were distracted. Even more so if

you knew what she'd done. The added bonus was that I got to
make sure that the cyanide actually worked. I read about it in
a book and I'm never entirely sure whether these novelists do
all the research they're supposed to.'

'But how— What if Maggie had refused?'

She smiled wryly. 'Between you and me, Charlie's cousin
was keen to get rid of Tommy and he had quite the eye for your
friend as well. I think he enjoyed spending time with Maggie.
From what I could see, the feeling was mutual.'

'She was drunk,' I said firmly. 'He took advantage of her
when she was in a bad way.'

'Maybe.' Carrie looked sorry for me, but in the way that a cat
regrets the last swipe that kills its prey when it was enjoying
the game so much.

'I still don't understand,' I said. 'Why are you telling me all
this? Why not just kill me, if that's your plan?'

'Killing you was never the plan.' Carrie's face changed then,
back to the girl I had known over the past four days. 'You were
going to be my scapegoat. The big family secret. You killed
Grandpa because he left you to grow up in poverty. Mama
wanted to send you money, she begged in her letters for it, but
he said you'd never get a cent. And poor Daddy, well, if he'd
only learned to keep it in his pants, then he'd still be alive. A lot
of people would have felt sympathy for you, Lena. I'd have got
you the best lawyer. An insanity defence gets you a nice stay
in a hospital, no need to even go to jail.'

'You sent Jack to my cabin?' How had a slip of a girl like her
known what he was capable of?

'I made sure that Daisy would come and save you. He does

it all the time. My nanny when I was a kid. That was the first time I caught him at it. This summer alone he had Daisy, a maid at our hotel in Berlin, some woman he picked up from the casino in Monte Carlo...' She leaned forward, handing me her whisky glass, and I took it without thinking.

'When I came up with all this, I'd never met you. The first time I even set eyes on you was the night that Tommy Scarsdale died, and you looked so – well, so beautiful up there on that stage. But so cold. Like you didn't really want to be there. Like Mama.'

I lifted the glass, chucking the whisky back in one go. 'Oh God!' I put my fingers to my lips, giving a start when my hand came away bloodstained, forgetting that I had cut it on the glass.

'It's fine, it's fine, it's fine.' In a trice, Carrie was beside me, her arms wrapped around me as I tried not to let the panic overcome me. She smelled of verbena and cigarettes. 'It's only whisky, I promise, Lena.' I felt her lips brush my forehead. 'You're safe. I promise, you're safe. It's going to be all right.'

'But how? How is it? How can it possibly be?' Her face was misty through my tears as she slid to the floor at my knee. 'Carrie, what have you done?'

'Only what needed to be done.' She took my hands in hers. 'I always wanted a sister and now I have one. I'm not going to hurt you. I won't let anyone hurt you.'

'Then how does this all end?' I wiped my face with the hand that wasn't bloody.

'Men seem to be able to get away with anything.' She glanced at Charlie and smiled. 'Except maybe for murder. I can't save you both, and Charlie knows too much.'

'No,' I said firmly. 'There's been too much death. You can't kill Charlie as well.'

'I have to.' She said it so matter-of-factly, drawing yet another logical conclusion, in her own mind at least. 'Lena, he wouldn't give up on his revenge. He hates you too much, and even I don't understand why.'

I stared at his unconscious body, sleeping peacefully as his fate was sealed. 'I didn't do anything to him. I barely remember him.'

'And yet he thinks you ruined his life, you and your father.' She patted my hand and eased to her feet. 'Time's up. All you have to do is walk away and I'll deal with the rest.'

I watched Charlie's chest rise and fall, his mouth slightly open as he slept on. I could save him, but he would punish me for it.

'It's him or you,' Carrie reminded me.

I nodded and got to my feet. I killed a man when I left Charlie Bacon alone with Carrie, as surely as if I'd held the gun in my own hand. And I don't pretend that it was the right thing to do but I'd do it again. He'd left me no choice.

To whomever reads this, please know
that I am sorry. I have done a terrible thing
and I must pay for my sins.
Charles Walker

35

Monday, 7 September
Queen Mary

Will was checking his watch as I walked briskly towards the
Pig and Whistle.

''Bout time,' he said, but he was grinning. 'I was ready to
get worried about you.'

'It's barely midnight!' I'd made it just in time, allowing
for a stop in the ladies' on the way to wash the blood from my
hands. It had felt more than a little symbolic. I was grateful
that the cut had stopped bleeding, but I tied my handkerchief
around it. If Will asked, then I could say that I'd been clumsy
and broken a glass. Not even a lie.

He bent and kissed me, prompting a round of whistles from
the men playing darts behind us. Will ignored them and took
my arm, walking us into the bar. 'Beer?'

'Please.' I wanted to wash away the taste of the whisky, forget
all about the last couple of hours. Already they felt dreamlike,
nightmarish. Lack of sleep had produced a haze over my memory
that allowed me to wonder if it had been real. Carrie's plotting,

Charlie's slow-burning revenge. If I tried to explain it to Will, would he even believe me?

Will left me with the band, who were playing dominoes in the corner, then ran off to get drinks. From the sly smiles of the men I could tell they knew that things had changed. I didn't mind that everyone knew about me and Will. Of everything I'd done in the past weeks, this was one thing I wasn't ashamed of.

'You gonna stay up until we get to New York?' Deon asked. 'We're only a few hours away now.'

'Won't it still be dark?'

'That don't matter. You'll get to see the city lights and the Statue of Liberty. If it's not too cold you can stay out and see the sun come up. Once in a lifetime view. And I should know – I seen it at least twenty times!'

'Well, when you put it like that...' I found myself agreeing easily, my close encounter with death leaving me eager to appreciate every opportunity.

When we disembarked, I would go to the Sherry-Netherland Hotel as planned. I could use the money in my carpetbag to pay for a room for a few nights. Afterwards, I'd go to a travel agency and arrange my passage back to Southampton as soon as possible. Third class if need be. I wanted to be home in London, home with Maggie and Cecil the dog. With my real family.

'Penny for 'em?' Will handed me a bottle of beer.

'I was thinking that I'd finally got my sea legs, just in time to arrive back on dry land,' I said. 'I sort of like the swaying now. I never even considered working on a ship before, but now I don't think it'd be so bad. You like it well enough.'

Will smiled gently. 'Life on this ship ain't real. You know that, right?'

'You think so?' I knew what he was about to say. That it had been fun, but it was time to say goodbye. 'It feels very real.'

The rest of the band had subtly drifted away, to dance or to join the darts match out in the corridor. We were alone and I couldn't catch my breath.

'Lena, this life is limbo. A day or two in port either end, then back on the ship, shuttling to and fro across the ocean. Every day is the same, pretty much, over and over, and I can't afford to take time off. This is my band. I lead them and I love them like brothers. This life isn't for you.'

I took his hand and swallowed down the tears. 'Maybe there's an even better life waiting for you somewhere, only you haven't been looking for it.'

'Lena, I'm sorry. I never meant for this to happen.' He looked distraught as he wiped the salt tracks from my cheeks. He shook his head. 'Can we enjoy our last few hours together? And, I don't know, maybe we can see each other in New York. Have one night out where I show you a good time?'

I nodded and tried to smile, not trusting my voice. I wanted to tell him that Broadway was off, that I was going back to England, but I couldn't. If we weren't going to see each other again, what did it matter? He was right, I had to forget about us having a future and enjoy these last moments before we docked in Manhattan and were immersed in reality once more.

Will dragged me up to dance and I threw myself into the music. Sweat poured off me but I didn't care. It was so good to laugh and to feel Will's hands on my waist, to see him smile and to know that, whatever happened next, I wasn't going back to live as miserably as I had before. I would take one piece of advice from Carrie: I would make a plan. I'd been drifting through life for too long. With no husband or children to tie me down, I was free to do whatever I wanted. It was time to take advantage of that freedom.

Sometime later a shout went up: New York was in sight. Singing and laughing, we formed a procession up into the passenger quarters, no one caring any longer who had paid for cabin and on which deck. We were all one by the time we reached the sun deck. A light breeze was blowing, a welcome relief, and the skies above us were still pitch black.

Had it really been less than five days since I'd first walked up here, that small brown bottle gripped in my sweating palm? During this short voyage I had found and lost a family, gained my independence. I felt hope for the first time since Alfie's illness had consumed him. That was quite something. All this death and now, having survived, I felt more alive than I had in months.

Will pushed through the crowd, pulling me after him, until we reached the railing. He stood behind me and I gripped the rough wood, peering out into darkness.

'I can't see anything,' I complained.

'Have a bit of patience,' he laughed. 'Hey, wait there. I need to go get something.'

He melted into the throng and I was so intent on catching my first sight of the city ahead of us that I almost missed the man to my left. I wouldn't have noticed him at all if he hadn't coughed. A single sound that caught my attention with its familiarity. A glance in that direction hooked on the neatly manicured fingers, then up to the sheepish expression on the face of Dr Richard Wilding.

'Hello, Miss Aldridge,' he said, smiling shyly.

'Dr Wilding! You're alive?' I was as shocked as he when I threw my arms around him, tears falling onto his shoulder. 'Oh God, I'm so sorry!'

'What a surprising greeting,' he laughed nervously. The good doctor didn't present his usual picture of tweedy respectability. Despite the night air, his forehead shone with sweat and his jacket was missing, his shirt sleeves rolled up to his elbows.

'Didn't you hear? Jack Abernathy was murdered! You went missing and we all thought something terrible had happened to you as well.' I wiped my eyes with my hands. 'I thought you were dead.'

'I'm so sorry, Lena, I honestly didn't think anyone would notice me gone. I did hear about Mr Abernathy. I've been staying down in the infirmary,' Wilding told me. 'I had a few... problems. Problems that I thought it was best to try and fix before facing the police. The chief officer knew where I was, but he agreed to keep it quiet.' His hands were shaking, I noticed. His bare forearms were bruised and marked. The syringe in his cabin drawer, the empty morphine vials in the wastepaper basket, it all added up.

'How do you feel now?' I asked.

He laughed. 'Damned awful, but better than yesterday. I lost track of time and came out here to be alone and get some fresh air. I didn't expect half the ship to join me.'

'No. Well, I'm glad to see that you're all right.' I patted his hand, meaning every word.

He managed a smile and moved away, his head down as he pushed through the growing crowd. Just as I lost sight of him, Will reappeared, a wide grin on his face and a bottle of champagne in his hand.

'A tip from a passenger. I figure this is as good a time as any to crack it open.' He popped the cork with ease and passed the bottle to me. 'No glasses though, I'm afraid.'

I took a swig and tried not to sneeze when the bubbles went up my nose. 'I reckon it tastes better this way.'

'Me too.' He took a swig himself, his other arm passing around my waist, and I leaned back in his arms.

'I was thinking,' I told him, 'that I might try and find out if any of my father's relatives are still around. You know where might be a good place to start?'

He was silent for a moment, thinking. 'I reckon I could help you out with that.'

The city lights began to appear in the distance, like stars twinkling through the clouds as we moved ever closer to land. A silhouette made itself known, her torch held high, her grand form emerging from the gloom as dawn began to break above.

Lady Liberty.

They were laughing when I saw them, so easy together, as though none of them had a single care in the world. Wilding walked away and left Lena with her beau. He's handsome, I suppose, for a coloured. It's odd the way she rejects all sense. Anyone who knew no better would think she was one of us except for the company she keeps. Still, the ship is its own world, with its own rules. She'll learn quickly in New York, I'm sure of it. Just look how quickly she learned to walk away. She put herself first and now Charles Walker is dead. Well, he deserved it.

I thought it would feel different. I'm writing this as we prepare to disembark. I can hear noise from the port, the hustle and bustle as porters charge up and down the corridors and stewards ferry breakfast to those who want to eat before we leave the ship. In the chaos, at some point, Charlie's body will be found. I wonder how long it will take for them to come and tell us. I hope we're at home when it happens. Mama is fragile already. I'd hate for us to get stuck on the ship for hours while they go through his belongings, though there's plenty there to help them figure out his guilt. A small glass bottle containing cyanide. The passport in his real name. The suicide note that took me no time to perfect, his handwriting so lacking in distinction. Daddy's monogrammed handkerchief, soaked in his own blood. The Bible from the bedside table, bookmarked with one of Grandpa's bearer bonds (my own little addition). An unsent letter that Charlie was foolish enough to write to his cousin back in London.

Will Mama ever tell me the truth about Lena? I don't know. What is certain is that Frankie will hit the roof if he ever finds out. He liked staring at Lena well enough, but he wasn't smart enough to see the truth. He's just like Daddy in that regard, seeing only what he wants to see. Taking the easy option instead of owning some integrity. No, I think that I will need to keep Lena a secret for now. I like the sound of that. A secret between sisters.

Isn't It a Lovely Day?

36

Park Avenue, New York

Standing up on the roof was magical, the whole world laid out before me. How incredible that I could be up on the eighteenth floor and not have my head in the clouds. Below me the tiny figures of New Yorkers scuttled along the avenue like tin soldiers propelled by an invisible hand, the cars like children's toys. The sounds of car horns and engines floated up around me from the street and I could smell the earthy scent of the chrysanthemums that bloomed in pots all around the terrace, a garden in the sky.

New York seen from above was like a toy city, something from the Hamley's shop window on Regent Street. Skyscrapers were growing up all around where I stood, like Meccano models, their height dizzying to look at. At street level the city had the vibrancy of London, but when you looked up you saw the dreams that people arrived here with. A literal representation of reaching for the stars. A promise of opportunity, though I saw the poverty too, the failure and the hangover from the Depression. One man's dream could mean a nightmare for someone else.

Hadn't Francis Parker built his empire at the expense of so many others?

'Lena!' I turned to see Carrie joining me on the roof terrace, a glass in each hand. 'Won't you have a drink with me?'

I took one of the glasses, the aroma of gin unmistakable, but I didn't drink. 'What's going on? I got a message from Eliza asking me to come here for five o'clock, but the maid showed me out here half an hour ago. Where is everyone?'

We were at Francis Parker's apartment, Daisy now the only resident, though I'd not seen her since the ship, woozy as she came round from the sleeping draught, embarrassed that she'd fallen asleep in my cabin and none the wiser as to what had actually befallen her. Walking through the apartment to reach the terrace, the rooms felt more like a museum than a home. The paintings on the wall looked priceless and the furniture appeared straight out of a stately home, polished wood that gleamed, cushions that had not a fray, as though nobody ever sat anywhere or touched anything. It was a strange place to meet, but I'd assumed that Eliza considered it neutral territory.

'No one else is coming,' Carrie told me, and I detected a twinge of nerves in her voice. She'd lost the confidence she'd displayed so brazenly on our last night on the ship. 'I wanted to see you, that's all. I'm sorry, it was me who rang your hotel, not Mama. I hoped that she would be up to it, but she's not been doing well since – well, you know how it is.'

Eliza. I'd hoped to at least say goodbye; it was the main reason I'd turned up at the apartment. To leave things on a brighter note, if such a thing were possible.

On our arrival in New York our party had been gathered in

the Abernathys' cabin once more. When Charlie hadn't shown up, the chief officer had used the master key to access his cabin, getting the shock of his life when he found the man lying dead on his bed, an apparently self-inflicted gunshot wound to his head and a suicide note by his side. Carrie had used a pillow to muffle the bang of the gun, holding Charlie's limp hand to the trigger so that no one would think twice. She made murder look easy, a thought that made me feel more than a little queasy now that I knew we were alone in the apartment.

I still felt numb about Charlie's death. If it were up to him, I'd have gone down for murder. Carrie had talked about a psychiatric hospital, but the alternative scenario saw me sent to the electric chair that they used to carry out the death penalty in New York. Though the thought made me shudder, I couldn't help but feel sorry for him. Without Carrie's influence, he would have never given me a second thought. We'd probably crossed paths before in Soho without me realising. So many years had gone by and yet he'd never been able to get over the hurt that he believed Alfie had caused him. He'd let himself be sucked into Carrie's tempest of vengeance.

'How did you do it?' I asked her. 'I mean, how did you convince the police that he was responsible for all those deaths? Are you sure they don't think I'm involved?'

'I can't tell you all my little secrets,' she said with a smile, 'but don't worry. I've made sure that no one will ever doubt poor Charlie's guilt.'

'He knew what you were capable of and yet he never suspected he was in danger.' I had to marvel at her audacity. At his stupidity. Was I making the same mistake? I moved away from the railing, frighteningly aware of how high up we were, and sat down at the small iron-wrought table, putting down my untouched drink. Maybe it was the altitude making me dizzy. 'Did he really hate me so much?'

'I doubt it, though he really did have a bee in his bonnet about your father. He was an opportunist. My grandfather had a whole stack of bearer bonds stashed away in his safe. He told me the combination after he got ill. He didn't want Daisy to get her hands on them and he thought he could trust me. I figured that no one else knew about them and he'd be dead before he knew they were missing. I promised Charlie five thousand pounds to get him onto the ship and the same again if it all went to plan.' She sparked a gold lighter and lit a cigarette as she took a seat. 'He didn't want you to know about the money, he thought it made him sound mercenary. Revenge is more romantic.'

'That's one way of putting it,' I muttered.

'It really was a stroke of luck, running into him in that pub. At first all I wanted was to find you. I'd disguised myself, you see. Wig and a lot of make-up. He thought I was a lot older, so he said, so he served me a drink and then we got talking. I didn't tell him that you were my sister, not right away. I think he thought his luck was in, but I wasn't that desperate to get him on my side. When he told me that Alfie had crossed him, I knew he was perfect for my cause.'

'So strange.' I shook my head. 'Honestly, I don't believe Alfie had seen him in years.'

'I don't really understand it myself, but I figure Alfie became a symbol of his failure. Not the real Alfie, some made-up version in Charlie's head. He couldn't take responsibility for it himself, so it had to be Alfie's fault. Why no theatre would touch him – nothing to do with him turning up drunk several times and missing his lines. Why he never married – couldn't have been 'cause he liked to hit his women. I hate to tell you, but he was a regular at the Canary. Had been ever since he realised you sang there.'

How had I never noticed him? But then, I'd never noticed any of the punters at the Canary. I just sang my songs and got off again. I'd lost my love for performance until I'd stood on that stage with Will a few days before.

'Anyway, I suppose you could call it kismet. Either one of us on our own probably wouldn't have done a thing. Even then it was nothing more than a crazy idea. The sort of thing you read in those cheap novels you love so much.' She smiled at me fondly. 'The way we saw it, none of the people who got hurt were innocent. They'd all hurt others. Well, apart from you, but Charlie didn't see it that way.'

'And killing Tommy? What had he done to either of you?'

'Tommy had crossed some very wrong people, you know. It suited Hargreaves to get Maggie to do his dirty work and keep his own hands clean. He didn't even ask for money, or any help. I gave him the poison to make it easier for Maggie. They say it's a woman's weapon.'

I could sense her taking a step back from her actions, as though Charlie and his cousin were the guilty parties rather than victims of her manipulations. Bad men, you might say. She wouldn't have done it if not for them. But she had been the snake, whispering in their ears. Giving them ideas. She had poured poison into her grandfather's medicine bottle, stabbed her father and shot her accomplice in the head, all in cold blood.

'Can you at least promise me that Maggie's safe?' I asked. 'That Hargreaves will leave her alone.'

Carrie smiled. 'He'll keep his mouth shut. I took pictures of him meeting Charlie at the Savoy, taking money from him the day after Tommy's murder. I've posted him copies. He says one word and he'll end up in prison for a heck of a long time. Send me a message if you need me to step in. And if it comes down to it, I've plenty of cyanide left.' Her grin broadened. 'It's in the dark room in our London house. Totally innocent in the right setting.' She took hold of my hand and squeezed it, smiling. 'I always wanted a sister. I know you don't feel the same right now, but I hope that one day you'll understand. I never wanted to hurt you.'

'You hit me over the head with a metal pole,' I reminded her, pulling my hand away gently. 'And you've admitted that you wanted me to go down for your murders, so forgive me if I don't believe you.'

She nodded but looked disappointed. 'I get it, Lena, I really do. I deserve it. But won't you reconsider? I'd love for us to spend some time together. I can help you to find a place to live, somewhere decent and close to us, and Mama might come around in a few weeks. She doesn't know that I know about you, but I swear she looks as though she's about to spit it out. Especially with Frankie being so obnoxious.'

'I'm going back to England,' I told her. I was glad that I'd checked out of the Sherry-Netherland earlier that day, storing the bulk of my luggage with them until my sailing to Southampton in two weeks' time, the next available crossing on the *Queen Mary*. 'I need to go and help Maggie.' I held up my hand to silence her as she opened her mouth to argue. 'I don't want anything from you or from Eliza. I've managed without your money for twenty-six years. I think I'll be all right.' I got up from the table. 'Take care of yourself, Carrie.'

I walked away without waiting for a reaction, the maid wordlessly calling the elevator to collect me. Right up until the moment that the operator shut the gate, I was expecting Carrie to come chasing after me. She'd got everything else that she'd wanted, so why let me slip out of her hands? I admit it – I was disappointed. She had committed multiple murders and yet I couldn't see her as evil. She was the result of an upbringing where everything was available, nothing denied, unless you were female. Eliza had paid a heavy price for her own youthful rebellion and I saw how her tragedy had infected her daughter, just as Jack's behaviour had influenced his son. The entire family had been corrupted by Francis Parker's overwhelming desire to control everyone around him.

Why am I so quick to defend her? Is there is a stronger connection there that I can't bear to admit to? The old 'blood is thicker than water' cliché? Perhaps that knowledge has influenced me in a small way. But more than that, I know that not a soul would believe me if I decided to tell the truth. I cannot prove my bloodline and I don't for one second think that Eliza would choose me over Carrie. In protecting Carrie, I protect myself. It might not be the noble answer, but at least I am honest.

★

When I reached the lobby, I picked up my carpetbag from the doorman and asked him how to get to the Harlem address that Will had given me. He stared at me as if I had two heads. 'You know the taxi cabs don't always want to head up that way.'

'That's fine,' I said. 'My friend told me I can take a train.'

'Your friend, huh,' he said, shaking his head as he wrote down the directions of which subway train to take. 'You take care, miss.'

I smiled at the idea that I couldn't look after myself and swung out into the early evening sunshine, a weight lifted from my shoulders. I was free of worry for the first time in weeks, even though I had nothing. No money but what was in my bag, no job, no place to live, not even a hotel room, but I'd get by.

Will had a friend up in Harlem, a librarian and writer who, along with her doctor husband, had a spare room they were happy for me to stay in. I had two weeks to trace any remaining relatives that Alfie had left behind when he'd departed for England thirty years before. My expectations were low, but I was looking forward to walking the same streets that my father had. This would be my last evening with Will before he had to sail back to England, but in a fortnight's time I'd be making that journey with him. Even if there was no chance of a future for me and Will, at least we could make each other happy for those few days. After everything, that felt like enough.

Acknowledgements

Several drafts of this novel were written during a global pandemic – thank you to all my friends and family who helped me to keep it together through this difficult time for us all. Huge thanks also to the NHS workers, who have worked tirelessly to keep as many of us safe as possible.

This novel exists thanks to my incredible agent Nelle Andrew, who convinced me that a very vague idea about a jazz singer, several murders – maybe on a ship? - was worth pursuing. You are such a brilliant champion and I'm grateful to have you on my team.

Thank you to the whole of Team HQ in the UK for your support over the past few years. In particular, I'd like to thank my editor extraordinaire Manpreet Grewal for believing in Lena and this book from the start. Also, Lisa Milton, Melanie Hayes, Joe Thomas, Georgina Green, Harriet Williams, Vicki Watson, Darren Shoffren, Angela Thomson, Sara Eusebi, Kate Oakley, Grace Dent, Angie Dobbs, Halema Begum and Tom Keane.

Thank you to Amanda Bergeron, Sareer Khader and the team

at Berkley for having such a wonderful vision for Lena. Your input has made this a far better book and I'm excited to set off on this journey with you.

This novel, like the last, began as a short story on the MA Creative Writing at Birkbeck. Thank you to Russell Celyn Jones and Jonathan Kemp for the constructive feedback. Thanks also to Julia Bell and Toby Litt. As ever, the Birkbeck #supergroup input has been invaluable – special thanks to Lou Kramskoy, Ruth Ivo and Karen Clarke in particular.

Shoutout to the D20 authors who have been such a support throughout the pandemic – launching our debut novels into closed bookshops has been mentally challenging. Without our Friday Zoom catch ups, I don't know where I'd be! The Wednesday Writers have been a weekly source of support. Thanks also to my fellow HQ authors Nadine Matheson, Luan Goldie, Kia Abdullah, Helen Monks Takhar and Anita Frank.

It's not been easy for any of us but the last couple of years would have been so much harder without my friends. Special thanks to Harriet Tyce, Josh Salter, Graham Hurt, Kat Liutai, Nikki Metcalfe-Dermott and Jane Dumble – for the support bubbles, dog walks, wine and gossip.

And last but not least – Mum, Dad, Rob and Tula (and not forgetting Maud and Pippa) – thanks for the quizzing and the Saturday night chats.

**Turn the page for an exclusive extract
from Louise Hare's atmospheric
and compelling debut, as seen on
BBC Two *Between the Covers***

Available to buy now

1

The basement club spat Lawrie out into the dirty maze of Soho, a freezing mist settling over him like a damp jacket. He shivered and tightened his grip on the clarinet case in his right hand. He'd best hurry on home before the fog thickened into a 'pea-souper', as they called it round here. The hour was later than he'd have liked; the club had been packed and the manager always paid extra if the band stuck around, keeping the crowd drinking.

'Done for the night?' The doorman leaned against the wall by the entrance, waiting for the last stragglers to leave.

Lawrie nodded. He'd been invited to stop for a drink with the band after the last set but he had somewhere to be. The night's moonlighting had been a last-minute call-out. He'd already arranged to take Evie out to the pictures but he needed the money and his name was just getting known around town: *Mr Reliable. Able to fit in with any band at short notice. Call Lawrie Matthews, he's your man; he'll play anything for a shilling or two.*

It might be after three in the morning, but the street was still open for trade. Across the road a couple of girls loitered, hardly dressed for the March weather, their legs bare and their jackets open. They sheltered in a shop doorway, huddled together as they smoked. One of them called over to him but he pretended he hadn't heard. That sort of entertainment wasn't for him. A few minutes of pleasure taken in a dark piss-scented alleyway could not outweigh the guilt. This he knew.

Even back home in Jamaica, he'd never felt confident in himself, not like his older brother Bennie, but this city forced him even further inside himself. It was a chronic condition, like asthma or arthritis; he could go a day or so feeling perfectly normal and then just a word or a glance was enough to remind him that he didn't belong. He liked working the clubs because he could just play his clarinet and get lost in the music. His fellow musicians respected him; many of them even looked like him. He revelled in the applause that came when his name was shouted out and he stepped forward to give his small bow and a smile, just the right side of bashful. But as soon as he left the warmth of the club, things changed. People looked and decided what he was without knowing a single thing about him. Most of them were well-meaning. Somehow that was worse.

He walked swiftly down to Trafalgar Square, putting on a sprint as he saw his night bus approaching, leaping on the back just before it pulled away and clambering up the steps to the upper deck. He sat down, panting slightly through exertion and relief.

Settled, he looked out of the window at the desolate streets rolling by. The city appeared defeated beneath the weak glow of the late winter moon, which lazily cast its light down on the abandoned remnants of buildings that looked flimsy enough to blow over in the backdraught, if only the driver would put his foot down. Almost five years now since VE Day, almost two years since Lawrie had landed at Tilbury, and the city was still too poor to clean itself up. Austerity they called it, as if giving it a name made it more acceptable to those struggling to make ends meet.

The double-decker wound its lethargic way south of the river and Lawrie tried to stay awake. His eyes were heavy but the draught through the window kept him shivering enough that he didn't nod off. He'd be home just in time to change into his uniform and swallow down some breakfast before heading out again to his proper job.

Jumping off at the Town Hall stop in Brixton, the last passenger left on board, he tugged his scarf up over his chin to ward off a wind that felt like icy needles stabbing against his face. By the time he turned the corner of his street his face was already numb and his gloved hand felt stiff around the handle of the clarinet case. He wiggled his fingers and looked down, checking they were still there.

Home at last; a chip of grass green paint flaking away from the swollen wood of the gate as he swung it open, the rough edge catching his glove. He let himself in the front door, careful to close it quietly behind him. Everyone would still be asleep; he could hear Arthur's less than gentle snores through the thin wood of the door that led to what had been the front room before Mrs Ryan had to let it out for much-needed cash. He silently pulled off his shoes and shrugged off his coat, hanging it up by the door, his trilby next to it.

Upstairs in his bedroom he stowed the clarinet safely away at the back of his wardrobe. He trusted his fellow residents well enough, but his mother had always preached that temptation could befall the best of men. That stick of rosewood had been his father's before him. Irreplaceable. Maybe one day he would pass it on to a son or daughter himself. He'd dared to mention that dream to Evie only a few weeks ago, and her smile had given him hope.

It was a room that his mother would have been ashamed to offer her cook. Besides the wardrobe there was only space left for a narrow bed and just enough room on the floor for his friend Aston to sleep on when he was in town, which seemed to be less often in recent months. The small window, with a view from the back of the house, let in a little bit of light and a lot of draught. Lawrie had rolled up some newspaper and jammed it into the gap between the window and its frame, but that wasn't enough to stop the inside of the glass from frosting over.

His uniform was ready on its hanger, but the cold had stiffened his fingers and it was a slow process; shedding the suit of a professional musician and putting on his everyday postman's uniform. He blew on his hands, trying to get some warmth into them, but he already knew that only a hot mug of tea would work.

Down in the kitchen, he expertly lit the flame on the stove and stared out of the window as the kettle boiled. He fancied he could see the sky lighten slightly as the hour grew closer to dawn. The kettle began its low whistle, and Lawrie lifted it off the ring before it could wake anybody with a full screech. Mrs Ryan would be up early so he made a full pot, tugging the hand-knitted tea cosy around it so that she could have a hot cuppa as soon as she came down. He always let it sit a good long while. He'd never been a big tea drinker before meeting Mrs Ryan, so he'd become used to the way she brewed it. He kept one eye on the time as he clasped the mug, his fingers softening, the feeling returning, as he sat at the table and enjoyed the silence and warmth of the kitchen.

When the clock hands read half past four it was time to go. Lawrie wrapped up again in his heavy coat and the deep burgundy scarf that Evie had knitted him for Christmas. Reluctantly, he forwent his beloved lined leather gloves for the bobbled fingerless ones that did what they could to protect his precious hands against the elements while still allowing him to work easily. Pausing before unlatching the door, he took an extra few seconds to adjust his postman's cap on his brow before the long, age-speckled mirror, his forehead bisected by a crack in the glass, courtesy of a V-1 that had fallen in the next street in darker days.

'Oi!' Derek, Mrs Ryan's son, stood at the top of the stairs, just out of bed and wearing only an off-white vest and pants. His mother would have words if she saw the state of him. In his hand was a brown paper package. 'Take these over to Englewood, would you? Usual place.' He threw the package down and Lawrie caught it lightly, nodding his consent. More black-market stockings, he guessed. Rationing had made Derek a fortune. He tucked the package away in the hallway cupboard to collect after his shift.

The sorting office was only a ten-minute walk but Lawrie had to be early. He had to be the first to arrive. He glanced up at the house next door as he pulled the front door closed behind him, but Evie's window stayed dark. Not yet five and she'd be fast asleep. Last summer the early dawns had woken her, the sun rising to greet the city as he left for work. He'd pause and wait, turning when he heard the scrape of her sash window opening up. They'd never speak – she'd hold a finger to her lips and smile down at him worried that her mother would hear, even though she was unlikely to. Agnes Coleridge took sleeping pills and snored louder than any man Lawrie had heard, the rumble audible through the party wall. He'd smile back and Evie would blow him a kiss as she rubbed sleep from her eyes. And even though the dark mornings had put paid to this small joy, he couldn't help but pause for a moment beneath her window. Just in case.

'You!'

Lawrie stifled a groan. 'Sir?' He turned to face Eric Donovan who was waddling down the aisle in his direction, his creased shirt already coming untucked from trousers whose waistband looked to be on the verge of capitulation.

'Get a move on today, boy, you hear? Second lot's gone out late twice this week already.' The words were barked around an unlit Woodbine that perched on Donovan's narrow bottom lip; the slimmest part of him.

'Yessir.' Lawrie had never headed out late, but he'd learned there was nothing to be gained in talking back to the boss.

'And don't forget my order.' Donovan lowered his voice, Lawrie nodding to show he understood. Donovan's sweet tooth kept Lawrie in his good books, Derek supplying bags of white sugar to maintain Donovan's addiction.

Lawrie put his head down and got on with the sorting while his fellow postmen straggled in, the air filling with a cacophony of male voices. Joining in with the general banter cheered him up by the time he'd got his bag packed, hefting it across his back and adjusting his stance to accommodate the weight. His walk took him back down his own street – past Evie's house – so he didn't complain, despite it being one of the heavier routes.

Evie answered the door when he knocked at the Coleridges', a round of toast in one hand and a shy smile on her face that brightened his mood in an instant. He didn't deserve a girl this beautiful, not after what he'd done, and yet here she was.

'Anything for me this morning, Mr Postman?'

'Always.' He leaned forward and kissed her lightly on the lips, one eye checking over her shoulder in case her mother made a sudden appearance. He didn't take it personally that he was forbidden to cross the threshold. He was sure that Mrs Coleridge would have said as much to any man who was wooing Evie. After all, his skin was barely a shade darker than her own daughter's. Evie's father had returned to wherever he'd come from without knowing he had a baby on the way, leaving Agnes Coleridge holding a mulatto child. No wonder she had a disposition as bitter as quinine.

'Evie! Shut that door, will you? D'you want me to catch my death?' The kitchen door slammed.

'Don't mind her.' Evie pulled the door to behind her and wrapped her arms around her body, a flimsy protection against the cold, standing there in a plain blue cotton dress, navy jumper and her house slippers. 'You got time for a cuppa? I can bring it out.'

Lawrie adjusted his bag across his back so that there was space for her in his arms, pulling her off the step and holding her tight to keep warm. 'Not today.'

'Is it Donovan? You should tell him what's what.' Evie fussed with his scarf, making sure his tender skin was protected.

'I can manage him just fine.' Lawrie stole another kiss before letting her go. 'Just one letter today, ma'am.' She laughed and took it, pressing the palm of her other hand to his cheek. 'I'll call round tonight when you're home from work. You have a good day now.'

She leaned against the doorframe and watched as he made his way up the street, pushing envelopes into letterboxes, just as she did every day, whatever the weather. It was a miracle she'd never caught a cold, but Mrs Ryan reckoned that love did something strange to a body – that if it could be bottled or turned into pills it would make penicillin look like an old wives' remedy. At the corner, he turned back to wave and blow a kiss. She never went inside until he was out of sight.

Towards the end of the day, as he sat in the police station, he would wonder if in this moment he'd jinxed himself – walking around with that stupid grin on his face as if he were the luckiest man alive.

The morning followed its familiar rhythm. First man back at the sorting office, first back out with the next delivery, smirking at the look of disappointment on Donovan's face. He had a little gossip with Mrs Harwood as he gave her a hand carrying her shopping bags home and thanked Mr Thomson for a racing tip that he wouldn't use himself but would pass on to Sonny who loved a little gamble. Lawrie clocked off in the early afternoon, declining the offer to join the others in the pub down the street. He tried to go with them once or twice a week, but only because he felt he should. He liked a game of snooker or dominoes but he really didn't have a lot in common with these men: mainly married, mainly ex-servicemen, all white. Besides, he still had Derek's delivery to make.

He made a short detour home to pick up his bicycle and the package. Englewood Road was on the south side of Clapham Common, a place that was close to home; that green expanse of open land beneath which he had spent his first few nights in England. He remembered arriving there, that summer of 1948, and wondering how the sun could be so bright and yet so chill. And then they'd led him into the deep-level shelter, laughing at his terror at being underground, and fed him tasteless sandwiches along with the rest of the *Windrush* passengers who were unfortunate enough to have nowhere else to go.

The south side of the Common was busy with traffic, those famous red buses no longer a sight that thrilled him. At weekends the paths that cut across the Common would be much busier: couples strolling, children playing, fathers teaching their sons to sail boats on the ponds or feed the ducks. This was where he'd first set eyes on Evie, and where they'd had their first real kiss the summer before, sitting in the deep grass on a long hot Saturday afternoon. In better weather the air would be full of the shrieks of young children playing games, the chatter of their mothers as they exchanged gossip and pushed their progeny in huge Silver Cross prams that forced Lawrie from the path and onto the grass.

On this cold March afternoon, only the odd dog walker had ventured out. At this time of day he often saw these middle-aged women with their precious pets emerging from the large houses that surrounded the Common to walk their pampered animals in circles. Their children were grown and their housework managed by a housekeeper or a charlady, someone like Mrs Coleridge who did for a family over on the north side. They came striding along with an entitlement that Lawrie would never possess, letting their dogs off the leash and looking the other way as their beloveds squatted and left the mess for someone else to step in. Just before he reached Eagle Pond, Lawrie looked up and saw one such woman coming towards him, veering to one side as she walked briskly down the centre of the path; there was a Jack Russell trotting along at her heels, and if Lawrie had learned anything in his postal career it was to watch out for those little bastards. The woman stared as he rode past, and he knew that if he looked back she'd be watching him. Making sure he kept moving and didn't hang around like a bad smell.

The lady who answered the door at Englewood Road was no better. Barely two words to say to him, neither of them wasted on thanks, but the money felt comforting in his pocket. Lawrie's cut was twenty per cent, bargained up from ten the year before. Derek needed a trusted delivery man, he'd argued. Someone who didn't look suspicious knocking on a door and handing over a brown paper package. Who better than the local postman?

Maybe he should take Evie out, he mused. Not just to the pictures. The boss of the club where he'd played the night before, he'd mentioned a few times that he'd get Lawrie a good table if he wanted to bring his girl along. Lawrie always smiled back and thanked him for the offer, said that he'd let him know. He wasn't sure what he was wary of. There was no shame in playing music for a living. It wasn't as though Evie didn't know what he did but he liked that she was separate from all that. The women who frequented the club, not all of them but a few, they reminded him of his mistakes. They reminded him of Rose.

He cycled back the way he'd come, recognising the woman he'd seen with the terrier as he drew close to Eagle Pond, but the dog was nowhere to be seen. There was something strange about the way she was moving, and he found himself slowing down. She was pacing up and down in front of the pond, looking for something. Her gait was lopsided and, when she drew closer, he saw that her face was wet from tears that were blinding her. She didn't notice Lawrie until the last moment, suddenly aiming towards him and coming up short as she took him in properly. She held herself rigid, her mouth gasping for air that her lungs didn't seem to want to accept.

'Ma'am?' Lawrie swung his leg and dismounted, making his movements slow so that she didn't spook. 'You all right? Can I help you?'

She looked over her shoulder but turned back to him, fixing her eyes on his uniform. Whatever she'd seen was more frightening than one skinny black man. And there was no one else in sight. 'You – you're... a postman?' Her tongue tripped as she spoke.

'Yes, ma'am. Do you need help?'

She nodded and pointed in the direction she'd come from, a ragged sob creasing her body.

He couldn't see anything out of the ordinary at first. There was the pond, and there he spied the terrier. The small dog was soaked through. Barking urgently at him, it ran back towards the water.

'The pond.' The woman squeezed out the words and he noticed now that her hands were filthy, her coat spattered with mud.

'There's something in the pond?'

It was useless. She had begun to shiver, her teeth actually chattering as shock took hold. Lawrie laid his bike down on the grass and headed towards the pond on foot. The dog was still barking in a fury, running laps between the edge of the pond and the path.

'What you got, boy?'

The dog splashed into the water, checking back to make sure he was being followed. There was a bundle there, a dirty blanket that once had been white. Lawrie crouched by the edge next to a smaller set of footprints that must have belonged to the woman. It didn't look like much, this wad of sodden wool, but that didn't stop fear from squeezing his chest tight as he reached out with his right hand, the palm of his left sinking into freezing mud as he tried to keep his balance.

15

He strained his arm and caught an inch of fabric between two fingers. Pulling gently, the bundle moved closer and he grabbed a tighter hold. The wool was heavy with water. White and yellow embroidered flowers peeked out from beneath the pond filth. Daisies. When he lifted it the bundle was heavier than he'd anticipated, but it wasn't the weight that sent him crashing to the ground – only sheer luck landing him onto the bank rather than into the water. His heart pounded his ribs so hard that he glanced down at his chest, expecting to see it burst out through his coat, scattering buttons onto the ground.

The blanket lay there on the grass, the bundle coming apart. A baby's arm had escaped, along with a shock of dark curly hair and a glimpse of a cheek. It could have been a doll, but one touch had been enough to convince him that it wasn't. The hand was frozen stiff but the skin gave as his fingers had brushed against it.

Someone had left a baby in the pond to die. A baby whose skin was as dark as Lawrie's.

ONE PLACE. MANY STORIES

Bold, innovative and
empowering publishing.

FOLLOW US ON:

@HQStories